PSYCHIATRIC REPORT	**BRINKVALE PSYCHIATRIC HOSPITAL**
IN THE MATTER OF AN APPLICATION FOR THE ADMISSION OF	**ADMITTANCE FORM**
Martin Grace	ASSIGNED PHYSICIAN: Dr. Reginald Gates
AN ALLEGED MENTALLY SICK PERSON	CASE NUMBER: 677319MG
	Date of Admittance: 09/14/2008

To the Superintendent or Physician in Charge of

BRINKVALE PSYCHIATRIC HOSPITAL of NEW YORK, NY
{name of institution} {location or institution}

The petition of STATE OF NEW YORK (Dr. Joanne Vest) , respectfully shows:

1. That he is 21 years of age or older, that he is a resident of NEW YORK in the county of Kings and that he is (if the petition is made by a public officer, so state, and of what country, city or town) forensic psychologist, NYPD or that he is of the alleged mentally sick person

2. That the alleged mentally sick person now is at the house of Kings County Psychiatric Hospital in the county of Kings

3. That the facts on which the application is based are as follows:

(The petitioner should state the facts observed by or the information known to him which would tend to show the existence of mental disease, such as irrational acts or statements, attempts at suicide and attempts or threats to injure others. It is important to describe any change that has occurred in the behaviour and character of the patient.)

Patient is a suspect in 12 murders; we require an evaluation to determine whether he is competent to stand trial. The murders were especially violent, and patient described exact manner of impending death to many of the victims. He claims he "saw" the deaths, but that they were carried out by a "dark man" whom he appears to believe is stalking him. After the onset of psychosomatic blindness, murders ceased.

Does not appear to be a suicide risk, but given suspect status in 12 murders and continued threatening statements about "dark man," strict security measures are necessary.

4. That he verily believes it to be for the best of the said alleged person that he be admitted to an institution for mental disease.

5. Upon information and belief that the said (ATTACHED) herein mentioned is not under a criminal charge or indictment.

5. Upon information and belief that the said (ATTACHED) is the owner of the following property (real and personal)

Call DA Taylor 212-714-7032 w/ diagnosis ASAP

PSYCHIATRIC REPORT
Martin Grace 677319MG

PERSONAL EFFECTS

DARK ART

J.C. Hutchins and Jordan Weisman

St. Martin's Griffin
New York

www.stmartins.com

ISBN-13: 978-0-312-38382-4
ISBN-10: 0-312-38382-7

First Edition: June 2009
10 9 8 7 6 5 4 3 2 1

If by some miracle I survive my twenties, I am certain I'll look back on today and think, This *was the day I began to lose my mind*.

Today was the day I coasted into work, still high from last week's breakthrough, my grin beating back the gloom of these crumbling halls ... and was unceremoniously shoved into a living horror show, a knife-sharp shadowdance called The Life of Martin Grace. That moment, there—me striding through Brinkvale, punching in on the Depression-era time clock, greeting my coworkers—was when my perception of terra firma reality shifted. Just a nudge. But enough.

I am stone-cold certain that Lina Velasquez was a meth-addicted hummingbird in a past life. The woman is pulled tauter than piano wire. She's all cat's-eye glasses and waving arms, a nitro-fueled perpetual motion machine. Her voice is a nasal blur in the background on any typical day. I don't know why sleepy Brinkvale needs an administrative assistant who's so damned kinetic, but I suppose everyone has a place ... and Lina was currently putting me in mine.

"Taylor!"

She was at her desk, behind the scratched, shatterproof window of the Administrator's Office, perched on the edge of her antique swivel chair, phone receiver pinched between shoulder and cheek. She was typing on her computer keyboard with one hand. I blinked and stopped, peering in at her.

Already exasperated, she rapped on the window with her free palm. The rings on her fingers *clack-clack-clacked*, insistent.

I cringed. Total principal's office flashback.

"In here, now," Lina said. "Dr. Peterson. Urgent."

I have never been an "urgent" kind of guy, but I'm getting better at handling moments like this. Late last week proved that. Still, before landing this gig, the word wasn't in the Zach Taylor vocabulary.

"Uh, what's up?" I asked. I glanced past Lina to the doorway of Peterson's dimly lit office. The old psychiatrist was at his desk, hunched over the scattered contents of an open manila folder. They glowed under an ancient gooseneck lamp. The septuagenarian's desk was cluttered with towers of precariously stacked papers. My mind captured the moment in charcoal-sketch caricature: Doc

Peterson, staring up at his own paperwork Tower of Pisa, cartoon hearts swirling around his bald head. I filed away the image, and tried not to grin.

"What?" I realized Lina had been talking. She pooched her lips and twitched them to the right. This was Lina's nonverbal Venezuelan shorthand: *Make your eyes follow my lips, make your feet follow your eyes.*

I walked past her into the dark room, uneasy of its dimness. It smelled of old books and stale coffee. The fat metal blinds were drawn shut. Peterson glanced up from the contents of the folder. He gestured to a chair in front of his desk and offered me a smile framing yellowed dentures. I didn't know if the man took pleasure in the act of smiling, but it didn't appear that way. The desk lamp's light glimmered in his saucer-sized spectacles.

My path rarely crossed with Peterson's. Three months ago, he'd interviewed me for an hour, then abruptly offered me the job of staff art therapist.

"Brinkvale provides a more, ah ... positive ... environment than you might imagine from the stories," he'd said as I left his office that day. Since our little chat, I hadn't spent more than five minutes with the guy. We've done the smile-and-nod bit in the halls ever since.

To hear the saltier veterans of the hospital talk, that's a good thing. They often suggest that the years here have put fractures of the larger-than-hairline variety in Peterson's sanity. He's known colloquially as the Madman in the Attic—"the attic" being the first floor of this building.

They don't call us Brinkvale employees Morlocks for nothing.

The old man's owl eyes blinked at me, that wide grin still stretching his jowls. I smiled back and sat on the edge of the black vinyl chair, a blocky thing that was at least a decade my senior.

"Hi, Dr. Peterson."

I shifted position in an attempt to see Peterson's face over the preposterous stacks of papers. I tried not to picture cartoon hearts over his head.

"It's a pleasure to have you in again, Zachary," he said. Peterson's voice had the distinctive lilt of the overeducated; each word clearly enunciated, starched and pressed. He nodded at a comparatively small pile of papers beside the folder.

"I read your report," he said. "I'm proud of you."

"From Friday?" I asked. "Spindle?"

Peterson gave a dry chuckle, and shook his head.

"*Spindler*. Gertrude *Spindler*. That is the patient's name, Zachary."

Maybe that was her name now. And maybe it had been her name for the first fifteen years of her life. But Gertie Spindler was "Spindle" for the dark era in between. She was calling herself Spindle when I met her a month ago and, in my mind, that's who she'll always be. Her lifelong obsession with strings, thread, fabric and patterns would have been merely eccentric had it not been for the secrets she'd been hiding with them. Hiding *in* them.

When you can see where the literal bodies are buried by matching swatches that were sewn into two quilts at either end of a decade, you've found a person so far gone, she can call herself anything she likes.

But not completely gone. Not last week, at least.

"Spindler," I agreed, nodding nervously. "Thanks. She'd been telling her story for years. I guess she just needed the right person to listen."

Peterson's smile spread. That yellow half moon was so unnatural on his doughy face, it seemed predatory. This is what a grocery store lobster must see, I thought, right before it's yanked from the tank. I shifted in my chair. The vinyl creaked.

"You have a lot of empathy for your patients," he said, tapping the file. "You tend to become *unusually* invested in their lives, and their therapy."

I flushed. Oh, hell. I knew this moment. I hated this moment. I've lived this moment a dozen dozen times in the past decade, in jobs, relationships, art projects, pet projects. This is how I'm wired. I fall in love with things, projects, people, even if just a little bit. I have to, in order to help them. To do anything less would be ... well ... *I wouldn't know how.*

"You know, about that, Dr. Peterson—"

The old man cut me off with a wave of his hand. His lips slid into a more natural, dour expression.

"Zachary, we have all been where you are. I could say that passion ebbs with age and experience, but I doubt you would listen, so I won't waste your time."

I frowned, off-balance. Was I being criticized or not? Peterson glanced down at the folder before him. From my vantage, I spotted a Brinkvale admittance form, with more attachments than most. A CD-ROM was in there, too. Peterson closed the folder. He pressed two fingers against its surface and pushed it a few inches forward.

"You are here because you are precisely what I need: bright and gifted at what you do," he said. "Your methods of connecting with patients are quite unconventional, but your success rate has been notable."

"I work from my gut," I said. "I don't know what's so unconventional about that."

Peterson tapped the stack of papers again. "Your first month here, you used a cassette 'mixtape' provided by Leon Mack's daughter to usher him out of a nigh-catatonic mute state. Last month, it was a rabbit's foot keychain that facilitated closure for Evan Unwin in the death of his infant son. Yesterday, it was needle and thread."

My frown slid further southward. "Dr. Peterson, art therapy provides opportunities for insight for both the patient and the therapist, and—"

"Of course," he interrupted. "But even more important is your willingness to embrace your patients as people. That's what I need right now." He tapped the folder. "This case is yours, and it takes priority."

I reached for the file. His hand did not move.

"You'll be expected to follow up with your other patients, of course; we are spread far too thin to give you a reprieve. But I imagine you knew that."

The understatement of the millennium. I nodded.

"I also imagine *you* wouldn't want to forsake those other patients," he said. "We're all committed to quality care here at The Brink."

His lips tugged upward into another smile, this one conspiratorial. The chief administrator had just committed the ultimate in-house *faux pas*. New employees learn two things their first day in this hole: where the toilets are, and that you never, ever call this place anything but Brinkvale Psychiatric in the presence of management.

He picked up the folder with a trembling hand and held it out to me. It bobbed in his hand, a boat floating over the sea of paperwork.

"Martin Grace. His transfer came down from County last night. He's due in city court in less than a week. It is a murder trial, and Grace is the gentleman with whom the district attorney's office has its grudge. He's also the prime suspect in eleven other deaths. You will engage the patient, and deduce in the days ahead if he is psychologically fit for trial. Consider it a bonus if he confesses that he consciously, willfully killed Tanya Gold and those other people and deserves imprisonment ... or another method of justice. This time next week, I expect to read your conclusions."

I felt my lips moving, heard my voice before I knew what I was saying.

"What if he's innocent?" I asked.

Peterson's forehead crinkled as his gray eyebrows rose above his glasses. He glanced around in the dimness, at the walls. His smile didn't falter.

"Zachary. He wouldn't be here if he was innocent."

I felt a bit sick as I accepted the folder. The thing felt cold in my hand.

Peterson's expression suddenly brightened, and his voice became dismissive, perfunctory.

"I suggest you take the morning to review the file," he said. "Conduct short sessions with your other patients after lunch. Then introduce yourself to Mister Grace. Leave the paint brushes and pencils in your office, if you please."

"Why?"

"Because Martin Grace is blind."

I don't remember much after leaving Peterson's office. I hope I appeared nonchalant as I performed my morning ritual: waving to nurses and orderlies, stopping at the break room to pour bitter, nearly burned coffee into my extra-large ceramic mug, working my way past doctors' and record keepers' offices to The Brink's sole, ancient elevator.

This didn't feel right. I hadn't yet read any of Martin Grace's admittance papers, but I didn't need to know his story to know I wasn't the guy who should be talking to him. The people I work with at The Brink aren't heading to trial. They're never players in an unfolding criminal case. My people—my *patients,* as Peterson would say—have either been convicted and need solace and treatment, or they're here because they're ill and have nowhere else to go. If you're at The Brink, you're at the end of the line. Only dead-enders need apply.

Make no mistake: I'm good at what I do, which is convince crazy people to express themselves with art. The pay is for shit, and this place is rock-bottom, but I'm making a small difference in this world, one misunderstood person at a time, and I find some peace in that. I try to save people through art, because art saved me. *Giddy-giddy,* as Anti-Zach would say.

So while flattered by Peterson's assignment on a certain level, I was also confused. Why would Peterson ask me, the proverbial new guy, to take this case? Enthusiasm, I got. Real-world life-and-death experience, not so much. And what in the hell was Grace doing here, in the ass-end of New York City's public mental health system, anyway? Multiple homicides perpetrated *by a blind man*—and they pick me? I felt like Bogey in *Casablanca:* "Of all the gin joints, in all the towns, in all the world ... "

Looking up, I realized I'd made my way to the elevator. I jabbed the metal "down" button and waited for the wheezing, hydraulic box to lurch to the surface.

I jerked sideways at the clap of a hand on my shoulder, nearly spilling my coffee. I turned around and faced a chest wider than a tree trunk. A name tag, yellowed and scuffed from abuse, met me at eye level. EMILIO.

I'm five-ten and change, but being in Emilio Wallace's presence makes me feel like a member of the Lollipop Guild. I stared up at his square jaw. In a former life, Emilio had been a semi-famous pro wrestler on the Southwest circuit. If the comic book hero Superman were real, he'd use Emilio as his *sans* spit curl stunt man. That resemblance allowed him to play ironic villainous heavies during his wrestling career, like George "Super" Badman, Samson "Man of Steal" Kent, and my personal favorite: Maximillian von Nietzche, the *Ubermensch*.

These days, Emilio is a Brinkvale security guard, known for pulling as many hours of overtime as the law will allow in order to fund a very personal artistic work-in-progress. Emilio grinned down at me, displaying where most of his paychecks went: a mouthful of ruler-straight, toothpaste-commercial-white teeth ... and a rogue gap here and there, the result of one folding chair to the face too many at the end of his former career.

Another unfortunate side effect of his days in the entertainment biz: mentally, the man's a half-bubble off plumb. He's got a thing for conspiracy theories and alien abduction stories. Hell, he believes vampires and werewolves are *real*.

Of course, maybe he's always been that way. Par for the course, here at The Brink. We work with what the Lord provides.

"Yo, Z," Emilio said. His voice was deep and low, an idling semi truck engine. "Just another manic Monday, yeah?"

"Right on, yeah," I replied. "You got any big plans tonight? Xbox with the boys?"

Emilio shook his head. "I see 'em next week. Got the new Madden. It's gonna be killer."

I nodded at this. I hadn't played a video game since college. My girlfriend Rachael was the gamer in my home. She played enough for the both of us—and probably the rest of the East Village, too.

"Clocking in some serious OT this week," Emilo continued. "New rooster in the coop. Blind dude. Spooky as hell."

My stomach tensed at this. The whine of the elevator was growing louder; it was almost topside.

"Spooky?" I said.

Emilio's blue eyes widened. "As *hell*," he affirmed. "Rolled in last night. I was there, took him to his digs in Max. He was mumbling to himself, those chains on his ankle cuffs scraping on the floor. Dude was like that Scrooge ghost, Bob Marley."

Jacob Marley, I thought, but I didn't correct him.

The elevator doors groaned open. Emilio and I waited for Malcolm Sashington, Brinkvale's omnipresent janitor, to roll out his mop bucket before we entered. Malcolm tipped us a salute as the doors began to close. I returned the gesture.

Emilio smacked the button for my level, 3, and then another for himself. Level 5. Maximum security.

The elevator began to slide downward, into The Brink.

"The guy is a panther," he was saying. "All coiled up. Didn't say anything to me until I got him in his room. Asked me if there was a camera watching him. Asked me if there was a chair. Asked me if the lights were on."

Yes on all counts, I knew.

"So he's blind, right?" Emlio said, grinning again. "He shouldn't care if the lights are on or off. But he tells me to turn 'em off when I leave and lock up. I'm like, 'Saving taxpayers' money?' He says no. Says the buzzing of the lights bothers him."

"Weird," I said, and meant it. The sound of florescent lights annoys me, too. Their constant *hmmm* reminds me of flies in a jar, and puts me on edge. But patient dorms don't have fluorescent lights. In fact, I couldn't think of any room in the place with florescent lights. When it comes to state funding, The Brink is as popular as the drunk uncle at the family reunion.

This meant Grace thought he could hear the hum of the *incandescent* bulbs.

"Yep, that's what I said, weird," Emilio agreed. "Dude asked me a bit about my family, the boys, then told me to scram. He switched on and off, just like those lights. Tough cookie." He gave me another nudge. "Pity the fool who's gotta crack that nut, huh?"

I took a sip of my coffee. I didn't know what to say.

The elevator shuddered, slowed and its doors squeaked open. Level 3: therapists' offices, quarters for higher-functioning patients, housewares, electronics ...

"Take it easy," I said, stepping out. Emilio gave me a thumbs-up. I took another sip from my mug and walked to my office. Martin Grace's folder felt heavier, and colder, in my hand.

✳ ✳ ✳

Brinkvale Psychiatric had a cursed existence before it ever existed. In 1828, the rapidly expanding city of New York was hungry for brownstone. Geologists were consulted, surveys taken, contractors hired. The following year, hundreds of laborers came to Central Islip on Long Island, about forty miles west of the city, breaking their backs for pennies to dig up blocks of brownstone destined for the city. The Brinkvale quarry—named after the idyllic apple farm snatched from its owner under the wily law of "eminent domain"—wasn't so much born as it was carved.

Nine years later, the Brinkvale quarry had closed, its resources depleted. Thanks to corrupt contractors and politicians skimming generous hunks of the quarry's budget off the top, New York's "Great Hole" had become a very unsafe place. In under a decade, more than ninety men had died digging that hole in the world. Worse, ten more died in "unrelated accidents" after organizing a committee to share their grievances with the city. Gallons of blood were splashed on those stones, literally and otherwise. The Brinkvale tragedies were partly responsible for the nation's labor reform acts of the 1840s.

For the next thirty years, the quarry lay quiet, a black dragon with its maw wide open, occasionally claiming the life of a curious child or soused thrill-seeker. But in 1875, the hole caught the interest of overwhelmed alienists desperate for a quiet locale, out of the public eye, in which to house the city's growing population of criminal lunatics. These were patients either too crazy for prison or too dangerous for the city's modest sanitariums. In the end, even cannibals, serial rapists, necrophiles, blood drinkers, ultra-violent schizoids and charismatic occult leaders need a place to sleep.

Brinkvale Psychiatric was not built over the quarry, but in it. Nine stories of howling, brain-boiling madness, stacked two hundred feet into the bedrock. The hospital was so large, so secluded, so wonderfully forgettable, it soon housed more than the howl-at-the-moon types. Brinkvale became an Ellis Island of the damned, an oubliette not just for the dangerous and deranged, but also the misunderstood and unwanted. Homosexuals. Troublemaking non-Christians. Ideologues. Opponents of the status quo. *Bring me your angry, your rebellious, your nonconformist masses yearning to speak freely ... and bury the wretches in a place where no one can hear them scream ...*

You won't find windows beneath the topside "attic" level, here at The Brink. There are only cracked walls, wildly uneven floors and a great many cramped, lightless places. The Brink has no sympathy for claustrophobes or nyctophobes, people who are afraid of the dark. People like me.

This is the place where I'd planted my flag to help people. This was where I'd been appointed to get answers from a blind killer.

And the room I finally entered—my fantastically disorganized office, more than sixty feet underground—was where I finally opened the manila folder in my hand, and suddenly realized how desperately I wanted to see the sun.

✱✱✱

My office is my refuge, the one place in Brinkvale where I can let my personality shine. One wall, covered in wall-to-ceiling corkboard, is the Me Wall, dedicated to people and things I love: many photos of my tattooed goddess, Rachael; pics of my slang-slinging, living spring of a brother Lucas and my father, Will; a faded, folded photo of my mother, Claire; a painting from my police lab-tech pal Ida "Eye" Jean-Phillipe (who had lent a more-than-helpful hand in achieving Spindle's breakthrough last week); a cover of the '80s *Creepshow* movie-adaptation comic (signed by both Stephen King and—an artist who I think walks on water—Bernie Wrightson); a half-dozen Salvador Dali postcards; some sci-fi memorabilia; and my own artwork. Charcoal sketches on cream-colored Stonehenge drawing paper, mostly.

Another wall—similarly swathed in corkboard—features my patients' art. Far less cheerful fare. Manic splotches of lush watercolors, pastel scribbles, wordless agony made visible. I use this gallery to showcase their progress, and to gain perspective on what I'm doing here. Strangers might see violent lost causes on this wall. I see glimmers, tiny penlights, of hope. If my patients trust me enough to craft these images, they might trust me enough, someday, to share their stories and secrets.

The rest of the wall space is dedicated to overflowing filing cabinets, bookshelves and sacks of art supplies. Clean freaks wince when they bear witness to my unique "organizational system," but even the fussiest anal retentives admit that the place projects an optimistic, cheerful vibe. That's a good thing, because it's a reflection of me.

But there was no solace for me here, not now. Martin Grace was whispering his past to me, whispering from papers and photos spread out on my desk. I sipped my coffee in silence, slipping further and further into the man's world.

According to his vitals, Grace was fifty-six years old, white, nearly as tall as Emilio, but slender. Single, lived alone, no children. An arrest mug shot revealed a pale, lean, curiously blank face. His green eyes stared impassively into the camera lens. I found this odd; aside from an acquaintance in middle school, I'd never personally known a blind person. But I vividly remembered that kid's eyes all those years ago, remembered the cloudy discoloration. And sometimes the eyes jitter; nystagmus, it's called. The kid back in school had a severe, stomach-churning nystagmus.

But Grace's eyes had none of this visible damage, no milky cloudlike appearance. Just a clear pine green. I kept reading, plucking a Berol pencil from the jumble on my desk.

Since his incarceration six months ago, Grace had been uncooperative with cops, lawyers and headshrinkers alike. The personal details in the admittance papers came by proxy, from police interviews with neighbors and colleagues. Martin Grace had lived in Brooklyn for two years, after living in Queens for three. He was a transplant from Buffalo. Before Buffalo, he'd spent a year in Albany ... and before that, one in Conquest, a town not too far from Syracuse. Before that, some time in Rochester, right across Lake Ontario from Canada. And before that, and before that, and before that ... the dude got around.

His most recent job was in the city, as an audio engineer. According to his coworkers at The Jam Factory, a music studio housed in a renovated jellies cannery, Grace was a quiet, talented technician with an uncanny ear for production and editing. He'd apparently memorized the studio's vast engineering consoles with dead-certain precision, manipulating hundreds of knobs and dials by touch alone. He also did some studio work as a keyboardist, the reports said. One employee called Grace "the forbidden love child of Stevie Wonder and Ronnie Milsap."

I actually chuckled at that.

Grace had worked at The Jam Factory for the same three years that he'd lived in Brooklyn. He was tremendously gifted, but remained aloof toward his coworkers. He was described as "cool" and "distant" and "off in his own world."

I flipped forward to the psychologists' verdict.

This is where the shit got weird.

Martin Grace had been blind for only two years. Stranger still, he wasn't physically blind at all. His diagnosis was "conversion disorder," something the rest of the world calls psychosomatic blindness. The man's eyes were perfectly healthy, according to an ophthalmologist hired by the city. Grace himself ... or rather, Grace's *mind* ... had simply turned his eyes *off*. I wasn't an expert in conversion disorders, but I knew that they could represent unresolved psychological conflicts, or a broken mind's way of willfully ignoring conflicts.

I pulled over my satchel and unzipped its main pouch. Out came my well-worn Moleskine sketchpad. I flipped to a fresh page and wrote.

PSYCHOSOMATIC = PAST CONFLICT? KEY?

I gazed at the words, rolling the Berol with my fingertips.

RESOLVING CONFLICT = SIGHT. HE NEEDS TO SEE TO TELL HIS STORY.

I flipped the pencil in my hand, the rubber eraser now facing the desk. I tapped out a beat on the metal as I continued to read. I made it a half-sentence before I realized what I was drumming: "Love Is Blindness" from U2's *Achtung Baby.*

Love is blindness, I don't want to see ... Won't you wrap the night around me?

Odd. I'd always preferred the cover version by The Devlins.

I kept tapping out the rhythm, kept reading. Martin Grace was a suspect in a dozen deaths, dating back at least ten years. More than half had been horrific homicides; the others, previously ruled as suicides or accidental deaths. But a pattern began to emerge. That's what happens to serial killers; at least that's what the movies say. They get lazy. They fall prey to routine, just like the rest of us.

The victims had a common connection: Martin Grace. One of the vics had been a lover, but the rest had been Grace's colleagues and friends, along with some strangers. According to these papers, Grace was practically a traveling salesman of death, bebopping from one city to the next in New York state, leaving a body (or sometimes two) in the rearview mirror.

He'd been running, that much was clear. But from what? Himself?

I scratched this into my notebook, then resumed drumming.

There was another twist: Grace seemed to have airtight alibis. Dinners with friends, drinks with the boss ... hell, even manning the cotton candy stand at a church fish fry. It didn't make any sense. Why did the cops have a hard-on for this guy? Did Grace simply have bad luck picking friends? Was he moving from city to city to start anew, get past the grief?

I flipped the page.

No.

The hairs on my arms spiked as icy gooseflesh rippled across my skin. Martin Grace had seen things, the report said. Seen things before they'd happened. Visions of death. According to recent interviews, at least a third of the victims' families said that Grace had told the victims that they were going to die before they actually did. And he didn't just tell them they were going to die. He told them *how* they were going to die.

And he was right.

Martin Grace would soon stand trial for the rape and murder of vocalist Tanya Gold, once a rising star in New York's hip-hop scene. According to the police report, Tanya Gold met Grace once— and only once—at Screamin' Soundz Studioz, a production house where Grace worked five years ago. There, Tanya recorded her contribution to a guest appearance on another artist's record. After the session, a panicked Grace pulled the woman aside, warned her that she was in danger ... that she would soon be "raped and ripped to shreds."

Understandably, the singer reported this to the police as a threat on her life. Motivated by pressure from Tanya Gold's headline-making manager (and whatever incentive he may have provided), New York's finest issued a restraining order and monitored both

Gold's and Grace's residence that evening. Martin Grace went to bed at around 10:30. Tanya Gold turned in a few hours later.

Per their orders, cops attempted to contact Gold the next morning. When she didn't answer her apartment door, officers entered and found a sight in the living room so freakish, one of the cops later reported that he thought it was "a reality show gag."

It wasn't.

Tanya Gold— a twenty-one-year-old who was as business-savvy and beautiful as she was talented—had been torn literally limb from limb. Ropes had been tied to her wrists and ankles. Those ropes had been looped through metal hoops in the living room's four corners ... hoops presumably bolted to the walls the night before. Either man or machine— Forensics was as baffled as the reporting cops—had pulled these ropes tauter and tauter, until Tanya Gold's body was ripped apart.

Coroner reports confirmed that Tanya Gold had been raped. Blood spatter analysis and the position of Tanya's torso (which had remained connected to her left leg, sweet Jesus) implied the rape likely occurred after the rending.

Martin Grace was arrested in his apartment that morning as he was dressing for work. He was questioned, mercilessly. There was no evidence that he'd left the apartment the night before, and—aside from his warning to the singer—no evidence linked him to Tanya Gold's murder.

From what I could surmise from other reports, it was Grace's town-hopping trail of terror that empowered the district attorney's office to prosecute the Tanya Gold case five years after the fact. The "visions" of death Grace experienced were numerous—and, according to the prosecution, damning.

He didn't just inform twenty-four-year-old musician Rosemary Chapel of Rochester that she'd hang herself. He told her which belt she'd use—her favorite, silver-studded black leather. Three hours later, those metal studs tore Rosemary's throat open as her legs kicked and twitched in space, suspended in her parents' garage.

Conquest resident Jerome Stringer was warned he'd lose not just a finger but a hand on his woodshop saw, and would pass out from the shock before he could call an ambulance. It happened three days later. Robbery gone wrong. Car accident. A horrifying (and preposterous, were it not true) homicide involving javelins. Martin Grace had precognitively seen them all, the families said. And in Grace's last interview with a psychologist at Rockland a month ago, the man finally corroborated this.

"Patient states he has a lifelong 'preternatural disposition' for clairvoyance, which recently transformed into precognitive 'visions' of victims' deaths," wrote the last doctor to work with Grace. "Likely suffers from delusions of reference/schizotypal personality disorder. Paradoxically, patient insists he did not kill these people, but is nonetheless personally responsible for their deaths. He calls himself an unwitting psychic sniper, 'the crosshairs for Death. For the dark.'"

My mouth went dry. I took a quick pull from my mug and read on, not blinking.

"Patient believes he is an earthbound 'catalyst' for human suffering and death," the doctor wrote. "His interaction with others incurs the interest and wrath of an otherworldy, monstrous entity he calls several names: 'The Inkstain,' 'Chernobog' ... and, most commonly, 'The Dark Man.' "

I shuddered at this, and at something vague and wicked and smiling very far away in my mind—and at the lyric I'd been absently tapping on the desk as I'd read.

A little death without mourning, no call and no warning. Baby, a dangerous idea. That almost makes sense ...

A dark man.

I placed the pencil on the desk. I read another page.

The murders had ended two years ago. The same year Grace went blind.

PRIMORUS MAXIMUS

3

There were more pages in Grace's report, most of them from the district attorney's office—that gothic letterhead was as familiar to me as the lines on my palms—but I didn't get to them. The silence of my office was shattered by skeleton song.

I jerked, nearly knocking the papers to the floor. I fumbled for my satchel. My cell phone played another round of cheerful xylophone music—I call it skeleton song, since bone-white rib cages are *always* used as xylophones in the cartoons—and then it went silent. I rummaged in the canvas bag, retrieved the phone and looked at its screen. Lucas had sent me a text message. I was thankful for the interruption. I flipped the device lengthwise and slid out its tiny keyboard. His IM flashed on the LCD.

STILL ON FOR GRAM? MEET AT Well7 @ 5?

"Yeah," I sighed, again brushing the hair from my eyes. "You bet, bro."

I typed this on the pad, added the words *IT'LL WORK OUT, CALL IF YOU NEED ANYTHING* and hit "OK." An animated pinwheel spun on-screen as my little phone talked to the cell tower sixty feet above and a half-block away. That blessed thing is the only reason we Morlocks get phone reception in the bowels of The Brink.

The phone beeped. Message sent. I slid the thing closed.

I leaned back in my chair, exhaling through my lips, feeling my body deflate as another emotion swept over me. The chair's springs squealed. I barely noticed.

Gram. She had warred with her cancer for four agonizing years—a physical and mental Hatfield-and-McCoy feud inside her—and then six months ago she'd emotionally checked out. She never told the family this, never told "her boys" that the pain was too much, that she finally wanted to join Grandpa Howard (who'd been gone for nearly twenty years), that she simply didn't have the steel for it anymore. No. She never confessed. But I knew. That mischievous, defiant glimmer in her gray eyes had vanished a half-year ago. I think my father knew, too.

But Lucas was different. Maybe it was his youth or his wide-eyed, adventurous soul that stopped him just short of understanding this truth, like a happy dog on a chain bolted to a doghouse. To that end, Lucas had clutched the hope, as bright as it was bittersweet, that Gram would recover, that the treatments would work, that the radiation and the chemo pumping into her veins would eventually do some goddamned good.

Gram gave up six months ago. But her body held on, driven by either Taylor Family Loyalty or sheer stubbornness (these things are not mutually exclusive) until last week. She wasn't talking at the end. She was just breathing. Sleeping and breathing.

And then, she was just asleep.

My boundless, bouncing baby brother was dealing with her death the best way he knew how—by channeling his frustration and emotions into his two current passions: filmmaking and parkour. Gram was cremated today, and her memorial service was tonight, at Selznick and Sons in the Upper East Side, near where my father lived. I would meet Lucas at "Well7"—my brother's peculiar nickname for Greenwich Village's Washington Square Park—at five o'clock. We'd stop by my apartment for brisk showers and shaves, and get to the service by seven. Rachael would meet us there. My father would likely arrive an hour after that, freshly stressed from his day at One Hogan Place, where he would undoubtedly have unleashed appropriately hellish retribution upon deserving ne'er-do-wells.

Dad had called last night and left a voicemail on my cell phone, telling me he might be late to the service. I swear to God, if he's late to his mother's funeral, it's a done deal he'll be late to his own. I hadn't yet shared this news with Rachael, who was baffled by my father's workaholic tendencies. She had good reason to be; my dad once told me he was so busy, he'd never even changed the passcode to his telephone messages from the "1234" default.

I turned back to the reports on my desk and shuffled through the papers until I again spotted that distinctive letterhead. These documents gave a macro view of the prosecution's position for the upcoming trial—thankfully, there was no legalese to bulldoze through—and they confirmed what Dr. Peterson had told me. Martin Grace was staring down a howitzer barrel: one count of homicide, and circumstantial evidence indicating eleven others. With Grace's alibis, I doubted the lawyers could pin all of the deaths on him, but they were giving it their fear-of-John-Houseman *Paper Chase* all. Things were not looking good for the blind man.

Hell. Come to think of it, things weren't looking good for me, either.

I glanced up at the letterhead.

New York County District Attorney's Office.

William V. Taylor, District Attorney.

* * *

By lunchtime, my mind was throbbing from a Google-, DSM-and textbook-powered crash course in psychosomatic blindness. (Did you know that, according to the Diagnostic and Statistical Manual of Mental Disorders, conversion disorders are very uncommon, representing only three percent of mental hospital admissions each year—and even fewer cases deal specifically with sight loss?) I was half-jumping at shadows, at Dark Men. Rattled. Something more than Martin Grace's graphic, delusional death visions was gnawing at my brain. It was something cold and faraway, familiar ... but ultimately unreachable.

At noon, I was thrilled to escape The Brink, if only for an hour. I surfaced and sat beneath Primoris Maximus, the hospital grounds' spectacular oak tree. Primoris' name was bastardized Latin meaning, "The first, the most important."

And it was. The tree was so old, awesome and iconic that a stylized rendition of its image played brand-friendly logo for the hospital. It was triumphant this time of year, leaves ablaze in autumnal amber and crimson. A crisp breeze rushed through the grass around me, rustling the large art pad in my lap, giving the sketch pencil resting on its surface a good reason to roll about.

I had just finished reviewing the notes I'd taken in my office, and slipped the smaller Moleskine sketchpad back into my satchel. Before coming topside, I'd concocted a vague strategy on how to approach Martin Grace, and had even settled on a personal mantra for my sessions with him: *Amazing Grace, how sweet the sound ... he's blind, but help him see.* The man was a musician. It suited him.

I reached into the wrinkled brown paper bag resting by my thigh and pulled out a Granny Smith apple. Lunches in The Brink's cobwebby cafeteria might be free for employees, but they're ashen, antiseptic things. Withered green beans, flavorless chicken breasts, meatloaf so soggy it was better suited for sloppy joes. Give me ten-cent fruit from a Chinatown street vendor any day. Make that every day.

I took a bite, grinning and grimacing at the apple's blissful tartness. The rest of my lunch—a peanut butter and jelly sandwich and yogurt—would have to wait.

The crux of my strategy with Grace was to learn more about his vision loss. This event two years ago had prevented him from killing even more people—or more appropriately, had coincided with the end of death around him. Unlike Dr. Peterson, I wasn't convinced that Grace had committed these crimes. According to the report, even investigators admitted that his alibis were solid.

He might have conspired to kill these people, but that would've required an accomplice. The district attorney's office wasn't charging anyone else with the crimes. Grace was the horse those folks were betting on, and they'd beat his ass until they crossed the finish line.

Grace's guilt or innocence was certainly important to me ... but I suspected I wouldn't unearth that information until I unlocked the secret to his blindness. What did it represent, in Grace's mind? Psychic self-flagellation? An escape for the chilling visions he'd insisted he'd had? A way to silence the killer's voice inside him, the thing he called the Inkstain?

Like basketball—an art form in its own right, a thing I reckoned more full-court dance than press—there are rules in art therapy, as well as tactics for sneaking past a sharp defense. These methods are cornerstones in sessions. Assume a calm and non-judgmental demeanor. Ask the patient to draw a tree, or a family, or a person. Have the patient discuss the picture, reflect about what's on the page and what it might represent. Armed with those techniques ... and enough backstory on the patient ... you can slowly guide him toward insight. Insight begets vision. Vision begets revelation. Revelations beget breakthroughs.

With Martin Grace, insight wasn't the only thing I was hoping for. *Sight* was my goal.

I'd had enough experience to know that my book-cramming and armchair strategies would only go so far. My job is a lot like the creative process itself: if you treat the playbook as gospel, you're doomed. Therapists must be adaptive, fleet-footed and improvisational. The way you interact with a patient—and the art the patient creates—must be as unique as the person you're treating. Unfortunately, my blind man in the basement was so "unique" he was in his own psychological zip code.

I leaned my back against the oak tree's rugged trunk and closed my eyes. I made an effort to listen, really listen to the world, its heartbeat. I heard the faraway voices of other lunching Brinkvale employees. The faint roar of a motorcycle on Veterans Memorial Highway, a quarter-mile away. I raised the apple to my mouth and took a bite, relishing the snap of its peel against my teeth. I savored the sounds and wondered if this is what being blind feels like.

I snorted. Even with my eyelids closed, the sunlight was creeping onto my rods and cones, warm and red. My eyes still worked. Grace's didn't. Or at least, a part of him thought they didn't. He had *willed* himself blind to escape his demon, his Dark Man.

The wind gusted again, colder now. I shivered. I sensed another faraway whisper in my mind—I knew this tickling sensation, welcomed its intimacy—and opened my art pad.

The creative inspiration swam and somersaulted inside my mind. I let my hand breeze over the paper in brisk elliptical motions, my pencil a half-inch above the textured surface, letting the tickle find shape. A moment later, the charcoal etched a light, curved horizontal line, and then—bisecting it—a longer, curved vertical line.

Yes. I'd thought that's where we were going with this. I let it take over.

The rest came in a blur of swift, gray arcs and tighter, darker crosshatchings: his eyes, sunken and sullen; the tiny trenches of crow's feet, stretching back to his ears; the impassive lines of his thin lips; the slight, asymmetrical nose, likely from a break long ago; the close-cut hair.

I pulled the pencil away for a moment, my hand still itching to say more, and saw Martin Grace staring back at me. The eyes. My pencil insisted that they weren't quite right. I darkened the pupils, made them bigger. *No.* Bigger still. Inspiration insisted, and I ran with it, like I always do, unthinking, filling the white space beneath his eyelids now ... *yes, more*, the tickle whispered ... and now the stuff was squirting from his tear ducts, spilling out onto his cheekbones, surging and gurgling like crude oil down his face, dark gray, darker now, no, black, blacker, *where are my brushes, where is my India ink, it's gotta be darker*—

"Wait!"

I snapped out of my zone—my creative place, my cave—and nearly yelped. The pencil slipped in my hand, slicing a panicked, manic line across the page.

I looked up at the person standing in front of me. A middle-aged woman gazed back, her expression equal parts wary and concerned. I felt hot blood swell under my cheeks, felt my eyebrows kick upward in chagrin. *Good God*, I thought. *So effing embarrassed*. Few people see this side of me, the spirit slice that takes over when I create and pour myself into that whole-wide-world of white space.

I blinked, and recognized the woman. Annie Jackson. Night shift.

"Ah ... heh. Hi, Annie," I said. I placed the pencil beside me and picked up the Granny Smith off the grass. Feeling stupid, I kept it simple. "Hi."

Still blushing. I wanted to scramble up the side of Primoris, build a treehouse and never come down. I smiled, praying I looked more Brinkvale employee than patient.

The look on Annie's round face softened, and she returned my smile. Annie was an eleven-to-seven gal. I was almost as befuddled by her presence here during sunshine hours as I was by the frenetic sketch in my lap. I glanced down at the pad. Half of Martin Grace's face was covered in hastily scribbled ooze.

"I didn't mean to interrupt." She gave a little laugh. It was a throaty, lovely staccato, a perfect complement to her Southern accent. "It's just, I thought, it's a fantastic portrait." She eyed the page and shrugged. The large purse under her arm bounced with her shoulder, its black strap a marionette string. "Too late now. Mind if I sit down? My dogs are barkin'."

I nodded, and patted my palm on the grass. My grin was a bit more genuine now.

"Take a load off, Annie."

The nurse rolled her brown eyes, but gave another chuckle. She tugged a long slice of blonde-gray hair behind her ear.

"Yeah, like I haven't heard *that* before," she said, groaning slightly as she sagged down beside me. "Still. Gets me every time. You know, my husband wooed me with that line." She dug a hand into her purse.

"No kidding?" I asked. I didn't know Annie Jackson very well—I'd only chatted with her the few times I'd burned the midnight oil here—but I knew that her wit was Ginsu-sharp, and that she smoked like a fiend. Sure enough, Annie produced a pink disposable lighter from her purse, and a cigarette so long and thin it looked like a joint run through a pasta press.

"Oh yeah," she said, lighting her smoke. "Met M.J. at a party. This was years ago, back in the '80s." She gave me a motherly smile that was so convincing, I barely noticed the sly twinkle in her eyes. "You were just a baby then, God bless your little heart."

I chuckled, feeling my tension ebb. I now knew Annie also had a gift for putting people at ease.

"Now *this* was a party, Zach," she continued. "I don't know how you New York kids do things, but in Atlanta, we do things big, and we do 'em *right*. There wasn't a place to put your buns, this party was so packed. So we're introduced, he's sitting on a comfy chair—'Annie Stormand, meet Michael Jeremy Jackson; M.J., meet Annie'—and that audacious soul slaps his lap with both hands, does a 'come hither' with his eyes and says what you just said."

I giggled, and took a bite of my apple. "What'd you do?"

"I said what any self-respecting woman says to a lyric-quotin' man named Michael Jackson," Annie said. She took a drag off her cigarette for dramatic effect. "I told him to beat it."

Now we were both cackling, Annie blowing smoke into the sky and me wiping away tears, and I was so grateful she was here because after the morning I'd had, the art my hand had just spun—and the somber evening to come—goddamn, I needed a good belly laugh.

We smiled in the noon sunlight, enjoying the buzzy, giddy after-glow you get after sharing a good joke. I reached into my lunch bag and pulled out my sandwich. She finally nodded at the art pad still in my lap.

"You're really good," she said. "Maybe it's even better than it was before. You get into a zone, don't you?"

I took a bite of my sandwich and nodded, enjoying the salty-sweetness of the peanut butter and raspberry preserves.

"Michelle's like that, too," Annie said. "Twelve years old, but she's gonna be a star someday. She bangs the hell out of those drums, Zach. Practices all the time. But when she *plays*, oh dear, look out. She's in another place."

"Yes," I said. "We all have that secret, safe place inside." I paused, noodling over her words. I tapped the sketch. "You said it was better than it was before ... "

She inhaled an emphatic *uh-huh,* and then exhaled. "This black stuff you drew on him. Makes it less real, but more ... realistic. I bet that's what he's like on the inside. I'm here today because I'm pulling a double shift, Zach. I was the one who admitted him last night. Midnight, to avoid the media." Her face faltered. Her voice was low now. "He's *cruel.*"

My stomach tightened, again. I stopped in mid-bite, felt the raspberry jam squirt between my teeth, sensed a glob of the stuff land on my shirt. I swallowed, hard.

"What do you mean by that?" I asked. It came out sounding more like a dry-throated croak than a question, but Annie didn't seem to notice. "I'm ... ah. Doc Peterson assigned me to him. I'm going down in a few hours."

Annie's chocolate eyes narrowed.

"Sonuvawhore," she said, and then immediately pressed a hand over her lips. Now it was her turn to blush. "I'm sorry about that, I truly am." I shook my head: *It doesn't matter.* Her eyes flitted to my art pad, then back to my face. "I just can't imagine why our attic madman would put *you* on this. You know this cat's story, don't you? You've seen the papers, right?"

"His admittance report, some of his background."

"Not *his* papers, hon," Annie said. She rummaged in her purse again. "Newspapers. Here."

She passed over a crumpled page torn from that morning's *New York Times.* I read the headline—*MURDER TRIAL BEGINS NEXT WEEK FOR 'BLIND' MAN*—and scanned the article, which was mercifully short. My eyes reached the end of the story. They stopped. They doubled back to the last paragraph.

There was my surname, in the walk-off quote.

"I cannot understate my office's dedication to convicting Mr. Grace," said New York District Attorney William V. Taylor. "We will not allow a serial killer to walk these streets. The man might be blind, he might not be. But he is guilty, and I'll personally *ensure that he is punished to the law's fullest extent—including the death penalty, if the jury allows it and the moratorium is lifted."*

"Oh shit," I said.

Annie placed her hand on my shoulder. Her voice was gentle, sympathetic. "Yeah. I'm sorry, darlin', but it looks like you're in a real professional pickle."

I pulled my eyes away from the newspaper, to Annie's worried face. So. She knew, too. I wasn't upset by this. I've never tried to hide whose son I was (well, not since back in my Anti-Zach days), but I've never flaunted it, either. Within days of being hired at The Brink, people had deduced that my dad was the D.A., confirmed it with me, and tweeted the news like little songbirds. I was a little surprised that the gossip had crept up the clock to the night shift staff ... but them's the breaks.

Annie patted my shoulder again. "I've seen him on TV. I bet he's just putting on a show for the reporters, right? You gotta be a bulldog on crime in this town. But I think it's just an act, just for the cameras."

I shook my head. "It isn't," I whispered. "It never has been."

After a minute of strained silence, Annie and I stood and walked away from Primoris Maximus, back toward The Brink. As Annie made small talk and I half-listened, I gazed up into the bright autumn sky, marveling at the battleship clouds scraping across the horizon, knowing that it would be sunset when I saw the sky again, knowing that it would be far darker, long before that.

It was time to make my rounds and tend to my people.

And then, time to meet Martin Grace.

Brinkvale is the mental health equivalent of Tatooine.

"If there's a bright center to the universe," my hero Luke Sky-walker once said, "you're on the planet that it's farthest from." My patients' stories are stranger than anything you'd find in that planet's intergalactic cantina, but luckily this day's sessions were brief and mostly positive that afternoon.

Understanding my patients requires patience, the kind reserved for puzzle boxes and correspondence chess. Today, I finally understood a message that Nam Ngo, a benign Vietnamese watch repairman from Brooklyn, had built into a sculpture. The man hasn't said a word in twenty years. But when I poured a boxful of clockwork parts onto his dorm table two weeks ago and asked him to tell me about himself, Nam's bespectacled face brightened, and he'd gotten to work.

Brinkvale staff now called him "The Clocktalker" (many of my patients seem to acquire these superhero-like nicknames), and I've been charged with deciphering the meanings behind his tick-tock sculptures.

Today, Ngo's sculpture was a man-shaped thing with a watch for a head. Nam twisted a key in the tiny mechanoid's back and beamed. The metal man ran in place, its head ratcheting to look over its shoulder. As it repeated this, Nam had made a circle with one hand and placed it to his eye. His other hand turned an invisible crank near his face.

Ten minutes later, I'd deduced that his favorite movie was *North By Northwest*. The compass-like position of the hands on the watch's face was the critical clue. The automaton's movements replicated Nam's favorite scene: Cary Grant being chased by the crop-duster.

That was the session. No blaring breakthrough "Hallelujah chorus"; Nam was simply telling me his story. I considered his case a long-term project.

After my visit with The Clocktalker, I spent time with "Bloody Mary"—Mary Winfield, a beautiful thirty-something with a phobia of reflective surfaces. When we met a month ago, she painted the same image, day after day, with her elegant brown fingers: Mary's mirror image, covered in streaks of blood, holding a decomposing infant. "Baby Blue" represented the son she'd drowned a year ago at a public pool in Queens.

Since then, Mary's art had slowly pulled away from this horror. In today's finger painting, Baby Blue was beginning to leave his mother's arms. The child would ascend as the weeks went on, I suspected—rising higher and higher on the canvas, until Mary finally found peace.

Jaded Morlocks say that The Brink's foundations slide a little deeper into New York's bedrock each year. The structure is home to vermin of all kinds: spiders the size of silver dollars, rats as fast as they are large, legions of fat, black cockroaches. Our charitably named "pest control problem" has been a source of shrieking, screaming madness for Gerald Carver, a former bug spray chemist.

Today, Carver—aka "The Bug Man"—drew pictures of his own hands, insects and worms burrowing tunnels deep into the flesh. Carver believed that the critters had finally corralled him here, in their territory, to exact vengeance. I admitted that the multi-legged masses have their run of the place, but gently insisted that Carver was neither the target of an insect conspiracy, nor victim of a karmic bitch-slap. I left the session feeling itchy, slapping at invisible fleas.

And there was Jane Doe, the amnesiac. And Jimmy "Park Place" Van Zandt, the *Monopoly*-obsessed autistic. And others. All of my visits were abbreviated, brisk things.

I wished for more time with them; I found the plights of these patients comforting, compared to the idea of meeting Martin Grace.

Which I was about to do right now.

***

"Hey, Taylor. Do me a favor, okay?"

I try to stay cool when I hear that grating, smug voice ... but couldn't help pressing the elevator button one more time, trying to make it go faster. Here he goes, and here I was, stuck in this can with him.

"What's that?" I replied.

Dr. Nathan Xavier indicated the paint smudges on my hands.

"Come by my office later. The walls could use a coat or two." He tittered.

I slapped the "5" button a third time and took the high road—like I always do with this guy.

Now, I'm one of those optimists who tries to see the good in everyone they meet. I've been told this is the Christian thing to do, and that's fine by me—God's a pretty awesome guy to have in your corner—but I also think it's the *human* thing to do. Everyone has their ups and downs. Everyone can be surly. And nearly all of us are loved by someone ... which means even the worst of us aren't that bad.

That being said, I think Xavier is an irredeemable prick.

I am absolutely committed to—and believe in—what I do, but I've lost count of the times this guy has disrespected my livelihood during the past three months. Xavier believes art therapy is the professional equivalent of bicycle training wheels and kindergarten safety scissors. The man thinks pharmacology alone will solve the world's mental and emotional woes. Naturally, the visiting drug reps love him.

Xavier has been employed at The Brink only a month longer than I have. He's a few years older than me and bears a strong resemblance to a Ken doll, plastic hair and all. Last week, he proclaimed that he'd picked up a "hot blonde bitch" at his tennis club. I asked if she had a sister named Skipper. He didn't get it.

Not completely satisfied that his "joke" had hit home, Xavier now nudged me and continued: "I'm thinking eggshell white. Maybe a robin's egg blue. Or maybe 'Baby Blue' blue."

The elevator pinged, passing Level 4, and kept chugging. I groaned.

"It's from my sessions."

"Oh, I know ... I'm just pulling your leg, man." He eyed his mannequin-like reflection in the elevator's doors and preened. "I totally get and respect what you do here, Taylor, really." He checked his teeth. "But finger paints won't help you with that blind head case. Peterson thinks you're perfect for the job. He obviously needs psychiatric treatment."

"Grace *will* get psychiatric treatment. But art therapy is a clinically recognized complement to—"

"I was talking about Peterson," he interrupted, and tittered again.

I ground my teeth, saying nothing.

"Honestly, though, Taylor. Art therapy ... for Grace? It's like asking a quadriplegic to break dance." He guffawed at his own joke. "He needs medication, not construction paper."

"I've got an angle," I said, adjusting my grip on the item I was holding. Xavier didn't notice.

"You'd better. This is the first high-profile case to come to The Brink in a long time. You're in the spotlight, so don't mess it up. There are plenty of people here who'd love to take the reins on that case."

"Like who?"

The elevator lurched to a halt. Level 5, maximum security. I stepped into the hall. Xavier chuckled.

"Oh, and bring a flashlight, Taylor," he said. "Peterson says your patient's got a thing for the dark." The doors started to close.

"Just like you."

✳ ✳ ✳

Emilio Wallace stood by the doorway of Room 507, his Superman face somber. He gave me a nod, twisted the deadbolt key and opened the three-inch-thick metal door. Its hinges squealed like fingernails raking across chalkboard. The slab swung past me and I stared into a dark room, a midnight vault.

Anxiety swept over me, cold and sickening. I clutched at the things I was carrying, closed my eyes, inhaled deeply and calmly asked my nyctophobia to shut the hell up. It didn't, not completely ... but the fear lumbered reluctantly back to its cage. Temporarily, at least.

I reached into the darkness and groped for the light switch. The hall light behind me flickered, casting a stuttered shadowplay across the pale-green tiled walls. I glanced back at Emilio. He gave me a bored smile and shrugged: *Hey, it's The Brink.*

I felt a half-second of sympathy for the security guard; the hospital's ancient wiring made the hall feel like a dime-store disco. The bulb strobed and buzzed, then finally resumed a steady glow. My hand found the switch inside Room 507 and flicked it upward.

There he was, sitting in a wooden chair in the center of the small room. His eyes were closed. He did not move. I stepped inside. Emilio closed the door.

Here we go, I thought.

"Hello, Martin," I said. I placed my papers and the plastic object I'd brought on the small table by the door, and picked up the wooden chair resting beside it. Like everything here, the chair was far past its prime. I placed it in front of him, about three feet away. It creaked merrily as I sat. "My name is Zachary Taylor. I'm Brinkvale's art therapist."

Martin Grace's middle-aged face remained still. He did not open his eyes. He did not unfold the hands in his lap.

"You should tell your friend that she is going to die before her time."

His voice was low and cool, gravel-rough. I tried not to shudder.

"Which friend is that?" I asked.

"Why, the *Suthun' belle*, Nurse Jackson," Grace replied. His impersonation of Annie's accent was unnervingly accurate. "She's all over you, her cheap Jergens hand lotion, the stink of coffin nails. That habit has her on the fast track to the grave."

I stole a quick glance at my Eterna. It was 3:30. I'd lunched with Annie more than two hours ago. I flared my nostrils, sucked in some air. My brain couldn't detect anything but the room's stale scent. I leaned back into the chair. It moaned.

"I'm sure Ms. Jackson appreciates your concern," I said. All right. The man wanted me to acknowledge his blindness. I obliged him. "That's pretty remarkable. Have your other senses also compensated for your sight loss?"

Martin Grace opened his eyes. His pine-green corneas stared into mine. No. Past mine.

"I imagine we'll have all the answers we need by the time you leave," he said.

He blinked slowly. Another moment passed.

"You're more direct than the others," he said. "Is that your personality shining through, I wonder, or the fact that you're on a deadline?" His thin lips teased into a smirk. "One week. Do you honestly care if the blind man steps before the firing squad? I certainly won't need a blindfold."

I shrugged. This was more adversarial than I'd expected. "I'm here to help you, Martin. I'd like to work with you, learn about your life, if you'll let me. I help people express themselves through—"

"Oh, I know what you do," Grace said. His smirk broadened, then flicked back to a flat line of impassivity. "In the great sea of quackery—where chiropractors and regression therapists splash about and make money hand-over-fist—perhaps the biggest, fattest ducks are *people like you*, Mr. Taylor. You're a two-bit Crayola salesman, nothing more."

I didn't move, but the head inside my mind was nodding. So. This was how it was going to be. I considered the notes I'd made this morning, the prep I'd done for our session.

"I thought you might have a better opinion of my profession, considering you're a musician," I said. My voice was neutral, professional. "I went on Amazon today and ordered some of the CDs you worked on at The Jam Factory. I'm curious to hear your keyboard work on Charlie Murphy's jazz album. Your coworkers say you're quite talented."

Martin Grace unfolded his fingers and made a theatrical flourish with one hand. His tone was condescending, acidic.

"Ladies and gentlemen, our Mr. Taylor is *invested*. My. I suspect you aren't even going to ask this fine institution"—he made another insulting hand flourish here—"to reimburse you for the purchase. Tell me that you at least scored free shipping."

I wasn't, and hadn't.

I looked into his eyes, my mind reciting Dad's quote in today's *Times*—"the man might be blind, he might not be"—and wondered if Martin Grace could see me now, puzzling over him. I resisted a childish urge to stick out my tongue and test this. I glanced up at the security camera in the far corner of the room. Yet another reason not to act like a goofball.

Grace gave a humorless chuckle. He placed his hands back in his lap and closed his eyes.

"You really are different," he said. "But not so different."

I didn't like this. I changed tactics, hungry to disrupt Grace's game of superiority. My goal was to establish a bond. Coax him into expressing himself in the language in which I was fluent.

"I'm confused, Martin," I said. "You've been indicted for a murder you say you didn't commit ... and you're suspected in nearly a dozen more. But you do nothing to defend yourself. Am I invested because I'm open to the possibility that you might be innocent? Am I naive because I don't want to see a man with airtight alibis sent to prison, or worse? If the sadness from these deaths has forced you to become blind, if this dark man—"

"You. Don't. Know. *Anything*. About the Dark Man," Grace hissed. He leaned forward, closing the space between us. He smirked again.

"Do you honestly think you understand the black ... because you're *afraid* of it?"

My stomach churned with slushy, slippery dread.

"How—" I began. Damn it. I couldn't help myself, I couldn't understand how he ...

"I can't see you, Mr. Taylor, but I already *know* you," Martin Grace said. "I smelled the stink of fear when you opened that door. Just look at you and your youth and your oh-so-comfortable clothes, and your baggy jeans, your button-down shirt hanging over an undoubtedly *very trendy* T-shirt, and your old wind-up watch—an heirloom from a dead relative?—and your broken-in sneakers that *just barely* squeak on this shit-hole's floors, and the sloppy glop of jelly on your shirt, and oh, your inexperience, all the paperwork you brought along, all your notes ... "

I couldn't blink. Couldn't say a word.

" ... oh, and be sure to *breathe*, Mr. Taylor," the blind man continued, "be sure to keep breathing while the patient yanks the rug from beneath you, *makes* you, pins your personality like a lepidopterist pins butterflies into glass boxes, pins you for the fraud that you are—you're an amateur, Mr. Taylor, an *artist,* a paintbrush-wielding *phony*—and somehow, you think I haven't heard this all before, haven't anticipated every question you'll ask, haven't a *brain* inside my *skull*.

"You want to save me, Mr. Taylor? You think I owe you explanations about the black, about the Dark Man, about *this?*" His eyelids flashed open like bad window shades, pupils not seeing his own waving hand before his face. "Here is wisdom. This world is cold, cruel and selfish, Mr. Taylor. We must tear the things we want from its grasp, claw our way inside, be worthy of the right to possess what we possess. You want to save the blind man? Get inside his mind like he's gotten into yours? Then fucking *earn* it."

Grace leaned back now. His eyes lowered to the hands in his lap. Whatever bond I'd hoped to make today had been depth charged, nuked and shot into the sun. My mouth made like it wanted to speak, but I was too stupefied to say anything.

"Stop trembling," Grace said. His voice was now passionless, bored. "And for God's sake, close your mouth. You sound like a beached fish."

He's ... cruel, Annie Jackson had said.

Yes. Yes, he was.

I stood up. I was numb, full-body numb. I watched my hands push the wooden chair back to its spot beneath the table. I saw my fingers slide across the table to the stack of papers I'd brought, and to the long, rectangular electronic device resting beside it.

This is what ... this is what prey *feels like,* I thought. *Cold and hunted and utterly alone.*

And yet. And yet.

I eyed the large Casio keyboard I'd placed on the desk. I heard my mantra for Grace's case in my mind: *He's blind, but help him see.* I felt my spine straighten, my shoulders rise, just a bit. I switched on the instrument, then turned to face my patient.

"You are a cold-hearted son of a bitch," I heard myself say. "And I'm going to help you if it kills me. We start again tomorrow, you and me, and I'm going to tear and claw the best I can, just like you said."

The man sneered. Opened his mouth to retort. I didn't let him.

"And you're going to meet me halfway, old man," I said. My fingers tapped a few keys on the Casio. Notes, sweet and bright, chimed from its speaker. Grace's eyebrows rose, curious. "You're going to play this thing tonight and find your groove and we're going to talk about it, because if you want someone with steel, Mr. Grace, someone to listen to your wretched stories about the Dark Man and your Life Before Blindness—and you *do*, as sure as I'm standing here, I *know* you do—then you've gotta earn that, too."

Martin Grace's eyes slid upward, in my direction. He actually smiled.

"We'll see," he said.

I twisted the metal doorknob to leave. "And that," I said, "is the goddamned point."

5

How did he know?

I asked myself this question over and over as the L line train *clack-clack-clacked* southeast, back on Manhattan Island, far away from The Brink, toward Washington Square Park and my rendezvous with Lucas. I felt slow, out of sorts. Martin Grace had done exactly what he'd said: pinned me, down to the six-month-old Vans on my feet. And he'd known what I was thinking. No, deeper and weirder than that. He'd known *how* I was thinking. I'd left Room 507 thirty minutes ago fully clothed, but stripped bare.

I stared at the passing darkness outside the subway, the occasional tunnel light (and accompanying graffiti) breaking the black. My eyes pulled focus from the tunnel wall to the window's surface. There I was, reflected, just as Martin Grace had described, a MySpace generation refugee, a shaggy-haired painter, an inexperienced poseur. My fingers rushed over the array of colorful buttons pinned to the flap on my canvas satchel. These were my cheerfully ironic, subversive broadcasts to the world; my personality trimmed down to punchy, half-sentence slogans. There Is No Spoon. At Least the War on the Middle Class Is Going Well. *Accio* New President. Rape Is Fucking Wrong. WYSIWYG. What Would Scooby-Doo?

They now seemed self-referential, hollow, immature.

The train trembled onward. I checked the time on my Eterna, which was indeed an heirloom bequeathed from my late grandfather. 5:30. I tightened my grip around my black Cannondale hybrid bike's handlebars. I watched my bicycle helmet hanging there, hypnotized by it swaying on its chinstrap.

How did he know?

I closed my eyes, silently asking for some enlightenment, for some distance from this throbbing, full-brain bruise I was experiencing. After a moment, the bespectacled, professorial side of me—the part that I always imagined sounded a bit like Leonard Nimoy—spoke up.

It's obvious, my logical side said. *Martin Grace isn't blind. He "made" you because he could* see *you. It explains his description of your clothes, the reference to what you ate at lunch (you had a jam stain on your shirt; you can see it right there, in your reflection), even the fear you experienced when you stepped into Room 507. He's not blind at all.*

I nodded slightly at this, let it roll for a moment. And what about the things he'd said about ... me?

Fascinating, my Spock-self replied. *If Grace can see, then he did what you do every day at The Brink: He watched your facial expressions and body language and modified his message for maximum impact. His comments were barbed, yes, but generic—after all, you're not the only twenty-something fretting about filling his professional shoes. Grace's assumptions about Annie Jackson are equally elementary: He discovered, somehow, that you had lunched together, and exploited that. It's Ockham's razor: All things being equal, the simplest solution tends to be the right one. Extrapolate. Grace is not blind.*

I frowned and opened my eyes. No. He was. I had a folder full of expert diagnoses saying he was. More important, I *knew* he was, I could feel it ... which meant he'd literally smelled my fear, heard things in my voice that I didn't hear.

Ah, and his *intent.* That's what spooked me. He'd wanted to break me. Martin Grace was an old, blind shark, all teeth and hunger. I'd been devoured in there.

So. How did he know? I smelled some truth in what my logical side was saying. If Grace did this evening what I do every day—excavate a mind's secrets—then what business did an audio engineer have knowing such things? That didn't make much sense. Not a goddamned bit.

My eyed slid upward, met the gaze of my reflection. There was something missing here. My brain nudged at this like a tongue probing the gap of a missing tooth. I needed more information about Martin Grace, things not in his admittance report. That folder told me what he was, but it didn't tell me *who* he was.

A secret smile rose to my lips. I knew a person who could help me. I just had to convince her it was the right thing to do.

The train screeched and slowed, rushing into the bright, tiled expanse of the 6th Avenue–14th Street station. I slipped my helmet from the bike's handlebars, plunked it on my head. I hefted my Cannondale toward the door. Enough shop thought, for now. It was time to meet up with Lucas ... and then with Rachael and Dad. And Gram.

✳ ✳ ✳

The sun had sunk past New York's skyline by the time I'd pedaled to "Well7," Lucas' nickname for Washington Square Park.

My kid brother is obsessed with slang, constantly inventing oddball words to describe the places and people around him—and always hoping those new words become mini-memes and spread beyond his circle of family and friends. "Well7" is an abbreviation-meets-amalgam of the "W" of Washington and the square you get making an "L" with your left hand and a "7" with your right. An unholy creation, sure, but I found it clever. Even my father, Mr. Windsor Knot, called the park Well7 now.

This pleased Lucas to no end.

I braked the Cannondale near a streetlight and watched my brother from afar. He was a hundred yards away, alone, burning calories around the park's *Arc de Triomphe*-inspired seventy-seven-foot marble arch. He was practicing his hobby, parkour.

The brainbendingly fast-paced maneuvers Lucas was performing around—and now on—the Arch have not officially been classified as a sport, although anything that requires this intense level of physical dexterity and stamina falls into that category as far as I'm concerned. Lucas tells me it's a state of mind, an urban survival philosophy whipped into blurred motion. He insists parkour is a discipline, a martial art whose opponent is the cityscape. I default to his expertise; he's been doing this for two years now. Last year, my father and I spent Lucas' nineteenth birthday in St. Vincent's emergency room after Lucas suffered a nasty drop from a second-story windowsill. Dad's fancy dinner plans were ruined. He'd fumed the rest of the night.

Them's the breaks.

Lucas is half-Wikipedia, half-evangelist about all his passions, so everyone he knows, knows a lot about parkour. The word is a truncated, modified version of the French term for a military obstacle course. It's also called the "art of displacement." The point of parkour is as simple as its execution is complex: traverse your urban surroundings in the most efficient and speedy means possible. If a fence separates you from your destination, jump it. If it's a wall, scale it. If it's a building ... well ... get all Spider-Man on it. Brick walls are sidewalks for the parkour-proficient.

This is a scrappy, dangerous pastime. I once watched Lucas rocket up the fire escape of a five-story New York University admin building, scramble to its roof in rapid-fire movements evocative of both crab and gorilla, make a running leap to a neighboring building, bound down *its* fire escape, and land on the sidewalk on all fours, like an unperturbed house cat. By the end of this performance, I'm sure my heart was pounding faster than his.

And here he was in the gloaming of Well7, again dashing toward its legendary Arch, now in the air, now bounding up its surface, side-crawling several feet, now shoving himself upward and backward, away from the marble, twisting his thin frame into a back flip, his body trapped in graceful silhouette for an instant—a black-and-white still of human ambition and freedom, I thought—now landing on his toes, tucking his body into a roll ... and now standing, panting, grinning in my direction, glancing back at the thing he'd conquered.

I pedaled over. Lucas yanked the bandanna off his head, freeing his long, curly brown hair, inherited from our mother. His fellow parkour practitioners (called *traceurs* and *traceuses,* depending on their sex) called him Socket, in honor of his shock-mop of hair and buzzy, infectious personality. (He usually acts like he's French-kissed an electrical outlet.)

My brother tugged off his battered backpack, unzipping it in one energetic motion. A cluster of black cables snaked from the bag to his body, down the neck of his loose-fitting long-sleeved T-shirt. I looked a question at him.

"Welcome up, buttercup," he said as he reached into the bag. He pulled out a compact notebook computer and fussed with a small box attached to the device. The laptop was a "Toughbook," a seemingly indestructible and very expensive device. Lucas could never afford something like this on the salary of his part-time clerk job at NYU's admissions office. This was last year's Christmas gift from our dad.

The cables connected to the PC sprang free. He flipped open the laptop and dropped cross-legged onto the concrete.

"Hey. What's up?" I asked. I nodded to the computer.

Lucas smiled, his teeth aglow in the LCD light. "You'll love it, Z," he said. "You'll *'dore* it."

He raised a hand high above his head. "Okay, so you've got bird's-eye view," he said, "and you've got worm's-eye view." His hand now shot earthward. "And of course, you've got first-person POV."

My brother's fingers now tapped the side of his head. I nodded. He was talking camera angles. Lucas was a film student at NYU. I couldn't fathom how Lucas' professors kept up with his super-sonic mind.

His eyes never left the computer screen. His fingers slid across the device's trackpad, double-clicking as he spoke. "But what about a hand's-eye view, huh? Or a foot's-eye view? Right? Yeah?"

He extended his arm. A small plastic gadget was strapped to the top of his hand. He tapped his sneaker, where an identical device was tucked into his shoelaces. Cables extended from these, up into Lucas' clothes. I blinked, doing the math. He'd rigged tiny vidcams to record his parkour moves.

"HAH!" Lucas cried, watching the ultra-jittery digital footage. "Steadicam, it ain't—but it works!" He finally looked up at me, gesturing at the cable on his wrist. "These wires are a pain in the conjunction-junction, but still. This'll come in handy for the project I wanna work on. Totally self-financed, fictionalized reality show. *Big Brother* meets crime-fighting parkour artist."

"And do you have a name for this zero-budget adventure?" I asked.

"*Traceur Fire*," he said proudly.

I laughed, wondering if this preposterous project would suffer the same fate as most of his invented words. My brother is one of the most ambitious, creative people I know ... but there are so many ideas whirring around in his head. He can't choose which project to prioritize, so he flits between them, hummingbird-style. Never getting too deep.

"I'll tell you all about it later," Lucas said as he unplugged the cables and cameras, stuffing the gear into his backpack. "But it's gonna be *epic,* man. So what about you, Z? You experience anything epic today?"

I laughed again. Yeah, you could say that.

I gave him today's highlights as we traveled from Well7 to my apartment on Avenue B in Alphabet City. We had about an hour to get to the funeral home where Gram's memorial service was being held.

I pedaled and Lucas bounded along beside me, occasionally busting out into a low-key parkour move. His body deftly pitched around streetlights and trash bins.

"Hey, how're you dealing with it?" I asked him. "Losing Gram?"

"Freedom's on the march," Lucas replied. "Seriously? Aching, but mending. All the signs were there, Z. I just didn't want to see 'em. But when she died, the pieces finally clicked into place, like Lego bricks. *Click.* She's gone. *Click.* We're still here. *Click.* We mourn, we move on."

"That's pretty damned insightful of you," I said.

"That reminds me. Hang on a sec."

Lucas removed his green backpack and opened it. He closed one eye, concentrating, as his hand dove into the pack. He looked like he was about to pull a rabbit from a hat. I grinned.

"Thought you'd want to see these," he said, passing me a cardboard box. "These were Gram's family pictures, going way back. There're some docs in there, too. I scanned some of 'em for the multimedia slideshow at the memorial."

"There's not going to be a dry eye in the house, is there?" I asked.

"Nope."

We stood there, smiling and thinking of her. It was an uncomplicated moment. Nice.

And despite what was still to come that night—the funeral home, my screaming father and the lunatic stranger, the folded slip of paper that would be pressed into my sweating palms—I can honestly say that this moment with my brother was the last time I've remembered feeling carefree.

The rest has been darkness and madness and terrible.

6

NOT ALL WHO
WANDER ARE
LOST.

The Selznick and Sons funeral home, like many in Manhattan, was
on the ground floor of a multistoried apartment building. And like
many other funeral homes in Manhattan, you'd never know it after
stepping past the polished brass-and-glass doors. The interior fea-

tured soothing cream-colored walls, a politely ticking grandfather clock, gold-framed paintings of flowers, stained glass windows. The colors in the windows matched the furniture, which matched the drapes, which matched the carpet. They were all muted, reassuring shades, not distinct enough to attract attention. Stately, serene, invisible.

Lucas and I arrived just before 7 p.m. Rachael waited for us in the lobby.

I felt giddy as she walked toward us, then felt guilty for feeling giddy. I should've been thinking about Gram, somberly preparing myself for the service. But as those few seconds of her approach stretched into delicious slow motion, as Rachael's hips rocked, as I gazed at her lips, I simply couldn't pull my eyes off her. She's a few inches taller than me, and God, did I like looking up to her.

Rachael. She's the reason balladeers were born. At least that's what I've told her, a thousand thousand times. She never gets tired of hearing it, though.

She wore an understated black dress and a matching long-sleeved sweater that hid the tattoos racing down her arms. The small tattoos on each of my wrists—the Chinese symbols for "courage" and "faith"—were covered by my dress shirt and jacket.

We clean up well, Lucas, Rachael, and me: today we were Opposite Day impostors, proudly displaying our Clark Kent alter egos for the AARP crowd. Rachael's magenta hair and the hoops in her nose and eyebrow spoiled the image a bit.

"Hey," she said, and gave me a quick hug. She kissed my cheek. "Right on time. You doing okay?"

I nodded. She smelled wonderful.

"Yo, *Hochrot*," Lucas said, a bit too loudly for my liking. I glanced around the hushed lobby. Solemn newcomers were stepping through the front doors. I gave Lucas a parental *shhh*. He took the hint.

"So tell me," he whispered. "Have you fragged your kids today?"

Rachael rolled her eyes.

"They're not 'my' kids, Lucas," she said, her voice low. "They're twerps on Xbox Live, screaming at their moms for chocolate milk. These guys, they *can't stand* getting beat by a girl."

"My geek goddess," I said, sliding my arm around her waist. "Mortals, behold her mad 'Onyx War 2' skills."

"Oh, poor Z," she said. She glanced up at a magenta sliver of hair that had fallen into her face, and blew it aside with a quick puff. "Onyx War was last week. It's Bloodwire now. This game's codemonkeys built it just for me. It's got the three Fs: First-person ... fully destroyable environments ... and *flame-throwers*. That stuff melts my heart every time."

Her blue eyes glimmered. She bared her teeth, playfully.

"Don't mess with PixelVixen707," she whispered diabolically. "Snarl."

Lucas snickered. "Snarl," he said.

"Speaking of messing with a good thing," I said, pulling my cell phone from my slacks pocket. I passed it to Rachael. "Dad's probably going to be late. Listen to the voice mail he left last night. Dial **212-629-1951**, and hit **3017**. That's my password. Unbelievable."

Rachael dialed in the numbers and pressed the phone to her ear. Lucas leaned in, curious.

The pair listened and exchanged more up-to-the-nanosecond slang. If you'd put a gun to my head at that moment, I still couldn't tell you what in the hell they were talking about. I think they were dissing Dad, but I wasn't sure. I needed subtitles when these propeller-heads got together.

At least Rachael had a professional excuse. In addition to being a part-time fact-checker for the *New York Journal-Ledger* and a freelance technical writer, she was the creator of PixelVixen707.com, a gaming blog bristling with "geek chica snarkitude." The site had started as a personal weblog, but the gaming-related posts had brought piles of readers—and ad money. I was the guy who'd created the splash artwork for her home page: a cartoonified Rachael in coveralls, welder's goggles perched atop her head, sleeves rolled high, flexing a tattooed bicep in the classic Rosie the Riveter "We Can Do It!" pose. She held a Wii remote in her clenched fist. A mutual friend had introduced us a year ago; my for-the-check freelance gig evolved into a life-changing romance. I couldn't image my world without this woman now.

And Lucas' excuse? He was just a hardcore gamer. And, well, he's Lucas. I can't comprehend half the things he says anyway.

A slender, graceful man stepped toward us, his pleasant face tinged with a hint of generic sorrow.

"Ms. Webster, are these the gentlemen you were waiting for?" he asked.

She nodded, immediately toning down her contagious smile. "Yes, these are Mrs. Taylor's grandsons, Zach and Lucas."

The man introduced himself as Mr. Kress, the "evening director" for Selznick and Sons. He efficiently ushered us past the staid, mahogany-accented couches and chairs and out of the lobby. He apologized to Lucas and me for our loss—I nodded blankly, it felt *weird* receiving such intimate condolences from a stranger—and then encouraged us to sign the guest book and fill out a memorial card before entering Gram's parlor.

I didn't know what a memorial card was, but Mr. Kress explained as he walked us to a desk just outside the open doors of the room reserved for us. I looked past him, at the group of silver-haired folks inside. My grandmother's urn sat on a table by the far wall, placed next to a small wooden box.

I smiled. My high school buddy Ida "Eye" Jean-Phillipe and her father Eustacio were here. As far as I knew, neither of them had known Gram, so I reckoned they were here to support the family. Eustacio was the flint-eyed deputy chief of NYPD's homicide division, and an old friend of my dad's. ("From the ramen noodle days," Dad had once told me.) Ida, an NYPD lab tech, was here for me. I hadn't known she was coming tonight. Very cool of her to show.

" ... so think of a memorial card as a message to your loved one," Mr. Kress was saying as we reached the desk. He picked up a small envelope and a pre-folded card and handed them to me, gave another to Lucas and one to Rachael. "Feel free to write anything you like—a favorite memory, a prayer, a story. It's a way to tell her that you're thinking about her.

"Then place the card in the envelope," he said, demonstrating. Lucas snorted. I flashed him a half-smirk: *We know how frickin' envelopes work. Jesus Christ.*

" ... and place it in the box next to your grandmother's cremains," Kress concluded. "We hope it will provide some comfort for your family to read these after the service."

The director thanked us, and softly withdrew. The three of us stood by the desk. We didn't speak. This was ... well, this was it, wasn't it? I stared at the card, suddenly feeling awkward and clumsy and cold and oh

—*be sure to* breathe, *Mr. Taylor,* I heard the reptilian voice of Martin Grace say, *be sure to keep breathing while the patient yanks the rug from beneath you*—

I shivered, there in the hallway. Rachael noticed, and gave me a concerned look through her black-framed glasses. Lucas, oblivious, bent over the desk and began writing a message to Gram with one of the fountain pens provided.

Rachael reached for my hand, entwined her fingers in mine and gave a supportive squeeze. I smiled. She let go, stepped over to the table and wrote her own message. Finished, they both looked at me.

"Give me a minute," I said. "Go ahead." They stepped further into the room.

And then it was me, a fountain pen and my grandmother.

Gram, I wrote, and paused. I watched the ink seep into the thick paper, a black cumulus cloud spreading into a pale sky.

Ink and Gram.

The two words that had carried me through so much of my life came from my grandmother. *Courage and faith, little Zachary,* she had said to me after my mother died, more than twenty-one years ago. As I stood here in the funeral home, I could remember that night as her hands brushed away my nightmare tears. The veins on her hands. Her palms, smooth and soft. *That's all you need, baby boy. Courage, to face the tough things. Faith, to endure them.*

She'd been right. Her words were still in my heart, on my wrists.

Thank you, I wrote finally. *I miss you.*

I blew gently on the ink, then closed the card.

I stepped into the parlor to join my family and friends.

✳✳✳

After I slipped my memorial card into the box by Gram's urn—brushing off the *weirdness* of knowing that the woman who'd helped raise me was now reduced to a canful of ashes—I worked my way toward Lucas, Rachael and Eye. The mood in the room wasn't jovial, but there was a joyfulness. We were here to celebrate Gram's life, after all.

Gram's friends all wanted to talk. *She always said such nice things about you. Your father was so blessed to have her there, to help. She loved you so much.* They were kind strangers, and I thanked them and held their hands and listened to their stories. I'm good at listening to people's stories.

"*Ou byen?*" Eye whispered to me as we finally hugged. "You holding up okay?"

"You bet," I said. "Thanks for coming. It means ... it means a helluva lot." I held her hand for a moment. My artist's eye took a picosecond of pleasure in the contrast of her black skin against mine. "We knew it was coming. It sucks, but it's ... it's over, you know?"

I knew she understood. Her mother died when she was young, too.

"And thanks again for the assist with Spindle," I said. "You did it, Eye."

"Oh no," she replied. "*You* did it, Z. I just helped a little." She added a quick phrase in Kreyol that I didn't understand, but her chuckle told me it didn't matter.

My high school girlfriend had lived in the States since she was ten years old, but she still peppered her conversations with phrases from her native language. I loved listening to her speak. I've always thought that if flowers could talk, their voices would sound like Haitian Kreyol, rising and falling, lyrical, like piccolos.

I glanced past Eye's shoulder at her father. Eustacio Jean-Phillipe was now pacing by the doorway of the parlor. He was talking on his cell phone.

"Is Papa-Jean on it?" I asked.

She grinned and nodded. "Papa-Jean" was our nickname for her dad. "It" was Spindle's thirty-year-old surprise.

Last week, I'd discovered that the locations of three bodies—and the buried treasure she and her two friends had vowed to hide—had been lurking in plain sight for years, sewn into Gertrude Spindler's quilt designs. I'd gone on a field trip, traveling to the "X" on the map—a rat-infested kitchen in a long-closed Chinatown restaurant, of all places—pried up some floorboards, and unearthed an arm-length metal tube. Ida Jean-Phillipe had opened the container in the NYPD forensic laboratory and extracted a sword in a stitched cloth scabbard. Her research revealed that the sword had an ancient, blood-soaked—and apparently "mystical"—history.

Ida didn't care for those silly *malchans* stories, and I agreed that we needed scientific evidence. Working off the books, Eye confirmed that Spindle's fingerprints were on the treasure. Using that information last Friday, I'd coaxed the rest of the story from Spindle. NYPD now knew what I'd discovered, including the identity of her dead cohorts, *sans* Eye's contributions.

"Papa's got some people looking into it," Eye said to me. "I know them. They're good cops. I think a few of them were a little embarrassed by that write-up in Saturday's *Post*, though. '30-Year-Old Murders Solved By Brinkvale Therapist. Crazy Quilter In Custody.'"

"Dude, you made the papers?" Lucas asked.

My face flushed red. I changed the subject.

"So yeah, Eye. I owe you some beer for this, next time we're at Stovie's."

"Ohhh, honey. Some? *Some* beer?" Eye took a quick step away from me, wedged herself between Rachael and Lucas, and playfully tossed her arms around their shoulders. There they were, my little family. I wished I had a camera. "Not *some* beer, *cooyon*. ALL the beer."

Beside her, Rachael giggled. "Girl, you are *so* my best friend," she said. She glanced at me, her expression pure, ah, geek chica snarkitude. "That's right, Z. *All* the beer."

I laughed quietly. "Fine, fine. All the beer."

Lucas beamed. "Katabatic," he said.

I glanced at my watch. A half-hour had passed since we'd arrived. We had another thirty until the memorial service. I looked back to the doorway, past Eye's father murmuring into his phone, to the hall. Was Dad really going to be late for this? Was he—

Huh.

A nearly bald man with a long silver ponytail stood next to the memorial cards. In his mid-fifties, he wore jeans, Chuck Taylors, and a photographer's vest over a black T-shirt.

I squinted. The T-shirt read: Not All Who Wander Are Lost.

As I watched, the man bent down to fill out a card. I saw the reflection of the creamy stationery in his round Lennon-style wire rims. Each wrist sported half a dozen bracelets. The guy was part flower child, part punk rocker. His face was twisted with worry, or dread.

I nudged Lucas.

"You know that guy?" He shook his head. I frowned. "You think Gram would've known that guy?"

"Hellzes bellzes," Lucas said. "No way, bro. Gram was Upper East Side, all the way. You know that. Unless ... " He paused. "Unless she was moonlighting at the local Freak Flag Manufacturer's Union or something."

"*Luc*-as," Rachael hissed. "Shut up. Uncool."

My brother shrugged at her innocently. I turned back as the man sealed the envelope and placed it in one of the pockets of his vest. He walked past Papa-Jean into the room, walking toward ...

Toward me.

"Are you Zach? Zach Taylor?" His voice was high, almost feminine. I glanced at my friends—they looked just as perplexed as I felt—and back at him. I nodded. He extended his hand.

The glittering charms on his bracelets clinked and chittered as we shook hands. Several crucifixes hung from leather straps. A Star of David. A Buddha. A pentagram. A mandala. The Virgin Mary. Other symbols, so many others that I couldn't place, including an armor-covered woman cradling an infant. His calloused palm squeezed mine, hard.

"I can't believe it," he said. His eyes glimmered with tears. "You're ... you're grown up. And *you*"—he was now gazing at my brother—"little Lookie-Luke. *Unbelievable.*"

The man was now emphatically pumping my hand with both of his. I didn't like this at all. My shoulders tensed. I tried to pull away. He wasn't letting go. I opened my mouth to speak.

"Listen," the man said. "I'm so sorry about your grandmother. You have no idea what she gave up for you two. She really protected—"

A hand slammed onto the stranger's shoulder from behind. The man did a full-body start as the atonal *shink-shink-shink* of his bracelets tailed off in a discordant jangle. I yanked away my hand, stepped backward, felt Rachael's hands steady me.

My father towered behind the stranger. His blue eyes were narrow slits. Eustacio stood beside Dad, like a club bouncer.

"Get out," Dad said.

The man turned and looked up, up, up at my father's face.

"Will." The man's tone evoked a showdown from a spaghetti Western. "Fancy meeting—"

Eustacio's dark fingers snatched at the man's forearm, his thumb digging into the tender meat just below the elbow. The skin went alive there, blossoming red. The stranger sucked in air.

"Take a walk with me," Papa-Jean said.

The cop didn't wait for a reply. Eustacio shoved the man away from us, toward the parlor door, his thumb still digging into the man's flesh. A heartbeat later, they were gone.

I looked at my dad, uncomprehending. I watched the haughty, frigid expression in his blue eyes glimmer, then vanish ... and saw the quivering muscles along his lean jaw line smooth as he unclenched his teeth. I knew this version of Dad. He wasn't merely angry. He was Defcon One, thermonuclearly furious.

"What was—"

"Drop it, Zachary," Dad said. I must've telegraphed that I was going to ask again, because he cut me off again, shaking his head once. I flinched. It was the nonverbal gavel bang. Court was adjourned.

My father has always been emotionally chilly—in fact, he wasn't present through much of our childhood; Gram did the lion's share of raising us cubs after Mom died—and he's never been one to tolerate backtalk. I suspect this hails from his ambition, and being the uber-hardass his job demands. A half-decade ago, when things were at their worst for me (*giddy-giddy pardner, let's get the posse and raise some hell*), his low threshold for defiance was pushed beyond its limits. He was the one who sent me away. Indirectly, he was the one who introduced me to my passion, my art ... and eventually, my career.

I don't think I could have disappointed him more. He once told me this "art therapy thing" was a phase. He offered me a "more respectable" position at his office, starting as a mail clerk. No disrespect to the profession, but I politely declined.

But *this*—this haughty, ice-cold snarling Dad—was a more recent development. For the past few years, he's been mean-spirited, high-strung, obsessed with work. He's changed. I didn't care for the man he has become. I guess we're even in that regard.

I closed my mouth, acquiescing. And with that, my dad became *normal* again. He hugged Rachael and Eye, tousled Lucas' hair, commenced with small talk about my girlfriend's writing and my brother's film classes and my friend's gig in the NYPD labs. My tribe wasn't stupid—they'd been around long enough to know that the wisest thing to do was humor New York County District Attorney William V. Taylor—so they smiled back, and answered his questions. Our eyes flitted to each other's, though, sending near-telepathic transmissions.

None of us knew what was going on with that stranger, but Dad's reaction was clearly bullshit. I was suddenly curious, hungry-curious, to learn more.

"—any interesting patients lately?" Dad was asking me.

"Uhhh ... " Great. Frying pan to fire. I couldn't get into this particular subject with my father right now, considering I was assigned to Martin's Grace case and Dad was on a mission to personally crucify the man. To me, Grace was already "a shit-storm onion"—a Lucasism, meaning layers and layers of trouble—without locking horns with Dad over the guy.

More importantly, I needed to know what had just happened here.

" ... yeah, Dad. Settled something on Friday, in fact." I faked a grimace, then checked my watch. "Lucas and Rachael can tell you a little about it. I need to hit the head before the service starts." I passed Eustacio as I left the parlor; we exchanged a nod.

And then I was off, trotting down the hallway, heading out of the lobby.

***

I caught up with the stranger a half-block down East 77th Street. Despite the autumn chill in the air, I was sweating from the run.

"Hey!" I hollered. The stranger turned, spotted me, and made to bolt across the street.

A taxi nearly clipped the man as he stepped onto the asphalt. He leaped back to the sidewalk, swaying wildly. In classic New York style, the cabbie screamed "fuck you" and then the car screeched off, leaving me alone with the man, both of us still panting.

"Look, I just want to know what the hell that was about," I said. The fellow shook his head, eying traffic for another opportunity to cross. He clutched his bruised forearm. I waved my hands in front of him to get his attention.

"I swear to God, man, my dad doesn't know I'm here. I just *need to know*. Who are you?"

The man barked a panicked laugh. "I'm nobody, Zach," he said. His spectacles reflected the passing headlights. "I'm the invisible man, the Ghost of Christmas Past, I'm an afterthought, a vapor"—and now his face twisted into a sneer as he spat out the words—"*vaporized* by your father, edited out of the history books, just like *him*."

I blinked. "Edited what? Who?"

"My God!" the man yelped. "It's all new to *you*—they never told you, did they? Of *course* you don't know. Gone, poof, a whole life ruined and erased. Your grandmother listened to Will—always the one with the answers, the one with the plans, the angles, the power—and she agreed! Decided it was for the best, to protect you. How could Will do that? Henry was a good man!"

"Who?" I asked. This was insane, The Brink brought topside, lunatic times, lunatic talk, *shink-shink-shink* jingle-jangle craziness.

"HENRY!" the stranger bellowed. "Will's brother. His own brother!"

Something small broke inside my head, like a cog popping loose. I cocked my head to the side, trying desperately to understand.

"My father doesn't have a brother," I whispered.

The Invisible Man was nodding now, his hand sliding up to his photographer's vest.

"Oh, yes he did," the man said. "Yes he *does*. Still alive, worse than dead. I came here tonight ... "

His voice trailed off. The man stared up into the night sky for a moment. A tear slid down his face. He looked back to me.

"I came here to finally tell her I was sorry, so sorry for not telling her Will was wrong, for not speaking out, for not standing up for your uncle—"

"I don't *have* an uncle," I said. That gear in my head was still rolling around loose.

"You do, Zach." The stranger's expression was pitying, sympathetic. He fished the memorial card envelope from his pocket and pressed it into my sweating palms. "You do. Hidden away, buried by your dad. But it didn't—"

He was looking over my shoulder now, the panic surging over

his face again.

"Fuck."

I turned and saw—and now heard—my father as he ran up the street toward us, shouting as he came. Damn it. Either Dad hadn't fallen for my "gotta whiz" sham, or good ole Papa-Jean had been suspicious and followed me. It didn't matter.

"Who are you?"

The Invisible Man shook his head again. He glanced into the traffic, then to me.

"I'm nobody, Zach. And so's Henry, right now. But know this: It didn't happen the way they said it did. It's all lies."

My father was screaming. The Invisible Man and I stared into each other's eyes for a heartbeat. He smiled and dashed across the street. The cars braked and honked, roaring around him. He made it to the other side.

And then, he disappeared into the darkness.

I gazed down at the crumpled envelope in my hand, a thing that—if this man was telling the truth—was a message from an alternate reality, a parallel universe. An uncle? Lucas and I ... had an uncle?

I pocketed the envelope. And then William Taylor, in all his Defcon-One glory, was upon me.

***

Call me the perpetual Young Man. I was a "young man" when I was six and accidentally dropped a jar of Skippy peanut butter on my kid brother's toes. I was a "young man" when I was ten and got caught watching a scrambled adult cable channel in our living room, well past my bedtime. (If you crossed your eyes just right, you could make out flashbulb pops of naked flesh through the snow.) And I was a "young man" when I was actually a young man: doing the Anti-Zach thing, breaking into high school lockers, acquiring mad skills with slim jims and stealing cars, getting stoned, picking locks, swiping merchandise, losing cops in alleyways and street crowds. And then the sin I committed, the unforgivable one that forced my father's hand and swept me away to a New Hampshire facility for "evaluation." I'm better for it. I hold back because of it. I'm no longer giddy to get *giddy-giddy*.

I'm sure I'll also be a "young man" when I'm fifty and my father is on his death bed.

"Young man, I want to know exactly what you're doing here," Dad growled now. Neither Lucas nor I had inherited our father's height, which was something he used expertly in times like this. He stepped toward me, looming like a thundercloud. He was far too close now, invading my personal space. I felt a desperate pang of claustrophobia; the tie around my neck felt like a noose.

Dad's blue eyes flared.

"Put some words into the air, son. Answer me."

I stammered and took a step backward, but he persisted, matching me footstep for footstep.

"Ah … " I heard myself say. "Dad, I just … "

"Just," he said. "What."

"Jesus! It was fucking weird, Dad!" I cried. I'd never seen him like this, this ferociously intent on getting answers. "What you and Papa-Jean did back there. Don't look at me and say that it wasn't! Can you honestly—"

"I'm asking the questions, Zachary." I heard his teeth click together on that last syllable. He took another half-step toward me. He was a playground bully, a junkyard Rottweiler, a lawyer vivisecting the accused on the witness stand. This was something he was dangerously good at. I realized then this was something he'd spent the past thirty years perfecting.

He huffed an exhale through his nostrils.

"I said. Tell. Me."

"I was curious," I replied. My shoulders jigged, shrugging madly. "I couldn't not be curious. You get all mafioso on some poor scrub, somebody who knew us—"

"He *knows* us because he's a criminal, Zachary," Dad hissed. "I helped send him up to Clinton twenty years ago, twenty-to-life. Must be out on good behavior ... and let me tell you that's a joke, young man, because there was nothing *good* about his behavior, not back then. Veterinarian. He had a clinic, clinic had a basement. He took his wife there, skinned her alive, *kept her alive*, and ate her skin. Cooked it like strips of bacon. He had enough training to know where to cut, *how* to cut, and how to stop the blood before she could die."

I shuddered, shaking my head. Breathing was very difficult right now.

"He did keep the blood that spilled, though," Dad said. "Kept every drop. And when she finally went, he went too, went out in the streets, naked, covered in buckets of her blood. God almighty. I had no idea he was out. Means he's been watching me—us—for a while."

The granite sternness in my dad's face ebbed, just a bit.

"You've always been like your mother, Zachary," he said. "You're caring and, yes, curious to a fault. And like her, you've always rushed into the fray, buying what people are selling, asking questions only after the damage is done. You needed history here, son. Context. You should have talked to me."

I didn't know what to say. Dad filled the silence.

"What did he tell you?" he asked. My father's eyes narrowed, predatory once more.

My reeling mind reeled itself in. I snagged on that question, coaxed my perspective into something more critical and defensive. Was Dad asking this because he was protecting me from a lunatic ex-con? Or was he asking because he was lying, lying right now, lying through his serrated lawyer teeth?

I thought of the card in my pocket, and what I'd been told. *It didn't happen the way they said it did. It's all lies.*

Fold, or call?

I lied back.

"Nothing. He kept saying he was the Invisible Man. Just said it over and over, Invisible Man, Invisible Man."

My father harrumphed.

"Yeah. That's what he said back then, too. That's why he bathed in his wife's blood. To finally become 'visible.' Now do you understand why I did what I did? Why I wanted to protect you?"

I nodded. The traffic on East 77th Street rushed past.

"All right, Zach," Dad said. "Let's put this to bed and get back to Gram." He smiled. "Cool?"

The wind gusted, chilly and unfriendly. He nodded.

The two of us walked back to the funeral home. I shivered the whole way.

I don't know which couple was hungrier: Me and Rachael, or Dali and Bliss. The cats were certainly the more vocal pair, tickled to see us as we entered our one-bedroom on Avenue B. Bliss served up throaty purr-chirps. Dali nuzzled our legs in his ecstasy to greet Those Who Provide Food.

"Hey kitties," I said. Rachael squirmed past Dali's snugglefest, beckoning me to pass her the takeout from YaKnowYa Szechwan It. I handed it off, and now both cats were doing figure eights around my legs, meowing.

Bliss pounced on my shoelace. *Feed us, human, or the worm gets it.*

Rachael strode into our postage-stamp-sized kitchen, snatching plates and chopsticks and a bottle opener from the cabinets. I shuffled to the pantry and liberated the Meow Mix. I resumed our conversation as I poured the food into the cats' hand-painted ceramic bowl.

" ... so yeah, Dad gets the Bond Villain Award for the night," I said to Rachael. "What a jerk."

"Hear, hear," Rachael said. She carried our dinner and two Rogue Chipotle Ales into the living room, and placed them on the battered steamer trunk that doubled as our coffee table. She plopped onto the couch with a tiny *oof*, slipped off her dress shoes, wriggled her toes. "You've been spooked since that guy came up to you. And you! Agent 007! What did that guy say when you chased him outside?"

She closed one eye and pursed her lips. She pointed an index finger at me, her thumb up like a gun hammer. *Kiss kiss, bang bang.*

I love Rachael. I love our life together. I love this breadbox apartment in which we live, on a street that's as electric and eccentric as we are. I love the comfort she brings to my life, the way she looks at me, the way she kisses me, fucks me, cheers me, knows me better than anyone else.

She takes care of me.

But if what the Invisible Man had said tonight was true, then this was rotten family history, emotional sludge. I didn't want to go there with her just yet. It was too soon, too new. Too *raw*. And hell, Dad could be right: none of it might be true at all.

"He was nuts," I said. "Dad said he was a killer, fresh out of Sing Sing or something."

"Gah. There's a million stories in the naked city," Rachael said as she pried off the cap with the bottle opener. "Why do you always get the weird ones?"

I gestured to the corner of the room where I made my art. Like my office, it was a four-car-pileup of sketches, easels, mason jars filled with muddy water, paintbrushes. "Guess it's the luck of the drawer."

Rachael mimicked a punch-line trumpet: *wah-wah-wahhhh*.

"Bad puns. A Zach Taylor specialty."

I gazed down at the cats, inspired. "Well, hello, Dali!"

Rachael laughed through her mouthful of noodles.

"Hey. Hottie." She slapped the cushion beside her. "Get over here."

I tossed my coat and tie onto the comfy chair in the room's corner, then sat next to my girl.

"Seriously. I'm sorry it happened," she said. She placed her chopsticks on her plate and cupped my face in her hands. I was deep-sea diving in those blue eyes. We kissed. I gave an appreciative *mmmm* as she pulled away. "Can I do anything?"

"Just accept my apology for Dad flexing his prick-fu action grip." I plucked up a slice of chicken with my sticks. "He was in rare form. So was Papa-Jean. Me and Eye, we've got ... single-minded fathers."

"They always get their man," Rachael affirmed. She reached out and stroked my arm. "Just like me. Hey. Don't wig. You turned out just fine."

My eyes flicked around the room and mentally cataloged the other rooms in our cozy, cramped apartment. Past the bookcases stuffed with comic trade paperbacks, video game guides, sci-fi novels and technothrillers ... past the paintings with "ZT" in their corners, the framed movie and video-game posters, the art prints ...

past Rachael's spectacular widescreen TV, sound system and racks of game consoles ... past our cramped corners where we performed our passions of writing and art ... past all of these things were Zach lights. Zach lights in every room.

Here in the living room, a string of cheerful chili pepper-shaped Christmas lights, stapled to the walls, glowed above us. In the kitchen and bathroom, light-sensitive gizmos plugged into wall sockets. In our bedroom, a desk lamp with a dimmer switch that was always on, glowing softly, always on. Rachael had learned to appreciate sleep masks.

I hadn't turned out just fine. I couldn't tell you why that was, just that it was. Broken Zach, scared of the dark. A blind man had reminded me of that, nearly five hours ago.

I faked a smile. "Maybe a little undercooked, but I guess I'll do in a pinch."

Rachael grinned, leaning her shoulder against mine.

"You're my fella," she said. "You're doing me just fine."

We shared a smile, and munched in amiable silence, surrounded by that warm blanket of familiarity and comfort. We ate our Szechwan, sipped our Rogues. Rachael chatted about the review of Bloodwire she was cooking up for PixelVixen707. I laughed at the probable headline: "Fan-fraggin'-tastic."

But the shadow-fingers slowly crept back into my mind. My father wasn't the only Taylor man to obsess about his work. I brought my baggage home, too: the whispers, the taunts. *You want to save the blind man? Then fucking earn it.*

Martin Grace.

"I've gotta ask you something," I said. Rachael looked at me, quizzical. I brushed a magenta bang away from her glasses. "I need a favor."

Beneath my girlfriend's electric hair, tattoos, piercings, and over-the-top online persona lurks the soul of a brilliant woman. My friends say Rachael's slumming, being with a guy like me. I've never disagreed. She craves precision in nearly everything she does. Her writing for PixelVixen sports a brass-knuckled humor and practicality that her readers adore. (Or 'dore, as Lucas would say.) Her freelance work as a technical writer is frills-free, logical and direct. And her tenacity is unparalleled as a part-time researcher and fact-checker for the *New York Journal-Ledger*. In the months after 9/11, she contributed to the two series that won Pulitzer prizes in the National Reporting and Public Service categories.

That's my girl. She's the rational ying to my emotional yang.

I told her about Martin Grace, the murders, his psychosomatic blindness, next week's trial. She frowned, horrified, as I recounted the ordeal in Room 507, and the conclusion I'd made as the train had rolled into the 6th Avenue-14th Street station. I needed to know who Martin Grace was. I needed more than what was in The Brink's admittance report.

Rachael took a sip of her beer. She glanced at the laptop resting on the tiny desk in her corner of the room. Her eyes came back to me.

"If you're going to ask me, Z, *ask* me."

She's so shrewd. I bit my bottom lip.

"I need your access to the *Journal-Ledger's* research library. I want to know everything about this guy: past addresses, income, taxes, marriages, whatever I can dig up. The cops and Dad have access to all that stuff—"

"Your dad isn't the attorney prosecuting the case, Z," Rachael interjected. She crossed her arms; the fabric of her sweater bunched around her chest. "He's an administrator now. Assistant D.A.s handle the cases. You know that."

She was right. She also wasn't through.

"You've had a lousy night, Z. I dig that," she said. "But if this is about you beating your Dad, forget it. And if it's about beating Grace, you can forget that, too. If you've got some vendetta working behind that very handsome, very kissable face of yours, there's absolutely no way I'll help. It's manipulative, and it's *not* who you are. I love you. I don't want to resent you."

"It isn't," I said. "Lookit, I've gotta be armed when I go back in there. I have to earn his trust, and the only way to do that is to get beyond the folder. I don't want to beat him. I want to *help* him."

She sighed.

"Zach, it doesn't sound like he wants to be helped."

"Maybe not," I admitted, and this was true. Grace had confounded every therapist he'd encountered during his hopscotch through the system. He'd mocked his doctors, sniffed them over ... and then snapped them over his knee. Grace was a self-proclaimed pariah, believing he deserved this fast track to Hell. Which didn't make sense. Despite those odd, so-called visions of death, his alibis were solid.

I thought back to this afternoon. Grace had torn a chunk out of me in that room. But I'd bitten back. He had admired that.

"Yeah, maybe not," I said again. "But I'm not going to know unless I try, unless I get some"—I thought of my father—"history. Context."

Rachael pushed her glasses up to the bridge of her nose. She took another sip from her bottle.

"You're not messing around," she said. "Not placating me."

"Not a bit." This was also true.

"Then you can come and play," Rachael said. She stood up, stretched, and pulled the black sweater from her body. The ink on her pale arms lanced from her shoulders, down to her elbows. I admired her for a breathless moment. Now *that's* my girl.

"But on one condition," she said. "I'm driving."

⁎⁎⁎

Over the next two hours (and more Rogue Chipotle Ales), I watched my girlfriend perform high-powered sorcery on her laptop. Using the biographical information I'd culled from The Brink's report, Rachael trolled a phalanx of governmental databases, collecting bits and bytes from the DMV, IRS, and other institutions. Since Martin Grace was under criminal investigation, some searchable information was also available in the NYPD's computer network.

My geek goddess was no black hat. She was a cybersleuth. If it could be legally found with the resources at her disposal, she could nearly always find it.

Tonight, she did—and it didn't make a goddamned bit of sense.

"You're not going to like this," Rachael said. She pulled a chewed pencil from the small bun she'd made in her hair a beer-and-a-half ago. "Look."

She tapped the computer's screen with the pencil's eraser. "I've got tax records from 1980 right here. Says Grace worked for Music Street Elite, a music store, in Louisiana. Cross-ref this—"

Her thumb and pinky executed a maneuver on the keyboard. A new window flashed on the screen.

"—with Louisiana local business data from the same year. Guess what? No Music Street Elite." She glanced at me, a tight frown on her lips. "Not in the Better Business Bureau, not in city or county property records—actually, they call counties 'parishes' down there—and not in the friggin' phone book."

"So he faked his taxes?" I asked.

Rachael snorted. "He faked a lot more than that." She tapped the screen again, reaching for the beer in my hand. I surrendered it. "This is nuts, Z. Nearly every tax report is bogus. The businesses don't exist. Even the homes he said he lived in don't exist."

She performed that same ninja move with her fingers, and the contents of the LCD flashed from one window to another (and then another, and another) in machine-gun rapid fire. As she did this, her pencil scratched check marks and question marks on a nearby notepad.

"Okay, I was lying," she said. "About half all of these addresses *do* exist, but according to residency data, the homes—many of which are apartments—were occupied by other families at the time."

"So he lived with friends," I said. "Roomies."

"Unlikely," Rachael said. She circled something on a sheet that had belched out of our laser printer. It was an address. "Look. 1985. Providence, Rhode Island. Do you really think that the Miller family—a married couple with four kids, crammed into a two-bedroom apartment—actually let Martin Grace crash on their couch for three years?"

I cringed. Six months ago, Lucas had roomed here for two weeks, after an unexplained falling out with some of his parkour roommates. I'd wanted to kill him by the end of the third day.

"Hell no," I said.

"Preeecisely," Rachael said. "Bogus employment record, bogus addys, no marriage certificates, no children, no criminal record, no IRS audits. Squeaky clean. On paper, Martin Grace is incorporeal, Z. He's a hoax. A ghost."

She whistled the theme from "The Twilight Zone."

"But these records here ..." I began, pointing to the steamer trunk. My notes from The Brink were stacked there.

"Yeah, I'm getting to that," Rachael said. She was buzzing, in the zone, and I was buzzing right along with her. It wasn't the beer. I loved it when she was like this, relishing in *the doing* of what she did. I wanted to kiss her then. I resisted this. She was on a roll.

"This is where things get legit," she explained. "Everything from ten years ago checks out. The jobs, addresses, tax stuff. It's as if Martin Grace, then 46, appeared fully formed in Rochester. He stepped out of the ether and started working for, ah ... Syncopation Productions, LLC. Music studio."

She executed another keystroke, and my patient's most recent state ID photo—from three years ago—winked on the screen.

"The folks working for your dad, they undoubtedly have access to this," Rachael said. "If they know anything more, it's coming from data I can't grab. They'll play those cards at the trial, I bet."

I took the bottle from her hand and took a pull.

"So what does it all mean?"

Rachael's pencil tapped the screen again.

"It means I don't have a clue who you're dealing with."

8

Two hours later, nearly midnight. I sat in the comfy chair near my corner of the living room, one leg slung over its upholstered arm. My angled thigh played easel for the sketch pad in my lap. Bliss sat on my other leg, purring, kneading my knee.

It was impossible to sleep.

Rachael and I had double-checked her research an hour ago, coming to the same conclusion: the man in Room 507 hadn't existed until a decade ago.

I made the connection not long after that.

That's when the killings began, I'd said. *When his "Dark Man" came.*

We'd held hands and chuckled about boogeymen, and then Rachael had gone to bed. She wasn't spooked—far from it. She simply had no expertise in where my mind was wandering. Data was her game. Therapy was mine. She'd left her laptop running, in case I wanted to search *Journal-Ledger* archives stories about the Grace murders. I'd told her I wouldn't be up much longer.

Now, sitting in my second-hand chair, I hoped I was right.

I stared up at the glowing chili-pepper lights. So. Ten years ago, a man named Martin Grace had punched a hole into the world ... and to hear him tell the tale, had brought a monster with him. It was ridiculous, to be sure; Grace's Inkstain was a psychological creation, a way to rationalize his supposedly precognitive visions. And those visions, I knew, represented psychological breakdowns in their own right. Delusions of reference, like Grace's last doctor had supposed? Schizotypal personality disorder?

That was inscrutable—at least, for right now. I'd have to hack-and-slash my way to the cause of Grace's psychosomatic blindness before I could learn more about the deaths. And I had to learn about the deaths before I could decipher what fueled his visions. To do that, I had to find out who this man was *before* he was Martin Grace.

I chuckled. It was a bitter sound.

Who is Martin Grace? Who is John Galt?

I gently shooed Bliss from my lap and picked up the wedge of charcoal resting by my sketch pad. I wasn't feeling the manic artistic urge that I'd experienced this morning under Primoris Maximus, but something was tugging at my hand. I let it flow.

It drew a large question mark on the page.

Ha. Yes. That was today, represented right here, surrounded by a field of white. Questions. Question after question after question.

The coal scratched smaller question marks as I chewed on this. I wrote the emotions I was feeling now, adding more question marks as I did so, quietly absorbed by the swirling motion of my hand.

Exhausted. Scared. Bruised. Determined, alone, invisible.

The doubt and curiosity came now. What if I couldn't help Grace? *Scritch.* Another question mark. *Scritch*, another word.

What was his history? *Scritch.*

What if I couldn't find what he was hiding?

Scritch.

What had he lost?

Scritch.

Why couldn't he see?

Where, how, when?

Scritch, scritch, scritch.

Ten minutes later, I mentally up-shifted and took a deep breath, examining what I'd created. Yes, question marks, all over the page— I expected that. I didn't expect, however, to find that the curved lines and dots were arranged in the shape of a man.

And there was more here. Some words were larger than the others. I read them and felt my eyes widen, then water. The coal trembled in my hand.

HIDDEN HELP

FIND LOST INVISIBLE HISTORY

I SEE ALONE

Oh my. This wasn't about Grace, not at all.

I was telling myself to find lost history … *invisible* history. From an Invisible Man.

My hand dropped the charcoal. My fingers, numb and stupid, slid to my pants pocket and tugged at the paper inside. I gaped at the crumpled envelope now in my hand, the thing given to me by the stranger. I opened the envelope and read the card.

An uncle who never was. A brother who wanted to hide him. A ... a mother who still loved him? It was all here, what he'd said as the East 77th Street traffic had rushed by.

I turned my head slowly, to the end table by our front door. There, beside a flickering scented candle, rested the box of photos Lucas had given me earlier that evening. The world assumed the syrupy slowness of a dream now. I went to it, brought it back to my chair, opened it and gazed into the past.

Most of the photos resting atop the stack were from the past year. These were pictures Lucas and I sent Gram as she'd grown ill, to keep her posted on our lives and loves. I held a photo taken nearly a year ago: My father, Lucas, Rachael and me, posing for a "Gram pic" in Central Park. Lucas was hamming it up for the lens, as always. Rachael and I held each other close, exuberant in our newfound romance. Her laughter at Lucas' cross-eyed expression had evoked a cheerful rise from Dad. We were all smiling.

It was a beautiful photo. I pulled my wallet from my slacks pocket and placed it inside, knowing Gram would want me to have it.

I dug further then, an archaeologist questing for I knew not what. In the middle of the stack, I found a yellowed sheet of paper, folded in thirds. As I pulled it out of the box, a scrap fell from its folds. I eyed the ragged cursive handwriting that stared back from inside in the box.

Suddenly have lots of time on my hands, it read. *Wanted to see how far it—or rather, we—went back. Did research. Hope you appreciate the history lesson, especially in light of recent events. Forever yours—H*

I squinted. Henry? Perhaps. Perhaps not. Perhaps Grandpa Taylor. His name was Howard.

I unfolded the paper and gazed at a small masterpiece, done in faded blue felt-tip ink. It was a tree, awesomely rendered in an obviously impressionistic, almost cartoon-like style. Superimposed over the tree were words, boxes and lines written in red felt-tip pen.

It was a family tree. It was *my* family tree.

I held the paper in my hands (they began to tremble again, I couldn't stop them) and glanced over the names, sped-read my way through history. There I was, my name boxed at the bottom of the page. Beside my name: *Lookie-Luke.* Lucas.

I held my breath as my eyes ticked up a generation. William Victor. There was a box beside Dad's name, but it was empty.

No Henry.

I exhaled. Not there. He wasn't there.

I gazed up and up, heading further and further back in time, curious to see from whence I hailed. I arrived at the top of the page, and felt my eyes widen as I read the name there, my great-several-times-over grandfather.

Zachary Taylor: 12th President of the United States, 1784-1850.

"No way," I said. My voice was loud here, in the empty living room.

Of course I knew the president—I'd been named after him, it was my mother's idea, Gram told me so—and I'd done more than a little reading on the guy in middle and high school. Those were the only American History assignments I'd ever enjoyed, and I'd considered myself a casual expert of sorts on the man. It felt *cool* to write a report on someone famous with whom you shared a name. It felt special, secret … like you might be destined for great things, too.

But the family tree before me didn't jibe with what I remembered from my high school research. I knew Zachary Taylor had six children: a boy and five girls. I'd had to memorize them for a presentation, and I could still recite the mnemonic device I'd used back then to remember their first names: A.S.O.M.M.R., pronounced Awesomer.

But according to this sheet, the prez had a *seventh* child, represented by a blank square placed next to daughter Octavia's name.

The generation beneath this empty box was represented by the name "Reginald Garrett Taylor," which meant the mystery child above had been male.

The bloodline from this branch of the tree—if this document was credible, which I was suddenly beginning to doubt—went down throughout the ages, and ended with …

… with Lucas and me.

"Bullshit distraction," I said, refolding the paper. I placed it in the stack beside me and went deeper into the box. I was looking for history, but not ancient history. I picked up another photo and smiled.

Here I was, gap-toothed, with a bowl-shaped haircut, playing with Lucas in the snow. I couldn't have been older than ten. Here was another photo of my brother, performing a handstand in our living room. A younger version of Gram beamed at him.

I went further back, and stopped. I *remembered* this. Summertime in New Jersey, parked near the Essex County Airport, watching planes soar from the tarmac. I couldn't have been more than four years old. Here was my mother, Claire, holding an infant Lucas, grinning at the camera. I was there, and Dad was holding me, telling me where the planes were going. I must stress: *I remember this.*

Love you, I'd said.

Love you back, buddy.

But this wasn't my father in the photo. I flipped it over. "Claire, Lookie-Luke, Zach and Henry at E.C. Airport," the note read.

It didn't happen the way they said it did. It's all lies.

Empty boxes in the family tree. Lives erased from history.

I stepped over to the computer. I opened the *Journal-Ledger's* archives, and did what my art told me to do.

I searched for hidden help. For lost, invisible history. I saw, alone.

And the memories, so many long-forgotten memories, rushed over me.

***

The wooden trains go choo-choo and the metal cars go vroom-vroom and the plastic planes go whoosh-whoosh here in Living Room City, where the roads are stitched into the Oriental rug and the buildings are painted shoeboxes and the airstrip is a neatly taped length of construction paper. I'm the four-year-old mayor of Living Room City, directing traffic, flying planes, marching children to the playground and, uh-oh, another thunderstorm's coming, we all have to go inside now.

I'm gazing up above Living Room City, airplane in hand, inbound for a landing but now in a holding pattern. I stop blowing air against the plane and its propellers stop swirling, like me, stopping, watching the thunderstorm on the walls.

I know it's not really a thunderstorm; that's just what I call these moments when I'm Mayor of Living Room City. I'm not silly, I know it's make-believe. The room goes dark, goes light, goes dark again, blinky-blink, peek-a-boo. Dad's colored-glass Tiffany lamp is a rainbow, now dark, now a rainbow again, and the lights on the walls wink like giant eyes, and Mister Rogers on the TV fades and comes back. He has a little city just like I do, with tiny houses and cars and stores. I watch the lights flicker, they've done this for the past two weeks, and when Dad is here and it happens he gets mad, and Mommy gets quiet and afraid, and I'm a little afraid too, because the thunderstorms have come back to Living Room City.

Wink-blink go the lights, *It's a beautiful d*—Mister Rogers' voice sings, and fades, and comes back—*eighbor, could y*—Dark, with the lights, now back!—*eighborly day for a beaut*—Off again! It's like twisting the radio knob in Dad's car. Dad doesn't like it when I do that.

I look around the living room. I'm the only one here, Mommy is upstairs, she's gone for just a few minutes, needs to feed Lookie-

Luke, the baby-baby, my baby brother, always hungry and cooing, his face is so round and his hair is so curly, and he squeals when I tickle him and then I squeal because it's *so funny* and—

Screaming.

Upstairs, screaming.

Upstairs, Mommy and Lookie-Luke, screaming.

I'm dropping the plane, and standing up, and I'm suddenly *very* afraid, I need to pee, and the lights are still out in Living Room City, but I see that the lights in the room by the front door, the place where the long, tall stairs are—the *foh-yay*, Daddy calls it—those lights are on, and I'm running toward the foh-yay, my blue Zips scattering the cars and trains on the floor like that monster I saw on television last week (*'ZILLA! 'ZILLA!*), and I really need to pee now, and the lights flick on in the living room and Mister Rogers is singing again and I pass the doorway into the foh-yay, my shoes are squeaking against the hardwood and there's Mommy, at the top of the stairs, screaming, her arm extended toward someone—

The lights here flash bright for a moment, and I squint, and then they explode like suns, tiny tinklings of glass falling from the walls, from the ceiling, from table lamps, and the lampshades are collapsing, clattering onto the tables.

I stare at the top of the stairs, watch my mother scream—Lookie-Luke is crying from the bedroom, it's so loud, it's all *so loud*—and something is clutching at her wrist, tugging her away from the stairs, something soaked in shadow, something grunting and snarling and black and hungry, roaring now, and

mommy pulls away, her face triumphant, and her eyes turn to me and

Mister Rogers is singing *let's make the most of this beautiful day*

and she falls

she falls down the stairs

since we're together

tumbling still, body smashing against the wood, face smacking against the banister, her head now *clack-clack-clacking* against
its white spindles, and something red and messy sprays against
the wall

we might as well say

stones rattling in a clothes dryer, she tumbles and tumbles and

would you be mine?

something wet and crunchy rises above the noise, I know the
sound, it's like biting into a carrot

could you be mine?

and Mommy's with me now, on the floor, her eyes wide open,
like they're asking a question, and the blood leaks into her left eye,
her legs are tangled, unmoving

won't you be my nnnnn

no, no, I look from Mommy's face to the top of the stairs and I
see it, the black thing hulking there, shoulders heaving, and Lucas
sounds like a police siren now, *eeeooooo—*

won't you, please?

and the monster steps forward, its midnight feet crunching on
the stairs, on the broken glass there, coming for me

won't you, please?

and I feel the pee rush down my legs and a feel a moment of hot
shame before I sway, feeling sick, head fuzzy

please won't you be

and the world goes black, as the dark man descends.

✳✳✳

I blinked, focused my eyes, coaxed myself to face the world again.
The memory was scalding, pure and new; I'd forgotten the last time
I'd even remembered that day. It had been buried under two de-
cades of fear and ... I guess ... a *need* to forget.

The documents I'd found using Rachael's *Journal-Ledger* back-stage pass were slicing a razor-sharp rift between Then and Now. I realized how easy it could be to let go, to shrug it all off, to slip out of the thin, dry snakeskin we call sanity. For the first time in my life, The Brink beckoned to another side of me.

The Invisible Man was right.

Henry Taylor, the uncle I'd never known—but *had* known, and ohhh, that was the terrifying thing about memory, how it could over-write old data, superimpose new identities over old ones, so easily "retcon" history, as comic book geeks say, to preserve one's sanity—was real, and among the living, buried away in a prison. I'd extracted a secret so rotten that I had to admire how it stayed a secret at all.

"Alive, but worse than dead," I said, gazing at the computer screen.

Digital scans of police reports and court records told the tale: Henry Taylor had shoved my mother Claire down a flight of stairs, in our then-Jersey City home. My father hadn't been home during the mid-afternoon incident.

Apparently, I'd been interviewed the day my mother died. The Administration for Children's Services report matched my long-for-gotten memory: The lights were flickering, a black thing shoved my mom down the stairs. This vision of a "monster" was indicative of emotional shock, the employee had written. The real culprit had been Henry Taylor.

The flickering lights (my Living Room City thunderstorms) were written off as bum wiring in a ninety-three-year-old home, typical for its age.

The justice system was uncharacteristically, blisteringly fast with delivering its punishment. This is because Henry's confession never wavered. He'd plotted my mother's death. He offered no reason, other than he wanted "to see the bitch dead."

A wave of hatred, thick and acidic, overwhelmed me when I'd read that.

He was sentenced to life in Claytonville Prison—New York's penitentiary equivalent of The Brink, a black hole for reviled offenders.

Henry had a long sheet of previous arrests and convictions—fairly harmless crimes, I'd thought. But the judge was merciless. Henry's possibility for parole: stone-cold, absolute zero.

And now, as I stared at the words *I wanted to see the bitch dead*, a ferret-like, desperate side of myself concocted explanations as to why my father wouldn't tell us about this.

He didn't want his children growing up with the public shame, the stigma.

He didn't want us to knowing the horror, didn't want us exposed to monstrous acts, crimes of passion, so early in our lives.

He didn't want his murderous brother contacting us later in life.

I laughed at myself, and shuddered. This was a mental shell game, the masturbatory act of a mind stinking drunk on bittersweet denial. They were excuses for an inexcusable betrayal.

And so, I clicked onward, finding mental footholds, jotting notes, seething as I skimmed. I re-read the police and court records. Both stated that Henry Taylor had remained *at the house* after the murder. The criminal did not run. Nor did he call 911, as unlikely as that would have been, to report two crying children and a dead body.

Instead, he'd called Dad. And Dad had arrived, unbelievably, with a restraining order against Henry that he'd filed earlier that day. The brothers had stayed until the cops arrived. Was that the behavior of an unrepentant killer? Not in my experience. And the NYPD officer who'd taken Dad's call and arrived on the scene? Eustacio Jean-Phillipe.

What had happened, during that gap between Henry calling Dad, and Papa-Jean's arrival? What had been said? This was not documented. Nor was the reason for my father's restraining order against his brother.

Further, the only person who'd apparently ever helped Henry in the past died that day. On every arrest sheet I reviewed, Claire Taylor was the person who'd bailed him out of jail.

It didn't happen the way they said it did. It's all lies.

Yes. My life was soaked in deceit, and I hadn't a clue. My father had erased his brother from our family history. Gram, for whatever reason, had acquiesced. And now Henry was back, back for a limited time only, call now, quantities are available for just one person. Me.

Why? Why did Henry kill my mother? Or had he killed her at all? The Invisible Man's memorial card—his final goodbye to Gram—insisted that Henry had been punished for a crime he didn't commit.

Troubled, I erased my digital footprints by killing the history and file cache of Rachael's web browser. I didn't want anyone knowing this. I rubbed my eyes and sighed.

Twenty-one years ago, I saw a monster push my mother down the stairs. But that wasn't true. No, the truth was far more terrible and sharp.

Henry Taylor was my personal Dark Man. He was the reason I was broken. The reason I was afraid of the dark.

9

I wiped my bleary eyes. I gulped a mouthful of The Brink's awful coffee. My office chair creaked like something out of a B movie, an undead creature slowly opening its own coffin.

Okay, shake it off, I told myself.

I stared blankly at the stack of artwork I'd collected from my patients last week. Scraps of torn paper mingled with larger sketches and paintings. Insects. Sharp teeth. A gingerbread house in the forest. A birthday cake with cartoon dynamite sticks for candles. A penis, apparently made of rusted metal and barbed wire. A blood-soaked mother holding her drowned child.

I wasn't up for this today.

I was preparing to digitally scan the art and post it on Brinkvale Psychiatric's new website. Doctor Peterson's recent hospital-wide memo about the site had been an obnoxious thing, banging the drums for "positive promotion for our excellent facilities" to evangelize our "world-class reputation." Excellent wha? World-class who? Naturally, Peterson had tapped me to administer its Art Therapy section.

And so here I was, placing Bloody Mary's painting on a flatbed scanner, transforming her trauma into ones and zeroes. The thing whined and whirred. My mind wandered, back to my own trauma.

I stared into space, past my giant ceramic coffee mug, eyes on the CRT monitor, but unfocused. The memory needled behind my eyes: baby Lucas screaming, Mom screaming, light bulbs bursting, the dark man howling. Tumbling, breaking, tumbling, bleeding, tumbling, blood running into her left eye.

And now there was blood on the monitor before me, oozing down the lined glass, bright and wet and glimmering.

I bolted back in my chair, screaming. The old chair's wheels squealed rusty laughter. My coffee mug somersaulted off the desk and shattered on the floor. I slapped my palms against my red-rimmed eyes.

Blood, no, can't be real, can't.

I pulled away my hands and swore.

The digital scan of Bloody Mary and Baby Blue stared back at me. The woman in the painting was drenched in watercolor red, nothing more.

You're going crazy, a splinter of my mind said. I blinked, shook my head. *Make a date with the Cheshire Cat, grin the grinnn of the—*

No, my rational self interrupted. *You're sleep-deprived. Anxious.*

"Thank you, Spock," I whispered. A wave of reassurance swept over me, followed by more doubt.

"Am I losing it?"

I suppose I would've heard a reply were it true. I snatched a roll of paper towels from my art supplies and yanked off far too many sheets for the job. I wadded the towels, dropped them onto the spreading mess, tamped them with my Vans.

Can't this be over before it's started? I thought. *Can't this be a dream? Can't the Invisible Man be nothing more than a con man looking for a quick buck?*

Maybe he was, but at this point the stranger was a more reliable source of information than my own father. That knowledge had tormented me all last night, and during the train ride here. The doubt, the damage … it was in my capillaries, piping into me, deeper and deeper. My father was a liar, that much I knew. But to what extent? How far did the rabbit hole go? He was falling far from grace, and I needed to salvage something, something *truthful* from our sidewalk conversation last night. Something to save him, in my mind, in some small way.

Does that make sense? I needed to believe him, believe *in him.* He's my dad. You can't just give up on your dad.

I gazed at the monitor. Mary was drenched in blood. Last night on East 77th, Dad said my stranger had flayed his wife, cooked her flesh, and paraded in public, covered in her blood. That had been, what?

"Twenty years ago," I said.

Yes. Twenty years ago. Something that grisly must've made big headlines back then, I realized, which meant folks older than me would remember it. People can't help but recall creep-show oddities like that—just as they rubberneck at the sight of a smashed car on the highway.

I needed someone's memory. I needed this to save myself from going crazy with doubt, to save my trust in my father. Even with last night's evidence pointing to the contrary, I needed to give him one last chance.

I stepped to my desk, picked up the walkie-talkie all Brinkvale employees are ordered to carry. I switched its dial from the open, nearly always quiet emergency frequency to the maintenance frequency.

"Malcolm," I said. "You there? It's Zach T." The 'talkie crackled.

"Yep."

"Gotta talk for a few minutes. Where are you?"

Pause.

"Library. Messy. Always messy."

"Right on," I said. I grabbed my satchel by the office door. "Stay put. I'll be right there."

✳✳✳

It's criminal, what's happened to Brinkvale's library.

When I first visited this cavernous room three months ago, I'd been amazed by its endless oak bookcases, curved walls and spectacular chandeliers. The room was designed in the art nouveau style, all sweeping lines, brazen and optimistic. The Brink's library was a paradox, a place that shouldn't exist in such a hard-cornered, utilitarian building.

But my amazement had immediately soured. Most of the bookshelves don't contain real books at all. The once-colorful murals painted on its walls are peeling like sunburned skin. The chandeliers are encrusted with rust and endless, ancient cobwebs. This subterranean cathedral was cursed by unsound architecture and sinful neglect. Patients rarely ventured here.

It was a lost, heartbroken place.

The library was maintained by Ezra Goolsby, a man as old and wretched as The Brink itself. The geezer had worked here for decades. Rumors about Goolsby abounded at The Brink: he'd suffered a stroke that made him physically incapable of smiling; he was a "true" Morlock, living in a small room behind the library; he had once been a Brinkvale patient ... it went on and on.

Worse still, Goolsby cared less about books than the people around him. But the man was a news junky, a periodical fiend. So while The Brink's library was a tragedy, its collection of bound newspapers and magazines dating back to the 1960s was awe-inspiring.

I entered the library, on the lookout for the grim codger. I heard the distinctive slop-slosh of a mop plunging into a metal bucket, and followed the noise. Malcolm was near the room's imposing main desk, the place where Goolsby typically reigned over his bibliofiefdom. Malcolm looked up, gave a low-key salute.

I enjoyed being in the presence of this man. Malcolm Sashington had serenity about him, a "let it ride" vibe that I appreciated, particularly in this madhouse. Whenever I saw him, I was reminded of locksmiths and secrets.

"How goes, Zach T?" he said. He tugged the mop from the wringer and flopped it onto the tile.

"Hangin' in there by my fingernails," I replied. My eyes ticked around the library, glancing through the rows of bookcases, across the large tables near us. "Where's the old man?"

"Gool's not here. Leaves as soon as he sees me. Were I your age, I'd think he's got a problem with me. Old enough to know better. Goolsby doesn't hate black people. Goolsby hates *everybody*."

I laughed. It echoed against the library's curved walls.

"Sounded like you needed something," he said, patting the walkie-talkie on his belt. His hand jostled the large metal hoop next to his radio. The keys there clinked. "Kinda urgent. You here to call in that favor?"

About a month ago, I'd gone topside to catch a breath of fresh air ... and caught a whiff of something else altogether: Malcolm toking up on his dinner break. In typical cucumber-cool style, Malcolm hadn't freaked. But he had asked me if I'd snitch. My reply had brought me a boon. A Malcolm Favor.

"I don't think this compares, but you be the judge. You got a good memory?"

Malcolm worked the floor with his mop. "If you're lookin' for history, talk to Goolsby. He's The Brink's elephant. Never forgets."

"Goolsby eats human souls," I snorted. "And it's got nothing to do with The Brink. Come on. You got a knack for remembering things or not?"

"How far we goin' back?"

"Twenty years."

Malcolm let out a low whistle. "Slippin' into favor territory. Let's find out."

"All right. I don't know when or where this happened, but it was probably in the city. Guy kills his wife, paints himself with her blood."

Malcolm leaned against his mop handle and gave me an insultingly bored look.

"That's it?" he asked. "You're gonna have to do a lot better than that, Zach T. Wouldn't even make a condo association newsletter in that town."

"Would it help if the guy was a crazy vet, and ate her skin?"

My friend nearly yawned now. "Son, lots of vets came back with lots of problems. Dime a dozen. You're looking at one, dig? So watch what you say about those who serve."

"A *veterinarian*," I replied. "Dude cuts her up. When she dies, dunks himself in her blood, streaks the town." I grimaced. "He cooked up her skin and ate it like bacon."

The mop stick banged against the floor like a gunshot.

"Oh hell yes," he said, his eyes wide. "Not twenty years back. Thirty."

"Thirty?" I asked. "But that doesn't ... Are you sure?"

"Hell yeah. Super Bowl Twelve, kiddo. Cowboys versus Steelers. I can't tell you who won that game anymore, but I remember opening up the paper that morning fully expecting to see a story about my man Harvey Martin and the Cowboys' 'Doomsday Defense.' Instead, we all got that story on the front page. Nearly puked in my Cheerios."

Malcolm stooped to pick up the mop. He stared into the bucket's brackish water.

"Mighty hard thing to forget," he said finally.

I nodded. "Cool, that's enough." I turned, now striding through the corridors of bookshelves, searching for the proverbial needle in this moldering haystack. I was surrounded by endless green books, each as tall as a man's arm, all identical save for the handwritten notes on their spines.

(TIMES) AUG–SEPT 1984.

(POST) JAN–FEB 1985.

I moved from case to case, shelf to shelf, finally finding *(TIMES) JAN–FEB* from thirty years ago. I hefted the book from its dusty slot, and brought it back to one of the tables.

If Malcolm was right, then Dad was wrong. I didn't want Dad to be wrong.

"Last chance," I hissed, flipping through the pages. Headlines, halftone photos and ads screamed by, time capsules of 1978 and '79: "Just when you thought it was safe to go back in the water... " ... Investigation Continues In French Tanker Explosion ... "We can do whatever we want. We're college students!" ... More Bodies Found In Gacy Murders ... "Ain't nobody can fly a car like Hooper!"

Finally, there it was, January 15, and there he was. The "Blood-bath Killer."

The face in the mug shot looked nothing like last night's Invisible Man. Not even thirty years (*twenty years,* I thought, *Dad said twenty years*) of hard time could've made a difference.

My stranger was Caucasian. The Bloodbath Killer was Asian.

My fingers dug into the yellowed paper, tearing it from the book.

✳ ✳ ✳

I slumped into a chair, tossing my satchel onto the table, ignoring how the *clunk* reverberated around the room. I glared at the ripped page in my hand, barely reading the story, finally spotting my father's name near its end, listed as a first-year associate. That was lawyer-speak for a lowly "assistant to the assistant" position. Last night, Dad pulled a memory from the earliest days of his career and ad-libbed. Lied.

"That's what he said back then, too," Dad had said. *"That's why he bathed in his wife's blood. To finally become 'visible.'"* But no such detail was mentioned in this news story. And why should it be? It wasn't true.

"Dad, you son of a bitch."

Tears, bitter and bright, filled my eyes.

"Hey Zach T," Malcolm said. He sat down across from me. "You okay, kid?"

"Past twenty-fours have been pretty rough," I muttered, wiping my eyes. "A real clusterfuck. Everything's different now."

"You talkin' about that blind man in Max? Martin Grace?"

I groaned. "Yeah, sure, why the hell not? I've been finding truths and lies all over the place. Grace is a frickin' ant in amber. Doesn't have a past, and doesn't have a future—not without my help, anyway. He's spent so long flogging himself for things he didn't do, he thinks he deserves it. He doesn't." I sighed. "None of us deserve it."

Malcolm tapped the weathered pages. "What's this have to do with...?"

"Oh, it doesn't," I said. "Not really. This is just my motif for the day, 'it ain't what you thought it was, kid,' life's way of taking a crap on you while you're down ... "

I shrugged, suddenly fed up with myself. "Sorry. Rambling. Usually not like this."

"I know you're not," Malcolm said. He leaned back in his chair. "So. You want some free advice?"

"Shit, I'll pay for it at this point."

He laughed.

"You ain't Charlie Brown, I ain't Lucy and the doctor is most definitely *not* in. I don't know what's going on with you or that blind man, or *that*"—he nodded to the paper in my hand—"but I know the sight of a man who's been beamed by more than a few curve balls."

I let out a knowing *heh.*

"Listen. People are smart," he said. "People usually know what they need to do at times like this, they know it in their hearts, but they gotta hear it from someone else. So I'm not going to say anything that'll surprise you."

I nodded.

"Okay."

Malcolm smirked, his face suddenly young and impish. He reached beneath the table, and pulled out his key ring. It clattered onto the table. Malcolm placed his hands on either side of the ring, palms flat against the wood grain.

"We walk a straight line, brother. Day after day we walk straight lines because it's easy to do that, because we need to do that, because it's efficient." He winked. "Preee-dictability. Right?"

I opened my mouth, but Malcolm slapped his palms against the table. I watched, befuddled to the bone, as he then banged out a thunderous drum roll. The keys between his hands trembled on the surface.

"But see?" he called over the noise, pounding harder now. "Shit happens! Earthquakes, curve balls, meteors from space!" I watched, mesmerized, as the keys bounced and skipped, slowly marking a drunken path toward the edge of the table, toward Malcolm's lap. "Can't walk a straight line in a earthquake, can ya? Well?"

"No!" I hollered. I couldn't help but grin. This was ridiculous library theater, a wind-tunnel "Afterschool Special."

"NO!" Malcolm cried, smiling. "Then what do you do?" The keys clinked merrily, dancing ever-onward toward the edge. Malcolm glanced from the keys to my face, his brown eyes now insistent. "What do you do, Zach T? Life's giving you lemons, life's sticking it in and breaking it off, it's got the ground shakin', and if you can't walk a straight line cuz walking a straight line is suicide, then what do you do?"

The keys were a half-inch from the edge now. Now a quarter inch. My hand snaked out, and snatched the ring just before it plummeted from view.

"You improvise," I said. The keys were heavy and strangely comforting in my hand. "Do the unexpected."

The janitor nodded.

"That you do," he said. "If the world is throwing you curve balls, learn to pitch. Learn the rules. Fire back." He nodded again to the newspaper story. "I bet it'll work for whatever you're dealing with there. Shoot, I bet it'll work for that blind man, too."

I tossed the keys to him. "Learn to pitch," I said.

"Yep." Malcolm scooted his chair away from the table. I watched him shuffle back to his mop and bucket. "You learn the rules, know how the dance goes, then you improvise. Dig?"

"Dug," I said. "Thanks."

I walked toward the library's curved doorway and the spartan hall beyond. "So. That favor. Did I just call it in?"

Malcolm looked up from his work and grinned.

"Hell no, Zach T! You ask me something that's easy-peasy to remember, and then you give me a chance to scream like a banshee and raise holy hell in Goolsby's castle. I nearly owe you *another* favor for the good times."

He shooed me with his hand. "Go on, git."

***

I returned to my office on Level 3, feeling a bit like my old self. Malcolm's advice would be good for handling Martin Grace later that day—in fact, I thought a had a solid improvisational curve ball to blast at the blind man this afternoon. Dealing with my father … that was a different story. I filed him away in my mind, buried myself in my work, anything not to deal with it.

Avoidance, yes. I knew it then, but couldn't put forth the effort to care.

I scanned my patients' artwork and posted it to The Brink's website. I made mid-morning rounds, briefly checking in with the patients with whom I'd worked yesterday and chatted with their psychiatrists, promising to file paperwork by day's end.

And then I was off to work with today's patients. These were the high-risk, disturbed, violent folk. The people probably destined to spend the rest of their lives here.

These devastatingly ill patients resided on the eighth floor of The Brink, the level dubbed "Golgotha." The only thing separating Level 8 from New York bedrock was Level 9, "The Sub," home to the boiler room and storage.

Perhaps Level 8's nickname was meant to be optimistic. After all, Golgotha was where things were at their worst for Jesus Christ, and yet he rose from the dead, good as new. Perhaps the name represented transformation; a beginning.

I couldn't think of it in such terms. The patients here were treated with as much dignity and care as possible, but this was where The Brink's dark legacy breathed on. This *was* Golgotha, the place of the skull, where crazies were sent to die in the dark.

I spent some time with John Palmetto—aka Lore—a patient here since the 1980s. Palmetto had drawn inspiration from local urban legends, using those stories like cookbook directions to kill eleven teenage girls.

I painted for—not *with*, but *for*—Diana Ellis, a woman so obsessed with the mutilation of human flesh that she'd spent two summer days in her Erie County farmhouse kitchen performing home-brewed autopsies on her family ... and had then amputated her own arms. Brink-folk called her June Cleaver.

I worked with a half-dozen Golgotha patients, and even through these sessions—positively harrowing by yesterday's standards—I tuned out the crumbling surroundings and found solace in Malcolm's advice. I found my footing. I improvised. It helped.

I took The Brink's elevator back to Level 3 to grab my lunch.

Dr. Nathan Xavier was waiting by my office door.

✳✳✳

"Taylor, you look like shit."

It was clear Xavier took perverse glee in saying this. He grinned his plastic Ken grin, then primly straightened his spotless doctor's coat. I brushed past him, unlocked the door and hurried inside. The room still reeked from this morning's coffee spill. He followed me.

"You're killing my buzz," I said. "What do you want?"

"Oh, just stopped by to drop off some paperwork. I don't agree with many of your conclusions about Nam Ngo, your 'Clocktalker.' I slid my comments under your door." He pointed at my feet. "You're standing on them."

I stared down at the crumpled papers under my Vans. I picked them up. These were carbon copies; the originals had been sent to The Brink's chief administrator, Dr. Peterson. *It is clear that Brinkvale's art therapist underestimates the psychoses of the patient,* it began. I slapped the document on my desk.

"What's your problem, Xavier?"

"*Doctor* Xavier," he said. He glanced around my office, wrinkling his nose. "This place is a sty, Taylor. It stinks." He nodded at the brown pile of soggy paper towels, still on the floor. "You're a slob."

I snatched up the dripping wad and tossed it into my wastebasket. I sighed. My left palm was now soaked with cold coffee. I considered wiping it on my jeans just to appall the guy, but instead I gritted my teeth and took the high road. Again.

"Xavier, what's this about? Is Brinkvale life so dull that you have to gun after me again? Didn't we just do this? Peterson's on my side. His email said so."

I might not have seen much of Peterson since I was hired here, but two months ago he'd served Xavier a polite smack-down after the young doctor criticized me during a staff meeting. Since then, Xavier's tormenting was less frequent, but more irritating. Until today, that is.

"It's about you being a failure," he replied. "Word around here is that you're fucking up the Drake case. You're losing it, cracking up."

"That's ... that's not true."

"You sure? I watched the security footage from yesterday's session with Grace. You let your guard down, lost control of the situation, and called the patient a son of a bitch. He might be crazy, but Grace was right about one thing: you *are* an amateur."

Xavier was spying on me? I clenched my fists.

"You had no goddamned right—"

"And you have no business treating him," he snapped. "Or anyone else, for that matter. Look, it's nothing personal, Taylor. It's merely survival of the fittest ... and you're making yourself an easy target."

He extended his hand now. His face was wicked and cheerful.

"But hey, congratulations on getting your name in the paper last week. You're out of your mind, playing the 'no comment' card with these reporters. And still, a star is born. Daddy D.A. must be so proud."

To hell with the damned high road. I shook his hand, gripping it hard. I clapped him on the shoulder with my other hand. I squeezed harder. He squeezed back, growling.

"You're an asshole," I said.

"And you won't be here much longer to say so," he replied.

I released him, fuming. Xavier grinned again, took a tiny bow, and stepped out of my office.

I slid into my desk chair, wondering how long it would take Xavier to notice the palm-sized coffee stain on his lab coat.

＊＊

I was opening my desk drawer to grab my lunch when someone else knocked at the door. I looked up. The stranger wore a business suit and a brown raincoat. I immediately thought of Karl Malden in those old American Express ads: *Don't leave home without it.*

"Are you Zach Taylor?" he asked.

I nodded. I was tempted to point at the plastic plaque bolted to the door. Xavier had pissed me off. I was sleep-deprived and famished. I just wanted some time to myself, and to prep for my session with Grace.

The man passed me his business card.

"Roland Smith, from Lifeplan Medical Alliance," he said. "I'll take just a minute of your time. I'm here about Martin Grace."

I stole a quick glance at the card. An insurance rep. I'd dealt with a few of these company men before. They're nice enough, but in the end, they're here on behalf of my patients' insurance companies—which means they want to ask questions about liability and payouts, things better suited for the Dr. Petersons of the world.

"I've got a lot of people asking me about Mr. Grace these days," I said. "If I gave every one of them a minute of my time—and honestly, people just say that, they want a lot more than a minute, don't they?—I'd be here until next leap year."

"Hey, 02-29," he said, smiling. "That's my son's birthday. Cool, huh?"

"Yeah," I replied, and it was. But I wasn't the guy Roland Smith needed to talk to. And I was hungry, for Pete's sake.

"Look, I know you want to know about Mr. Grace's condition, but—"

"How's he doing?" Smith asked. His voice sounded concerned, but his brown eyes were inquisitive.

"I can't tell you that," I said. "It's a patient confidentiality issue."

Smith nodded. "Lifeplan Medical Alliance just wants to know his status, considering next week's trial. You understand."

"I do, but we both know I'm in the clear here. You want to talk to an administrator about this."

"Yes, of course, but perhaps—"

I tossed his business card on my desk, scooped up my Brinkvale-issued walkie-talkie and stood up. Smith stopped talking.

"See this?" I said, raising the radio. "On the other end of this is a 260-pound security guard who used to be a pro wrestler. He loves his boys more than the world, but I bet he still gets a kick out of cracking skulls. You want me to call him?"

Smith's face had gone pale. He shook his head.

"You'll direct all formal inquiries to Brinkvale admin, then."

He nodded.

"I'm glad we settled this," I said. "Have a great day."

The insurance man left. I checked my watch.

"Damn it all," I muttered. Too late to head topside.

I plopped into my chair, unwrapped my sandwich, and ate in silence.

***

That afternoon, I was greeted by another B-movie disco-theque light show on Level 5. The hallway's incandescent bulbs still sputtered and stuttered like yesterday, still victims of ancient wiring and INSUFFICIENT FUNDS reports. My stomach churned at the darkness.

I saw Emilio Wallace's tall form directly ahead, about a hundred feet away, still standing watch by Room 507's door. He waved at me. The flickering lights transformed the fluidity of his arm into choppy stop-motion footage. He walked quickly toward me, meeting me halfway.

"Yo Z," he said, and gave me a broad smile. His capped teeth looked disturbing in this light, like blinking Chiclets. He clapped me hard on the shoulder.

I looked closer at Emilio's face. His Superman chin was covered in a Brillo-pad of stubble. His eyes were a little wild, feral.

"Hey man, you okay?" I asked. Above us lights buzzed on and off. "Dude. No disrespect here, but you look a little hellish."

"Heh, nope, none taken," he replied. "It's ... it's just good to see someone, you know. For hours and hours and hours, it's been just me and Martin here—t-t-to the max."

"*In* the Max," I corrected. "Martin ... Grace? You guys been talking?"

Emilio nodded. "Come on, Z ... when was the last time we had anyone in Max? Gotta k-k-kill time somehow. It's just been m-m-me and Martin, shootin' the bull."

I nodded back, and shivered. Goddamn, it was cold down here.

"G-good to see you, is all," he said. "They gotta get these lights fixed. Mess with your head. Between them and all the OT, I been seein' ... "

His voice trailed off. He looked up at one of the lights, then shrugged, helpless.

"What?" I asked.

"Nothin'," Emilio said. He placed his large hand on my shoulder and gave it a firm squeeze. "Just need some sleep, that's all. Damned good to see you."

We walked toward Room 507. Emilio asked about the paper bag in my hand; I told him it was for Martin Grace. I asked

Emilio if he'd heard Grace playing on the electronic keyboard I'd left yesterday.

"Nope, but I wasn't here this morning. That was Chaz. Not sure if he heard anything. Didn't mention it. Is it important?"

We stopped a few feet short of Grace's room.

"Might be," I said. "I'll find out soon enough."

"Well, if he doesn't tell you if he got all Liberace on—"

The lights above us suddenly flashed brighter and quicker than before. A bulb far down the hall—near the elevator—popped and shattered. Sparks and glass fell onto the cracked tiled floor. I gasped. A tiny shriek echoed from the nurse's station. Emilio gave a low, appreciative chuckle.

"I'll call maintenance, don't worry," he said. "That's the second one to go today. Listen. Like I said, if he doesn't want to talk about it, you can always play back the CC tape."

I thought of Xavier and harrumphed.

"The room's vidcam."

"Roger," Emilio said. He stepped over to the door, unlocked it. "Okay, get to work. Give a shout if you need me."

He tugged it open. The hallway's light show flashed wicked shadows into the void beyond. I could see the dark outline of Martin Grace, still in the center of the room, still sitting in his wooden chair. I thought about Malcolm. I thought about improvisation.

My hand slid into the inky blackness, fingertips groping for the room's light switch. I found it. The room blew up bright, forcing me to squint.

Martin Grace's eyes were closed. His face, impassive. Dead.

The lights outside the room stopped blinking. Now, there was perfectly steady, innocent incandescent light ... everywhere.

Martin Grace was grinning now. Grinning like a crazy person.

I felt a bead of sweat trail down my spine.

"Huh," I heard Emilio say. I stepped into the room, toward my patient. The door closed behind me.

Grace kept grinning.

It was as quiet as a tomb.

$$* * *$$

I stood still and watched the man closely, not speaking, wanting to defy his expectations. I'd done the predictable thing yesterday, had taken my lumps, learned my lesson. It was time to test *Grace's* predictability now.

"Good afternoon, Mr. Taylor," he said finally. His grin didn't waver. "What's in the bag?"

I wasn't surprised by this. I'd expected it. Cool.

"Something for later."

I placed the sack on the table by the door, next to the Casio. I dragged the other chair to the center of the room, and sat.

"Did you relay my warning to Nurse Jackson?" he asked. His voice was low and smooth, a night-drive radio DJ. "About her early date with the maker?"

"No."

Grace's lined face slipped into a frown. "Ah. Well, I must say that doesn't sound very gentlemanly," he said. "Doesn't sound like someone concerned with the fate of his fellow man. That's why you're here, after all, isn't it? To make a—"

His voice dipped low, dripped with condescension.

"—*positive impact* on the world. To give something back."

I crossed my arms, knowing that my chair's creaks would telegraph this. The man's head tilted slightly. A ghostly, knowing smirk was now on his lips.

"Behold the indignance of youth," he began. "It's no wonder

the leaders of this great nation worry—"

"Do you smell that?" I asked.

Martin Grace stopped speaking. I watched his nostrils flare slightly, his eyebrows rise, appraising. He said nothing.

I leaned forward, placing my elbows on my knees. "You smelled the jam on my shirt yesterday, and that was only a smudge. Surely you smell this."

"What," Grace said. It wasn't a question.

"Bullshit," I replied.

I was learning to pitch.

Martin Grace's face tightened. Twisted. Went crimson, like a cartoon. His knuckles flared white as he clenched his fists.

"Just who do you think you're talking to? Do you have any idea who in the *FUCK* you're talking to?"

"I know who I'm *not* talking to," I said. "I'm not talking to Martin Grace."

The man's eyes opened. He stared at my face, his pine-green eyes burning hot and furious.

"You know what I mean," I said. "Don't insult me by saying you don't. Let's get a few things straight, Martin. One: No, I do not know who in the fuck I'm talking to. But I'd like to know. I'd like you to tell me who you really are, not who you claim to be. I'd like you to work with me, get talking and playing on that piano, expressing—and *helping*—yourself, for God's sake. Two: You were right yesterday. I'm not 'like the others.' You're stuck with me, so lend me a hand here. I'm going to find out one way or another, I really am. I'll keep digging."

Martin Grace spat at my feet, missing my sneakers by a half-inch.

"Dig," he whispered. "Dig all the way to hell. That's the only way you'll find me, maggot. I run the red show, the hellshow."

I had no idea what that meant.

"Who are you?" I asked. "Who were you?"

The man's face smoothed over, went cold. At that moment, Martin Grace reminded me of my father.

"You seem to think that if I *see*, everything will be all right," he said. " 'Praise the Lord, it's another Mr. Taylor miracle, he saved The Mole Man.' That's what they're calling me now, you know that, don't you?"

I didn't. The smile on Grace's face told me he knew this.

He tapped his temple, drawing my attention to his open, sightless eyes.

"But your mind doesn't understand. Even if you save me, you're not going to save me. You're going to kill people ... probably yourself. I'm doing you *a favor*. Protecting you."

"You know, I'm getting pretty damned tired of people trying to protect me," I snapped. "The past is what it is. You can't erase it no matter how hard you try, or how far you run. What are you so afraid of?"

Martin Grace's head tilted slightly, as if he had heard something. He closed his eyes. He raised his head slowly, the light bulb above him illuminating his lined face. He was handsome and horrifying in the silence.

"Oh, you *know*," he said.

The Dark Man, yes—but I shook my head. "I honestly don't. You're crippled by remorse for murders you didn't commit. These visions you had, they have explanations, Martin. Roots from before, from before you were Martin Grace. If you tell me about your life, if we go down that road together... "

I paused. Grace wasn't listening. He was still smiling up at the ceiling.

"I want you to find peace," I said simply. "I want help you find—"

"You know ... what's ... *here*," he said. "I *know* you do. I can smell it all over you, the thing I've smelled on myself every day for ten years now. You're my midnight kin, my haunted brother, my tormented son. You've *seen* it, you've *felt* it, you know it's here, been here all along, been close, hosting Black Mass in the corners of your mind, in the corner of every room, behind every closed door, under every bed—"

"Knock it off, man," I said.

"—and you *know* it's here—"

"Stop."

"—right now. With us. Right. Now."

The light above Grace flickered. I gaped up at it, unbelieving.

"I hate that sound," the blind man said.

The light buzzed again.

I had a hand to my mouth now. I could feel the blood rushing from my face. I couldn't help it. I felt slow and stupid, like a child. Frightened. I couldn't stand, couldn't think straight. Was it getting colder in here?

"There's not a single bulb in my apartment, you know," he said. "Nary a one. Keeps things *quiet*. Keeps things *sane*. When I'm alone and I'm thinking about it, it does this. Plays with the lights. It's not far, never far, is it?"

I looked over my shoulder, to the wall by the door. The light switch had not moved from its "on" position. The light above flashed more Morse code.

"The Dark Man, Mr. Taylor. Can you see it?" Grace's voice purred. "Your friend outside certainly can. He's been seeing it for a day now; it's been prowling the hall like a panther, driving him mad."

Shadows splashed across the bare walls as the light went berserk. Could I see it? Christ, could I? Something black there, in the corner? An absence of ... everything? Light? Something breathing, shoulders heaving?

Was it real?

Would you be mine? Could you be mine?

"Emilio thinks it's a *vampire*," Grace whispered. He said this as if it were a wink-nudge secret between two friends. I shuddered. "But it's so much worse than that. Don't you agree?"

He spread his arms, a priest at the pulpit. The light continued to flicker. "This is where the Inkstain lives. You're wise to be afraid of the dark. It hunts best in the pitch."

I'd made plans for today's session. Wanted to rattle him, put a chink in his impenetrable suit of armor. This hadn't been on the agenda—God no.

"It's in every exhale, every other heartbeat, every third eye blink, and you want me to set it free? No, Mr. Taylor. That would be unwise. Just do what your father wants you to do. Forget about the blind man, the lost love. Keep him buried in The Brink like he wants, if only for another week, so Daddy can bury him someplace worse. Father knows best. Forever and ever, amen."

And then the room went dark for a breathless, terrible moment.

Something skittered in the blackness. Millipede feet.

This isn't happening, I told myself, *this is the power of suggestion, bad wires, bad lights, bad, broken Zach, nothing more. There's nothing else in this*

Skitter, from behind. *Tktk.*

in this room goddamnit, just me and the blind man and

The bulb flashed bright again, steady. Grace lowered his head and looked at me.

I fought every urge to turn around, look for the thing that was never there. I took a deep breath, bit my tongue to focus.

"What ... what do you know about my father?" I finally asked.

The man chuckled. "Now who's insulting whom, Mr. Taylor? If you're curious, ask him, not me."

He lowered his arms.

"Now are you going to tell me what's in your bag of tricks before you leave ... or will you be coy and make me guess? Because I assure you, Mr. Taylor, our session is over. You'll stare at me and ask me question after question, and I'll say nary a syllable. You may be stupid to think you can crack me ... but you're smart enough to know what I say is true."

And I did. My shoulders slumped. No improvisation from me, no history from him. No. Not in this room.

But what about ... outside this room?

My eyes turned to the Casio piano by the door. Learn to pitch, Malcolm had said. I'd soon see if my patient had stepped to the plate last night. And tomorrow, I'd see if he'd play today's game, too.

I strode toward the room's table. Grace smiled at the sound of the bag I'd brought today. It crinkled in my hands. I pulled out a long, flat, rectangular box, and a sketch pad. I flipped open the top of the box. "They're pastels, Martin," I said. "They're more than a hundred here. And paper."

Grace laughed, a full-belly guffaw.

"You've giving a blind man *crayons?* You're the worst art therapist the world has—"

"You know, I *knew* you were going to say that," I replied, and I had. The curve ball was in my hand, small, but finally there. I needed these unexpected maneuvers, if I wanted to evoke something from him, some expression beyond this game-playing. "You're a one-trick pony, Martin Grace. Let's see if you have the balls to evolve. Draw for me, blind man. I'll come back tomorrow to see what you've created. We're going to talk about it."

He opened his mouth to retort. I didn't listen. I grabbed the Casio piano from the table and left the room.

"He knows," I said to myself, walking the hallways of Level 3. "Somehow he knows when the lights are going to flicker."

I was still shaking from the beast I'd seen in Room 507. Either I was losing my mind, or Martin Grace was manipulating me. Neither prospect was good.

"Yeah, gotta be it," I murmured. "Uses it to scare me, throw me off-balance, gain control of the session. He's shutting me down when I start to get personal."

My rational side—my personal Leonard Nimoy—spoke up.

Why would he do that?

"Because I'm close. Close to something. Something he doesn't want me to know."

And what does that mean? Mr. Spock asked.

"It means that's my in. If I can't get in the front door, I gotta squeak through a basement window. Personal. I've got to get personal."

So how can you do that?

I turned the corner toward my office, hefted the Casio synthesizer in my hand.

"I'm working on that," I said. "Let's see if he met me halfway."

I unlocked the office door and went to my desk. I placed the piano on its side.

"Memory card," I said, and smiled. I pushed a release and a tiny plastic rectangle popped from the device. Before yesterday's session, I'd configured the Casio to record everything played on its keyboard.

I launched the media player on my PC and slid the memory card into a small reader.

"Did you get curious, you coldhearted sonuvabitch?" I said. "Did you get creative?"

I held my breath as the contents of the card were accessed. An audio waveform appeared on the screen.

I tapped the spacebar. There was silence, and then a very brief and cheerful, if chaotic, series of notes.

I nodded. That had been yesterday's dinner bell, when I'd played a few keys to get Grace's attention. I looked at the remaining waveform.

The Casio had automatically truncated the "dead space" between this and the next notes, reducing hours of silence into seconds.

The audio program continued to load the file. I listened. Given his pro work, I expected Grace's music to be jazz. It wasn't.

It was classical music. Masterfully played classical music.

The song sounded familiar, like something used in a movie. Something Kubrick used in *2001: A Space Odyssey*? Or perhaps "The Blue Danube," or "Also Sprach Zarathustra"? No. Older.

A whirlwind stream of notes, delicate, high things, scattered before booming, menacing low notes. Now, syncopated blasts. It was on the tip of my tongue.

Now a second, much more familiar tune interrupted—this one coming from the satchel at my feet. Beethoven's *Fifth*. I grabbed my cell phone. *Bum-bum-bum-bummmmm*.

Dad was calling. I sneered and let it ring again. I didn't want to talk to him.

I flashed back to my time with Grace just minutes ago. What had he said? Something about me doing Dad's bidding, burying the blind man. What did that mean? What did Grace know that I didn't ... and more important, *how* did he know it?

"Just frickin' ask him," I said, and answered the call.

"Zachary. You lied to me."

I blinked. *I* lied to *him?* "What?"

"Please, don't waste my time, young man," he said. His voice was calm. If I hadn't lived with the man for eighteen years—and hadn't watched him become bitter about his job during the last few of those—I'd think we were about to have an intellectual conversation. I knew better.

"Your hand is in the cookie jar," he was saying. "I know it and you know it. You're a liar, and not a very good one at that. Transparent, son. You threw your friends under the bus last night, deflecting, thinking I'd forget. Crass. "

"Dad? I don't under—"

I heard the ubiquitous crinkle-crack of a newspaper, the rattle-pat of a finger tapping its surface.

" 'A Brinkvale Psychiatric employee who spoke on the condition of anonymity confirmed that Grace is being evaluated at the facility,' " he said. "Was that you?"

"Of course not," I said.

The line roared as I heard the paper being torn and wadded.

"Now that, son, is what the truth sounds like. But could it get worse?" Dad said. He was raising his voice now. "Of course it could! 'Dr. Theodore Peterson, the hospital's chief administrator, confirmed that art therapist Zachary Taylor—son of New York District Attorney William Taylor—is assigned to Grace's case.' Quote, 'Zachary is a world-class art therapist, and I see nothing wrong with assigning one of my most talented staffers … ' "

"Dad," I cut in. "What's the problem?"

He laughed without mirth.

"We don't have an hour for me to enumerate, son," he said. "First and foremost, you *lied* to me. You didn't say *anything* about Martin Grace when I asked you about work last night. You said you needed to piss. We both know the only thing you did was piss. Me. Off."

"I didn't lie," I snapped. My initial shock was ebbing, but I could feel a high tide of rage taking its place. Getting torn apart in Room 507 — and the hours of being haunted by Henry, the *truth*—had finally found a target. *He* was pissed off? "I didn't lie. I just didn't answer your question. I didn't want to watch you pull the same bum's rush bullshit you and Papa-Jean pulled on the Invisible Man, bully me into—"

"—oh, listen to you, you're—"

"—spilling my guts there—"

"—so righteous, I didn't raise—"

"—during Gram's *fucking funeral!*" I screamed. I blinked, mentally reminding myself to *chill*, I was as work, this wasn't the time.

But I couldn't help myself. "Besides, what I do here at The Brink is *absolutely* none of your business. I have the same therapist-client privilege as our psychiatrists."

"Not subpoenaed, not in court," Dad said.

"No," I shot back, "but we're not in court right now, and we weren't last night." My fingernails dug into the cell phone's plastic. "Tell you what, Dad. I'll confirm that Peterson gave me the Grace case. That's all you're getting. Anything else is protected information."

"I'm your father," Dad said. His voice rose a half-octave, warmed just a little. "I'm trying to protect both of us. You have no idea what kind of danger you're in—how over your head you are. If you've seen Grace's dossier, you know what he's capable of. He hates the weak. He hates … *doctors.* You're sharing space with a *multiple murderer.* Don't you understand what that means? You're at risk, above all."

"I'm not weak," I said. My mind flashed to this morning's rounds with the Golgotha patients. "I work with murderers every day."

"Not like *him,*" Dad replied. His voice had gone cold again. "And you are. I'm sorry son, but you are. You're no match for him. She was no match him, she couldn't help him, and he killed her, tore her open."

I frowned. "Tanya Gold was a singer, Dad. Not a doctor."

He paused, and didn't speak for a long time. I gritted my teeth.

Finally: "I *need* to know these things, Zachary. You're supposed to tell me everything."

Oh, I'd fucking had enough of this.

"Just like you tell me everything, right, Dad?"

More silence. His voice came back, low and threatening.

"What is that supposed to mean, Zachary?"

"We don't have an hour for me to enumerate," I said, mocking his voice. I wasn't about to tell him about Henry. Not now, maybe not ever. "See, no one comes to The Brink unless they're doomed. Your office is *burying* this man, Dad, railroading him into a hole so deep and dark—there's *no way* a proper psychological evaluation can be made in the time before the trial. Your people have rigged the game, and you think I should tell you *anything*? What are you really after?"

"Let it go. Please."

I felt myself straighten in my chair. The sound of Taylor Family Loyalty being strained to its limit.

"No."

"This is a conflict of interest," Dad said.

That wasn't my father's voice anymore. I was talking to the district attorney now.

The newspaper rattled again, forty miles away.

"I'll spoon-feed this to you," he said. "This story is hinting, young man, *hinting* that Grace's lawyer can leverage this into an investigation against my team's practices. Maybe even grounds for mistrial. That's not going to happen. Grace belongs in The Brink, but not with you. We're both at risk here. I'm pulling you off his case."

I felt my jaw unhinge.

"You don't have the authority," I said.

"Anyone can make a phone call. This is all going to be over today. I've got de Luca heading to Brooklyn in two hours for one last pass, and I'll be calling Dr. Peterson as soon as I get off the phone. Come five o'clock, we'll have what we need, and you won't be working with Martin Grace anymore."

"Why?" I asked. "Why are you doing this?"

"Why are you making me, Zachary?" he countered. "I'm doing this for both of us. It's for your own—"

I snapped the phone shut.

All of my bravado was gone, cut like marionette strings. Like that, just like that—*snick!*—my chance to change Grace's life for the better was over.

My eyes trailed from my cell phone to my monitor. This song was the closest I'd been to Martin Grace, and I had no idea what it meant.

I knew the true keys to saving Grace were things like this. Personal things—things that could make a positive effect. They were stories not found in his Brinkvale files, not in The Brink. They were in the world beyond.

Personal things. Positive effects.

Personal.

Effects.

I bolted upright, checked the Eterna on my wrist. Two-thirty. I did the math, cussed, then snatched Grace's files from my satchel. I scanned the first page and nodded. It was an hour-and-a-half ride on the LIRR, barely enough time.

I schemed for another minute. I'd need help. A lot. The cell phone was in my hand already. I hit the speed dial.

"Welcome up!" Lucas cried into my ear. "What's shakin', bacon?"

"Where are you?" I asked.

"I'm with the *chica*," he said. His voice went off-mic for a moment, barely audible. "And my-my, is she *muy delicioso*."

I heard a woman giggle, say something in Spanish. They laughed. I grinned; I couldn't help it.

"I need to know if you're interruptible," I said. "Like right-frickin'-now interruptible. For a … for a little adventure."

I heard another chuckle, this one in my mind. *Giddy-giddy, pardner.*

I closed my eyes, shook my head.

"Dookle, sounds intense," he replied. "Where do you need me to be?"

I told him.

"Katabatic. On my way, meep meep," he said.

I hung up, and turned to the walkie-talkie on the desk.

One more call.

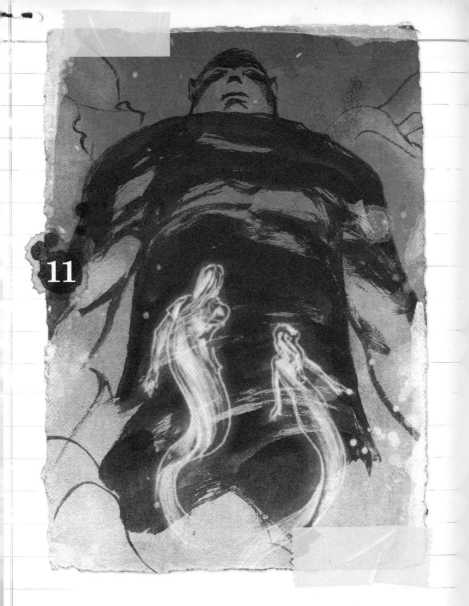

11

Malcolm stood beneath the mighty tree Primoris Maximus as I pedaled up on my Cannondale. He eyed me, a smoke in one hand, a
lawn rake in the other. I'd buzzed him less than ten minutes ago.

If he's already here, then it's a no-go. Crap.

I braked near the trunk, stealing a lungful of the aroma around me. In a few weeks, the trees would be aflame. This was my favorite time of the year. If the world is a tiger, then autumn is that brief but awe-inspiring moment when the big cat yawns and stretches—all claws and shifting colors and glorious, trembling muscle—before settling in for a long nap.

Malcolm looked mournful.

"Bad news, huh?" I asked Malcolm. "Couldn't get 'em?"

"Oh, I got 'em," the old man said. He patted the breast of his beat-up brown corduroy jacket. "But we need to talk first, Zach T."

I dismounted and leaned the bike against the tree.

"Look, I know I told you to dance during the earthquake, but this isn't really what I had in mind," he said.

He pulled a large manila envelope from his coat. The words INTER-DEPARTMENT DELIVERY were stenciled on its flap. There were dozens of names on the envelope, all marked through with bold Sharpie strokes, save for the one at the bottom: *Martin Grace.*

"They'll fire you for having this stuff," he said. "That ain't even what I'm really worried about. *I* can get fired for taking it. You need to request these things, Zach."

"That'll take too damned long for what I need it for," I replied. "I *need* Grace's personal effects. Look, I'm getting it from all sides right now. Grace is creaming me, not giving an inch. Xavier's sniffing around, looking for a way to boot me off the case. My own dad's out to get me. If I don't start making connections *now* and helping him *now,* it's over."

I glanced at my watch. I needed to catch the train to Grace's house before dad's man de Luca cleaned it out.

"It's a leap of faith, Malcolm," I said, urgency in my voice. "I wouldn't ask for help if I didn't need it."

Malcolm shook his head deliberately.

"You didn't *ask* for help," he said. "You know how I roll, Zach. I don't help anybody. Them's the Malcolm Rules. I owe you, but it ain't enough."

My heart sank a little.

"Sorry I troubled you," I said.

Malcolm passed me the envelope, turned, and walked back toward the building.

"Toss in a fifth of Grey Goose and we're even," he said over his shoulder. "Now, go on. Git."

I got.

✳ ✳ ✳

"Get out, *getoutoftheway!!*" I screamed as I piloted my Cannondale down the steps of the LIRR train station, tires skidding on the cobblestones, arms trembling as I successfully kept the bike under control. I was a sight worthy of a Hollywood action picture—a *Bourne* chase scene … if an international spy ran with the eighteen-speed crowd.

I braked at the foot of the stairs, hefted the Cannondale onto my shoulder and made a mad dash to the shimmering, ball-busting turnstile. MTA tokens spilled out of my hands as I madly shoved a copper coin into the slot … now ratcheting through, grunting, heaving the bike … now dashing to the train doors as their *ding-dong* warnings blared … and then, inside the car, panting, smiling sheepishly at my fellow straphangers.

What can I say? Lucas isn't the only Taylor who's got mad skills.

It would take around ninety minutes to get to Brooklyn from here. If Lucas met me on time—and if the 5 P.M. deadline Dad had mentioned was accurate—we'd have twenty minutes to investigate Grace's apartment unobserved.

The real question was, would Lucas show up on time? My brother wasn't the most punctual—

Cheerful skeleton song, xylophone music, interrupted my thoughts. Text message from Lucas.

HERE. LOUNGIN'. CHICA LIVED NEARBY. :P

I texted back: *OK. BE THERE IN >90.*

I looked at my reflection in the train window. *You're really going to do this?*

I patted my satchel. "Not technically breaking and entering if I've got his house keys," I said. A nearby passenger, thinking I was speaking to her, inched away from me.

And if you find anything worth taking? Are you going to steal it?

"Ain't stealin' if you intend on bringing it back," I whispered. My voice was low, a little hoarse—and Dixie-fried enough to give me a troubled pause.

Anti-Zach. I began to shiver. I squeezed my eyes shut, gripped the handrail tight.

"I'm not going down that road with you," I hissed. "Not again. Never again."

It—he—wasn't your fault, I could almost hear A-Z say. *Wrong place, wrong time…*

Hush.

I opened my eyes and stared at my reflection again. I was about to invade an alleged serial killer's home, disrupt an investigation by the Manhattan District Attorney's office, and most likely tamper with, and remove, evidence.

My cell phone chimed again, this time a ringtone of "Birdhouse In Your Soul" by They Might Be Giants. Rachael.

Not to put too fine a point on it, say I'm the only bee in your bonnet.

"Hey," I said. "What's up?"

"—ach?" Rachael said. "—alling to check in. Haven't heard fr— all day. You okay?"

"Ah, sorta," I said, straining to hear. She must've been at the *Journal-Ledger's* offices. Those thick-stoned Midtown buildings wreaked havoc with cell reception. My thumb tapped the side of the phone, boosting its volume. "Things are a little hectic over here right now."

"—at The Brrrrrrk?" her voice said. "—oesn't sound like it. Noisy. Rattllll … Are you onnn*nnnnn*—"

The phone whined in my hand. I winced.

"—train?" she finished.

"Yeah," I said. "Had to split early, Rache. Nothing I can't handle though, don't worry."

"Didn't catch that last part," Rachael said. "You're—ouble?"

I frowned. This was exasperating.

"Listen, I'm heading over to Martin Grace's apartment in Brooklyn. That's it, just looking for something to help him. Like I said, nothing to worry about. But Rache, sorry to get all high school on you, but don't tell my dad, okay?"

The line whined again, garbling whatever Rachael was saying now. I hung up.

The phone vibrated in my hand. I hit the "talk" button without looking at the screen.

"Hey Rache," I said.

But it wasn't Rachael. For a heart-pounding moment, I heard Martin Grace speaking to me … and beneath his voice was the husky breathing of his Dark Man, *tktkssssssstttt*—

"—ust got off the phone with your employer," my dad was saying. "Young man, you're in … "

"Oh, fuck you," I snapped, and hung up. Disgusted, I switched off the phone.

I spent the rest of the train ride in troubled silence.

When I arrived at Grace's brownstone, Lucas was showboating for
no one, deftly juggling concrete shards from the broken steps.

I pulled up on my bike, tugged off my helmet. He grinned, tossed the concrete, and sprung from the steps like a Pop-Tart.

"Chica sends her regards," he said.

"No she doesn't," I replied. I dismounted the Cannondale.

"Nope," Lucas affirmed. "But it's the polite thing to say. Let's stash the Black Stallion there."

I followed him to a tight alleyway beside the brownstone. Grace's building and its neighboring identical twin loomed over us, blocking out most of the afternoon sun. Rusty fire escapes raced down their sides.

My brother pointed to a graffiti-tagged Dumpster. Black sacks of garbage lay inside. I groaned.

"Lucas, this bike cost more than a grand," I said. "I'm not gonna leave it in the trash."

"How far up?"

"Five floors."

"Well, you could make like a Sherpa ... "

I sighed, checked my watch. We were already down to fifteen minutes. I prayed Dad's crony was trapped in Brooklyn traffic.

"Come on," Lucas said.

"Shit, okay. Just help me hide it."

We stowed the bike on its side near the Dumpster, covering it with sacks of trash. Our camouflage job was effective; it would take more than a glance for a passerby to spot the bike. I reminded myself that we'd only be gone for fifteen minutes.

We trotted to the front of the building. I unbuckled my satchel, stuck my hand into the envelope Malcolm had given me. Based on the admittance papers, I knew there were three items Grace had had on his person when he was admitted into the system: A wallet, a cellphone and a key ring.

I found the keys. There were tiny, textured stickers on each one. Braille.

Jesus, this was crazy. I looked at Lucas.

"Don't fret, Z," he said. "Superglued to your hip. Thick as thieves, you and me."

"You have no idea," I replied. "I'll give you the score on the way up, okay?"

As Lucas nodded enthusiastically, I slid a key—amazingly, the right one—into the brownstone's deadbolt. We were in.

✳ ✳ ✳

I can only imagine what we must have looked like, skulking past the battered doorways and water-stained wallpaper. *Poseur* secret agents, mostly likely. But nobody saw us as we climbed the stairwell.

We faced Grace's door. Apartment 512. The words *Sealed by New York City Police Department DO NOT ENTER* glared at us from a vertical strip of tape covering the seam of door, where the door met the frame. It lanced from eye level down to the deadbolt.

"Shit," I whispered. I had the door key in my hand, but…

Lucas reached into his jeans pocket and removed a foldable multitool. As he coaxed a blade from its handle, I shook my head. Cut the tape to get inside, leave proof that an intruder had been here. No go.

"Did you come this far to turn back now?" he said. "Trust me, bro. We'll put it back."

He slid the knife's edge under the tape, gently nicking the wood. Soon, he'd tugged away enough of the strip to grip it with his fingers. He pulled the tape now, slowly peeling it from the door frame.

I nodded, and slid the key into the deadbolt.

From across and down the hall, the tinny rattle of a doorchain against wood. *Shuck,* went a deadbolt. *Shuck,* went another. Fuck. 509's tenant was coming out.

"Wind chill," Lucas hissed. He nudged me and gave the tape a frantic yank. It snarled as it snaked from the wood. "*Motorvate,* dude."

I unlocked the door. It swung open, and Lucas shoved me inside. I stumbled as he followed, the key jangling in my hand, and I heard the door's latch snap home behind me, and was I gasping now, like a asthmatic, head reeling with fear, it was slick and sickening and *everywhere*

fuck jesus dark, dark not a pinprick of light, fuck

I staggered backward, banging against the door, my hand swishing out into the black, finding nothing.

Blind. Truly blind.

I heard the rapid-fire *click-clickclickclick* as Lucas flipped a light switch, heard him swear at the thing, it was firing blanks, mocking us, *there's not a single bulb in my apartment, you know*, Grace cooed in my ear, *keeps things quiet, keeps things sane*. Shitshitshit sane, sane for whom, shit

Lucas' hand was on my bicep, firm and reassuring.

"Right here, Zach, right here, one sec ... "

He faded away, lost in the ink. I couldn't hear him. I could only hear my heartbeat, a terrible derailed L line train thundering and smashing inside my skull, and my screeching gasps, hyperventilating now, there wasn't enough air in the world for my lungs, not now, not in the black.

Light, flaring and explosive, filled the room. Lucas looked up from the Sony Handycam in his hand, its pop-up light glowing like a beacon. He dropped the open backpack in his other hand and reached for me. I clutched at his arm, blinking, sucking down air. Ghoulish shadows scratched at his face, lit from underneath.

Lucas' eyes swept over me, his face grim with concern. He squatted, sweeping the videocamera's light around Martin Grace's living room. His free hand fished inside the backpack. I watched the spotlight traverse an unremarkable couch, an easy chair.

He passed me a tiny flashlight. I clicked it on.

"He's blind," I whispered, breathing easier now. I slid Grace's keys into my satchel. "No need for lights."

"Con Ed must hate the bastard."

We squinted in the gloom. The absolute absence of light in Martin Grace's home was unsettling, but even more was its absence of ... of what? I flicked my flashlight this way and that. It was an eerie, spartan place. Bare walls. A coffee table, its surface unblemished and blank. Built-in bookshelves near an unused fireplace, all empty. The mantle above the fireplace, also empty. This place was creepy in its whiteness, its utter lack of personality.

Lucas frowned at the curtains beside him. He pulled them aside. The white LED of his vidcam blasted back into our eyes.

"Aluminum foil on the windows," he said. "This guy's got a fuggin' phobia."

I turned away, flashlight probing my half of the room. "Come here," Lucas hissed suddenly. "Mother lode."

Stacked against the wall was a tower of rack-mounted audio equipment—digital receivers, amplifiers, two massive multi-disc CD changers. No recording gear ... just premium-brand, audiophile stuff, made for listening.

"Nice," he said.

"Pan right."

The shelves of a prefab bookcase sagged with the weight of hundreds of CDs. On the spine of each jewel case was a tiny, Braille-stenciled sticker. Every disc was a clue, a peek into Grace's mind.

"There's no time to write all this down," I said dispairingly.

My brother looked at me with an expression so comical and cartoonish, I nearly giggled. One of his eyebrows was cocked impossibly high on his forehead; his lip was curled in a sneer. He looked like a frizzy-haired Elvis Presley.

"Bitch, I've been rollin' since I flipped this on," he said, nodding to the camera. "I'll get this, and then stand watch by the door. Wanna make sure our neighbor out there isn't scheming. You check out the rest of the apartment. How much time?"

I checked my watch. "Ten minutes." I walked out of the living room into the cramped hallway. My footfalls echoed off the naked walls.

This tiny flashlight was doing a piss-poor job of beating back the darkness. The day-night slipped around me like a glove, oppressive; I felt it soak my clothes, seep into my pores.

I gave the bathroom a once-over. Nothing of note here; no prescriptions, only store-brand toiletries. The kitchen was equally devoid of personalization. I thought of my apartment; how Rachael and I had done everything we could to make that place special, ours.

How could a man live an invisible life? I wondered. *There's gotta be something here, something his, truly his, something hiding.*

I nudged the door at the end of the hall with my foot. The bedroom door swung inward, its hinges stutter-squeaking like a giggly child. The blackness was overpowering here. *It hunts best in the pitch,* I heard Grace say. I licked my lips. My nyctophobia was slobbering, ravenous now. Gooseflesh was having its way with my skin, cascading down my arms, my chest (I felt my nipples stiffen, and shivered), my balls were digging up inside me, every hair standing on end.

The flashlight in my hand sputtered, spiraling the room into a candlelight flicker show. My teeth gnawed into my bottom lip as I shook the thing—work, work, goddamn you.

The door slammed shut behind me.

I couldn't scream … and if I had, I would not have heard it now, Jesus Christ, the sound of skittering leaves, of gravel tossed upon hardwood. *Tktktk.* Blood squirted into my mouth, my incisor gone too far into the flesh, lip cut.

The shadows swirled and jittered and the flashlight failed me. I slapped its head against my right palm now, and there, in my peripheral vision, a shape high on the wall, a thing with horns, now without, a thing with snakes for arms, dancing, looming, and I could hear it speaking now, a cicada hum—

"Would. You. Be. *Miiiine?*"

The flashlight winked out … and then flashed bright again.

I stared at the wall, wracked with shivers, not blinking at the shade-thing towering above me. It no longer danced. It no longer spoke. But its snake arms still jittered, frightening things.

I blinked. Looked down at my trembling fingers. The fingers on my right hand. The light surged past them, casting their shadows on the wall. My fingers. My fucking fingers.

I pulled my hand away from the flashlight, and the monster disappeared.

"Get a grip, you idiot," I said. I swallowed the bitter blood mixed with spit in my mouth and swept the light over the room.

It showed a bed—fastidiously made, taut sheets, military corners—an empty night table, a chest of drawers, an open closet door. I looked inside the closet, up to a shelf above hanging khaki pants and dress shirts. It was empty. Light kicking south now, to the floor. Two pairs of shoes. One set were expensive, gleaming Italian dress shoes. The other was a pair of pristine Reeboks.

A search of the nearby chest of drawers was equally fruitless. Socks, briefs and white undershirts glared up at me, their slumber interrupted. God, it was so dark in here.

"Focus," I said, and did my best to.

I aimed the flashlight toward the far corner of the room. There, beneath another curtain-covered window, was a full-sized electronic keyboard resting atop a metal card table. Its white and black keys gleamed in the light. I thought of Emilio Wallace's haunted face from this afternoon, of his too-white teeth and the hollow gaps in between. A tiny, ancient television sat beside the piano.

Why would a blind man need a TV? I wondered, and then immediately cursed myself. That was the selfishness of my sighted life spilling into this one. One need not see to watch. Grace had proven that already, hadn't he?

I leaned in, looking more closely at the twelve-inch TV. What *did* the man watch? I snatched my untucked shirttail and used it as an impromptu glove. I tugged on the silver volume knob.

It didn't switch on. I checked the power cable—it was plugged in—and twisted the chunky VHF knob. It dutifully clack-clacked, trying to switch stations. Nothing.

I spun the UHF knob beneath it. It made a subtle ticking sound, like a stopwatch.

I stiffened. I knew that sound.

You surely do, Zach. That's a tick-tick that takes us way back. Giddy-giddy.

I growled at the voice in my head and leaned closer, nearly placing my ear against the plastic box. I turned the knob slowly. It'd been more than five years, and here I was, sliding on this suit, quietly alarmed at how easy it was to do so ... and how well it still fit.

Tick-tick-tick-CLICK.

"Two to go," I whispered.

The other tumblers soon fell, and the front of the television popped open like an oven door. I looked inside.

The bedroom door behind me screeched open, and I nearly screamed. More light surged into the room.

"We're in deep shit," Lucas said. His face was flushed and manic in the light of his Handycam. He slammed the door behind him. "Cops. Lots of cops. Spotted them from the hallway window. Coming up the stairwell now."

"Cops? I thought it'd be some D.A. intern—"

"Shut up, man. We gotta bolt!"

I reached into the hollow television and pulled out a metal box, about the size of a large paperback book. I slapped it into his free hand, shut Grace's home-brewed safe and gave the combination knob a spin.

Lucas shook the box. The tinny sound of cardboard or paper clicked against the box walls. But there was something else clanking inside, too. It sounded small and metallic, like a silver dollar.

"Hold this," he said, passing me the Handycam. He pulled off his pack and slipped the lockbox inside. With one efficient tug, the pack was zippered tight, and our work here was done.

We grinned at each other in the darkness.

"Okay. Katabatic," Lucas said.

And then the fury of New York's finest descended upon us.

***

The voices were not voices; they were monstrous roars, banshee-screams from an unholy two-hundred-foot *daikaiju*, window-rattling wails.

NYPD! GET ON THE FLOOR! ON THE FLOOR NOW DO IT NOW WE'RE COMING IN ON THE FLOOR NOWONTHEFLOORNOW!

From beyond the room and down the hall, I heard the pistol-shot of wood shattering, hinges swinging madly, a doorknob bashing into drywall. I started, staring at the closed bedroom door.

Lucas punched my arm, hard.

"Help me!" he hissed. I turned and watched him tear the dark curtains off their cheap aluminum rail, watched the plaster dust—exquisitely captured in my trembling flashlight beam—puff into the air as the rail's screws were ripped from the wall. The curtains tumbled. I dashed to my brother, wrenching the card table, keyboard and TV away from the wall.

We shoved upward together against the window frame, our faces reflected and warped in the foil taped to the glass. I was in sync with my brother, hoping what he was hoping, hissing the same prayer he was hissing.

LIVING ROOM CLEAR! the monsters screamed. *TAKE THE HALL!*

"Come on, you fuckin' foolbiscuit," Lucas snarled.

The window shot upward. We squinted together, blinking at the sunlight and the rusted metal of the fire escape beyond the sill. Lucas was a blur now: one leg through the window frame, now the other. He wasn't a person, he was a snake, sliding his torso through now, head dropping low, now completely on the other side of the glass.

"Gimme-gimme," he said, hands beckoning. "*Hurry.*"

"Wha?"

"Your *bag*, dude. The *camera!* Nitro your ass, hand 'em over!"

BATHROOM! CLEAR!

I didn't hesitate. The satchel was off my shoulder and in his hands. In another whip-snap maneuver, Lucas slipped the thing over him, its strap crossed across his chest. The Handycam went in next. He twisted his body on the rattling fire escape, his back facing me now.

"Careful on the way down," I said.

He glanced back, his eyes glimmering and gleeful.

"I ain't going down, bro. I'm going *up.*"

And then he was off, his left leg swinging toward the handrail of the escape, his foot planting on its rusted surface, his leg tensing, propelling himself skyward ...

... and then he was soaring, falling, soaring.

✳✳✳

My brother plummeted toward the concrete below, his lanky form—now in a crazy primate, parkour-predatory shape—arcing toward the building across the alleyway. He slammed onto the railing of the neighboring brownstone's fire escape two floors down, grappled there for a half-second, legs swinging in space, and then pulled himself onto the grated landing. He didn't look down, didn't look back. He simply ascended the escape, determined and single-minded. Destination: roof.

Boot clomps, a stampede, behind me.

KITCHEN! CLEAR!

"Shit fire, here we go," I said, and wedged my body though the window frame. I was nowhere near as fast or as elegant as my kid brother. My head slammed against the wooden underside of the window—*pow*—and bright flashbulbs filled the world. I shook my head, scrambling outside, my Vans *ping-pinging* on the metal, my arms snatching at the fire escape ladder.

NYPD WE ARE COMING IN ON THE GODDAMN FLOOR DO IT NOW NOW NOW

I took the rungs two at a time, scrabbling like a mad crab. Letting go now, feet slamming on the landing below. The frame of the escape groaned and trembled, displeased.

NOW

Another ladder, hand over hand, sneakers squeaking on metal.

DO IT NOW

A crack above; the sound waves blasting through the open window like a discordant bass drum, sound of the door splintering.

My feet slammed against the next landing. *Gong,* down here everybody, heart thundering now, running, I'm running like the old days, the bad days, Anti-Zach is here, breathing and laughing again ...

A voice above, crisp now, like a flapping bed sheet: *RUNNER! HE'S RUNNING! STOP! NYPD! STOP!*

But I didn't stop. No, no, no, I didn't stop.

✳ ✳ ✳

Space, empty space, free falling, ten feet, zero-g, *2001: A Space Odyssey; I'm sorry Dave, I'm afraid I can't do that.*

My body slammed onto the alley concrete. Another comic-book *pow* of pain surged through me, this one from my elbow. I heaved myself upright, staggered to the pile of trash where I'd left my bike. I stole a half-heartbeat to glance at my arm, saw the blood flowing through the torn fabric of my button-down—*Rachael got me this shirt for Christmas, ah jeez, ah shit*—and tuned out the pain. The trash bags were airborne now, victims of my adrenaline rush, and then the Cannondale was up on both wheels again.

Helmetless, hopeless, I mounted the bike and pedaled away from the building's entrance on East 32 Street, heading east, toward New York Avenue. The passage's end was closer now, the light at the end of my tunnel, if I could break through this then I'd be home free, could call Lucas, catch up, see what was inside the dark man's box *and oh yeah, giddy up pardner, what a fuckin' rush, Zach, we're back on the wild ride, ohhhhh*

" ... no," I said.

A police cruiser swept into the alley, its metal rear fishtailing and rocking, emergency lights spattering blue-white-blue on the brown bricks surrounding it. It screamed up the narrow space toward me.

But I didn't stop.

The Crown Vic's tires squealed as it braked, headlights flashing, siren yowling.

I saw the reflection of myself in the interceptor's gleaming black push bumper. I saw the cop inside, a young black guy, barking into his radio. I thought I could hear the flickering bulbs inside the cruiser's light bar, a samba beat, *cha-cha-cha*.

The Cannondale's front tire was cocked in mid-air now, a wheel-ie. I pedaled faster.

My bike raced up the hood of the car, spider-cracking the cruiser's windshield, rubber treads squealing, triumphant.

Bouncing over the light bar now, *cha-cha-cha*, down the rear window, out of the alley, into the free and clear.

But my grace and luck had limits. The bike's handlebars twisted in my hands. I fell and slid, slid past the sidewalk, past screaming pedestrians, past it all, into the traffic of New York Avenue.

William Taylor

13

The last time I'd been in handcuffs, they'd really been handcuffs: cold metal digging into bone, pitiless things, strictly business. Now, the shackles *du jour* were flex-cuffs.

I rubbed my wrists. My fingers traced the raw, dented flesh where the tough plastic had been zipped against my skin. Flex-cuffs weren't nearly as iconic as their predecessors, but they were just as merciless.

Pain. I was a knotted twine ball of it right now. My bandaged left elbow, gashed from when I'd dropped from the fire escape to the alley. Wicked-raw road rash on my right forearm and calf from where I'd lost my Cannondale mojo and slid onto New York Avenue. I was not looking forward to peeling off these clothes when I got home.

I looked up from my wrists, past the scratched metal table before me, to the wide mirror on the cinderblock wall. My nicked, weary face gazed back.

If I got home.

The cars on New York hadn't made me road kill, of course. Not even close. I'd been cuffed by New York's finest, received the long-forgotten (but well-deserved) kick-slaps to my sneakers, forcing my legs to spread to shoulder-width; the classic slamming of the torso onto the cruiser hood; the brusque street-side interrogation: *Am I going to find any needles, anything that's going to stick me, when I go through your pockets? I better not ...* ; the pat down.

I turned away from my reflection, disgusted with myself. I'd been sweating it out alone in this interview room for more than an hour. I hadn't been formally processed yet. No mug, no prints, no charges. An unsmiling cop had wordlessly escorted me here, passed me a bandage for my elbow, and locked the door.

Cops.

Why had cops kicked down the door at Grace's apartment? I'd expected a stuffed-shirt D.A. intern, maybe a NYPD lab liaison—someone like my buddy Eye. But not cops, and certainly not cops in wild-dog mode.

Had that neighbor seen Lucas and me? Had Dad set me up?

Before last night, it wouldn't have occurred to me to even ask.

I heard a bump against the room's thick door and then the cheerful jangle of keys. It swung open. A middle-aged sergeant stared at me. He spun the key ring on his index finger. A faded tattoo peeked out from the cuff of his long-sleeved uniform shirt.

This little key trick didn't appear to be a power trip, wasn't a "do not screw with me" message for the incarcerated. It had the resigned nonchalance of a thing one does to keep from nodding off.

"Taylor. Let's go."

I followed him. This was it. They'd book me, pitch me in the holding cell with the rest of the criminals. But we soon passed the door that lead to a vast, bustling room called "Processing."

"I don't ... " I began.

"Save it," he muttered. The man's voice was a sleepy flat-line, a Ben Stein carbon copy. He yawned. "Poor kids check in, they don't check out. Rich kids come in, they get a 'get out of jail free' card. That's Monopoly. It's a game."

"I know what ... "

"Uh-huh, a game," the cop said, as we walked further into the bowels of the building. "See, most of us get stuck being the iron or the dog. And most of us are happy with our little green houses on Oriental, right next to the Reading. That's the railroad."

I gave a nervous laugh. "Heh, I know. I've played ... "

The sergeant whirled around and shoved me against the wall. I gasped. The man's jowls were quivering now, furious. He jabbed his index finger into the center of my chest, poking my sternum, poking hard.

"And a blessed few of *us*—"

Poke. I sucked air through my teeth, in pain.

"—get to *live*—"

Poke. Shit!

"—on the Upper East Side." The cop's eyes bored into mine, hating me. His finger was relentless now. "These folks move around the board, do whatever they want, in their silver *race cars,* wearing their *top hats.* Free pass. Just visiting. *Get ... out ... of ... jail ... FREE.* Understand?"

He stepped backward, finger still pointed at me. I nodded, not understanding, not at all. I wasn't a rich kid—hell, Rachael and I eat hot dogs and mac and cheese one week out of every month to keep the lights on. No, I didn't understand, but I nodded with manic gusto, anything to stop this craziness.

The cop's finger swung to the right, toward the end of the hall.

"Sign for your bike and belongings down there," he said.

The sergeant smiled. It was an unapologetically, infuriatingly fake smile.

"You won't be getting everything back."

He stepped off, away from me, back toward the interview room. The keys jingled, spinning, on his finger.

✳ ✳ ✳

The tires of my Cannondale crunched on the gravel parking lot as I pushed it away from the 67th Precinct's impound garage. The tiny building was behind the station proper. I navigated the bike around the potholes. I was exhausted.

I checked my watch, biting my lip when I saw the jagged scratches on its glass bezel. It was just after 8 p.m. Damn it all. I'd neglected to sign out of The Brink, had been gone for hours, hadn't told Dr. Peterson where I was going, hadn't filed paperwork, hadn't planned, not one bit. I was fired, had to be. The day couldn't get any worse.

I spotted my father at the edge of the parking lot.

"Yes it can," I said softly.

The wind sliced through the hole in the elbow of my shirt, making me shiver. My father waited for me just beyond the lot's chain-link gate. His black overcoat fluttered and flapped in the breeze, like bat's wings. He looked like an undertaker.

In a normal family, a moment like this—a meeting like this—would begin with the father asking if his son was all right, just once, just to make sure, just before digging in with the fire-and-brimstone paternal fury. I didn't think my father would do that. William Taylor hadn't been a normal father for some time now.

I was right.

Dad nodded at the pothole directly before him. The murk inside the divot shimmered like a sleepy brown eye. Dad leaned his head forward, gazing at me in the puddle's reflection. He reminded me of a kid, about to spit into a pond.

"You see me here, young man," he said. His voice was ice, Defcon One.

Not knowing what else to do, I nodded.

"Tell me. Should I get on my hands and knees and give myself a good dunk here, right here in this filth? Does that seem like a good idea to you?"

I felt my lips trembling. I said nothing.

Dad's blue eyes flicked up, met mine. "Well, it should. After today, it should come as second nature, a basic instinct. You see, you seem to be doing everything you can to drag my name, this *family's* name, through the mud. You must want to destroy everything I've worked for, son. That's the only explanation I have for the absolute, bloody abortion of a day this has been."

I flinched.

"Martin Grace's lawyer called my office," he continued. "She's gunning for an investigation because of *you. Your* involvement at Brinkvale. It doesn't matter if it holds up—she's going for it, which means there's a perception of injustice, sloppy management. Perception is an illusion, young man. But perception is *everything*."

He exhaled. I waited, shivering.

"Why didn't you listen to me? I said you were in danger. I said I was doing this to protect you. Do you know how many calls I made to dust-broom this? How many favors I owe so the press doesn't catch a whiff of this ... this ... "

He blinked twice, searching for the word that would convince the jury to convict.

" ... this *ruination?* Do you know? Six. Six calls to six very powerful men." He nodded to the police station behind me. "I had half a mind to let them crucify you in there. But no. Perception defines reality. This is a reporter's wet dream. Me, you, the case, you breaking into that killer's apartment ... "

His eyes, pained, looked into mine.

"You could've been killed going down that fire escape. And for what? For trying to help a man who doesn't deserve to breathe. Not after what he's done."

He kicked a shoe-tip's worth of pebbles into the puddle.

"The universe itself conspires against me," he said. "Your friend Peterson isn't pulling you from Grace's case. He says you're the best The Brink has for this sort of thing."

I raised my chin, surprised. Something inside me shifted and glimmered. This news was ... unexpected.

"That man just committed career suicide—whatever career he had left," Dad said, "but that'll come later. This is about you, Zachary, and the great, grand mess you're in. The mess *that I just pulled you out of*. Understand me?"

I suddenly did.

"I ... I owe you," I said.

My father nodded. I thought of Malcolm and his damnable currency, and the envelope of Grace's personal effects—the envelope Lucas still had, wherever he was. And the lockbox.

So many clues. So many insights. So close. And yet …

Wait. Dad was right: this was all about me. He hadn't mentioned my brother, or a nosy hallway neighbor who might have spotted us. *Play this out,* I thought, *like you know how, like you do every day. Just another minute.*

"I just wanted to look around, Dad," I said. "I just wanted to find something to help—"

"You're lucky you didn't," he said. "No number of calls could've saved you then, young man—and we both know how many calls I've made for you over the years. This is a tired rerun, Zachary … and it ends now. If you're going to lose all control again, you'll do it on your own, and God help whoever you pull down with you. But this is the last time I'll ever do anything like this for you. You would've been in felony territory … "

He kept talking, but I wasn't listening. My brain was beginning to stir. The steel inside me was encouraged by this. Lucas hadn't been caught. Dad's people hadn't found the TV safe—and if they had, they knew I didn't have whatever was inside. This was as scot-free as it got.

It didn't have to be over. As my father droned on, I realized that I didn't *want* this to be over. Hell, with the things we'd found at Grace's apartment, this was just beginning. I couldn't let go. Saving him—saving me, maybe?—was what mattered.

I clenched my teeth. I was about to cross a line here, and I didn't care. *Let's see this to the end and try to save the blind man. I told him I'd help him if it killed me. Hi, world. Watch me call my own bluff.*

"No," I said.

My father stopped in mid-sentence. "What?"

"No, Dad. I'm not dropping the case."

I expected another bout of Defcon-One Dad. I did not expect him to glance first to the left, then to the right—likely looking for cops or peds—and then lunge toward me with such fury that I damned-near regressed and pissed myself.

His dress shoes splashed through the puddle as he rushed me, his hands out of his overcoat pockets now, reaching for—now grabbing and tearing—my shirt. The Cannondale slammed against the gravel. I screamed, stepping back, my hands digging at his wrists. He'd never done anything like this before; not a slap, not a swat, not a spanking, not ever.

"Dad!" I cried. "What the f—"

"*Ungrateful*," he hissed, his fingers tight on the fabric now, wrenching me toward him. My emotions were a frantic, swirling hurricane: terror, disbelief, embarrassment, fight or flight.

"I pulled your ass out of the fire," he snapped, yanking me back and forth. I was suddenly a stupefied doll in his hands, a flopping Raggedy Andy in his Rottweiler fangs. "There is no 'no' this time, Zachary. Walk away from this. The stakes are too high, for me, and especially for you. He'll ruin me … and he'll *kill* you. I told you, he hates doc—"

"Dad! *Dad!*"

"Be quiet and understand. Don't you understand?"

Anger now. My hands lashed out. They crashed against his chest, shoving him away. Dad's lungs went *hooooo*, and he staggered back, his feet splashing through the puddle again. He glared back at me with the kind of eyes I'd seen in The Brink, wild and unhinged.

"Jesus Christ, Dad. What's crawled between your ears?"

He steadied himself, wheezing. "Let. It. Go."

Goddamned stubborn bastard. I took a step toward him, two days' of fury unleashed. I couldn't stop this train if I'd wanted to, and at that moment, I didn't want to. In a move that was as inexplicable as it was gratifying, I kicked hard at the gravel, peppering his slacks and shoes. I was a baseball catcher going postal on the ump. I kicked again.

"No fuckin' way," I barked back. "*You* answer *me*, goddamn it. The hell's going on, Dad?"

My father recoiled. I pressed onward, took another step, kicking a third time, nearly dropping my own shoe into the murk. "What *is it?*"

"He killed her!" he screamed. "He killed her—and goddamnit, I'm going to make it right!"

My father's words stopped me where I stood. As if blinking from a trance, Dad suddenly became very aware of where he was. He glanced around again, this time like an animal. I watched him, more curious than furious now. His body sagged, suddenly defeated.

"Who, Dad?" My voice was calmer, but still insistent.

As I watched his mouth find the words, I thought: *If he says the words "Dark Man," if he says that thing killed Mom, I'll lose my mind right here.*

"No one you know," he said.

"Not Tanya Gold."

"No," Dad muttered. "Sophronia Poole. Last vic. Two years ago. You ... you didn't know her."

"But you did," I said. Shame flared inside me as I heard myself. Damn it, even now, I was doing what I do. Dad was wrong about me trying to destroy him—but he was right about second nature and basic instincts. It's in me, this need to know.

Dad nodded, staring at something far away. He was old, *so old*, right then. He was beaten, real ... human. A tumbler quietly clicked inside my mind. I realized that my father would die someday.

And then his bright blue eyes glimmered. I knew this look. I'd felt it myself minutes ago. Steel. He pointed at me. If a six-shooter were in his hand, we'd be in the Old West, duelin' time.

"You *are* dropping this case, Zachary. It's just like Grace's lawyer said. Conflict of interest."

I shook my head. "You're the one with the conflict, Dad. You're making this personal."

"It's *always* personal," he replied. "That is what justice is. Truth and conviction and punishment are always personal."

I stepped backward. I wasn't appalled by this, wasn't frightened. I was saddened.

The man who'd lied to Lucas and me for more than twenty years—who'd erased his brother's existence from our lives, from his life—was schooling *me* on justice and truth. I resisted the acidic urge to laugh at him, and tell him what I knew.

Instead, I stepped over to my bicycle and lifted it upright. I didn't care who Dad was protecting—me or him. I couldn't care, not anymore, because I couldn't trust him.

I kicked my leg over its black frame, clomped my Vans onto its scratched, punished pedals.

"Goodbye, Dad," I said, and rode off.

14

Richard Drake
Agent Extraordin...

"You know, for this kind of hands-on treatment," I said, wincing as
my brother smeared the Nelsons Cuts & Scrapes cream on my right
shoulder, "I prefer the digits of my lady friend over there."

Lucas snickered as his palms rubbed the last of the ointment on my wounds. He glanced from the comfy chair in which I was sitting to the couch. I glanced at Rachael, who was shaking her head. The living room's chili pepper lights above made her magenta hair pop like a road flare. For the first time in this white squall of a day, I felt anchored.

"I've seen this dude's wang a thousand times," Lucas told her. "Not interested." He turned back to me. "Your girl's not a *traceur*, Z. There aren't enough fingers in the world to count the scrapes and bruises I've taken care of. I'm a frickin' field medic."

"Hyperbole," I said.

"Hold still."

He gingerly spread the Nelsons over the road rash on my right forearm. As he did this, I told my tribe about the day's events: the failed, second session with Grace; the music from the Casio's memory card; my arrest and release; Dad's role in it. As Lucas wrapped a bandage on my cut elbow, I finally explained why Dad was obsessed with burying the blind man.

I did not tell them about his lies, or how he'd damned his brother to Claytonville.

"You ever heard of her?" I asked Lucas. "A woman named Sophronia Poole? Two years back. You were still living at home then."

Lucas stood up, shaking his head. I pulled myself up and slipped on a fresh T-shirt. I hobbled across the room, gracelessly splashing down beside Rachael. I smelled like a medicine cabinet. She patted my thigh.

"Smooth, babe," she said. "And what have we learned today?"

"Never run from the cops."

"Mmm-hmm."

Lucas, oblivious, dug into his backpack. "Sophronia. Nope, don't think so. Maybe a colleague? A girlfriend? Though I don't know about that. He's all work-work-work."

"Hell if we'd ever know." I looked over at Rachael. "He's never told us about his extracurricular activities."

"Don't kiss and tell," Rachael said. "Good policy."

It didn't happen the way they said it did. It's all lies.

"Maybe," I said.

I pulled in a deep breath and exhaled, looking at them.

"Okay. No bullshit, no sales pitches. I'm probably fired come tomorrow morning—but if I'm not, I'm committed to this. I'm going to help this guy. If you don't want a part in it, I don't blame you, so—"

Lucas slapped Grace's lockbox onto the steamer trunk in front of us. He looked at me, a wily smile on his lips.

"Taylor Family Loyalty, bro," he said.

Beside me, Rachael tugged my satchel off the floor, placing it beside the metal box. She pulled out its contents. The folder with the admittance papers and our research from the night before. The crumpled Brinkvale envelope containing Grace's personal effects. She shook the envelope. Out clattered a cell phone and a wallet.

"You're trying to do the right thing. I'm in," she said. "But this is serious business, Z. I'd be out the door if I liked you less ... or if you weren't such an amazing lay."

"Tee Em Eye," Lucas muttered. "Knock it off."

"Okay then," I said, motioning for the folder. She passed it over. "Can you fire up your laptop? And Lucas, find something to open that box."

He blinked. "Uh, can't you just go old school, get a paper clip and ... "

"I've done enough of that today."

He shrugged and headed for the kitchen. Rachael powered up her PC as I flipped through the folder, locating the CD-ROM that contained the police reports. Rachael slid the disk into the machine.

Seconds later, there she was: Sophronia Poole. Age 47, lived on Central Park West. There was a photo of the woman here, probably culled from her DMV record. She was black and beautiful; her eyes twinkled behind tiny, trendy glasses. High cheekbones, full lips.

My eyes ticked down the report. Poole had been a psychiatrist. As with the other deaths, the only M.O. commonality was Martin Grace himself: *Suspect was a former patient of victim,* the investigation paper said. *Victim's files reviewed. Victim believed suspect suffered from paranoid delusions; suspect felt "followed and hunted." No clear motive from victim's files.*

Sophronia Poole died on August 18th, two years ago. I asked Rachael to scroll down the screen.

"Oh my," I whispered. "Oh my God."

On August 19th, Sophronia's downstairs neighbor had called 911. Jacob Kellerman hadn't heard anything unusual the day before. He'd called because blood had seeped through the upstairs floor and left Rorschach stains on his ceiling.

Sophronia Poole was found on the living room floor of her condo, gagged. Her heart had been removed.

I closed my eyes. My father knew her, wanted to avenge her.

"It's no wonder," I whispered. "No wonder."

Lucas bounded into the living room, armed with a flathead screwdriver. One of our cats, Bliss, pranced behind him. Lucas proudly pointed to his leg. Dangling from the carpenter's loop on his jeans was our five-dollar claw hammer.

"I missed my calling," he said, jabbing the tip of the screwdriver at the hinged lock on the box. He tugged the hammer from its loop. "Part-time carpenter, part-time locksmith."

THWACK!

The lockbox's lid shot up like a jack-in-the-box, making a tinny exclamation as its top smacked against the trunk. Pop went the weasel—and pop went Bliss, a foot into the air. She was gone in a furry blur.

The three of us leaned forward simultaneously; I'm certain we were all aware of this, how silly it must've appeared ... how very *theatrical,* how very *Pandora* ... but we were drawn to the mystery inside.

Resting atop a stack of documents was a creased envelope. It was sealed.

I scooped up the screwdriver and used it as a makeshift letter opener, tearing the paper.

My fingers found a small stack of photos inside.

I pulled them free.

We gasped at the monster staring back at us.

✳✳✳

It had been a person once, a woman captured on faded Kodak photo paper. She was young, about my age. A desert sunset glowed from somewhere behind the photographer, soaking the woman in hues of amber and tangerine. Her blonde, feathered hair and bell-bottoms told me this was the 1970s.

But she wasn't a person anymore. She was a ghoul. A furious tangle of black lines covered her eyes and mouth, unholy and in-human—worse than a scream, worse than wide-eyed terror. She was howling.

The ballpoint pen ink was scratched deep into the photo, torn well past its emulsion. I flipped to the next photo. Two more ghouls—once children, now small, feral things with swirling holes for eyes—glared back from a wooden seesaw. Along the edge of the photo was written, *At the tot lot, 1982. Jenny, 5. Danny, 7.*

"What in the hell is this?" Rachael said.

"His past," I said, shuddering. "Back to haunt us."

"Bad juju," Lucas whispered. His face was pale. "Uckin'-fay ooky-spay."

I reached back inside the lockbox and removed several yellowed documents and an envelope. At the bottom of the box were a pair of military dog tags and a bronze disc, slightly larger than a fifty-cent piece. Rachael held this to the light. In its center was a starburst; above that, an eagle's head.

"'Central Intelligence Agency,'" she read. "'For Valor.'"

I looked at Lucas. "Not ooky-spay. *Ook*-spay. Jesus, who is this guy?"

My eye returned to the photos in my hand. I flipped through the rest. They were all defaced. Entire heads were covered in black permanent marker in some; others simply had slivers of black tape covering the subjects' eyes. A much younger Martin Grace was in one of these photos. He stood before the Grand Canyon with the ghoul-woman and the tot lot ghoul-children. I couldn't tell if they'd been smiling when the picture was taken. They were wailing now.

"'Dear Rick,'" Rachael recited, holding a creased sheet of paper in her hand. "'It's been two weeks since you called. Danny, Jenny and I pray you that you're safe, sleeping soundly at night, dreaming of us.'" Rachael's eyes flitted to the end. "'Keep fighting the good fight. We love you.' It's signed 'Lucy,' dated March 10th, ten years ago."

"Here's something from the CIA," Lucas said, tapping a sheet. "It's for that medal. For, uh, 'acts of extraordinary heroism involving the acceptance of existing dangers with conspicuous fortitude and exemplary courage.'"

"Name," I said.

"Distinguished Intelligence Cross," he said.

"Not the medal, doofus. *His* name. There's gotta be a name."

"Oh. Richard Drake."

Richard Drake.

"Hot damn," I said.

My mind did the math, concocted a question. Was Martin Grace really a man named Richard Drake? I thought back to my research session with Rachael after Gram's memorial service, and what she'd said then: *Martin Grace is incorporeal, Z. He's a hoax.* I flipped the Grand Canyon photo and read the names on its back. Lucy, Daniel, Jenny ... and Rick. Yes.

"So we've got a name, and we've got a family," I said. I picked up the medal. "And we've got a job, I think. Don't know what he did, exactly, but we know he was good enough to get this thing."

Eager now, Lucas and I examined the other documents. There was a letter from the CIA, also dated ten years ago. *LETTER TO: Richard K. Drake,* it read. *SUBJECT: Discharge from the Agency.* I read the two-paragraph note. According to this, the CIA would formally process Drake's discharge upon his "return to the United States," and per procedure for "compromised agents of your expertise," appropriate steps would be taken to ensure a "safe, expedient transition" into civilian life. The letter promised the same assistance for Drake's family. It was CC'd to a woman named Amelia Ramoo, Director of Operations.

"This shit's right out of a Le Carré novel," I said. "Instant, government-approved history. They gave Grace—er, *Drake*—a fresh slate ten years ago."

"The same year the murders began," Rachael said.

Lucas gave a low whistle. Another sheet was in his hand now.

"Your bad boy just got worse," he said. "Skipping the commercials, getting to the good stuff. Letterhead: 'Smith, Whitmore & Gifford: Albany, New York.' Says here, '...if they could find a body, they would extradite and press charges.' Ten years ago."

He tapped the paper. "Oh, and the 'they' are the Russian authorities."

Now Rachael gave me a nudge. The dog tags swung from her fingers, clinking on their chain. "This isn't English, Z. Cyrillic, I think."

I gazed at them. Russian authorities, Russian dog tags.

"Don't you have a Russian buddy at the paper?" I asked her. "Tech reporter. Nicky-something?"

"Nicolina," she said, frowning. "She's Bulgarian, but she's old enough to speak the language."

I nodded. "That's fine. Keep holding them, just like that." I fished my cell phone out of my pocket and navigated to the camera. I snapped a closeup of the dog tags and asked Rachael for Nicolina's cell phone number. I attached the photo to a text message asking for help, and sent it.

"We'll get the name of our unknown soldier soon enough," I said. "Could be that body Lucas just read about."

Rachael shook her head. "This doesn't make sense. You're the CIA. You've got a badass spy guy who's clocked in enough time to get a new identity ... but then he starts killing people when he goes back to civilian life. Would you allow that? I mean, if these guys are like they are in the movies—"

"—then you whack the loose cannon," Lucas said. "Totally. Convention of the 'rogue agent' genre." He tore open another sealed envelope at the bottom of the stack.

"Maybe it's not like the movies," Rachael said.

I nodded. "Or maybe they knew he wasn't the killer."

"Huh," Lucas said. He passed me one of three forms from the envelope. This was paper-clipped to a second sheet of paper. "Birth certificate," he said.

"And death certificate," I replied, gazing at the second page. "Oh man, this is weird. The birth certificate is for a 'Lucinda,' but death certificate says, 'Veronica Grace.'"

Rachael peered over my shoulder. "The whole family got instant histories. The pink slip said so."

She began to type on her laptop. "Screw this. I'm Googling this guy."

I nodded. "Name change, right. Wife was in a car accident, on ... shit. Lucas, what's that discharge letter say? What date?"

"October 7," he replied.

"About a month after Drake came back to the States," Rachael affirmed. The computer screen glimmered in her spectacles. "Poor bastard. At least he was there to take care of the kids."

"*Kid,* singular," Lucas said, reviewing another sheet. "The 'daughter-formerly-known-as Jennifer Drake' died in that accident, too. 'Crushed cranial ...' ah, gross-o. Wormy-squirmy. I does not want."

He tossed the papers onto the trunk, his expression sour.

"Drake killed 'em. Must've," he said. He pointed to the photo booklet. "That's why he scratched out their faces. It's a hit list."

I leaned back into the couch. "No. When Grace—shit, when *Drake*—could still see, he believed that if he looked at you, you'd be marked for death. He was protecting them."

Lucas shook his shaggy head. "Then why scratch out their faces at all, if they were already dead?" he asked.

Protection in the afterlife? I wondered, but didn't say it.

Rachael glanced up. "Okay. Zero hits for 'Richard K. Drake' and 'Central Intelligence Agency,'" she said. "Same goes for *Times* and newswire archives. Your patient's true identity has been scrubbed ... at least in the databases I have access to."

I nodded. "But we've got a hint at what he did back then. Probably stationed in Russia—"

"Soviet Union," Rachael corrected.

"—okay, the Soviet Union, and he probably killed someone," I said. "We've got a medal. We've got a wife and kids, but they're all dead. What else ... "

"The boy's not dead, bro," Lucas said. He stood up and paced, restless. "Well, he's not a boy anymore, but he's still alive. Birth cert was in the envelope, but nothing about his death."

I leaned forward, groaned again, examined the document.

"Daniel Drake," I said. "Aw hell, but his name's changed now. Rache, is there ... ?"

"I'm on it," she said. "Pass that over here. I'll need his DOB, middle name, social."

I leaned over, kissed her neck, told her to work her sorcery.

Daniel Drake. The key to a lock. The only living connection to a blind man's past.

✳✳✳

As Rachael pried her way into Daniel Drake's life, Lucas and I sipped Dogfish Head beers and viewed the footage he'd recorded at the blind man's apartment that afternoon.

I was amazed by the images on the screen. Even there, in the darkness of Grace/Drake's spartan living room, Lucas had artfully composed each shot: rule of thirds, depth of field (as much as the Handycam could accommodate, anyway), the proper balance inside the frame that coaxed the eye, unconsciously, to focus on specific objects. Without words, he'd masterfully told a story, and evoked a mood so spooky, I felt myself transported back there, breathing the place's stale air, praying for light.

The kid had it. He really did. But he'd make a lousy documentary filmmaker. The things I'd wanted him to record—the names of the CDs on the bookshelves—had been all but obfuscated in the name of artful angles and evocative cinema.

Lucas didn't seem to notice this as he watched. I didn't have the heart to mention it.

The movie concluded, we learned what Rachael had found so far. Remarkably, public records indicated my patient's son had changed his name *back* to Daniel Drake less than a year after his father had returned to the United States.

Rachael had scored Daniel Drake's address and a New York driver's license number minutes after she'd queried his name in her online resources ... but she had pressed on, conducting an impromptu background check, cross-reffing with criminal records.

As she did this, the cell phone in my pocket vibrated and played skeleton song. Text message. I flipped the phone open and read the message from Nicolina, Rachael's friend.

DOG TAG NAME READS, "PIOTYR I. ALEXANDROV," Nicolina's message said. *RANK: LT. COLONEL. HOPE THIS HELPS, SEND <3 TO RACHE.*

I scribbled the name "Alexandrov" in the open notepad on our steamer trunk, and shared the news.

"We'll follow up on that later, babe," Rachael said, peering over the screen of her laptop. "I'm busy ... and so are you. Get crackin' on Drake's other stuff."

Right. Papa Drake's effects from The Brink. Lucas and I exchanged a quick grin — we motherless Taylor boys knew who ran *this* operation—and began to examine them.

People my father's age think that I'm a tech-head because I can work a computer and cell phone and appear to know what I'm doing. It's bogus. I'm an analog man. I appreciate the *tangibility* of doing things without a mouse: the dusky smell of pencil shavings, the splash of paint on a canvas. I dig phone calls more than Facebook messages, prefer week-old postcards to eye-blink emails.

So I gravitated to the wallet while my brother gleefully poked through the menus on Drake's cell phone. It was an expensive thing, brimming with programs for the visually impaired. In addition to the standard calendar and address book, it featured a GPS receiver and map software, both of which were voice-enabled and did text-to-speech.

"Cracked case, off-brand," Lucas observed as he eyed the phone. "The guy's got some archived voice mail, but we need a password to get to it."

He sat in the corner comfy chair, his face glowing ghost-white from the phone's large LCD. The screen sputtered, and my brother frowned. "Bad battery?" he said, looking at me. He knocked it against the armrest and the screen flicked on again, feebly.

"Jeez, careful with that," I said. "It's been banged around enough already today, riding shotgun during your fire-escape stunt work. You're the one who probably busted it."

"I accept no responsibility," Lucas sniffed, tapping the screen. It glowed bright again, like before. "I did not have sexual relations with that woman."

"Just tell us what's inside before the thing croaks."

He nodded and began tapping the phone's buttons again. "Lots of numbers in the addy book—whoa—including Dad's friend, Sophronia Poole. And hey! Tetris!"

Tinny eight-bit music streamed from the phone's speaker now, a goofy *beep-boop-bleep* version of the game's anthem, "Korobeiniki." I snickered. An old Russian folk song about peddlers, now forever associated with falling bricks.

"Love that game," Rachael murmured from beside me. She hummed along as she dug into New York State's criminal database.

Music.

I sucked in a quick breath. The tune was reminding me of something. Something familiar, important. What was it? A ubiquitous song, yes. *Something you've heard before, but couldn't quite—*

"Lucas, I need that film geek brain of yours," I said. I pointed to our entertainment system. "Grab that stereo cable over there, the one we use for the iPod."

I glanced at Rachael's laptop. "That thing takes memory cards, right?"

Click. Double-click. "Mmm-hmm."

I rummaged in my satchel, finding the memory card I'd used to record Drake's Casio jam session. I pressed it into the appropriate slot of the computer. Rachael gave me a cool look over her specs: *Watch it, bud. I'm driving here.*

Lucas triumphantly slapped the cable into her palm. Bliss, who'd taken residence on the couch arm near Rachael, batted at it. Well ahead of me, Rachael plugged the cord into the PC's "line out" port. She opened the card's audio file and launched a program to play it.

"Name this tune, Lucas," I announced. "I know it sounds familiar, from a movie, but I don't—"

The disorganized notes I'd played to bait Grace yesterday thundered from the speakers. We winced. Dali and Bliss hit warp speed, scrambling from the room.

"Uh, 'The Kittyfright Concerto,'" Lucas said.

I gave him the middle finger. He stuck out his tongue, then turned down the volume.

And now, Drake's song was playing, that whirlwind stream of high notes ... followed by booming low ones. Lucas' head began to bob along. He snapped his fingers. The bob became an enthusiastic nod. Rachael hit the "stop" button on her program.

"Natural twenty, baby," he said. "It's from *Fantasia*, the Disney film. We watched it for my History of Animation class last month."

"That movie's effed up," Rachael said. "If there were ever a movie to see stoned ... "

"That and *The Wall*, yep," Lucas agreed. "Anyways, the song's called 'Night on Bald Mountain.' Chart-topping classic, nineteenth century. There's a monster in it, he drags souls to Hell. Heh! And guess where the composer's from?"

"The Soviet Union," I said.

"Russia," Lucas and Rachael corrected. I sighed.

"So what does *that* mean?" I asked. "The song. You've got a Russian connection, and the Dark Man, maybe? Dragging people to Hell? Babe, can you ... ?"

"Uh-uh. Baby steps, snookums. Working on Daniel Drake here."

Right. I gazed down at Drake's personal effects scattered on the steamer trunk. We'd examined everything: the letters, the photos, the dog tags. They told a story that ended a decade ago. I wanted something more current, to fill in the gaps. The cell phone was a good lead, but ...

The wallet.

I picked it up, glanced at my tribe. Rachael was pointing-and-clicking. Lucas was still standing, thumbs tapping on Drake's phone, reinvested in Tetris.

As my fingers slid across the wallet's brown pebbled grain, I felt a sudden rush of guilt. Of all the things I'd done over the past two days—digging through databases, breaking into the man's house, stealing his lockbox—this felt wrong. Voyeuristic.

I unfolded the wallet and gingerly removed the items. Some cash. A state-issued ID. A credit card. An insurance card.

I tugged at the contents of a small pocket. Two items fell onto the table. One was a white card, featureless save for a row of Braille on its surface. I set it aside, frowning.

The other card was well-worn, its ink slightly faded. It was an appointment card, dated for August 7th, two years ago. The appointment was with a Dr. Sophronia Poole, Psychiatrist.

I gasped. *He hates doctors,* my father had said.

"She was Drake's shrink," I said. "Poole, Dad's friend."

I flipped it over. On the back, in crisply-drawn letters, was a list. Payard chocolates. Coltrane, Davis. Sunflowers. J. Deaver, D. Baldacci. Sushi (spider roll).

Beneath this, in more ragged lettering: W. Taylor. D.A. B-friend.

"Man oh man," I said. "I think he had a thing for her … and so did Dad. Poole and Dad were dating, guys. I have no idea how Drake found out—shit, *we* didn't know—but it's here. The man wrote a grocery list of the things she dug, including Dad."

"*Ménage à* yeesh," Lucas muttered, glancing up from the game. "Patient falls for his doctor. That's pretty commonplace, right?"

"Transference, yeah."

"Let's hope he doesn't fall for *you,*" he said.

Rachael looked up from her computer. "Boy, you pick the winners, Z. Daniel Drake has been arrested four times in as many years. Disorderly conduct, driving under the influence, two counts of assault. Loves the bottle. He lives up north in Haverstraw. Rural area. No current employment record—he's on disability for a bum leg after he was involved in a hit-and-run last year; he was the 'hit.' I don't have a phone number for him. It's unlisted."

Lucas interrupted, reciting seven digits from the cell phone's screen. "It's here, under 'Danny,'" my brother said. "Can't tell if he ever called the guy, though."

I waved my hand, motioning him to toss me the phone. I snatched it in the air, saw that Daniel Drake's number was highlighted, and hit the "call" button.

"What are you doing?" Rachael asked.

"Besides mooching off the dude's minutes," Lucas said.

I put a finger to my lips. The phone on the line rang once. A woman's voice announced that the number was disconnected.

Haverstraw. Rural. That's where Claytonville Prison was located. Uncle Henry.

"I have to see them," I murmured. "Get answers."

"'Them?'"

I glanced at Rachael. "Him. We've got a good start here. But what was Richard Drake like before he started hopscotching the state, running from his Dark Man? What did he do in the Soviet Union? I need more. Maybe his son can deliver."

Rachael closed the laptop, gazing at me over her glasses again. "More what? Zach, you're supposed to find out if Drake's fit to stand trial, that's it. You're not supposed to *cure* him."

"I'm not trying to ... "

My voice trailed off. That was a lie. I was trying to, or hoping to. The blind man was broken. I'm a fixer. To shoot for anything less would be ... wrong. And was there even more to it? Didn't I want to prove something? Didn't I want to prove the world wrong about Drake? About me?

"It's what I'm wired to do," I said quietly.

She leaned over and kissed my lips. Her blue eyes met mine.

"I know. Take my car tomorrow, head up there. I'll work from home and see what I can dig up on this Alexandrov guy."

She yawned. It was contagious.

"Aww, night-night time for the oldsters," Lucas said. He walked to the front door. Lucas always knew when he was welcome, and when it was time to go. He'd been that way that since we were kids.

"Yo, take the blind dude's keys when you go," he said, opening the door. "If his kid's phone number's in the cell, maybe he's got a key to the place, too."

"I do *not* want a repeat performance of this afternoon, thanks," I said.

Lucas eyed me. "Can't hurt to have 'em. I know you can't argue with that."

I sighed and nodded, and looked on the steamer trunk for Drake's key ring. It wasn't there. I rummaged in my canvas satchel — I'd slipped his keys inside when we broke into his home, I *remember* that—but they weren't there, either. What the hell?

I heard the smug voice of Monopoly Cop, the bastard who'd grilled me in the halls of the 67th Precinct police station: *You won't be getting everything back.*

"Fuck," I said. "The keys are gone."

"Want me to help you look?" he asked.

I shook my head. Either they'd spilled out of my bag as Lucas had escaped, or they were spinning on some cop's finger right now. Either way, I wasn't going to go hunting for them.

"Splitsville for me, then. Hey, *Hochrot,* if you want help with this spy stuff, let me know. I'll swing by after morning class."

Rachael snickered. "You just wanna frag the Bloodwire noobs on the widescreen."

"In surround sound," he agreed. "Martini shot, everybody."

He closed the door. I heard him bounding down the hallway, and then the wall-trembling *clomp-clomp-clomp* as he took the stairs, likely two at a time, to the street.

"One thing before," Rachael said. I turned to her. Her face was worried now. I reached for her hand.

"I'll be careful tomorrow," I said. "I will."

"Oh, it's not that," she said. "It's about us. We don't lie, you and me. We don't hide anything from each other."

I thought of Uncle Henry. My stomach tightened.

"*I'm* the reason why the cops crashed Drake's apartment," she said. "It was me. I called you today. You were on the train, said you were in trouble. Said to tell your dad."

I began to breathe again. "The connection was bad. I said to *not* tell my dad."

She gave a half-chuckle. "Yeah, I gathered that later. He called after we were disconnected, said you'd turned off your phone. Asked after you. I was worried; I told him."

I raised her hand to my lips, kissed it. "Hey, it's okay. You did what you thought was right. It worked out."

"Bad communication," she said, "sucks."

She brought our hands to her cheek. She kissed my finger. "I 'dore you, ya know."

I smiled at the Lucasism, but my heart ached. I couldn't tell her. Couldn't.

" 'Dore you back."

"You're worried about the keys," she said, looking at me.

"I'm worried about a lot of things. The keys. The case. The job. Mostly the job."

"All will be well." She leaned in now. "Let's get you to bed, 007."

She kissed me. Her tongue slid inside, swirled around mine. She stood. Her smile was sly, delicious. "I'll be your Bond girl, if you have the energy."

I watched her hips as she slinked into the kitchen, toward our bedroom.

I had the energy.

✳✳✳

We'd never done this on stairs before.

We moaned as our bodies moved together, arms and legs slipping against each other, slick with sweat. We faced each other, gasping, now kissing. Her fingernails dug into my shoulders, leaving red crescents on my flesh. My tongue rushed to her neck, trailed up to her ear. I told her to keep doing what she was doing, God yes, and she commanded me to go harder, deeper, that's it, fuck, that's it, right there.

Her legs, lickable inked skin, wrapped around my waist, pulling me closer. I gripped the wood behind her, my knees digging, rubbing, burning, against the carpet beneath me. My toes slid on the hardwood floor. Her hands raced down my chest, then hers. My lips found her breasts, and I nipped and sucked to our rhythm.

She cried out, fingers tearing through my hair. We rocked, building up, edging closer, growing hotter and brighter together. I heard music now: faint, delicate notes, like leaves scattering in the wind.

And then the world went dark. Cold.

I looked at my lover. Rachael's face was covered in electrician's tape, two black Xs where eyes should be. Tar-like oil began to spew from her nose, her mouth. It rushed down her chest, pumping out of her as I pumped inside.

I shrieked, bolted backward, nearly falling on the slick floor. Before me, my anchor, my darling, my love ... *liquified*. She lost form and mass, bursting into a black mess, splashing against the wall and stairs.

I looked down. The floor was gone, replaced by more liquid. Blood. A face emerged from the shin-deep pool, smiling up at me.

Would you be mine? Mom said. Crimson bubbles—dozens, tiny things—rose from her lips. *Could you be mine?*

A hiss, from atop the stairway. My skin was awash in wave after wave of gooseflesh, every hair electrified. My vision blurred as I wept, as I looked. Looked up.

It was there in the shadows, holding Lucas in its snake arms, and Lucas was a baby again, *Lookie-Luke, he giggles when I tickle him.* My brother wailed.

I went to climb the stairs. My mother's hands clutched at my legs.

Mine, she gurbled.

Mine, the dark man affirmed ... and Lucas slipped into its inky chest, black quicksand, filling my brother's tiny nostrils as his arms flailed. And then, he was gone.

The music grew louder. Thunder.

The dark man did not descend this time, not like before.

He screeched ... and then pounced.

15

The nightmare haunted me long after it woke me, a little after four; I couldn't fall back to sleep. I paced the living room, fretting about its meaning and obsessing about my state of employment. I hadn't smoked a cigarette in more than six years, but Jesus, I wanted one that dark morning.

It was seven o'clock—time to call. My fate and the fate of Richard Drake hinged on the next five minutes. I'd been reckless yesterday, leaving work early. And there was the embarrassing matter of Dad calling Dr. Peterson, trying to yank me off the case. If I was done at Brinkvale, Drake was, too.

Peterson was a "first to come, last to leave" kind of manager. I dialed The Brink. He'd be there.

The sleepy switchboard operator patched me to Lina Velasquez, Peterson's ever-present hummingbird assistant, who then put me on hold. As I endured a horrid Muzak version of The Beatles' "Love Me Do," I imagined Peterson at his desk, surrounded by piles of paperwork, pining over an office supply catalog. ORGANIZE YOUR LIFE, its cover read.

"Peterson here."

"Uh, Dr. Peterson," I blurted, "do I still have a job?"

I immediately blushed, feeling very young, very graceless ... and very stupid.

"And good morning to you, too, Zachary." The old man chuckled. "This must be about yesterday."

"Yes, sir."

"Well, of course you do. In the future, the Brinkvale team would appreciate notification before you take an unexpected leave. Our patients expect us to be completely dedicated to their well-being. I also expect no less."

I exhaled, felt my shoulders unwind. "Of course."

"Dr. Xavier did complain about the day's missing paperwork, however."

I gritted my teeth. "Of course."

"But yes, yes, all is well," Peterson said airily. "Since I have you on the phone, I'd like to discuss your progress with Martin Grace. But first, how is your lady friend?"

"Rachael? Uh ... "

"Malcolm told us about the emergency, why you departed so unexpectedly. Something about your lady friend taking a fall?"

"Oh," I said, smiling. Good old Malcolm. Now I owed *him* a favor. "She's all right. Just a few stitches."

"And your patient?"

I had to be careful here. I didn't want to lie any more than I already had, but ..

"Honestly, Dra—ah, *Grace* is resisting treatment," I said. Peterson gave an *mmm-hmm*, as if he anticipated this. "But I've used some resources beyond his admittance report to learn more about him. Internet, mostly. I've found a family member who may tell me something to help, ah, facilitate a better bond. I plan on meeting him in person."

"You're tenacious, Zachary," Peterson said. "Going outside the box. I like that."

More like inside *the box—the lockbox,* I thought. *And lock-ups, too. Meeting another long-lost relative along the way.*

"I'd like to take the morning to see him," I said.

"That sounds wise," Peterson replied. "Be sure to follow protocol, identify yourself as a Brinkvale employee. You've done off-site interviews before. You're aware of the responsibilities."

I bit my lip. Responsibility.

"Listen, Dr. Peterson, about my Dad—"

"Zachary," he said. "Did I not convince you of your qualifications when I assigned you Grace's case? Your enthusiasm and dedication are reasons enough, to speak nothing of your talents. Besides, there are people far more important than your father who are interested in the outcome of Grace's trial."

I frowned.

"Like who?"

The old man paused.

"The families of the victims, of course," he said, his voice suddenly hasty. "My point, Zachary, is that your father's insistence has clashed against my obstinance. Unless a higher authority than your father orders otherwise, you're the one I want on the job."

"Thanks," I said. "I should be back at The Brink this afternoon, easy."

"*Brinkvale*, Zachary," Peterson replied. "And yes, good luck with your interview."

I thought of the day ahead, of the strangers I would soon meet.

Luck. Yes. I needed all the luck I could get.

✳ ✳ ✳

I piloted Rachael's red Saturn, heading to Haverstraw and Claytonville Prison. The long upstate trek was an autumnal art show. Hillside trees rushed by, glowing golden in the early morning sunlight.

What would I say when I finally met him?

Hi, Henry. I think every memory I have of my dad from early childhood was actually of you. You're the loving father Lucas and I should've had. So why did you kill our mom?

I thought of the nightmare and my mother's face, the blood-bubbles streaming from her mouth. *Would you be mine?*

I shuddered, suddenly desperate for distraction. I switched on the radio, jabbed the "scan" button, growled at the lousy reception. I attached my iPod to the stereo and hit play.

Richard Drake's piano rendition of "Night On Bald Mountain" surged from the dashboard speakers. This was the only genuine clue Drake himself had provided me—and he wouldn't have done even that, had he known about the Casio's memory card.

I listened to the entire song, puzzling over its significance. Did it represent Drake's time in Russia? His fear of the Dark Man? Something else?

The exit sign for Claytonville emerged on the horizon. I took the exit and drove toward the prison, toward a past I never knew.

✳✳✳

As I was processed through Claytonville's "visitor" system—and as far as I could tell, I was the only visitor of the day—I saw enough to know that to be incarcerated here was to be sentenced to an earthbound Hell.

From the outside: Fence after fence of rusted razor wire and desolate weed-strewn prison yards; guard towers and sharpshooters; chair leg-thick ivy vines enveloping the building's crumbling limestone walls. The air was still and silent, as if the land itself was too frightened to breathe.

Inside, water dripped from cracked ceilings. Hallways sloped. Stone walls writhed with fearless spiders and cockroaches. The place reeked of piss and disinfectant. Men howled in their cells. Everywhere, the shriek of warning bells and rattling of bars. This was Brinkvale's Golgotha on its worst day.

A corrections officer—a dull-eyed bulldozer of a man—opened the rusted door of the visitor's room and waved me in. I was alone, facing a row of ten semi-private nooks. Each nook had a chair. Each chair faced a floor-to-ceiling pane of thick shatterproof glass. Beyond that, a chair for the inmate.

There were no tables in these nooks, nowhere to lean or take notes. Both inmate and visitor were completely visible here. A half-dozen security cameras swept the room. Claytonville trusted no one.

I felt naked. All of my belongings, from satchel to spare change, had been confiscated during processing. A cheap plastic visitor's pass, which I had to return when I left, hung from my shirt.

I sat down. There was no phone receiver like in the movies. Just a circle of finely drilled holes, resembling a sink strainer, at eye level. I couldn't quite believe I was here ... and I couldn't quite believe this was happening.

From beyond the glass, a trilling alarm bell sounded. The metal door at the room's far wall opened.

Out stepped Uncle Henry. A guard followed him.

Henry walked the length of the room, toward me. His stride was slow, deliberate.

"Ten minutes," the guard said. My uncle nodded.

I didn't move, but I was reeling on the inside—feeling seasick from a wave of memories. It was an onslaught of half-remembered things, flashbulbs of smiles and high-fives and piggyback rides and *love yous*; things I thought Dad and I had done and said. But Dad was barely there back then, I realized. It had been Henry, all Henry.

He was tall and thin like my father, but more handsome in a rugged, weathered way. He was bearded now, something he wasn't in the old photos I'd seen of him. His gray hair graced the shoulders of his orange jumpsuit. A bracelet jangled from his left wrist. It was identical to the Invisible Man's bracelet I'd seen two nights ago.

I wondered how many years it had taken for Henry to earn the privilege to wear that bracelet again.

He sat before me, his blue eyes cataloging my clothes, my hands, my face.

"I did my part. I stayed away," he said. His voice was a dusky baritone, low and smooth. "But I knew you'd find me eventually. So curious, just like your mother."

I was trembling now. Yes, there was anger here inside me, and heartache, twenty years' worth. And swirling confusion and fright. And a hunger, in my marrow. A need to know.

"Why did you kill her?" I whispered.

Henry's eyes stared into mine.

"I loved your mother," he said. "I did everything I could to save her. Your home, the family, had been under attack for weeks. Will, proud and stubborn and skeptical Will, wouldn't listen. And when it finally came for one of you—likely you or Luke, we'll never know—it was … *intent*. It had been paid, paid in blood, and was there to collect."

I blinked. "Who?"

"The Dark Man."

A tear slid down my cheek. This was my 4 A.M. nightmare, yes, I was still locked in the dream, locked in the lockbox, I could feel my head nodding now, stupefied, drunk and stoned all at once, nightmare, yes, *Could you be mine?*, yes, no. No.

"No."

"It was there," Henry said. "You saw it."

I shook my head again, more resolute. "*No. I saw you. I saw you kill her. Killer.*"

"There were villains that day, son. I wasn't one of them. I'm sorry you lost her. I'm sorry you came away marked, different. I saved your brother, if that means anything to you."

"No, it was you," I heard myself say. Christ, was this really happening? "It could only be you. It must have been. I read the report."

"Gods as my witness, it wasn't," he said. "Claire was my best friend."

I leaned forward, wiping away my tears with a hand jittering so hard, it was nearly worthless. I wanted to pound through this barrier, pound at him.

"Then *who*? Who did it? And don't you talk to me about the Dark Man, don't you dare say that to me again, fucking lie, you don't know, you can't *possibly know* what kind of misery ... "

He looked at me, his eyes sympathetic.

"Of course I do," he said. "Of *course* I do."

"All right. Why?" I asked. "If you're innocent, why are you here?"

"The same reason you are," Henry said. "Dark art. I read the *Times* story about you and Martin Grace. I saw those words—'the Dark Man'—and I knew. I knew you were coming."

My mind frantically scrambled back to yesterday, to my office. Dad screamed at me about the Drake case. He tapped and tore at his copy of the *Times*. *Taylor Family Loyalty ... let it go.*

"Lie. No reference to the Dark Man," I said. I looked up at him.

"I'm talking about *today's* story," Henry said. "There's a leak at The Brink. Somebody's feeding the press. They want to sink you."

"Three minutes," the guard said.

"Listen to me, Zach," Henry said. "The Dark Man is a mercenary. It's a thing summoned from the black to exact vengeance. Terrible vengeance, not justice. Do you understand the difference?"

It's always *personal,* I heard my father say.

"It isn't real," I said.

"That's what the atheists say, but God's still up there."

He leaned toward the glass, meeting me halfway.

"If Martin Grace is haunted by the Dark Man, then he did something unspeakable, unfathomable. Someone paid the black with blood. Someone wants your blind man to suffer. Just like they wanted us to suffer, all those years ago."

"It's a psychological breakdown," I insisted. "A super-fueled guilt complex, paranoid delusions, conversion disorder—"

Henry smiled. God, I *remember* that smile now.

"You'll find the path," he said. "Or the path will find you. Either way, know this: I'm proud of you. I read in the *Post* about your other patient, the quilter. You listened to her, you worked through her madness to right a wrong. You *believe* your patients, Zach. You understand that there is truth—sometimes only a speck, but always enough—in what they say. That is wisdom beyond your years."

He reached out and pressed his palm against the glass.

"So very proud of you," he said.

My trembling hand met his. I smiled back.

"'Dore you," Henry said.

"What ... ?" I squinted at my uncle, not believing.

"Time's up, Taylor," the guard said. He took a step toward Henry.

"What did you say?"

"I said, I adore you," he replied. "I love you, son."

He stood, nodded goodbye and followed the guard to the metal door. I was out of my chair, walking down my side of the room, keeping pace, wishing for more time. The men paused as the guard tugged at his keys.

"Gram ... Gram's dead," I called.

"I know," he said. The guard was unlocking the door now, twisting its handle.

"Why did she cover it up? Why didn't she ever mention you to us?"

Henry gave me a bittersweet smile. "Because I asked her not to."

The alarm bell rang. The door boomed closed.

He was gone.

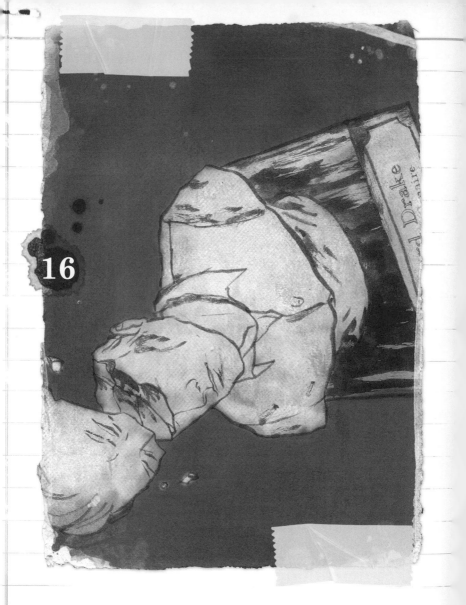

16

The Saturn's tires slopped through the long, muddy driveway that led to Daniel Drake's house. I downshifted, letting first gear do its methodical thing. It was a little after 10 A.M. I wasn't in a hurry; Daniel was unemployed and would probably be home. Of course, that wasn't guaranteed, but I couldn't check because his phone was disconnected.

I was happy to be away from Claytonville and my uncle. Our reunion had played over again and again in my mind on the way here. And the further I drove from civilization, the louder that one-man band became.

The Dark Man is a mercenary, Henry had said. *Someone paid the black with blood. Someone wants your blind man to suffer.*

I couldn't believe it, not all of it. The demon plaguing my patient was a self-made myth, pure fiction. Wasn't it?

I loved your mother. That wasn't your mother. You saw it.

Yes, I had seen a dark man that day. But being four years old, I'd probably seen pink pterodactyls flying in the kitchen a week before. My past self wasn't what I'd call a credible witness. I'd been in shock. The Administration for Children's Services report from that day had said so.

And yet, beneath this supernatural babble, I trusted Henry. He'd been a surrogate father to Lucas and I back then, according to my freshly excavated memories. And even when trapped in a place far more hopeless and wretched than The Brink, he'd followed my life the best he could, through pinprick-sized broadcasts in newspaper stories. He'd cared enough to watch me grow, from afar.

Another side of me spoke up now, its Spock voice cool and logical: *You can love a person and still do terrible things to him. A crime of passion. A murder of a mother.*

"She bailed him out of jail, again and again," I whispered, slowing the car as it neared Daniel Drake's home. "She was his best friend. Explain that."

Madness defies the microscope, Zach-Spock said. *The evidence is there. He loved her, he killed her. Some things are inexplicable.*

But the devil's in the details, I knew. Tiles slide without grout; houses tumble without nails. There were far too many details I'd read and experienced to condemn him in my heart. Dad's mysterious restraining order ... Henry's waiting at the house until Papa-Jean arrived ... my uncle's sincerity during our conversation... No, I couldn't do that, not yet.

He said he was proud of me.

I couldn't remember the last time my father said that.

I trusted Henry in that unquantifiable, ocean-deep way you trust a parent or a spouse. It felt *true*.

I pulled up beside an ancient, primer-coated Chevrolet pickup truck. My canvas satchel was in one hand now. My other killed the engine and yanked up the Saturn's parking brake.

I stepped out into the crisp country air and eyed the sagging one-story wooden house before me. Like Brinkvale and Claytonville, this place was heartbreakingly lonesome, forgotten. A thin trail of smoke puffed from its chimney.

I trudged through the muddy front yard, stepped up to the porch. An overturned garbage can pointed toward the house, undoubtedly the work of raccoons. Fat, sleepy flies buzzed over half-eaten TV dinners and sandwiches. I held my breath, and knocked on the splintered front door.

It trembled in its frame, then bucked open. Daniel Drake stood in the dimness beyond, his pine-green eyes tight with suspicion.

He pulled a smoldering cigarette from his lips and gave a loud, wet, rattling belch.

"Who the fuck are you?" he said.

✳✳✳

I smiled and extended my hand. Daniel did not reciprocate; his right hand held a beer can. He brought it to his lips and took a long swig, his eyes never leaving mine. I lowered my hand.

"Mr. Grace, my name's Zachary Taylor. I'm a therapist at Brinkvale Psychiatric. I'm here about your father. He's my patient."

His eyes widened a bit. He was tall like his dad, but far more stocky and muscled. The last ten years had not been kind to Daniel Grace. He was pushing 30 but looked more like 40. He sported the hollow-cheeked appearance of a heavy drinker: worn-down, perpetually nonplussed, run through a meat grinder. His greasy brown hair hung in his face, covering bloodshot eyes.

I was again reminded of my Anti-Zach days, my personal road to ruin — and my discovery of the art within me, my personal salvation. I wondered what I'd be like now, had I not turned that corner five years ago.

Daniel belched again, this time blowing the stinky air out of the corner his mouth. His stubbled, sunken cheeks puffed as he did this. I noticed a long, pale scar along his jaw line.

"From where?" he asked.

"Brinkvale Psychiatric." A fly buzzed between us in a half-assed loop-the-loop. The stench from the garbage was nauseating.

"Brink's not nearly deep enough for that sonuvafuck," Daniel said. "But I bet you already knew that. What do you want?"

"Next week, your father will be prosecuted in a homicide case," I said. "He's a suspect in a dozen killings, all told. I've been assigned to see if he's mentally competent to stand trial—and, if I can, to learn if he committed the murders. Richard is being—"

"Difficult?"

"Yes, he's resisting treatment."

Daniel gave a low chuckle. He raised his eyebrows, telling me to continue.

"I need to know about his past. I'd like to ask you a few questions."

Daniel killed the beer in his hand. He sucked down the last of his cigarette and flicked it past me, into the muddy yard.

"Haven't seen him in a decade. Past is all I got. Why's he in The Brink and not in county lock-up?"

"He suffers from psychosomatic blindness," I replied. "He hasn't seen in two years."

Daniel turned and stepped inside the house.

"Good. Means the monster can't hunt any more."

He glanced back, flashing a brown-toothed grin at my expression.

"You coming or not?" he said.

I followed him inside, shoving the door closed. Its underside scraped against the floor. I watched his gait, looking for an indication of the "bum leg" from which he qualified for disability money. There was none.

Mid-morning sunlight streamed into the living room, past dusty curtains. Despite this, the room was a cold place, oppressive in its gloom. Everything here, from the walls to the worn furniture, seemed old and bruised. Empty beer cans and whiskey bottles rested on a nicked coffee table; more lay on the floor. An open bag of Rold Gold pretzels lay abandoned on the sofa, its remains strewn across a stained cushion. A meek fire crackled in the fireplace.

An old boombox sat on the sooty hearth, surrounded by a dozen presumably dead "D" batteries. I didn't recognize its brand. Static-filled classical music whispered from its speakers. Beside this was a small stack of hand-chopped wood and a hatchet. The place stank of cigarettes, body odor, beer and vomit.

Several framed family photos smiled from a shelf above the hearth. The pictures behind the glass were awkwardly shaped things. Younger versions of Daniel Drake and his late sister were on display, as was their dead mother. A large hunk of each photo had been cut out. Magazine photos of Kurt Russell were taped over the absent father. This was Daniel's own attempt to "retcon" his past. I felt a pang of sympathy for him.

A cockeyed slab of wood hung above the shelf. GOD BLESS THIS MESS, its hand-carved letters said.

No kidding.

"Sit," Daniel Drake said, motioning to a chair near the fire-place. "Beer?"

"No, thanks."

"Smoke?"

I shook my head. He grunted and left the room. Above the music, I heard the tinny clank of aluminum cans, the click of a lighter, the *thunk* of the refrigerator door.

He returned with two cans, a lit cigarette in his lips. He plopped onto the sofa. He opened one of the beers with a *crack* and slurped at its frothy head.

"No lights," he said, pointing to an oil lantern near the couch. "Didn't pay the bill. Phone bill, neither. Beer's warm, tastes like piss. Still does the job."

He exhaled, and tapped his ash into a nearby empty.

"So. Daddy."

I nodded. He shrugged.

"Fire away. Memory lane, fuck if I care."

I marveled as he chugged half of the Coors.

"I'd like to connect with your father, and I think the best way is talking to him about the past," I said. "But I've had a hard time learning about Richard's early career. From around—"

"Oh, I *know*," he said. "From before the big shittin' change, back when we were the Drakes and not the amazing Graces. When things were normal, whatever the hell 'normal' means."

"What did your father do? Before the 'change'?"

"That's *classified*," Daniel said. He put a finger to his lips and gave a wicked grin. "Back then, Jenny and I thought he was a trav-eling bank executive or something. Never home."

He glanced out the window, surrounded in vaporous smoke. In this, Drake's son and I were alike. Absent fathers.

"But when he was here, it was good," he said. "He knew just what to say, how to talk to us. He wasn't hard on us, didn't need to be. It's like he knew we were gonna break the rules before we did. Heh. 'Think about it,' he'd say, just out of the blue. 'Do the right thing.' It was weird, like he was reading our minds."

He turned back to me. His eyes were glassy, a little angry. He finished off the can, crumpling it in his hand.

"I learned a little more ... later," he said. His stomach lurched, and another burp hissed from his lips. "Mindbender. Fuckin' sigh ... cology. Prisoners." His eyes squinted cheerfully, as if he'd heard a joke. "Detainees is what they call 'em now."

"I don't understa—" I began.

"Did you know he destroyed us?" he interrupted. "Did he tell you that? 'Course he didn't. He comes home from his six-month trip, spooked to shit, and then we had to leave, change our names, our fuggin' lives. It was like that show, "The Pretender." Brand-new identity, tear up the past, it never happened. You ever watch that show?"

I told him I hadn't.

"Changed our *names,* man. Fuck him and his war. I changed mine *back.*"

He cracked open the second beer, staring at the floor, saying nothing. A faraway symphony hissed from the boombox.

"You said Richard was frightened," I prompted, "when he came home. Came home from where?"

Daniel hummed a melody I didn't recognize.

"Eh? Right?" he said, his eyes wide now. "National fuckin' anthem, See-See-See-Pee. Moscow or something, I don't know. We moved, it wasn't explained. I thought he'd blown a whistle on some bank fraud or something. Witness protection, Dad was a hero, he thought about it and did the right thing. And then ... "

He took a deep drag of his cigarette.

" ... and then Mom and Jenny were killed, and it was just me and Dad. And he lost it, man, he just fuckin' lost it, started obsessing about death, jumping at shadows—literally jumping at shadows—and then we moved out here to B.F.E. He said we'd be safe here."

"From what?" I asked.

"From the monster ... but .... but I didn't know that then." Daniel blinked slowly now. The man was hammered. "Life in the fucking boonies. But people were nice, at first. One lady, Bethany Walch, dropped by a few weeks after we came here, introduced us around, took a—hah—a keen interest in the Widower Grace, if you catch my drift."

"They had a relationship."

"Depends on your definition. The next week, she got threshed right along with the hay."

His glazed eyes glittered.

"It's quiet out here. We heard her scream three miles away."

"That's terrible," I said.

"Few days later, he sits there, right where you're sitting, and tells me that he's responsible, he killed her. Which is bullshit, and I said so, cuz he was standing next to me when she died. He doesn't listen." He opened a fresh can of beer. "Then he tells me something worse is coming. He tells me my girlfriend's going to die on the Scrambler, he's seen it, and he's telling me about it now so he can stop it from happening."

"Scrambler?"

"Carnival ride, pitches you around, makes you wanna fuh"—Daniel belched here, wiped his mouth with the top of his wrist—"fuckin' puke. Here's the thing, mister, the thing that'll crack that fuckin' brain of yours. I didn't have a girlfriend when he told me that. And then a few weeks later, I did. And the carnival came, and I didn't listen, and we went."

"And she died," I said.

He touched the long scar on the side of his face. "Yeah."

"Did your dad know the girl before he told you this?"

Daniel Drake looked at me. The cigarette hung from his lips. Smoked streamed into his watering eyes.

"He saw her picture in the paper. It was Ms. Walch's daughter. Her picture was in the Sunday paper, the day after her momma died."

Daniel's face twisted into a snarl. He plucked the cig from his mouth and pitched it to the hardwood floor, mashing it with his work boot. His voice was cold now.

"He left the next day. Fucking *coward* left his eighteen-year-old son with a paid-up house, a shitload in the bank and a letter on the kitchen table. Says he's a 'death-bringer,' he's cursed, seein' things—a giant, living Inkstain sliding across the walls. 'Unholy retribution,' he says, some convoluted monster-movie bullshit, and he's leavin' to save my life, not coming back, and I shouldn't look for him."

He threw his can of Coors at the fireplace. I flinched. The can bounced off the hearth, spraying foam and beer onto the floor.

"And by fuck, I didn't."

I looked up from the mess to Daniel's face. *Four arrests in as many years*, I recalled. *Two for assault.* I had to tread carefully now.

"What ... What did you think of that?" I asked.

His bloodshot eyes locked with mine. The music filled the silence.

"About. What."

"About what he said in the letter."

Daniel Drake stood now, towering above me, his body swaying. His face had gone blank, impassive. Just like his father's.

"My girlfriend's head was cut clean off her shoulders," he said. "I swallowed so much of her blood that day, I can still taste it. Mister, I believed every word."

I didn't need the drunk to walk me to the car—and frankly, after the spook story I'd just heard, I didn't want him to. But Daniel Drake insisted, and so we trudged through his slop-soaked front yard toward the Saturn. I tapped the remote entry button in my hand, and the doors unlocked.

"Nice car," he commented. "Yours?"

"It's a friend's."

He nodded to his blue, battered pickup truck. Behind the shitheap's cracked windshield was a faded, handwritten FOR SALE sign.

"Everyone needs wheels. Got a guy comin' tomorrow to see it. It's yours for two hundred now, if you wannit." He snorted through his nostrils, sucking phlegm into his mouth. He swayed, spat and smiled. "Cash or check, it all spends the same."

I opened the car door and smiled back.

"I'm good. Listen, I really appreciate you talking to me. It's been really helpful."

"One man's trash is another man's treasure," he said.

I extended my hand again. This time, he shook it. His calloused palm squeezed far harder than I liked.

He leaned toward me. The air turned rancid as he spoke.

"Mister, you're not trying to cure him, are you? Make him see again?"

"I ... I don't think he wants that," I said. "I just want to do my job."

Daniel's green eyes probed mine. "What's dead's buried. You'd be right to leave it alone."

I can't leave it alone.

"Thanks again," I said, and climbed inside the car. My feet found the clutch and brake pedals. I switched on the ignition. The Saturn purred.

Being inside was literally a breath of fresh air. I leaned my face toward the cartoon pine tree dangling from the rearview mirror, and inhaled. I suddenly felt as if I were in a Glade commercial: *Fresh forest scent! Ahhhhhh!*

Ah.

I looked at the dashboard. There, in its center, was my iPod. My brain made the cross-reference: Richard Drake, the song he played at The Brink, Russia, the classical music streaming from Daniel Drake's boombox. If there was anyone who might know ...

"Daniel!" I called, rolling down the window. "Daniel, one quick question!"

The man turned in the yard, spat again, and walked back to the car. Goddamn, he was burly. He slapped his hands onto his knees and peered into the car. He flashed me his brown teeth, gleeful.

"Changed your mind about the Chevy, huh?" he said. I shook my head.

"Actually, it's about your dad. I heard the music inside, and it made me think of something. Your dad played this, on a piano. Does it mean anything to you?"

I tapped the iPod. The opening high notes of "Night On Bald Mountain" were playing now, leaves scattering in the wind—

"NO!" he screamed. "NO NO NONONONONO! Heard it enough then, still hear it in my fucking sleep! Turn it OFF! Turn it OFF, you motherfucker!"

"Wait, just—"

His hands were inside the car now, his scarred, crimson face an inch from my ear. His fingers tore at my face. I felt blood surge down my cheek.

"OFF, YOU MOTHERFUCKER!"

And now I was screaming, no words, just screaming. My right hand slammed onto the gearshift and thrust backward, putting the car into reverse. Foot off the brake, hitting the gas. The car lurched, but didn't move.

No

—music thundering in the car, a lunatic roaring in my ear—

fucking

—TURN IT OFF, his boots thumping against the car door now—

way.

My hand found the parking brake and slapped it down. The Saturn roared, spraying mud into the sky as its front-wheel drive let loose.

Daniel Drake screamed at me past my windshield ... and now, as I twisted the wheel, heaving the car into an ungainly one-eighty, he was in the rearview mirror, chasing me, growing smaller and smaller.

The shakes terrorized me for the first half-hour of my drive south. Eventual destination: The Brink. I recalled Malcolm's pep talk in the library yesterday, about learning to pitch and walking through earthquakes. As I eyed the scratch on my cheek from Daniel Drake's attack, Malcolm's optimistic sermon rang hollow.

I was running on four hours of sleep and adrenaline, wracked with an ever-present full-body tremor. Screw baseball and pitching. The earth beneath *me* was pitching; I couldn't find the ball anymore.

I was ravenous for normalcy. As soon as Daniel Drake's home vanished from the rearview, I called Rachael. The cell flashed a mocking "NO SIGNAL" message. I cursed and drove on, slick with fright and sweat.

I said nothing. I tried not to think.

As I neared Claytonville once more, my cell phone played its skeleton song. Reception, finally. I checked the screen, saw a new voice mail message and dialed in.

"Welcome up, bro," Lucas' recording said. I smiled at his upbeat voice, the youthful exuberance. It was rejuvenating.

"Me and your girl are catchin' big fish on the 'net," he continued. "Think we found something about that Alexandrov dude, you know, 'Comrade Dog Tags.' You'll want to hear it. Call when you can, meep-meep."

I dialed his number. Lucas picked up on the first ring, and put me on speakerphone.

"Goddamn, I'm happy to hear you guys," I said. "My powwow with Daniel Drake went into 'X-Files' territory. I think I need a new pair of shorts."

Rachael's voice purred in my ear. "There's a clean pair of panties in the glove box."

"Really?"

She laughed. "No. You okay?"

"Getting there," I said. "Everyone gets a 101 in the twisted history of the Drake clan when I get home tonight. What's Alexandrov's story?"

"You're gonna love this," Lucas said.

"Here's the deal," Rachael said. "Core information about Drake, we don't have. Stuff like his DOB, real tax and property records, bio. But we do have lots of peripheral info: the dates on the lockbox CIA letters, the Soviet connection via the dog tags, the name 'Alexandrov,' that stuff. If wasn't much, but it was enough to eventually get us to a website called 'YoureNotMeantToKnowThis.com.'"

"Subtle," I said.

"Actually, it's fairly off the beaten path," she replied. "Not a lot of people frequent it; it's not mentioned in any of the conspiracy subculture websites I started with. That's what we're talking about here, Z. Tinfoil hat territory. It's run by some anonymous guy. I tried tracking him down, but there was no useful registrant information on the website address. So this is fourth-hand information, understand."

"Rumorville," Lucas chimed in. "They've got a mill there."

"You're a dork," Rachael said.

"I prefer 'dweek.'"

I rolled my eyes, grinning. Grateful.

"So you're at this site," I said. "What happens next?"

"This place specializes in U.S. intelligence community cover-ups," Rachael said, "or so they say. There's a post about the sad, sad story of Piotyr Alexandrov—though the guy sounded like a Grade-A asshole."

"Foolbiscuit."

"Shut *up*, Luc," she said. "According to this, Alexandrov was once a high-ranking Soviet Spetsnaz officer. These Spetsnaz guys were hardcore special forces, Z, bred to be bad. Anyways, it looks like our comrade got into the black market weapons business after the collapse of Communism. Remember the stories coming out of Russia ten, fifteen years ago?"

"Not really," I admitted. "That was high school. Too busy reading comics and listening to Alanis Morissette to care."

"Heh. So was I, but my dad's gig gave me a nose for news. The nineties were awful for Russia. Power vacuums, chaos and corruption abounded. The mob ran the streets. Now according to this site—"

Lucas: "YoureNotMeantTo—"

"Goddamn it, *hush*. He's been like this all morning, Z. Twitterpated about this spy stuff. Don't make me pull over this car, Lucas."

My brother cackled.

She sighed. "Okay, so the site says the American government approved of some of this Russian mob activity—even supported it, in back-door dealings. Factions that were willing to push U.S.-friendly agendas were left alone, even assisted."

"What kind of agendas?" I asked.

"Doesn't say," she replied. "But our benevolent Uncle Sam frowned greatly upon other factions, like arms dealers. There was a network of these jerks called 'the cowboys.' They were ex-military—had access to guns, bullets, bombs and worse. They paid off corrupt officials, stole the weapons and sold them to anyone who had the money."

"That's bad news for a fledgling democracy," I said.

"It's bad news for *everybody*, Z. They were international exporters. These guys had air fleets. Armed every African civil war in the '90s, kept Columbian drug cartels well-stocked … "

Lucas' voice came on the line. "So here's where we think your blind guy enters frame. Site says CIA spooks were sent to Russia to track 'the cowboys' and find out who was the end-level boss running the operation."

"Alexandrov," I said.

"*Bzzzzzt*, nope," he said. "Lemme finish. The CIA team was lead by a small group of spooks specializing in, ah, 'infiltration and interrogation.' The operation was code-named 'Red Show.'"

My mind snagged on this. Dominos fell, puzzle pieces clicked.

"Holy shit," I said. "That's what Drake said yesterday. 'I run the red show, the hellshow.' And today, Daniel called him a 'mind-bender,' something about prisoners."

"We just jumped from lukewarm to hot," Lucas said. "Katabatic. So Alexandrov's apparently a 'trusted lieutenant' in the cowboys' operation, the right-hand man. Mini-boss. Now this is where our tinfoil types bust out their violins. 'Did he deserve such inhumane treatment?' they say."

I frowned. "What's that supposed to mean?"

"Put it together, bro. Drake and his boys apparently nabbed the dude and interrogated him. Site says that a few days after Alexandrov disappeared, U.S.-friendly Russian mobsters wiped out a cowboy safe house. *Ka-boom*, Bruckheimer style. They were gunning for the leader."

"And?"

"Fee-ass-co. There weren't any cowboys to smear. They blew up a house where Alexandrov's wife and daughter were staying. And our Spetsnaz dude? Fade to black. Never seen again."

I remembered the letter from Drake's lawyer.

"Because Drake killed him," I muttered.

Rachael, now: "Likely, from what we suspect. Now it's brass tacks time, Z. The sources for this report are *very* sketchy: innuendo, supposed off-the-record conversations with former collaborators and low-level U.S. intel officers, alleged 'translated Russian documents.' There's not a named source or cited doc in the entire thing. It stinks. But."

"But," I said.

Lucas made a farting sound.

"What are you, two?" she said. "Yeah, but. We've got enough in the lockbox to put Drake in the CIA, in Russia during the late nineties, *and* there's that damning connection to Alexandrov. If what his son said was true—"

"He hated the guy," I said. "I don't think he was lying."

"Then the story checks out, as much as it ever will."

I nodded. So. This was the information I needed to get past Drake's smug-faced defense. That day back in Russia, ten years ago—the day he made a terrible wrong turn, a decision that somehow killed Alexandrov and his family—that had sparked his eventual journey to The Brink. This was the pry bar.

Henry's voice echoed in my mind.

He did something unspeakable, unfathomable. Someone wants your blind man to suffer.

"The Dark Man," I whispered.

"What's that?"

"I said I'll be back when I can." I glanced at a road sign ahead. Twenty miles to the exit that would lead me to Brinkvale, and Drake. I finally began to feel good about this day, confident again. "Today's the day, I think. Thanks for the data dump; I'll be home right after work."

"Later gator," Lucas called.

"Be careful, and cool," Rachael said. "So long, hottie artist."

"Bye, geek goddess."

They disconnected. I stuffed the phone into my jeans pocket and drove on. For the first time, I felt truly ready to face Richard Drake. I could now help him confront his past. I could help him forgive himself.

I could help him see.

NOV

Saturday

18

1998

The Brink's elevator lurched, stopping at Level 5. I might have been puffed up by the footwork Rachael, Lucas and I had accomplished today, but I wasn't stupid. An hour's worth of rediscovered confidence doesn't trump a lifetime of nyctophobia.

I braced myself for the bizarre hallway strobe show.

The doors groaned open. The lights in max were bright and steady.

"Miraculous," I said, smiling. I walked the hall, whistling and singing the walk-off anthem to *Hair*, the musical: "Let the sun shinnne .... Let the sun shine ... The sunnn shine iiiin."

Emilio Wallace wasn't at his post by Room 507's door. In his stead was Chaz Hoffacker, an impossibly short, unfriendly butterball of a man. He and Emilio were buddies—I assumed it was a watchman thing. I'd tried to befriend Chaz my first week here, but had failed his ironclad compatibility test. He asked me what I thought of Ziggy.

Not Stardust. Not Marley. "Ziggy," the newspaper comic.

He'd kept his distance ever since. It was for the best, really. His affection for "The Family Circus" was equally boundless.

The man looked up from the comics section of the *Journal-Ledger* and harrumphed.

"Hey, Chaz," I said. "Where's Emilio?"

He shrugged.

"Took a personal day. Said he was overworked, needed some rest. Gig was gettin' to him. It happens."

I felt apprehensive about this. Emilio *never* took time off, he was a Brinkvale legend for that. Then again, he had looked worn down yesterday. Said he needed sleep.

Chaz unlocked the door. Room 507 was dark, as always. But the hallway lights were humming, and I was buzzing, let the sun shine in. I wasn't afraid. I stepped inside and flipped on the light.

I gasped.

Richard Drake sat silently in his wooden chair, an impish smirk on his lips. Beyond him, to the left, was something new and wonderful and horrible.

I gazed, suddenly punch-drunk, at a floor-to-ceiling mural. Its beauty was eclipsed only by its epic chaos. Vibrant, colorful swirls and manic, jagged lines shimmered on the cinderblocks. There was no message here on this wall, no approximation of form or conscious organization—just zigzags and spirals and broad swooshes. I spotted a scribble-swirl of black up in a far corner, near the ceiling.

I thought of the children in Drake's photos—the tot-lot ghouls with the vortex eyes—and shivered.

The long box of pastels rested neatly on the table, seemingly untouched. My eyes slid to Drake. His grin widened.

"This is tremendous, Martin," I said, careful to use his pseudonym and trying not to sound as dumbfounded as I felt. I reached into my pocket and grabbed my cell phone. "I'm going to document this. It's truly remarkable work, I'm impressed."

Drake opened his eyes. I snapped a photo of the wall with my phone's camera.

"Would you tell me what it means?" I asked.

"I would, Mr. Taylor," Drake replied, "but I *can't*." His voice as smooth and cruel as ever. "Last night, I heard growls, scratches and oily smearings against the stone. It sounded like people fucking. But I did not draw whatever is there. You'll have to ask the Dark Man what it means."

He pointed now, with uncanny precision, to the room's corner.

"He signed his work, did he not?"

I grabbed the room's other chair and placed it before him. It gave a creaky shriek as I sat.

"Martin, I admire what you've done here," I said. "It's breathtaking."

"I'm sure it is. It took everything you had not to wail in terror."

Two days ago, I would have been alarmed at this "outing" of my fear. But I had a better bead on Richard Drake now. Then, he was an audio engineer, determined to infuriate his therapists. Now, he was a government-trained mindbender, an interrogator, someone who lived to sense weakness and rend wills. I couldn't match his skill—I wasn't naive enough to believe that—but I had one important fact on my side.

"The Dark Man did not draw that," I said, "because the Dark Man doesn't exist. We both know that. In fact, we both know I can access the security tape for this room if I wanted, to prove that he didn't. I'd see you in night-vision footage, working on this art project."

"I prefer to think of 'him' as an 'it,'" Drake said. He raised a finger. "It's like talking about God. The Creator is beyond human reason, and therefore beyond gender. So is the Dark Man. Don't anthropomorphize it, Mr. Taylor. Its teeth are obsidian razors. Its claws are ebony ice. The only human thing about it is its insatiable appetite."

He folded his hands and stared into space.

I stayed quiet. This was a chess game. I was white, he was black—and black had dominated the board from the beginning, had deflected nearly every advance I'd made, had punished me for trying to play.

It was time to castle.

"I know who you are," I said.

The blind man kept smiling.

"I know who you *were*," I said.

Drake's eyelids fluttered.

"I know about the CIA," I said, "and Russia, and Operation Red Show and Alexandrov ... "

His face went bone-white. His eyes blinked madly now.

" ... and I know about what happened to his family ... "

"Stop," he whispered.

" ... and I know you were discharged from the Agency ... "

"No."

" ... and that you came back, terrified ... "

"God damn you, stop."

" ... and I know you abandoned your son after Lucy and Jenny died, after Ms. Walch's daughter was killed—"

"STOP!" Drake screamed. A mist of spittle sprayed from his lips. His green eyes flicked back and forth, doing madman's math. He was a coiled thing now, sliding lower and lower into his chair. Its wood growled beneath him.

His breathing went high and ragged. I watched him closely. If he began to hyperventilate, I'd grab Chaz. We'd take care of him.

"Leave me alone," he panted. "Don't. No. Go. You're going to the black place. You're tempting the Dark Man. Its *wraatttth,* oh no, Almighty God, no—"

"The visions you saw, Richard, they're a manifestation of your guilt—from a terrible misstep you made in Russia. The monster isn't real, Richard. The monster is *you,* how you see yourself."

Drake cringed in his chair, feral. His eyes continued to flit around the room.

"The people who died, they meant something to you, or your family," I said. "They represented intimacy, happiness, a new beginning, healing. And just as the Dark Man doesn't exist, neither does your ability to see things before they happen. It was your psyche—acting like a lance, a sword, a thing that sliced at you—that wouldn't let you move past the horror. Can't you see? Those people you're accused of killing were milestones, Richard. Positive roadside markers that led away from what happened in Russia.

"Tell me Richard, please. It's the only way to break through this. *What happened in Russia?*"

His eyes flickered. His voice had an edge now.

" 'Eye for eye, pig-fuck American,' " he said. " 'Blood for blood.' A vow. Curse. It came across the ocean and found us. Killed Lucy and Jenny. I took Danny and ran, and it followed me, getting into my eyes, showing me what it was going to do. *Who* it was going to do."

"No, Richard," I said. "It's not—"

"And YOU!" he snarled. He clenched his fists. "*You*. You'd just better shut your fucking mouth, Mr. Taylor. It *is* real. It hunted, and it's still here, hungry, because *I'm* still here. You've seen it; I smelled you see it. Why would you possibly want to free it from the cage?"

No. Oh, no. This wasn't supposed to happen. Confrontation, realization. And then self-forgiveness. So close ...

"There's no Dark M—"

"*Yes! There! Is!*"

He was out of his chair, rushing toward me, hands flailing in space for only an instant—and then they clamped onto my shirt. He yanked me out of my chair. The thing shot backward, cracking against the wall like a thunderclap.

"GET THE FUCK OUT!" he bellowed, shaking me. My head bounced forward-and-back, forward-and-back, like a boxer's speed bag. "Get OUT of my LIFE!"

I opened my mouth to scream, but he released me with a shove. I stumbled backward, back slamming into the door. I heard a cry from the other side, and then Chaz was inside, brushing past me, clomping toward a man nearly twice his height.

I'd never see a man so tall go down so fast.

***

The walk back to my office was circuitous, silent and despondent.

I was shaken by Drake's outburst—*It's obvious these Drake men must address their rage issues,* my logical side had quipped—but I was more depressed that he still believed in his Dark Man delusion. A decade of self-hatred is a hard thing to shake, I knew, but I thought I'd been close. Really close.

And that was what truly troubled me: Drake's unyielding belief in the Dark Man. He hadn't killed those people—the empirical evidence of his alibis was enough for me to trust that—and yet he welcomed the chopping block. He was a self-appointed whipping boy, ready for the flaying, gleeful for blindness and banishment. It didn't make sense ... but then again, as my inner Spock had said this morning, *madness defies the microscope.*

I trudged the halls of The Brink. It was brass tacks time, as Rachael would say. "Come to Jesus" time, as Lucas would say.

When Dr. Peterson assigned me this case, his instructions were clear: Deduce if the patient was mentally competent to stand trial. Nothing more. But I'd taken up a crusade to fix the blind man. Yes, looking back now, it had been my intent from the beginning. Even my clever mantra had been a road map for this case: *Amazing Grace, how sweet the sound ... he's blind, but help him see.*

How fair was that for my patient? For me?

Drop it, Zachary, my father had said.

Practically speaking, I *should* have—should've saluted and done the uncomplicated thing. But I couldn't, and damn it, that was infuriating.

What was the *purpose* here? What was powering this thickheaded quest?

Was it ego? Was I like that haughty pissant Dr. Xavier? Someone anonymous was feeding the press inside information, all of which was designed to make my life—and my father's—more and more miserable. I reckoned he was behind that. And me? Was I fueled by ambition, focused on some invisible, mythical scorecard that's somehow supposed to define me and my reputation? Was this about job security?

Was this about defying my father? A bohemian urge to clash with the control freak, The Man? Rage against him and the secrets he'd kept from Lucas and me?

Did I want to impress my girl? Prove my worth to a woman who was out of my league, a woman who could pick damned-near any man—or hell, probably any woman, for that matter—but chooses to settle for me?

I held back a bitter chuckle here. I had no mother. Wasn't I just high-maintenance enough with my broken mind and nyctophobia and rabblerousing and checkered past to evoke a maternal instinct in my empowered geek goddess? Was I expecting her to fix me? Had she? My God, was I that fucked up?

I turned corners and passed doorways and looked inside myself for the answer. I was brutal, and I was honest.

Yes.

There were slivers of truth to all of those things. But those slivers, as small and shiny as they were, were dwarfed by No.

No.

I wanted to save Richard Drake because he deserved to be saved. We all do. We all deserve a chance to forgive ourselves for a pitch-black past, and pick up the shattered pieces of ourselves to start anew. I'd lived that, after the accident, the soul-grinding *wrong place, wrong time* catastrophe that wouldn't have happened if I hadn't been on the wild ride with my *giddy-giddy* pardner. But I'd clawed my way out. The paintbrushes, papers and pencils that my father mocked ... that Xavier mocked ... that Drake himself mocked ... had saved me.

Perhaps that was an impossible thing to want for Drake, but damn it, that's what I wanted.

But it isn't up to you, my rational self said.

This was true.

Perhaps Drake was too far gone to be helped by me or anyone else. Perhaps he and his Dark Man were forever entwined, conjoined, inseparable. And if *that* were true, then he was fundamentally broken. Psychologically unsound.

Unfit for trial.

I knew where Drake would go, were I to sign that form and pass his lawyer an insanity plea. His destination would probably be a place different from prison and cosmetically better than The Brink. But it would be more hellish than either.

Drake's essence—his brilliance—would be obliterated by a system that cared for neither breakthroughs nor progress. It cared only for status-quo pacification. He would rot in a room, unliving a ghost-life, gazing through a miasma of pharmacological cocktails and solitary confinement.

That's not treatment. It's barely existence.

It was no way for a man to live. And that's why I couldn't let it go.

I walked the final hallway on Level 3, reflecting on my session with Drake, replaying his confession, his outburts, his absolute insistence on the Dark Man's existence.

Eye for an eye, he'd said.

I stopped, five feet from my door. There was something odd about that bit, something itchy, like a scab. I gave it a scratch. My exhausted, sleep-deprived mind said no more.

I shrugged, closed the gap, fished for my keys.

An eye for an eye.

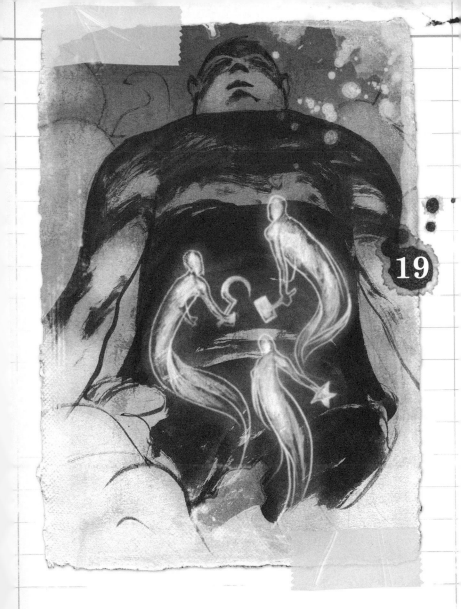

19

I'd packed my things and was about to lock up for the day when the office phone rang. I sighed, then smirked. Of all the battered third-hand equipment I'd been assigned at The Brink, this yellow-and-black beauty was my favorite. Row of sleepy-blinky extension lights, frayed cord, cracked receiver. It was the Charlie Brown of office phones.

Its broken bell gave another surly trill. I picked up.

"Zachary. A moment, please." The voice was crisp and formal.

"Of course, Dr. Peterson. What can I do for you?"

"I have reviewed the incident reports you and Mr. Hoffacker filed today regarding your altercation with Martin Grace. Frankly, I'm surprised ... and disappointed. Very disappointed."

I stiffened. "Disappointed?"

"Yes. The patient's assignment to Level 5 was merely a formality, in accordance with the court's request. Grace's files indicated that he was belligerent, not violent. If I had thought your safety was in jeopardy—"

I exhaled, smiling. "Oh, I'm fine, Dr. Peterson. It was a brief outburst, nothing more than that. He was blowing off some steam."

Peterson clicked his tongue, impatient.

"I become concerned when multiple murderers 'blow off steam,' Zachary," he said. "Your colleague, Dr. Xavier, is of the opinion that the patient would benefit from medication and sedation. Xavier also volunteered to appropriate the assignment, should you feel threatened or overwhelmed."

I nearly growled into the receiver. Goddamned Xavier.

"With all due respect, sir, Drake is *accused* of those crimes," I said. "And while I appreciate Dr. Xavier's concern for his safety, he hasn't worked with the man. This was a fluke."

"Drake?"

Fuck-fuck-fuck.

"Grace. I said Grace."

"Well, I believe Xavier's concern was for *your* safety," Peterson said.

I snorted. The guy was a snake—and as phony and hollow as the toy he resembled.

"There's nothing amusing about this, Zachary," Peterson said. "Grace's behavior today could be a harbinger. The stress of the impending trial may be influencing his behavior. If I decide that medication or restraints are the best solution, then that's how it shall be. But your point is well taken: No one at Brinkvale has spent more time with Grace than you. Tell me. Will he become violent again?"

I heard Grace's voice, bellowing: "Get out of my life!"

"It's ... unlikely," I replied.

"You don't sound entirely convinced."

"That's because I don't honestly know," I admitted. "Look, Dr. Peterson, I'm getting closer to determining Grace's mental competency, and I'm using information from his past to do that. I need his mind clear, focused, lucid ... not reacting to a mule-kick of Dr. Xavier's dope."

"There must be something wrong with our connection, because I thought I just heard you criticizing the technique of a Brinkvale colleague," the old man said.

I winced. "I'm sorry. I'm asking you to trust my judgment. I'm making a leap of faith in my patient. I'd appreciate it if you made one in me."

The line was silent for a moment. Peterson then gave long *hmmm.*

"I'll defer to your expertise," he said. "But understand that time is very short indeed for Grace. Come tomorrow, you will have three business days to make your conclusions."

"I know," I said. "Oh, I know."

∗∗∗

I called Rachael on the drive home, hoping she and Lucas would be up for supper at Stovie's, an eclectic pub renowned for its beer, bacon cheeseburgers and buffalo wings. Rachael was game, especially for a brew—"I'm feeling like something hoppy, an IPA," she'd said—but Lucas had bailed for the day. Apparently his "brilliant, exotic chica" had called with dinner plans. Lucas was loyal, but he was no fool.

We met at the apartment and walked the three blocks south to Stovie's, on Avenue B and East 8th. For decades, the space this bar now occupied had been an appliance store. According to Stovie's lore—once told to us by its seen-it-all barkeep Mendel—the store closed in the 1980s. Its bankrupt owners left behind their merchandise. Rather than pitch the appliances, Lenny Reynolds—an East Village resident legendary for his industrial art—re-imagined them for use in his new bar. Refrigerator doors became tables. Oven doors became bench seats. Electric stove tops lived on, re-engineered as wall-mounted light fixtures. The chrome of vintage logos glittered from every nook.

And magnets. Everywhere, thousands of refrigerator magnets on every conceivable surface, nearly all of them donated by Stovie's patrons. There were enough colorful plastic alphabets here to spell out the *Encyclopedia Britannica*.

Only in the East Village.

The bar would soon overflow with NYU students craving Thursday morning hangovers. Right now, the scene was sedate. Rachael and I sipped our beers as I recounted my traumatic morning with Daniel Drake (I'd cleaned my scratches at The Brink; they looked worse than they actually were), and the session with his father. I even confessed to my hall-wander realization that a sliver of my Drake obsession was fueled by a desire to impress her.

Rachael placed her pint of Klass' Bitterest on the metal table and frowned.

"Zach, you *do* impress me. It's your default setting, babe. I'm smitten, and blind man or no, I'm staying smitten. Call me the luckiest girl in the world ... or a five-state radius, at the very least."

"I second that," came a lilting voice from behind her. Ida "Eye," the fourth member of our little tribe. "Yep. Sampled the Zach goods back in high school. Yummy."

I winked. "Not yummy enough."

"Oh, no man's yummy enough anymore," the forensics lab technician said. "As a matter of fact, I'm waiting on Adrian right now."

"Now *she's* yummy," I said. Rachael's Doc Martens clacked against my shin. "Ow! Save me, Eye! Have a seat."

She slid next to Rachael, grinning. Her brown fingers tapped my ever-present Moleskine sketch pad. It lay open, beside my beer.

"Been thinking about this," she said. "Can you do a sketch of Ade for me? I want to surprise her with a present. She's got enough watercolors from me—but I thought I'd give her something special, from the best artist I know."

I blushed a little.

"Well, Christmas *is* coming, and the goose is getting fat. I'd be honored."

She beamed.

"Thanks. So how's this case going, with the blind guy?" she asked. "I'm reading all about it in the papers. You'll be a rock star before this is all over, Z."

"I don't want to be a rock star."

"Well, you certainly rock my world," Rachael said. She rocked her head like a head-banger, her hands raised in a glam-rock "devil's horn" salute. My cheeks were warmer now. I laughed, fanning my face with my hand.

"So what's his deal about a 'dark man?'" Eye asked. "Sounds racial."

"Oh god, it's anything but," I said. I picked up one of my pencils and doodled absently on the sketch pad. "It's his ... well, 'inner demon' is the best way to put it. It's a long story—and honestly, I'm kinda at a loss at this point. We've dug up just about everything we can on the guy, and it still doesn't seem to be enough.

"I mean, we know about the Alexandrov-Russia debacle now; he refused to confront it, and is still trapped within the delusion," I continued. "We've exhausted his personal effects from The Brink ... and I don't think there's anything more we can glean from the lockbox. It's like driving in the suburbs: roundabouts and dead ends everywhere."

"Somebody poke me when you start speaking English again," Eye said.

"Sorry. It's complicated." I glanced up from the page, to Rachael. "And then there's our boozing, belching 'Son of Drake.' He lost it when I played 'Night On Bald Mountain.' I wish I knew what was up with that song. All he said was, 'Heard it enough then, still hear it in my fucking sleep.'"

"So Grace played the song a lot after he came back from Russia," Rachael said.

"Yeah, but *why?* Lucas knew more about the song than we did. We should call ... "

I reached for my cell phone, but Rachael shook her head. She pulled her Blackberry from her hip pocket.

"We don't need that bouncing Red Bull commercial," she said. "Besides, you don't want to interrupt his date with 'exotic chica.' Let *your* chica handle this."

Eye watched us, bemused.

"Still waiting for that poke," she said.

Rachael's thumbs tak-takked on the Blackberry's keypad, accessing the internet. As she did this, my pencil etched vague, shaded shapes in the Moleskine pad. My hand was suddenly itchy, wanting to tell a story. I rode shotgun, watching it do its thing, finding the image as it moved.

I drew two curved lines near the center of the page. They looked like the beginnings of wings—or fluid, jointless arms. I teased the lines with crosshatchings, wondering where the pencil would go next.

"God bless wireless networks, Wikipedia and Google," Rachael said. "'Night on Bald Mountain.' Composed by Modest Mussorgsky. Song's best known for, yep, *Fantasia*. Lemme cross-ref with *Fantasia*."

On my page, new lines slipped down from the top endpoints of the curves. These, too, arced toward the center of the page. Ah.

These weren't animal wings. They were horns. I kept going. So did Rachael.

"Looks like Disney called this character 'Chernabog.' But the critter's better known as *Chernobog*, with an *o* ... as in, 'oh what a difference a vowel makes to the copyright office.' Here's the skinny. Comes from pre-Christian Slavic mythology. Nocturnal demon, tormentor of souls, a 'dark and cursed creature.'"

"Putting the poke on layaway," Eye announced. "I give up."

I barely heard them. My pencil was screaming across the page.

Rachael, from faraway: ... *also a bringer of grief, darkness, evil and death. Now* here's *a job title for you: 'Chernobog, Servant of the Black'*... .

The pencil lead snapped in my hand. Still staring past my sketch, I dropped the pencil, groped for another.

... *brought forth by black magic* ...

Found it. Continued.

... *curse lifted when the karmic scales are re-balanced* ...

"Z," Eye said, grimacing, "beloved, I got no love for whatever you're drawing."

I blinked, and gazed, a bit repulsed, at what I'd sketched so far. It resembled the head of an emaciated bear, with black swirling holes where its eyes should be. Instead of ears, hideously long horns sprouted from its skull. Spit—or blood, it was unclear—oozed from its snarling fangs.

It was a gut-churning sight, but I wasn't embarrassed of the image, as I'd been with Annie Jackson under Primorus Maximus. My tribe was initiated. I shrugged.

"This is how it is," I said. They exchanged a look and nodded. "So, Rache. Cherno—"

I cut myself off, still staring at the black bear-monster. Something flickered in its eyes, in my mind.

"Chernobog," I said. "I *know* that."

And I did, I was certain of it. Had Lucas said the demon's name last night, as he'd listened to Drake's song? No. This detail, this hook in my brain, felt a bit older than that. I hit my rewind in my mind, eager to remember.

"Night On Bald Mountain." Chernobog, Black God of Death. Obviously, it was an allusion to Drake's monster, much like this new sketch. The Black, aka the Dark Man, aka The Inkstain, aka ...

"He's called it Chernobog before," I told them. "It was in his admittance report, from a past psyche evaluation."

They looked at me, their eyes anticipating.

"And?" Eye asked.

And ...

I dropped the pencil onto the table, exasperated. "Fuck if I know."

I sighed, cupping my hands over my eyebrows, conjuring tunnel-vision on the sketch. The beast's eyes howled. Madness defied the microscope.

"It's more Sisyphean bullshit," I snapped. "Questions, answers, more goddamned questions, and here I am, waving from the bottom of the hill again. Pisses me off, man. Why? Why did Peterson pick me?"

"Oh hell," Rachael said. "You know why."

I rubbed my eyes. "I honestly don't, not anymore."

Eye raised her beer. "The aforementioned world-rocking," she said, and drank.

I coaxed a feeble smile for her.

"Z, if you really want to ask 'why,' I've got a better one for you," Rachael said. "Why is NYPD going all out for this guy? They're rooting through homicide cases that are ten years old. Those are cold cases, babe. Why the arctic excavation? Why now?"

"Oh, that's easy," Eye said. Her brown eyes met mine. "Your dad, and mine."

"My ... huh?"

"Well sure," she replied. "It's all because of your dad's ex. The lady who died, your patient's psychiatrist."

Rachael took a sip of her Klass' Bitterest. "Sophronia Poole."

Eye peered at me. "I'm a little surprised you didn't know about this, Z. My dad's been working on it for, what, two years now? All done during his off-time, once it went cold. It was a personal favor for an old friend—your dad. Heh. You know a little about that, pinging someone in the NYPD for help."

I nodded. It *was* handy, having a contact on the inside—and William V. Taylor, Manhattan District Attorney, had asked his friend Eustacio Jean-Phillipe to keep the case on life support. And the Homicide Division's deputy chief had done just that. I imagined how meticulous Papa-Jean must've been to discover Richard Drake—and then piece together the horrors my patient had fled.

How many hours of personal time? Dozens? Hundreds?

What's dead's buried, I heard Daniel Drake say. *You'd be right to leave it alone.*

"I never knew about her," I said.

"You're kidding," Eye said. "There was an entire room in my father's house dedicated to her. Well her, at first. By the end, it was mostly about your blind man. Did you know he had a crush on her?"

I thought of the appointment card in Drake's wallet and nodded. He'd "made" Sophronia Poole during their sessions, had taken notes on what things she liked: sunflowers, Jeffrey Deaver novels, spider rolls, my father. He'd planned to woo her.

And then her heart had been carved out her chest, taking my father's heart with it. That final murder had crushed Drake's heart, too—and his mind. He'd fallen for Sophronia, in the way patients experiencing transference sometimes do. She was his savior, an angel, an object of affection and desire. Love? Had he fallen in a kind of love with her?

Perhaps. She'd been someone he cared about. He'd gone blind after that.

My eyes fell back to the page. Chernobog glared back with its sightless eyes. The Black. Whirling circles, spirals, hypnotizing, look into my eyes.

Eyes.

Eye

I groped for my pencil. Yes, something. Something finally.

Eye for eye.

I leaned into the page ... and the pencil was a living thing in my hand again, sending a transmission and I was listening, *tune in, Zach, can you read me, read between my lines, yank words from my curves, from my scratches? there's something scratching at your door*

I was nodding now, my nose an inch from the table. I drew, drew from inside.

something important, yes, almost there, draw the beast, finish the piece, complete it—eye-for-eye—*draw the letters-not-letters, shade it, make it real*—killer of loved ones—*a test of your mettle, make it metal*—haunted for all your days—*now meddle, meddler, welder, weld it, put it together*—

I yanked my sweaty face away from the sketch pad, gasping. Rachael and Eye watched me, speechless. Despite their familiarity with this part of me, their expressions were both distracted, worried. I grabbed my glass of beer and gulped a mouthful. It was gloriously cold.

I looked at my art.

The bear-beast's head hadn't changed ... but something had grown from its neck. The remainder of the page was filled by two large, shimmering metal rectangles. Rune-like letters glinted from their centers.

"Dog tags," Rachael whispered, understanding.

I nodded. Yes. Oh, yes.

Oh, no.

"What if Alexandrov is still alive?" I asked. "What if he's been killing them all along?"

20

I barely remembered showering and dressing the next morning. Every element of the morning ritual—pedaling my Cannondale to the subway station, the rumbling ride on the LIRR train, chaining my bike outside The Brink, morning coffee, coworker conversation, elevator ride—it all streaked by like a traffic time-lapse video, all forgettably anonymous and unimportant. I did not visit my other patients this morning. I had a single purpose. Richard Drake.

I strode down the hallway of Level 5, taking a heartbeat to appreciate the steady lights above. I spotted Emilio Wallace, back at his post by Room 507, and waved. He raised a hand and made a half-hearted motion in return. The gesture reminded me of the ubiquitous robotic wave of a pageant contestant. He wasn't smiling.

I repressed a shiver as I slowed my pace and drew closer. The hallway's strobing mania may have disappeared, but Emilio appeared to have inherited it. His eyes blinked and twitched like a paranoiac's. Black Samsonite bags hung above his cheeks. He hadn't shaved. His lips trembled; he alternately pressed them together and blew air from them, sputtering nonsense.

I stared up at him. It was incomprehensible, whatever had happened to my friend. Emilio's massive shoulders were unnaturally tight, kicking well past his collarbone. The man's meaty hands seemed electrified, grasping at nothing, fingers playing invisible notes on a piano.

"Emilio," I whispered. "Oh my God, man. Are you ... feeling okay?"

His chiseled face crumpled, then twisted into a spasmodic smile. The flesh around his bloodshot blue eyes crinkled. His capped teeth chittered. I wanted to hug the man. I wanted turn and run.

"Fffff. Fuh-fuh-fuh." He squeezed his eyes shut, concentrating. It was heartbreaking. "Fuh-*fine*. Juh. Juh."

"Just?"

He barked a laugh, nodding enthusiastically. The sound echoed in the empty hall. "*Just*. Just chillin'." His crazed smile eked even wider.

"Dude, come on. It's me. Zach. You know, 'Yo, Z.' We're buds. What happened?"

"Ffffollowed me," he said. "Huh-huh-home. Huh-haunted. Haunted ... *housssse.*"

I felt the blood leave my face.

"What followed you?"

Emilio glanced past us—right, left, down the hallway—and leaned down, as if to tell me a secret. His wild eyes widened. He tittered.

"Thh." His voice was a conspiratorial whisper. "The *vuh-vampire.*"

He was sick. No question. Absolutely none.

"You should go home," I said.

"Home is where the *sssstart* is," Emilio said. His face devolved into a bitter, saddened sneer. His voice was a low rumble. "Sss-starts there. Whi-whispers. Ink on the wuh-walls. Sluh-sliding across the walls."

I took a step backward, and immediately hated myself for doing it. Emilio didn't notice.

"Vacation," I heard myself say. "Get away from this place, man. Take a week, damn, take two. Far away."

"Need the muh, muh—"

"No you don't, not this bad," I said. "You should really go. Like, now. Think of your boys, man. You gotta be right—um—ah, fuck it. You gotta be right in your head for them. You gotta be their dad."

He brightened ... as much as his ticking muscles would allow. He nodded again, more slowly this time. More controlled.

I nodded back. "Okay, game plan, buddy. Let me in. I'll be there for a bit, but when I come out, we're going to the infirmary, getting you once-overed. After that, your ass is taking a holiday."

" 'Kay."

"Katabatic," I said. I gave him an encouraging smile. "Let's do this."

Keys jittered in trembling hands. Tumblers fell. Hinges shrieked.

I entered Room 507, for what I hoped would be the last time.

✳✳✳

The room blazed white as I flipped the light switch. Richard Drake sat in his chair—I wondered, fleetingly, if he ever stood, or slept—and his eyes were open, blankly staring at the thing before him. The second chair. My patient had been busy, planned for company.

My gaze shifted to the wall on my right. Holy shit.

He'd been *very* busy.

It was another full-wall mural, drawn from the pastels I'd left, etched in the same incomprehensible, scratch-swirl style as its twin across the room. I pulled the cell phone from my pocket once more. The phone *pinged*, a new photo stored inside.

"It's another amazing piece, Richard. It really is."

"Don't call me that," Drake said. His voice had the inflectionless tone of an insomniac. "Go to hell. Go away."

"I can't," I said.

"You *won't*."

"No. I can't. Not built for it. But you've known that feeling."

Drake's eyes blinked slowly. "Yes."

I sat down, watching him. His face was expressionless, inscrutable.

"I'm heading to my office soon, Richard. I'm going to fill out a form ahead of schedule—and for me, that's something just short of miraculous—and I'm going to sign it. My boss will smile his peculiar elfish smile and say, 'Very good, Zachary.' My father will be furious. And your lawyer will do the Snoopy dance.

"You've sensed me spin and hustle these past four days, dribbling through my legs, trying to squeak past your defense. But you're impervious. You're a pro. And while I scrambled and fumbled and dug in, dug into your past, dug straight to Hell like you told me to, your tactic remained the same, Richard. You clutched to your sins and your guilt, convicting yourself, wrapping that black blanket tight."

I sighed. The ancient chair beneath me sighed, too.

"You are not mentally competent to stand trial."

Drake stiffened. His eyes widened slightly.

"I didn't hear you," he said.

"Yes, you did," I replied. "I don't know if that's what you were gunning for—I don't think so, but I'll be damned if I'll ever know. You've made sure of that. You're a Gordian knot, Richard, and I just can't find a sword sharp enough to cut through. The well's dry. I'm out of gas. You're so certain that your delusion is real, you've half-convinced *me*. You're mentally ill. The key to freedom is in your hand—in your mind—but you've either forgotten about it, or you've chosen not to use it.

"And that forces my hand, because this is the last stop. There are no other doctors to stymie, no other mindbender tricks to pull. It's just The Brink ... and me. And you did it. You've broken me."

Drake shook his head.

"No."

"Yes," I said. "There's no other conclusion I can make."

Fire glimmered in his eyes. His lean jaw tensed.

"*No.*"

I placed my hands on my knees. My voice was sympathetic. *I* was sympathetic. It tore at me to say this, to admit this. *He's cruel*, Annie Jackson had said, and he was ... but he had a *reason* to be, he was tormented by a life-changing error, a thing my heart knew I couldn't live with were I in his shoes, and he deserved a fate better than the one he'd now endure. The one my signature would help sentence him to.

"Richard, the endgame isn't next Monday. It's now. Your view of the past is so resolute, so brazen, so *inflexible*, that there's no reason to waste our time anymore."

"I said *no*, damn you." There was a tremor now, on the edge of his icy voice. "I'm *sane*. I *know* what I've seen, and it's real. You know it's—"

I spoke over him, insistent, my voice still low and sincere.

"Have you ever considered, just for a moment, that the past didn't happen the way you think it did—or prayed it did?" I asked. "I'm not talking about rewriting history. What's dead's buried; that's what your son said. But what if there was never a burial ... because there was nothing to bury?"

Drake's head cocked to one side in an agonizingly slow arc. His ear nearly kissed his shoulder now. He shook his head, as if trying to shake away a dream.

"I ... don't ... "

"No, I don't think you ever have," I said, "and I don't know if it's true, but can you loosen your grip on the past to consider—for only a moment—that Alexandrov is still alive?"

His green eyes were the size of half-dollars now. His voice was a whispered hiss.

"*What?* How did—"

"They never found a body, Richard."

"How could you possibly *know that?*"

I leaned forward now, leaned in close. "This is it. The end of the line, the bottom of the ninth. If you're going to convince me that you're the crosshairs for Death—that you're *really* the cause of all this misery despite your alibis—then you'd better do it now. So here's the pitch. What happened in Russia? What is the Dark Man? Why 'Night On Bald Mountain?'"

Richard Drake's voice pitched low as he spoke. It was unsettling, unbalanced, like a warped LP record. This side of my patient was new. I watched him closely.

"In all my years—all those jobs—I never spilled a drop, never bruised a knuckle," he said. "It's classless, inhuman. No way to treat a living thing." He sighed. "Until ... "

"Until 'the cowboys,' the gun runners," I said.

"Until *him*. Every game, every trick, every con, every incentive, even drugs. Nothing. The Ivan was bedrock, unflappable."

He looked up at me now, and for a heartbeat, I thought he could see again. But his pine-green eyes still stared past me, vacant.

"We needed to know who ran the operation," he said. "We *needed* it. I had to, you understand. I *had* to. Desperate measures."

"You beat him," I said.

Drake shook his head quickly, squinting, terrified by whatever he was seeing inside his mind.

"No, no, so much worse than that," he said. "The things ... Jesus ... that was *me* ... his face, his thumbs, his teeth, the *saw*, oh Christ, the saw and the blood and the sutures and the screams and *laughing,* always laughing at me, 'pig-fuck-American,' 'fuck-your-mother-American.' Trained. Better. Better than me. And through it all, I played that fucking song on the boombox, over and over and over again. Was it the music? Was it the broken bones and blood he'd lost? Seeing what was left of his face in that mirror? I don't know ... but I broke him."

He dragged the back of his hand against his lips.

"He gave me an address, said it was the boss' safe house. It was my job, my call. I didn't order recon, didn't think there was time. The house was a heap of ash when the goons were done. But."

"Was it a double cross?" I asked. "Did he ... "

"Did he willfully sentence his wife and daughter to death? I doubt it," Drake said. "He'd been in Red Show custody for *four days* by then. That's enough time for a paranoid mob boss to split and whip up a double cross of his own, should the right hand try to stab him. These people trust no one. Evil. There's a special place in Hell for people like them. People like me."

Drake leaned back, the wood settling around him.

"He was the one who told me, you know. Alexandrov. I don't know how he found out—either he had a mole, or one of us had gone hostile. Doesn't matter. My career was finished, fucked. He told me that I'd killed his family. He sat there, chained to that chair, bleeding out of every hole God gave him, and he laughed and spat and cursed me. 'Eye for eye, pig-fuck-American.' Payment in blood. Spoke in a language I didn't understand. Then told me that I'd be haunted for the rest of my days. I'd be the eyes of death, 'the black harpoon.'"

His voice was flat now, businesslike.

"And so I hit him until he stopped laughing. Damned-near all of his teeth were gone already, so that part was easy. I took his tags and dumped him in the Volga."

I stared at him, silent. His face was slack and expressionless.

"Eye for eye," I said.

He nodded. A tear slid down his cheek.

"Your orders killed his wife and daughter—and a month later, you lose *your* wife and daughter. That's not the work of a demon, Richard. That could be the bloodlust of a man you tried to kill. And perhaps the debt hasn't been paid in full, not in Alexandrov's mind. Perhaps he watched from afar, followed, preyed upon your friends, creating the illusion of the Dark Man ... and you, so damaged from Russia, driven so desperate by the blood on your hands, made the illusion a delusion. The sinner needed punishment. What better punisher than Chernobog, Servant of the Black?"

Drake began to moan as he wept freely now. His chest heaved, wracked by his sobs. He wasn't a killer now, wasn't a *cruel* man. For this moment, this heartbeat, he was a child, lost in the dark.

"I don't know if he's out there," I said quietly. "But I think he *could* be. You didn't physically kill these people; you've admitted that. If Alexandrov is out there, pursuing a vendetta, then that could help prove your innocence. You could even help me, feed me enough information that the cops—the feds, the CIA, who-ever—might find this guy. If he's still alive, he's a ghost now. That means he's safe. You could give him bones and blood again, make him catchable ... again."

I couldn't tell if Drake was listening anymore. He covered his face, shuddering and weeping. He gave a low wail inside his hands, and now my vision was blurring, moved by the move-ment of his soul.

"Richard," I said, "I can't ... Jesus ... I can't begin to imagine the fear you've felt, the terror of feeling watched, or hunted. I don't know what it's like to flee a new home, a new life. I've never lost friend after friend, town after town. What happened in Russia, I can't fathom the pain ... the *ache* ... of that mistake—and I'm sorry that I can't reach that, imagine it."

My hand fumbled to the wallet in my back pocket. The chair creaked as I tugged it free, flipped it open, pulled out the photo from Gram's shoebox.

I stared down at the trembling thing: me, Rachael, Lucas and Dad. Taken a year ago, when things were less complicated, less broken. I began to weep now, too. I wept for the face that wasn't there.

"But I know ... God, do I know ... what it's like to lose family. I saw her die, Richard. A soul doesn't recover from that. It's bruised, crushed. Your wife and daughter, gone. There's no worse punishment. But ... "

I looked at him now. His long fingers smeared the tears into his skin. His eyes were closed, but he was pulling out of it, listen-ing again.

"Alexandrov *might* be alive," I told him. "The Dark Man might *not* be real. Can you open your mind to that? That sliver of possibility?"

I reached out, slowly, and placed my hand on his shoulder. His body flinched, but he did not pull away. His face turned toward my hand.

"Can you open your eyes and see that world, a world that might be?"

The room was silent.

And then, Drake did.

He sucked in air through his teeth, squinting at the comparative brightness of the room. His eyes fluttered, cataloging the hand on his shoulder as if it were a new thing. His expression was exquisite and bittersweet.

Something that sounded like a laugh—a genuine, joyful laugh—surged from his throat. It sounded gruff and rusty, out of practice. I watched his eyes roam from my hand to his shoulder, then down to his chest. He pressed his hands there, drummed his fingers along his ribcage. His eyebrows raised, hopeful.

I'd never seen a smile so beautiful or truthful. He laughed again, more confident this time.

His gaze shifted down to his slacks, his loafers—he was tapping his feet now—and then racked focus to my Vans.

The smile changed. The glee transformed into something more serious and straightforward.

"Thank you," he whispered.

His pine-green eyes followed up my leg, to my knee and to the hand there, holding the photo. And then they flicked to my face. Tears spilled anew, down his red cheeks. The expression on his face was new, too.

He was ... *terrified.*

His voice was hushed, quaking, barely audible. "Oh no. You're wrong, so wrong." His eyes flicked over my shoulder, and he uttered a low sound: *rrrrrnnnnn*

The light above us flickered. The strobe show was back.

A noise, wicked and unholy, rumbled from my right. The sound of something large scraping against the cinderblock mural ... now the screech of knives, sharpened on stone ... of breathing now, lascivious and wet and hungry ... and the *clickity-click* of dogs' claws on tile.

"—*nnno* God, no." Drake's face had turned pale, sick. "The Dark Man is here, behind you, whispering, showing me how you're going to die. Here. *With me.*"

And that's when the room went black.

I gasped, reeling back into the chair. It was black and cold and oh no, black, no, dark, oh dear Christ Almighty, breathe, please help me breathe, no air, no light, no *anything*—

Richard Drake screamed. I felt a rush of air, blisteringly cold, rush between us. I saw nothing in the ink, but yes-no-yes, I could sense something growing there, growing taller between us, rising from a feral crouch, now towering above us. The frigid wind came in waves now, as if hailing from a paper fan.

As if it were dancing.

And then, that sound. Autumnal leaves.

Tktktk.

"No! God, no!" Drake shrieked. "*Not just you.* Your family. It's showing me ... how your family will die, too. *No! NO!*"

The light blasted bright again, and began its manic Morse Code stutter, *bzzzt bzzzzzt, bzzzt.*

I bolted from my chair, whirling around, eyes wild, searching for the thing I'd heard. Nothing. Not a goddamned thing but me and the painted walls and Richard Drake. I turned to him, chest heaving, my heartbeat a thunderstorm in my ears.

He'd covered his face with his hands, was screaming like a damned man. I stumbled backward, toward the door, my gaze irresistibly locked on the crazy man in the chair.

"*CURSED!*" he howled. "*TOO LATE!* Too late for me, Mr. Taylor, and too late for you and yours. I *warned* you, and now it's *free*, the cage broken, I can *see*, it's here to *play* ... and it'll play, Mr. Taylor, play with you like a cat plays with a mouse ... "

His next word was either *prey* or *pray*. I couldn't tell, and I didn't care. My back pressed against the metal door. I slammed my palm against it. I made a fist, and pounded. My voice was high, cracking like a teenaged boy's.

"EMILIO! For fuck's sake, GET IN HERE!"

The bolt clacked open and Emilio's hands were on my shoulders, yanking me from the room. I was airborne for a half-second ... and I then was bounding into the hall, nearly spilling onto the floor.

Emilio was a tree-sized blur, cannonballing into Room 507. His massive form was soaked in the stuttering light as he reached out, ready to restrain the still-sitting, still-screaming Drake. Emilio tore Drake's hands away from his face. He leaned low to give Drake a verbal warning, per procedure—*calm down*

Their faces were inches apart. Drake's scream rose in pitch, impossibly raw now, like shattering glass.

I dashed from the doorway, down the hall, head spinning, brains popping like a bad fuse, emotional overload, tilt, tilt. Tilting, the world was tilting.

The lights out here weren't flickering, weren't growing dimmer. They were getting brighter. *How is that possible...*

Emilio bellowed, like a tyrannosaur. I spun on my heel, eyes focusing on the doorway.

The world went slow.

Emilio Wallace ran full-speed from the room, his muscled arms flailing, as if aflame. His voice was a tornado, a battle cry, a thing his fans heard years ago in Southwestern convention centers. *Nuh-nuh-no, not them,* he was screaming, *I wuh-won't do it, not my boys* ...

... and then his six-foot-five, 260-pound body smashed into the tiled wall opposite the door.

He bounced off and staggered, stupid. His broken nose gushed crimson, covering his mouth and Superman chin in a horror-show goatee. He swayed once, then slapped his palms onto the wall to steady himself.

He stared at the cracked tiles and snarled. He swung his head forward, bashing it against the wall. Ghoul's paint sprayed against the pale green.

"Nuh-NO!" he howled.

I couldn't move. Couldn't speak.

Emilio drove his forehead into the tiles again and again, growling, now howling. A nightmare of flesh scraps and blood spritzed forward—then upward—as he hammered his skull against the wall. His face was covered in gore. His forearms and hands were slick, misted with blood.

And bashed again.

A tile broke loose and shattered on the floor. It was like a pistol shot. I ran toward him.

Roaring, he bashed again.

Meat spilled into his face.

And again.

A sickening, soggy crunch rang in the hall. My friend's shoulders sagged. A terrible gurgle pushed through his blood-soaked lips ... *hhkkkkk* ... and he fell.

I stopped at his bloodied body. My eyes refused to work, to blink. It was impossible to look away.

The lights in the hall began to flicker. I shivered.

From behind me, I heard a skitter-slide of feet, the sound of millipedes and bad dreams. I felt something watching me, a thing old and awful, and very cold. And then, a blast of ice. A breath on my neck.

My eyes fluttered, rolled upward.

For the first time in my life, I was grateful for the dark.

21

My bicycle weighed less than twenty-five pounds, but it felt oppressively heavy on my shoulder as I trudged up the steps of my building. The carpet-covered wood creaked beneath my feet. The old light fixtures struggled against the dimness of early evening. My Cannondale's rear tire spun sleepily as it skipped against the wall.

Tick-tick-tick, went the wheel. And then, skitter-slide: *tktktk.*

I stopped, clutched the banister, sensing something unfamiliar. There was no breeze here in the stairwell, but it was chilly, as it always was this time of year. I sniffed, smelled plaster and wood polish. The air felt damp, heavy. It pressed against me like fog, another skin, claustrophobic.

Tktktk.

I shuddered, resisting the urge to turn around.

It was the Cannondale, yes. It was the Cannondale's tire whirling round and round, and the air had changed because people were heating their apartments now. That was all, an elementary deduction; my Spock-side would be proud. I leaned against the handrail, inhaling deeply. The whirlwind days and sleepless nights were catching up with me. They'd come, finally, to collect.

Tick-tick-tick, went the wheel.

"Oh, shut up," I said.

I clomped up the second flight, relieved to be home.

***

Rachael and Lucas were waiting in the living room, their faces pinched and fretful. I smiled. It was a weary-faced farce. They knew it, too, and I loved them for that.

My brother pulled the bike from my shoulder and wheeled it to the hallway closet. I heard him hang it on the door rack.

I gazed at my woman standing in the center of the room, surrounded by our red halo of chili-pepper lights, drinking up the sight of her. I went to her, hungry to feel warm, held, beloved.

Her inked arms pressed me closer. I sighed. The steel cables in my shoulders slackened a bit. I kissed her, breathed in her scent of shampoo and skin. Goddamn, this was perfect. Holistic. Necessary.

"You should've let me pick you up," she whispered.

I pulled away, gave her lips another quick kiss. "No. I needed to be alone. Needed to think."

Lucas stepped into the room, a fresh beer in his hand. I accepted the bottle and slid onto our couch. Compared to the stiff hospital bed and metal chairs in which I'd spent nearly my entire day, this felt luxurious. Rachael joined me. Bliss hopped into my lap, delighted. Her other half, Dali, was nowhere to be seen.

"Tell, bro," Lucas said.

I sipped the beer, unsure of what to say. Drake's personal effects lay strewn about the steamer trunk before me: wallet, phone, envelopes, letters ...

"Failure," I said finally. I suddenly wanted to cry, but I didn't have it in me.

They waited. Lucas sat on the floor.

"So there was an accident," I said. "I told you that. And I'm fine. But ... I ... this morning, I watched my friend head-butt his brains all over a wall."

"Oh my God," Rachael said. "Why?"

"Because he'd been hacked, like a computer," I murmured. "He'd been reprogrammed by that son of a bitch. Our CIA interrogator spent days spooking him, slow-boiling him like an egg. Today ... today the shell came off. Jesus. Emilio is ... Emilio *was* always a little off-center. Drake exploited that."

"He's dead?" Lucas asked.

I nodded slowly, my lips trembling.

"He must be. They took him topside. A chopper medevaced him out. No one's told me anything, but there's no way a person could survive that."

In my mind, I heard the Brinkvale tile shatter against the hall-way floor. I shuddered.

Emilio was dead.

"No way," I repeated.

"This just ... happened?"

I turned to Rachael.

"It's my fault. I told Drake my theory about Alexandrov. He broke through, he actually *saw* ... and then he broke down. Starting screaming about the Dark Man, how it was going to hunt us, kill us."

"Oh, babe," she said. "I'm sorry."

"Who's 'us?' " Lucas asked. His voice was low.

"Us three, and Dad."

I watched him. He pulled his knees up to his chest. Now, he hugged his shins. An incisor dug into his bottom lip. Oh, no.

"Lucas, relax," I said. "It's bullshit."

But it's not, cooed a slippery voice inside me. *You've been marked. Time's running out. Tktktk-tock.*

I shook my head.

"It's a con, Luc. A way he controls his life, and others. It isn't real."

The voice in my mind tittered.

"It's *not,*" I said again, more insistent. "Paranoia only has power if you buy what it's selling. You have to *believe,* man. Emilio was like that, God love him. He was eager. He was unbalanced. He bought into it."

And you? the slippery voice said. *Aren't you in line to buy? You heard it, scritch-scratch, tktktk. You felt its breath on your neck.* And now the voice was Richard Drake's: *You're wrong, so wrong...*

"Don't be eager," Lucas was saying. "Heh, right. Dookle. What's the opposite of 'eager?'"

"Skeptical," Rachael and I said simultaneously.

The three of us smiled. I felt a little better. I rubbed Bliss kitty's head. She hopped from my lap.

"Are you done with Drake?" Rachael asked. "Is it over?"

I shrugged.

"After I watched Emilio ... ah, jeez ... after I saw it, I fainted. Woke up in the infirmary. They fussed over me. Dr. Peterson came down, personally conducted the interview for the incident report. *That* was awkward. Cops took a statement. Of course, no Zach Taylor screw-up would be complete without a cameo by Nathan Xavier."

"Is that the prick who looks like a Ken doll?" Lucas asked.

I nodded.

"Plastic prick," Rachael said. "Doctor Dildo."

I smirked, grateful for the joke. "I spent most of the afternoon in a counseling session. I had questions about Drake, but everyone was giving me the 'wait and see' line—probably because Xavier is gunning for the job. All I know is that the man has completely shut down. He isn't moving, talking, eating. Near-catatonic state. Oh, and he's blind again."

"Everything's undone," Lucas said.

"Pretty much."

I sighed.

"I don't know what to do. I was ready to sign him off as unfit to stand trial, I really was. He'd never given me a reason to believe otherwise. Therapists and patients are supposed to work together. You give, you get. But Drake never gave an inch."

I pointed at the belongings on the table.

"I had to *steal* whatever I got," I muttered. "Goddamn. Do you realize that I've been more like Anti-Zach in the past four days than I have in the past four years?"

"That's not true," Rachael said. "You've been trying to help."

"I haven't helped anybody. I killed my friend."

"Z, you didn't—"

"He gave you the song," Lucas interrupted. "'Night On Bald Mountain.'"

I paused. Yes, the song. But Drake hadn't given that willingly, either. I never told him the Casio recorded his every note. Sure, the tune was another glimpse inside him—another validation of the Dark Man. But that was worthless now. Everything I'd done was worthless. In fact, that stupid song had been the only "art" this stupid art therapist had extracted from his patient. I *was* a fraud, a boy pretending to be a man. I'd been so desperate to—

Wait.

Wait just a damned minute. It *wasn't* the only art …

My hand shot to my jeans pocket, nearly spilling my beer. Both Lucas and Rachael looked on, perplexed, as I pulled out my cell phone and pressed my thumbnail against its side-seam. A moment later, a black plastic rectangle was in my hand.

I passed the memory card to Rachael.

"We need your computer," I said.

***

As the laptop's photo editing software imported my two photographs from Room 507, I quickly explained the pastels I'd left for Drake, and the wall murals he'd drawn.

We crowded around Rachael's tiny desk: she was driving, Lucas and I stood behind her, leaning in like cartoon vultures. I sipped my beer as the photos blinked onto the screen.

"Windchill," Lucas said, rubbing his arms. "This … is some spooky shit."

Yes. Yes, it still was. The photos couldn't evoke the *scale* of Drake's murals—the jaw-dropping awe of their size. But their frantic, fluid mania was here, captured in pixel-perfect precision. Inelegant curves, swirls, zigzags … blotches of color here and there.

It was an on-screen acid trip, incomprehensible, a half-remembered dream.

"He didn't tell you the point of this," Rachael said, her finger teasing at the laptop's touchpad. "Didn't give a hint."

"No. He said the Dark Man drew them."

Lucas squinted at the image of the left wall—the first photo I'd taken. He trailed his finger along part of the image in a vertical, vaguely S-shaped path. He didn't touch the LCD; he'd been around Rachael enough to know better.

"See that?" he asked. "These curving vertical lines here and here, and down there. They're incomplete. They start and stop, so this is easy to miss. But watch. Try to imagine, *hmmm,* heh. Yeah. Think of a long spaghetti string."

He finger repeated the motion, and the pattern became more clear. These lines were not connected—globular gulches of color separated them—but it was clear they followed the S-shape Lucas had illustrated.

"There's something like that over here," I said, pointing to a series of lines on the other side of the photo. They lanced downward in a diagonal formation, also separated by manic patches of color.

"Kinda like missing data," Rachael said.

My eyes flicked to the second on-screen image. The photo I'd taken this morning.

"No. Encrypted data. Look."

The right wall's mural featured the same "spaghetti string" lines Lucas had identified, as well as the diagonal ones I'd just found. But there was a twist. This photo's lines represented the *missing* content from the other photo. The stuff that filled the gulches.

"No fucking way," she said. "He's blind. There's just ... no fucking way."

Lucas' voice was a whisper. "Do it, *Hochrot*. Merge the pictures."

Her finger slid against the track pad as she created a new file. Tap. Click. Double-click. Click-click.

Tktk.

I shivered, suddenly cold.

She pasted the first mural image into the new file's blank canvas. The mouse pointer rushed to the second photo. Copy. Now back to the new file. Paste. The mouse highlighted a tiny number in a sub-window. *100%*, it read.

Her finger tapped the "down" arrow on the keyboard. *90. 80. 70.*

The second photo faded with each keystroke, slowly revealing the first photo beneath it.

60. 50.

"Stop," I said.

"Windchill," Lucas muttered, shaking his shaggy head. "Windchill, holy shit, *windchill*."

The two images were now perfectly visible together, stacked like plates of semi-transparent glass.

The lines Lucas had spotted were now complete. The picture itself was ... complete. Two halves made whole.

"This isn't possible," Rachael said. She reached up, absently tugging the bottle from my hand. She downed a hearty gulp. "This can't be happening."

We stared at the screen, too stunned to say more. The once-manic crosshatches and half-swirls now made a kind of sense, meshed together. Triangles popped from the colorful ether. Diamond shapes. Serpentine lines. There was still no overt message here ... but there was *purpose*, and that fascinated me.

It also frightened me.

A clatter rang from our bedroom. The three of us flinched simultaneously then gazed past the living room doorway, through the kitchen, into the dimness beyond. Bliss hissed from the shadows. An invisible Dali spat, then meowed.

Rachael turned back to the screen. "Play nice together," she whispered, distracted. "Play nice."

I shivered, again. The air in here felt heavy and wet. Claustrophobic. I glanced around the living room, feeling foolish—feeling crazy—as I did an inventory of the walls. I looked up, at the ceiling. Had that water stain been there before—

"The Black," Lucas said.

I blinked.

"What did ... " My tongue was thick and dry in my mouth. " ... you say?"

He tapped the LCD this time, his fingertip smudging the screen. Rachael was too engrossed to complain.

"There's black here and here. Dig it. Half swirly-moon on the right." My eyes slid leftward as he spoke. "Half swirly-moon on the left."

The black scribbles—which had been etched into the high corners of Room 507's murals—were near the top of the merged image, each positioned equidistantly from their respective vertical edges. Lucas was right. They looked like half-moons.

My eyes trailed down the picture, following a straight line from one of the black stains. A column of strange colorful shapes ticked down the photo. A "U" on its side. Three bars stacked atop each other. A thumbnail-sized crescent moon. Others.

"You see that?" Rachael asked. She took another pull of my beer.

"Yeah," I said. "I do."

Lucas gave a little yelp then snapped his fingers. Rachael and I gasped.

"Print," he said, patting her shoulder. "Print, sister, print. Control-P. Nitro-like, meep-meep."

She executed the keyboard command. The nearby laser printer whirred and hummed. Lucas snatched the color photograph before it hit the tray and bolted back to the steamer trunk. I was a half-step behind him. Rachael closed the laptop and followed.

He cleared a spot on the table's center, shoving Drake's personal effects to one side. He slapped the picture onto the trunk and looked up at us, his eyes gleeful.

"Pole of gob-gook here," he said, finger dragging down one column of runes. He jabbed at the other black splotch. "Pole of gob-gook here." He repeated the move.

He grinned.

"Now watch this katabatic shit."

He folded the photograph into vertical sections then overlapped the paper, accordion-style, until the black halves became a full moon. The process reminded me of the puzzles on the back of *MAD* magazine.

There were words on the page now.

" 'RETURN TO SENDER,' " Rachael read. She looked at me. Her face was white. "This *can't* be happening."

Lucas' fingers were a machine gun now, tapping the photo.

"New stuff, all over the place. Those weird shapes from before— they're *new* shapes. Hey. A long red line, going from here ... "

His finger pressed against the bottom-right corner of the page. It slid upward in a slow, leftward arc.

" ... to the top of the page, over here. Little green boxes, bam, bam, bam. Big-ass bluish thing here. And look. From the Earth to the moon."

A vermillion tentacle snaked from the large red artery, dead ending at the center top of the photo. The swirling black hole.

"Map," Rachael said.

I nodded, numb.

"Yeah," I said. I knew it. I'd seen it. "It's a map leading to Daniel Drake's home."

We jumped at the sound of thunder.

* * *

Beethoven's Fifth Symphony blared from my cell phone's speaker. The thing jigged on the steamer trunk, vibrating.

Bum-bum-bum-bummmmm.

"Christ, not *now*," I growled. I glanced at the others. "It's Dad."

"Pick it up, bro," Lucas said.

I turned to him, surprised.

"Dude, no," I snapped, appalled. I grabbed the phone. "He wants to sabotage my career for some bloodlust vendetta!" I stared at Lucas, incredulous. "Dad's been keeping shit from us for *years*, man, rotten stuff, for *fucking years,* burying, re-writing ... "

I stopped myself. *No.* Not now. Maybe not ever.

The phone rang again. My thumb jabbed the button that would send the call to voice mail.

Lucas crossed his arms.

"So he didn't tell us about Sophronia two years ago. So what? Have you told me every girlfriend *you've* ever had?"

Faraway, in the bedroom, Bliss hissed again. Dali growled, an air-curdling *rrrrreow*.

"Knock it off," Rachael called to the pets. "Lucas, he said he doesn't—"

"I get it, I do," Lucas said. "You're pissed, he's pissed, it's a Pissapalooza. But he's family, and this"—he pointed to the photo—"is *windchill* shit, too spooky to be anything but real. Can't you feel it? Dude, look at your arms, you've got pebbles for pores. You're shivering. It's fucking freaky."

"Th-that ... ," I stammered, "that doesn't make it *real.* This is all explainable. Every bit of it: Drake's Dark Man, the killings, that map. Just because someone says you've been 'marked' doesn't make it so. You wouldn't even be wigging now if I hadn't told you!"

Lucas took a step toward me.

"Aren't you afraid?"

"I don't—"

"Aren't you?"

"Of *course* I am. How can I *not* be, with the week I've been having? But Luc, being scared doesn't mean I—"

Another hiss, louder this time. Then came the delicate scratching of cat claws on hardwood. And then: *tktktk.*

"Did you hear that?" I whispered.

The phone buzzed twice in my hand. I nearly screamed.

"Z, please. At least play the message," Lucas said. "I need to know he's okay."

I nodded, because I needed to know, too. Far too much was happening now—this now, right now, this moment, this heartbeat—to ignore the message. I was learning to hate him, but I loved him. I still loved my father.

I tapped the speakerphone button and dialed into voice mail.

The air around us roared; Dad had called from the car.

"Zachary, it's me. I'm a few blocks from your house right now. I heard about what happened at The Brink today. Incident, ah ... "

I heard the flick-rattle of paper.

" ... incident report 507-482. My God, young man ... "

I pointed at the phone. *See?* I mouthed. Lucas shushed me. The engine in the background surged, accelerating.

" ... Zachary, that could've been you," Dad said. "The next time, it might be you. And it *can't* be you, Zach, I won't allow it. I'm coming there right now to discuss this, and if you're not there, I'll sit and wait and *whatthehell*—"

Car horn now. Tires screeching, sliding. My father, howling.

The phone trembled in my hand, its speaker overpowered by the explosive clap of an impact ... and then shredding, squealing metal. Steel laughter.

The line went dead. We stared at each other, immobilized, disbelieving.

From above, from the ceiling: *tktktktk.*

And then the lights flickered

The lights blinked off, the entire apartment black now, inkswimming

The cat hissed

Lucas moaned, horrified

Light now, on the table, something buzzing on the table

Bzzzzz

Richard Drake's phone, screen glowing

Bzzzzz

Vibrating

Bzzzzz

INCOMING CALL

Bzzzzz

SOPHRONIA POOLE

In my ear, so close, like a lover

Tktktk.

The three of us moved together. Wrenched open the front door. Pounded down the apartment stairs.

Screaming.

22

We scrabbled down the concrete front steps of our building into a world of darkness. Every light bulb on this block of Avenue B was dead. People around us yelled and cursed with frustration. The sound-scape of the city played kick-drum backbeat to our high, ragged breathing. The wind howled.

Lucas was gasping, his limber knees bent, his pose feral. Rachael's eyes burned bright with confusion. I was sweating, bone cold, paralyzed by panic and fright and a sudden certainty that'd I'd been wrong all along, that the thing was here, alive, snaking around us, constricting.

"What the hell's going on, Z?" Rachael screamed. "What's happening?"

"Blackout," I said. "I don't know."

Oh yes, you do. Tell the bitch she's been damned, that she'll be devoured, that you did it, Zach, you killed her just like you killed Emilio, cursssed cursss—

"LOOK!" Lucas wailed.

He pointed north. Far beyond our block—and the darkened block beyond that—was East 14th Street. Blue and red strobes flashed on the horizon, from its major intersection.

"Dad's accident!"

"Luc, you don't know th—"

But he took off at full speed, not listening. The door of Seventh City Comics, a ground-floor shop in our neighboring building, swung open. Blake Lafferty, Seventh City's owner, dashed onto the sidewalk, swearing at the blackout. Lucas was nearly on him, about to plow into—

Lucas leaped sideways, his body soaring parallel to the ground. His hands slapped onto the metal light pole by the curb, and his body tucked into a ball, sneakers screaming toward the pole. Their treads slammed into the metal—*bong!*—and he shoved off at an angle, flying past Blake like an agile tree monkey. Lucas somersaulted on the sidewalk, found his footing and tore off north again, toward the intersection.

This all happened in the span of an eye blink.

"Come on!" I yelled to Rachael.

We followed him, shouldering past a wide-eyed Blake.

Lucas was an urban kangaroo. He bounded, rolled and slid past pedestrians, every footfall a close call, every leap reckless and magnificent. The world was his Autobahn, his junglegym. Store awning supports became monkey bars. Fire hydrants, rocket launch pads.

We ran and ran, screaming his name.

My brother did not see the shopping cart until it was too late. The homeless man's cart, overflowing with cans and clothes, rattled directly into Lucas' path—and from my vantage point a quarter-block away, I thought he was done. But Lucas pushed further, faster and dove ... *forward.*

Again, his hands slapped home first, gripping the top edge of the metal basket ... and in an instant—stretched thin like taffy—his arms took over, wrenching his torso skyward. My eyes freeze-framed him there, a Central Park handstander, a Cirque de Soleil performer ... and then his momentum propelled him forward, and his hands were free. His body backflipped, feet smacking safely onto the concrete.

But he tumbled. He smashed into a cluster of strutting boys, none of them a day over seventeen. They toppled like tenpins, howling. Lucas was up now by the street curb, patting the boys, manically barking "dookle, sorry man, dookle, sorry, real sorry." One of them shoved him. Lucas flopped into the arms of another boy. This one punched him in the face.

My brother reeled, snatching at a third boy. He grabbed the kid's jacket and—in a blurred miracle maneuver—performed a simultaneous foot-sweep and toss. The kid blasted into the puncher, and they went down again.

The first kid pulled a gun.

"Fuckin' cap you, yo!"

I barely heard the gunshots over my screams.

Either Lucas was fast, or the kid had lousy aim. The three bullets went wild, one of them splintering a store window across the street. And that's where Lucas was bolting now, into traffic, away from the danger, still heading toward East 14th. His body made a graceful slide across a car's hood, like a '70s cop-show hero.

The world around us plummeted into pandemonium. Bystanders ran from the gunfire, others dropped to the pavement. Still others rushed toward storefront doors, bottlenecking the entrances. The block had gone raving mad.

"Coincidence!" Rachael yelled as we ran. Her voice was raw, manic.

"What?"

We were in the street now, dashing alongside the cars, questing for a gap in which to cross.

"Rationally explainable," she gasped. "The pictures, timing—yes—timing, all bad timing, the call, blackout, call on the phone, call from a dead person, not dead, battery's bad, transistors going, we saw that earlier, bad screen, cracked case, number belongs to someone elll—"

She stumbled and spun, her body flailing into the street. My goddess' magenta hair glowed neon. Her glasses glittered like a mirror ball.

Headlights.

"NO!" I bellowed.

I leapt beside her, snatched at her arm. The tires screamed.

The car's grille stopped inches from her face.

I pulled her up and we crossed the remainder of Avenue B, still tracking Lucas, ignoring the verbal diarrhea spewing from the terrified driver's mouth.

Tracking. Hunting.

Oh yes, I thought. *Drake was right. It's here. It's real. We're all being hunted now.*

***

We finally arrived at the intersection of B and East 14th. I was reeling on an adrenaline high, wheezing, legs burning. Rachael gasped beside me, her face pale and sweaty.

The cityscape here was soaked by the strobes of a police cruiser, stopped in the center of the intersection. The Crown Vic's rear bumper was a crushed, mangled mess. Behind the cruiser was a black BMW, its hood crumpled. Smoke billowed from beneath the steel.

Lucas stood by the Beamer. He'd been right. Dad was there, pressing a handkerchief against his bleeding nose. The cop was gone; I figured he'd responded to the gunfire.

"You're okay," Dad said as he saw me approach. He sidestepped Lucas and strode toward me. "Thank God. *Now* do you believe me? What I said about Grace?"

"I don't want to talk about it," I said. "I'm just glad—"

"You're going to tonight, young man." He threw the handkerchief onto the asphalt. "This gets settled tonight."

"Pop," Lucas said, "he doesn't want t0—"

"Shush, goddamnit," he snapped. Lucas flinched. Dad's eyes re turned to mine. "You can undermine me all you want, Zachary, and I can live with that. But you've undermined my case. The media is circling like sharks now over this so-called 'conflict of interest.' *I'm* the victim here. *You're* the perp. Why couldn't you just drop this? Taylor Family Loyalty, son. Thicker than water, thicker than profession—we always tell each other the tru—"

I wanted to punch him in the face.

"You're a fucking hypocrite, Dad," I said. "I'm glad you're alive."

I turned around and walked away.

***

As Rachael, Lucas, and I walked the East Village streets in silence, a war raged in my brain.

The rational and irrational sides of my mind screamed at each other, one-upping each other in vitriolic arguments and counter-arguments. *This is textbook paranoia,* my Spock-side said. *When the mind looks for patterns, it finds them. The Dark Man is a delusion; it's always been.* The emotional side of me—the part that powered my sketches, that spoke through my art—insisted that an unholy thing was set to feast on my friends and me.

Unprovable, Spock said.

That's what the atheists say, came the reply, *but God's still up there.*

I smirked, nodding at this. I was quoting Henry, my uncle-who-never-was. Henry had been put away for a crime he said he didn't commit—a crime my heart didn't believe he could commit. Twenty years ago, the Dark Man had been paid, paid in blood, and had destroyed my family in the name of vengeance.

Vengeance for what, I did not know. But I knew it was back. I'd sensed and seen enough today to finally understand that.

And I knew, with steel-bladed certainty, that I wouldn't let that fucker harm my family.

You'll find the path, Uncle Henry had said. *Or the path will find you.*

Oh, yes. In this eclipsed world, the path blazed bright.

I strode between them, my hands in my pockets, wincing at the wind.

"We have to talk about this," Rachael said. "Make sense of what happened tonight. Explain it. We have to understand those photos, and that effed-up phone call. Coincidence. Timing, bad timing ... "

I wrapped my arm around her waist. I think I loved her more right then than I ever had. There was Rachael, her purest essence bared on a Manhattan street corner: my better half, the brains of our operation, looking for answers.

"You're right," I replied.

Lucas glanced up from the sidewalk.

"Dude, there's no way I'm going back to your apartment."

I threw my other arm around his shoulder, drawing him close. What happened at the apartment had been terrifying ... but for Lucas, I think our father's actions had somehow been worse.

"Don't sweat it," I said. "You guys head on over to Stovie's. It's a few blocks away and I bet the power's on over there. I'll go get Drake's map and cell and meet you there. We'll talk over burgers and brews, sort it all out."

My brother's face brightened. I grinned back at his thousand-watt smile.

Rachael nudged me.

"Z. Babe. What about the dark?"

I looked into her eyes. The wind gusted, again.

"We all have to face our fears at some point," I said, and kissed her.

Autumnal leaves swirled around us, skittering against the sidewalk.

Tktktk.

✵✵✵

The kitchen match scorched to life in my fingers as I stood in the front doorway. Our living room flared in a dance of amber and shadow. I picked up the nearby scented candle and lit it. The thing flickered feebly, beating back the black.

I made quick work here, harried by the surroundings.

Drake's bizarre mural map went into my back jeans pocket. I slid his cell phone and the rest of the personal effects into my canvas satchel. The Brinkvale files went in, too. I thought of where I was headed and considered liberating Lucas' pen flashlight from his backpack. Instead, I retrieved our stocky Maglite from the kitchen tool drawer.

I scooped up my pencil and small Moleskine sketchpad from the steamer trunk. I tore out a page, placed the pad in my bag.

There. Nearly ready now.

I stopped at the end table by the front door, bending low to write my note by candlelight. They'd hate me for this, and I loved them for that.

Dear Rachael and Lucas,

For the past four days, the "Dark Man" has been a fiction for me, a boogeyman myth painted in rumor and shadow. An unreal thing.

And yet, somewhere in the unreality of today, I found reality. Belief. I don't know if the Dark Man is a tangible thing, a monster capable of murder ... but I realized tonight that if it is, I will not let it hurt you.

I love you—I 'dore you—more than the world. You're my tribe. So I'm going north, to pull its gaze away from all us … to just one of us. Me.

Drake's map, a thing that was undoubtedly drawn by his subconscious (and I know a little something about that, don't I? hee) leads to his son's home. Answers wait for me there. Answers, I think, from Drake himself.

Is Amazing Grace trying to redeem himself? 'Was blind, but now he sees?' I don't know ... but I hope that whatever I find ends this. I hope it saves him. I don't know what I'll find there. I don't think Drake knew when he drew his map. But there's something important there; the secret to all of this, I hope.

I'm sorry I don't have the courage to tell you this in person. I'm sorry I know you well enough to know what you'd say.

If The Dark Man is real and hunting us, it'll come for the person coming for it, the man driving on the red road, toward the map's black moon. I'm going there, and I'll be back soon.

I love you,

—Z

I blew out the candle, locking the door as I left.

The countless, shimmering confetti lights of the city finally relinquished their hold on the passing landscape, allowing sleepy suburbs and townships to emerge on the horizon. Then they, too, disappeared in the Saturn's rear window ... and all was dark. Inky penumbrae of trees and hills now blurred past the windows, illuminated briefly by the high-beams, now gone. The moon glowed like a spotlight, fat and full.

I drove, alone.

I wasn't alone.

The beast was here, slithering in the back seat—I could hear it, the sound of a spoon swirling through cottage cheese, a wet, *slurp-swish* that rushed from the right side of the car to the left, restless and hungry.

Glancing into the back seat or rearview mirror was pointless. It didn't want to be seen. And yet it loomed, always invisible, sliding its tongue against its fangs—*obsidian razors, Mr. Taylor, tktktk*—huffing its gelid breath against my neck.

I twitched, wide-eyed, hands frozen to the steering wheel. The Saturn's heater was set to high. It blew cold air.

The car sped on, northward on the interstate. I craved distraction from the sounds behind me. I fiddled with the radio, tapping the "seek" button with a trembling finger. The manic side of me—the side that had split this morning as Emilio's skull split against Brinkvale tile, the side of me now drinking the Dark Man Kool-Aid, *glub-glub-glub, refreshing ice-cold India ink, it hunts best in the pitch, paid in blood, ohhh yeahhhh*—wasn't surprised by the music that slipped through the speakers.

Blue Oyster Cult's "Don't Fear the Reaper." Stevie Wonder's "Superstition." The Doors' "This Is the End."

I barked a crazed laugh when Queen's "Another One Bites the Dust" hissed through the static on the FM dial.

"I get the fucking point," I said.

The radio snatched another station. A wicked, never-ending cackle roared from the dash. I shrieked. Vincent Price laughed on and on in his timeless walk-off from the Michael Jackson song "Thriller." The Dark Man, it seemed, had a sense of humor.

It'll play, Mr. Taylor, play with you like ...

" ... a cat plays with a ... "

Tktktk.

I switched off the radio.

"Grih-grih," I muttered. I squeezed my eyes shut and opened them, focused on the road ahead. Watched the highway's dividing line tick past the car hood.

"*Grip.* Get. A. Grip. Zach."

The air from the dashboard vents blasted hot, drying my eyes. I blinked, savoring the cascading warmth. The Doberman behind me growled, as if suddenly understanding.

"You're not real," I said. "You're a psychic virus. A transmythssion. A figment."

The thing's jaws snapped now, hollow fangs clicking in a vibra-slap staccato. The sound of skulls.

"That's right. Drake was patient zero, brainwashing us with his CIA training, spreading his sickness. But you're paranoia. You're delusion. You're ... not ... real."

An awful sound hailed from behind me—the sound of slop dumped from a bucket. The heater still blasted, but my body jolted uncontrollably, wracked with shivers. The thick splash hadn't come from below. It came from above.

It was on the ceiling.

"Not real," I whispered.

My hair stood on end. Icy spider legs swirled across my arms, my neck, my face.

Jesus Christ, it's on the ceiling and it's sagging now, the sound, *dear God, milkshake sucked through a straw, no, not real, colder, getting colder in here, Antarctic wind, no, not*

" ... real," I hissed. "Not."

Loud, by my ear: *TKTKTK.*

I screamed.

The cell phone in my hip pocket sang "Birdhouse In Your Soul."

Rachael. I pulled out the phone, hit "talk," smiling, relieved and grateful—so goddamned grateful.

"What kind of macho bullshit is this?" she snapped. " ' ... So I'm going north, to pull its gaze away from all us ... to just one of us.' What's gotten into you, Z? You don't just *do* this, you can't just up and leave without telling us. We *waited* for you. Waited for more than an—"

"Baby, I'm sorry," I said. The gooseflesh relinquished its hold on my skin. "I couldn't, just couldn't. You and Luc are all I have. I—"

"What?"

"You guys are it, babe, all I've got. You were nearly killed tonight. If this thing's real, I won't let it—"

"—eaking up," Rachael's voice said. "—amn it, Z, we're suppos—"

I gripped the wheel. No. Goddamned cell phone reception failure, not now.

"Rache, listen. I'm the bait, it's the only way. I wouldn't be able to live ... "

My voice trailed off, distracted. The car was warm again. No, the car was *hot* again. No feeling of being watched, no slither sounds, no bucket of Black sloshing in the backseat.

Flash-bulb memory: Drake's last word to me yesterday, as I ran from Room 507.

Pray. Or prey.

"Oh no," I said.

"—ach, you're ... —ouble here ...—ow ... no ...—eam—"

"No," I said. I stared at the midnight wilderness before me. "Don't you dare, not her, you fucker. No, oh no, no-no-no—"

"—help—"

The line went dead.

The dashboard vents whirred merrily, filling the interior with white noise and hot air. My fists pounded the steering wheel as I wailed, sweat suddenly streaming from my pores. The phone was worthless. I threw it into the passenger seat, snarling, sick at heart.

Tears made the yellow line ahead blur and shimmer, a night-time mirage.

You've damned her. Damned them all.

The wheel's leather grip moaned as I squeezed tighter. I hated myself. Hated Drake. Hated the inky thing hunting us.

Uncle Henry's voice: *Sometimes you find the path ...*

Too late. Too late to turn back.

My foot punched the accelerator. Eighty. Ninety. Past ninety.

"Come and get me, you cold-hearted son of a bitch," I growled to the Dark Man. "I'm heading to your home. Come and get me."

I drove, alone.

Daniel Drake's house rose out of the blackness like a theater prosce-
nium, blasted bright by the Saturn's headlights. The thing reminded me of a rotten tooth, mottled with decay, covered in filth and

splinters. The one-story building felt taller than it had yesterday morning. Impossible, I knew; a trick of the light. But it loomed and leered at me, its darkened windows now eye sockets.

Watching, like tot-lot ghouls.

I killed the engine and the headlights. I slung my satchel onto my shoulder and stepped out into the chilly midnight air. I clicked on the Maglite. My eyes adjusted to the stark contrast of bright and darkness. Above me, the moon was fat, nearly full.

I was grateful for the flashlight: it wasn't enough. I felt my nyctophobia pumping fear into my brains, my veins—but for this moment, the emotion was far away, glimmering like a lighthouse beacon. There were other emotions throbbing in my mind—anger, determination, concern. What overpowered them all was the flat sensation of sleepwalking ... of arrival without travel ... of inevitability.

Daniel's blue pickup was gone. I peered at the building, listening. Music rose and fell from the living room, muffled by the walls. I walked through the muddy front yard to the porch. The house remained lightless, lifeless.

The music was clearer now. "Night On Bald Mountain."

My knuckles rapped against the cracked front door. No answer. I knocked louder, calling Daniel's name. I pounded. I yelled. My voice echoed in the night. I thought of Bethany Walch, the woman who'd befriended Richard Drake and his son ten years ago. The one who'd been threshed right along with the hay.

We heard her screams three miles away.

No answer.

I stepped from the porch, skulking to the side of the house, comforted by the heft of the Maglite in my hand.

Its bulb did not flicker, didn't strobe as I'd seen a dozen times in the past few days. The Dark Man didn't want to warn me this time. The bulb inside blasted ultra-bright for a moment—far too short a time for me to realize what was happening until after it'd happened—and then it shattered, the tiny shrapnel shards tinkling against the lens glass.

I stopped, glancing first at the dead weight in my hand and then to the sky, looking for the spotlight above. My fear of the dark surged like a wave, cold oil on my clammy skin, as a cloud swept over the moon.

Black. The whole world had gone black.

I doubled over, dropping the flashlight, clutching my arms, my stomach, gasps hissing from between my teeth. The fear ... was a swarm.

My mind flickered, on-off-on-off, just like the Brinkvale hallways, Room 507, the hellshow, a horror strobe light. Bile, sweet and sickening, gushed against my tongue, filling my mouth.

Nonsense filled my head. I seethed, breath screeching as I hyperventilated, thick spit oozing from my lips, *and this is how it ends Zach, alone in the dark, gobbled by black flies, shoo fly shoo, shoes, pinned me down to my six-month-old-Vans, pinned like a lepidopterist pins a-mazing Grace how sweetthesoundthatsavedawretchlikeme*

My knees buckled. I fell. The phobia was my blood, my air, the pillow pressed to my face. And my God, the faces came now, all painted black, eyes and teeth frightfully white: Emilio (*Vuhvammpire,* he said) and Drake (*Be sure to* breathe, *Mr. Taylor*) and Henry (*mercenary, a thing summoned from the*) and oh God, there was Mom, pupil-less, blood bubbling from her mouth, singing me a nightmare lullaby. *Would you be mine? Could you be mine?*

My cheek pressed into the cold mud. Black vacuum. Airless. Soundless.

A century passed. An eon. And then, finally, the cloud's tendrils swept past the moon. The world around me brightened slightly. Air rushed into my lungs.

I stood, body quaking, eyes blinking. I remained still, waited for the lights in my brain to come back on. I didn't move until I was certain I wouldn't piss myself.

The sound came from ahead, from behind the wood-frame house.

Tktktk. Tktktk.

"Back," I said, slinging a palmful of spit from my mouth. My voice sounded alien, unused. I was drowning in the fear now. I coughed a manic laugh, recalling an AC/DC song.

"Back In Black," I said.

Tktktk.

I stepped forward, nodding at the noise, heading to the rear of Drake's home. I passed a waist-high pile of chopped wood. Yellow eyes glittered from the gaps between the blocks. Raccoons. Or darkling friends, perhaps.

The grass field behind the house rustled, whispered. I came to the back door and tried its knob. Locked. I brought my nose to the cracked window, gazed into the kitchen. The world inside was soaked in black velvet.

"DANIEL!" I shouted.

The wind swept in, carrying away my voice. The field whispered. And now my mind whispered ... whispered slippery, boozy confidence. Oh, I knew this voice. It purred, the voice of a slut, the voice of sin, the voice of the doppelganger—the side we deny ourselves because it always brings misery and madness.

Hi there, Zach, it said. *Long time.*

"Anti-Zach," I replied.

I'd lost my mind. I was certain of it now.

We're back on the wild ride, ain't we? Finally? Repeat performance.

"One night only," I agreed, staring at the doorknob's cheap lock.

Oh, gooood. Giddy-giddy.

Yes. Giddy-giddy. I opened my satchel and let my fingers slide inside, groping for the folder containing Drake's Brinkvale admittance papers. I plucked a paperclip from the stack and pulled it from the bag. It glimmered in the moonlight.

I tugged at the wire, fingernails bending and denting it, using my teeth when I needed to, just like the old days, the A-Z days.

See, Z? You oughta keep me around. You need me. I ain't as bad as you think.

"No," I said, jigging the pick into the knob. "You're worse."

Ouch, partner. And can you live with that? Can you live with me being in your head?

The lock clicked. The door swung open.

"Let's first see if I can live through tonight," I said.

I stepped inside, on a mission to find the "X" on Drake's mural map—the thing he'd brought me here to find. The darkness enveloped me, and I could feel the beast here, could nearly hear the saliva dripping from its black fangs.

Anti-Zach had enough sense not to follow.

✳✳✳

The kitchen reeked of bacon grease, rotten food, cigarettes ashes and beer. My hand found a light switch by the door and toggled it up, then down, then up again. No dice. Daniel Drake's electric bill was still unpaid.

The room felt like a walk-in freezer. I shivered now, marveling at the vapor puffing from my lips. The walls were alive, crawling with shadows, creaking, *tktktking*. I wondered which ones were the Dark Man, and which were my fright-trip imagination.

"Night On Bald Mountain" played on and on from the living room ahead, presumably from a CD.

The fear-needles poked at my skin, a thousand cold fingernails nicking and scratching. I told myself to breathe, to stay calm, that there was light in here, there really was, look, see, light.

My eyes adjusted to a keyhole's worth of moonlight streaming through the window. It wasn't nearly enough. I pressed my body along the wall, determined to traverse the room along its perimeter, inching against its walls and counters and

BONG.

I flinched, swearing. My hand flailed in the darkness, searching for the thing against which my hip had struck. Metal, smooth, pebbled with grime, grease-slick. My fingers found the wrought-iron cooking grates, and I nodded. Stove.

The walls tittered.

I stepped around the appliance, hand now sliding across its surface, now feeling the steel give way to pocked countertop. My fingertips parted a sea of crumbs, then pressed into something half-eaten, mushy. For a heartbeat, I was more revolted by this room than I was afraid of it.

The meager moonlight began to wane, victim of another cloud. I held my breath, desperate and sick again. No. Not now. Please, Lord. Not now.

My hand brushed against a small cardboard box, and I picked it up, praying for a box of matches. I shook it. The ex-smoker in me heard the ubiquitous rattle of cigarettes inside. I pitched it

The kitchen was darker now. From the living room, the music began to stutter, fade in and out.

My hand groped again, and my panic rose again, blazing red-hot, blowing hypothermic in this icy room. Come, damn it. Come on.

"Come on," I whispered.

The music roared louder, surging with static.

My sweating palm grasped the hilt of something plastic and I fumbled with it in the dark, hungry to understand it, see it by touch alone. Plastic handle, metal nozzle. A grill lighter—the thing with which Daniel Drake lit his gas stove, his cigarettes.

I sighed, index finger sliding past the trigger guard. I pressed its switch. The room flared to life.

Daniel Drake stood before me, his eyes bloodshot and murderous.

A whiskey bottle hung from one hand. In his other, a hatchet.

"You again," he muttered, swaying.

I was stupefied, scared stiff.

"Never *here*. He was *never here.* And when he finally came home, Mom and Jenny died."

His breath was putrid from the booze. My mouth tried to find words, but my brain was stuck, vapor locked. I suddenly needed to pee.

The living room thunderstorm raged on, even louder now.

"Obsessed, he was insane, obsessed," Daniel said. He shrugged his broad shoulders. "He ruined *everything*. He ruined our brand-new life out here. My life. *Her* life. And. And then ... "

He dropped the whiskey bottle. It shattered on the floor.

" ... he ... "

Daniel snarled, hefting the hatchet in both hands now.

" ... left."

The radio trumpeted a final crescendo, then fell silent.

"It's *you*," I said, backing away, the lighter's flame still flickering between us. "You tracked them, all of them, all of his friends. *You* killed them.

"You're the Dark Man."

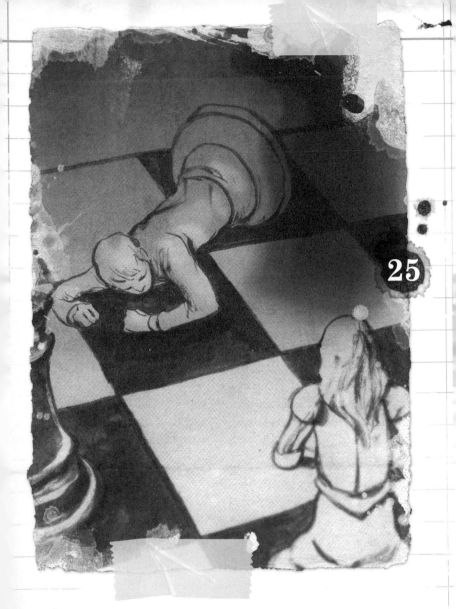

25

Daniel clomped forward, closing the gap. The countertop dug into my ass, immovable. I glanced about in the shadowdance, frantically doing an inventory of the cramped kitchen. Stove beside me.

Refrigerator across the room. Between them: counters, sink. In the kitchen's center, a weathered thrift-store table and two rickety, mismatched chairs.

An open jar of peanut butter on the counter. Empty booze bottles in the sink. Skillet on the table, writhing with roaches. Unwashed plates there. Crumpled cans of Coors.

GOD BLESS THIS MESS.

I resisted a suicidal urge to laugh.

"No. No, fucker," Daniel Drake said. His massive form swayed in place. He grinned knowingly. "No-fucking-comprendo. Dad's the killer, was always the killer. He brought something back with him from the See-See-See-Pee. A curse. An Inkstain. He could see the future, see the blood a-comin', and he ran. God, *all the blood* ... "

His hollow, hopeless face twisted into a sneer.

" ... and oh, the blood that'd come and gone, Jesus, the things he did. I *know*. I *saw*. Extra-shittin'-extra, read all a-fuckin'-bout it. Them people he killed in Russia. All the letters that came here after he left, all them government letters, letters from fucking lawyers— oh, he *knew*, he *knew* I'd see 'em, knew they were comin', I know he *knew*. I read 'em all. I burned 'em all."

He glanced down, at the stained throw rug beneath his feet. His mouth curved into a toothy, meat cleaver smile.

"Well. *Almost* all of 'em."

"Daniel, put the hatchet down," I said, still holding the grill lighter between us. "I'm here because your dad sent me. He wants me to find something here, in this house, something that can help him. Maybe it's you, the things you've read. You've gotta come back with me, come back to The Brink. Your father needs you. Your ... your *family* needs you."

The walls seemed to rattle as the man laughed. The hatchet's thick blade shimmered in his hands. He leaned in. The fire's reflection burned bright in his eyes, turning them coal-red.

"ME?" he cried. "Sounds like he needs you more than he ever needed *me*. You, the stranger, the meddler, the gravedigger, diggin' it all out, bringin' it all back, filled with worms and bugs ... "

Tktktk.

" ... and you wanna fix 'im, cure 'im, so he can see. And then what, gravedigger? I'll tell you what. More. More killin', more dyin'. No. That can't happen. He's earned this. He *deserves* this. He's the walking dead. And you. ... *You.*"

He puckered his lips and blew. The lighter's flame vanished.

"You're just dead."

I heaved my body to the right, away from the stove, as the darkness spiraled upon us. An instant later, the room filled with the splinter-blast of axe blade meeting Formica. The lighter slipped from my hand, clattering into the ink.

"No, Daniel!" I screamed, but the man's raspy breath devolved into another grunt, and I scuttled further, nearing the sink and window above it.

The hatchet was a thunderclap, shredding the dish cabinet where my head had been. The blade gave a shrill, throaty squeak as Daniel yanked it from the wood. I stumbled on, hands smacking against the booze bottles in the sink. I stole a half second to look down, using the moonlight from the window as a spotlight. I grabbed a bottle, held it like a club.

The man chuckled in the darkness. A hand fired from the black, clapping hard against my chest. I snatched at something—anything—to keep from falling. Miraculously, my fingers gripped the sink's faucet. I used it for leverage, staying upright, gasping in dread as the metal began to bend. Bottles clinked cheerfully as my forearm clashed against them.

"*Gotcha*," Daniel hissed.

The hatchet roared downward again, destroying the bottles in the sink, missing my hand by an inch. I felt the bee sting of glass slicing my skin. Daniel wrenched the axe wildly upward. Its blade blew through the kitchen window, scattering thick shards across the countertop. They tinkled like knives nested together in a drawer.

I found my footing, madly swinging the bottle in my hand. It detonated against the axe handle, spraying razor-edged jewels that sparkled in the dim light from the window. Daniel roared. He dropped the weapon, hands pressed against his face.

I lunged toward the floor, intent on grabbing the axe. A steel-toed work boot bashed into my stomach, blowing the air from my lungs in a surprised scream. I slid, nearly fell ... but Daniel's hands snatched my shirt, yanking me skyward.

I felt my feet leave the ground. Zero-G.

He slammed my back into another cabinet, leaning close, his grinning, blood-soaked face glowing bright in the moonlight. Glass shards glittered in his cheeks, his chin. One flashed from his gums, bathing his teeth in a gushing stream of blood.

He shoved again, sending my back into the cabinet. The dishes inside clattered, cheering for more destruction.

"KILL YOU," Daniel roared.

And then I was airborne, heaved in a one-eighty, a boneless scarecrow in free fall ... and now, my body collided with the kitchen table, smashing through it, finally impacting on the floor. Plates and beer cans shattered and clanked around my face. The skillet bonged, bouncing across the linoleum, landing near my arm.

Stars filled the room. Blood filled my mouth.

Daniel was relentless. He crouched low. His fist smashed against my face. I cried out, asking him to stop, no, I didn't want to die in the dark. The world rocked as he punched me again.

My hand groped in the darkness, searching for the skillet. Daniel saw this and kicked it away. It clanged against a wall, out of reach.

My fingers still crawled forward, grasping nothing ...

The wet crunch of knuckle blasted through my skull.

... grasping air ...

Daniel was wheezing. The shadows on the ceiling were laughing in the dimness. *Tktktk.*

... grasping the hatchet's handle.

I let loose a war cry and swung the thing. It was unbalanced and heavy in my hand. The blade whooshed in the darkness for a breathless eternity, and then sank home in Daniel Drake's shin. The room filled with a nasty *thock* sound.

He staggered, his back striking the sink cabinet. I heard him tug the axe from his leg—the sound of tearing wet lettuce—and he was screaming now, screaming loud and long, like a child.

"You want ... want t0 ... KNOW MY FATHER?" he shrieked.

His hands were tugging at something beside me—the frayed, filthy throw rug.

"HUH, gravedigger?! HUH? You want to KNOW him?! Go JOIN him!"

I stared dumbly as his finger snaked around a metal ring in the floor. I tried not to choke on my own blood, not to hear the skitter-scratches screaming in my ears.

Daniel opened the trapdoor.

"Be BURIED with him!" he screamed.

His boot crushed my side. He swung his fist. Another lightning bolt blasted across my eyes.

I felt my body being dragged slowly toward the hole in the floor. I struggled. It didn't matter. Nothing mattered.

I fell. The door slammed shut.

And the dark ... began to speak.

26

The lizard part of my brain—the part hardwired for instinct and survival—ran the numbers and grunted a deduction. Cold ground beneath me. The overpowering, stale aroma of earth, dust, rat shit. Boards creaking less than two feet above my prone, bleeding body. Crawl space.

And that was my last rational thought for a while.

Blind. Blind like Richard Drake. Eyes open now, staring into the abyss, and yes, yes, it stared back at me, an ancient thing, a thing from before *before,* and I was sinking into its planet-sized onyx pupil, drowning in its inky aqueous humor, feeling my body pull into itself, crushed by the absence of light, warmth, sound, everything.

Everything ... but the fear.

Fingers like rail spikes ripped at me, impossibly cold, burning my skin. Shrieks fell short in my throat; there was no air in which they could be heard. But my mind was alive with sounds: the marching of spider's legs, the rising drone of locusts, the swirling scattering of autumn leaves—*tktktkt*—the roar of rockslides

stones rattling in a clothes dryer, she tumbles and tumbles

and now the soul-rending sound of a chuckle, the noise thunderclouds make as they collide and devour one another, growing fat and black for the storm to end all storms.

The Dark Man breathed. Panted, like a hungry dog. I imagined its forked tongue slick with crude-oil drool. It was omniscient. Omnipresent.

"Not ... real," I muttered.

But the shadow-chill slid over me, wrapped tight like a wetsuit, and I could feel the black, January lake water seeping through the membrane of my skin, full-body inoculation, a cure for *life*—life, the disease, the virus, the thing that must not be. It spoke back to me in its non-voice, a liquid language, sloshing affirmation in my inner ear: *oh-so-real, tktktk, oh-so-mine ... .*

Certainty. This was where I would die. This was my grave. The grave for the meddler, the gravedigger, dead, dead's dead, what's dead's buried, you'd be right to leave it alone.

Buried.

I rocked, weightless in the void, my mind seizing upon this. Join him, Daniel had said. Be buried with him. What did that mean? Was Richard Drake's body buried down—

I howled. The black stuff streamed *into* my eyes now, tears in reverse, piercing my ducts, turning my eyeballs into cold marbles.

—no no, focus, think of something else, Drake, yes, buried here? Then who's the blind man in The Brink? Body in the crawl space ... I need light, I need to see.

I screamed. Razor blades tearing beneath my fingernails now. I screamed again. Echoless.

no. no-tktktk-no-light-so-dark-no-light-now

No. No matches, no lighter, no flashlight in my satchel, nothing in the bag to beat away the

BZZZT.

What the f—

BZZZT.

This wasn't happening. I wasn't hearing that.

BZZZT.

I'd gone mad.

The black poured on in earnest now, slithering into my nose, tugging up my lips, squirting though my clenched teeth. I felt it surge through my pierced earlobes (*Christ, I haven't worn hoops in five yeaaaowww*), the ink squirming through them like tapeworms.

My frozen hands fumbled to my satchel, to the buzzing thing inside—the impossible thing, no signal, no sender—my stupid fingers finally wrapping around Richard Drake's cell phone. The cracked thing vibrated in my palm as I pulled out into the black, its LCD screen an impromptu flashlight, a beacon.

I read its screen, not daring to press it to my face, too frightened to listen. INCOMING CALL: SOPHRONIA POOLE. I held it high. The crawlspace came alive in its pale light—floorboards above, rotten earth beneath, limestone foundations. Three feet away, to my left: a crumpled, mold-soaked shoebox.

And there, looming near the box. Him.

It.

The Dark Man.

***

Picosecond glimpse

obsidian fire, shape of a man, crouching, depthless

Nothing made sense

shifting, intelligent, soundless black flames

anymore

torn paper, burned paper

Madness standing

electrified contortionist, jointless sea-snake limbs jigging, kicking wild

by the box

arms conducting palsied, unholy Butoh *dance*

It's guarding

ice-pick fingers twitch-blur-tugging invisible upright bass strings

the box

head rocking side-to-side, gleeful mania, seesaw-seesaw, cheeks clapping against obsidian shoulders

So what's

head of horns, head of vipers, head of smooth, polished stone

inside

faceless, but inside the nothing: beyond-black eyes ... beyond-black teeth

the box?

Tktktk.

I gritted my teeth, trembling. I pointed my makeshift lantern at its face.

"Would you be mine, motherfucker?" I whispered. "Could you be mine?"

The Beast roared.

✳✳✳

I clawed my way toward the crumpled shoebox, toward my boogeyman. I tasted dirt on my lips, felt it turn to bitter sludge against my teeth. This box was the "X," the thing Drake knew/didn't know, the thing his subconscious prayed was here. Endgame secrets, covered in decay.

The shade-shape splashed onto the crawl space ceiling, screeching, talons swiping the earth, raising no dust, leaving no marks. I edged closer.

"Unfinished business?" I growled, holding the glowing phone ahead of me. "Someone holding on, on the other line?" I gripped it tight, groaning as I inched forward—my body was beaten, nearly broken. "On the other side, maybe?"

Or maybe coincidence, bad timing, Rachael's voice said from a lifetime ago, as we'd chased Lucas. *Bad battery, battery going dead ...*

The phone's plastic case squealed and snapped in my hand. A hunk of plastic dug into my palm (*the battery cover,* I thought, panicked) then tumbled away. The cell's screen flickered. The device gave a malcontent chime. Fuck.

"Not stopping," I said, shivering. Vapor surged from my mouth as I gasped. "Not done. Can't let it go."

My torn, bleeding fingers pressed against the shoebox. The phone chimed another warning. The Dark Man wailed a laugh, and descended.

Earth became tar and we sank together into this new murk, his shark's teeth gnashing my legs, my ribs, and I still clutched the sputtering lantern, still tugged at the box bobbing on the slick, viscous surface. It tipped, and the contents of the box were swirling in the ether now, barely visible in the phone-glow.

My capillaries seized, freezing. My eyes fluttered, lungs burned.

I snatched a swirling sheet of paper—

Dear Danny, I have to leave, and I want you to know why...

—and then I gripped the document beside it, the copperplate letterhead already familiar to my mind—

CENTRAL INTELLI...

—and then my fingers found the photograph.

The phone peeped a feeble chime. Battery nearly gone. Its splintered screen light dipped from white to gray.

Do not humanize the Inkstain, Mr. Taylor, Drake cooed, far away. *The only human thing about it is the souls it shreds.*

The Dark Man began to shred.

The last of my air was lost in a churning, gurgling scream. The pain was indescribable. I stared at the photo with dead man's eyes.

A short man, angular face, crew cut, unfamiliar military fatigues. ALEXANDROV, PIOTYR, the typeface said in the photo's yellowed border.

DECEASED, it said.

The tearing and gnashing ceased. Sweet oxygen rushed into my lungs. I gasped, sucked in the air, terrified and grateful.

As the broken phone's light dimmed to nothing, I looked at the crawl space, at myself.

No new gashes, not a tooth mark. My clothes were intact. The letter and photos lay by my face, bone-dry.

The Dark Man ... if he was ever here ... was gone.

I closed my eyes, and passed out.

27

The crawl space was marginally brighter when I awoke. Slivers of sunlight peeked through cracks in the foundation around me and the floorboards above.

I shifted in the dirt, slapping a hand over my mouth to suppress a sudden shriek. The Dark Man may not have left a mark, but Daniel certainly had. The muscles in my torso and face sang from his beating; the pain was exquisite and loud, a full-body cathedral choir. My tongue teased at a loose tooth. My right eye seemed to move in a viscous syrup—the beaten, bruised flesh around it had swelled, nearly sealing it. I gritted and groaned, sliding across the filth toward the place I'd landed last night.

I longed for Lucas and his parkour-honed "field medic" talents. I imagined him in my Alphabet City living room, hand over contemplative mouth, considering me ... and then turning to Rachael: *Now* this, *my dear Hochrot, is the face of a foolbiscuit.*

I grinned ... then fretted over the loose tooth.

Lucas and Rachael. My tribe. I couldn't wait to—

"Oh, shit," I whispered. My voice was hoarse, ragged.

Richard Drake said they'd been marked. When Rachael had called last night, the car's heater had surged back to life, and that feeling of being ... *hunted* ... had vanished for the duration of my drive here. Had the monster rushed back to the city? Had it devoured my lover? My brother? Then returned to confront me down here?

"Oh, shit," I said again.

The Dark Man is here, behind you, whispering, showing me how you're going to die...

Yes. Richard Drake had said that. And he'd said that Rachael, Lucas and Dad were going to die, too—but he say didn't how, or when. Rachael's last word to me as the cell phone died in my hand had been "help."

My hands trembled as I stuffed the shoebox documents and photo of Alexandrov into my satchel. I spared a moment to look at the fragile cell phone that had saved my life. Hunks of its plastic case and buttons were missing, exposing blackened circuits. A vertical crack bisected its dark LCD screen. I flipped it over and gazed at the exposed battery. It was covered in barnacles of corrosion.

I placed it in the shoebox and closed the lid. The phone—*or its caller,* I thought—deserved to be, finally, at rest.

And now, I needed to get out of here, man, right now, *giddy-giddy.* I tore through the earth, reaching the trap door, bracing for the pain that would sweep over me as I would shove open the trapdoor, bolt out of the crawl space and run to the car. God, this was gonna suck.

Wait.

I paused, did as I was told. My lizard brain was growling. I listened. If Daniel Drake were somewhere in the house, waiting to finish me off ...

Chill, Z. Take a breath. Go slow, for God's sake, go slow.

I placed my palms against the door and pushed upward, gently. Its hinges creaked.

My eyes rose above the scuffed linoleum like a periscope. Daniel's body lay in the center of the room. His legs were splayed across the remains of the shattered kitchen table. The man's left shin—obviously the leg I'd hit with the hatchet—was wrapped in a blood-soaked dishtowel and cinched tight with a leather belt. The hatchet rested against his belly. Daniel's glass-shredded face was covered in dried blood. He was snoring.

I pulled myself up through the trapdoor, hands sliding in the tacky blood on the floor, desperate to be quiet.

Daniel blew out another foghorn snore ... and then his ass tooted a fart, almost like an exclamation point. I choked back a half-laugh, half-sob of pain. I hated him, but I couldn't leave him like this. I told myself to call an ambulance when I had access to a working phone.

Seconds later, I was up and gone, hobbling through the back yard, past the grass field. Its tall blades swished in the morning breeze, a thousand-thousand fingers waving goodbye in the eastern sunrise.

Working the Saturn's pedals was an excruciating chore.

The rotten-tooth house finally sank into the rearview mirror, and I sighed, grateful to be gone.

And when the car hit the interstate, I slammed the accelerator to the floor.

Cell phone reception.

I needed cell phone reception.

***

Speedometer: 85 MPH. Dashboard digital clock: 7:22 AM.

Nausea swirled in my belly and I dry-heaved with fright. It was a wordless drive, surrounded by the dim roar of the passing road, punctuated by the screams in my mind. The screams of a World Without.

She's my anchor, my sail, the second half of my heartbeat. She grounds me, electrifies me, excites me, astounds me with her brilliance and talent, and loving her is the easiest thing I've ever done ... effortless, natural, true. Always there, my cheerleader, my coach, my teammate, my perfect fit.

Kid brother, trusty sidekick, ever-present reminder to bounce, to stay lively and propitious, to never take life too seriously. Pop Rocks for the soul.

Father, the man to whom I owe my skepticism, my rationalism, the Bedrock of Me, the source of my hunger to do right, to fix the world ...

Rachael's tattooed chest gushed blood, flayed by a maniac. Now, her body was bisected on subway tracks, shoved by a stranger. Raped. Worse.

"No," I muttered.

Lucas' face flaking black, house fire flames consuming his body. Head crushed on concrete, a parkour move gone bad. Shot, bam-bam-bam, strutting Alphabet City punks back to settle their tenpin score.

"Please, no."

Dad's screaming face, dunked in a men's-room toilet in One Hogan Place, parole violator dead-set on payback.

"God, if you can hear me ... "

But He didn't.

The visions blasted on, kaleidoscopic, tungsten-flares of midnight murder and mania, of my beloveds' lives ending terribly, quietly, slowly, bullet-train fast. And then, a life's worth of feeling the gaping World Without, with a new breed of nyctophobia: a darkness of the heart, no reason to keep beating. My fuel, my fire, gone forever.

Forever.

Tears slid down my smashed face. I glanced at the dash-board clock.

7:23 AM.

Nightmare minute.

If they were dead, it was my fault. All. My. Fault.

"Please, God. *Please.*"

90 MPH now.

***

And then, as the car screamed ever-southward, just miles away from Claytonville Prison: skeleton song.

I'd already been clutching my cell phone, watching for reception bars to wink on-screen. My thumb frantically jabbed the "voice mail" button; the thing could've dialed in at warp speed and it still wouldn't be fast enough.

First message. 10:38 PM last night. Rachael.

Z? Lost you. Come back to the city—don't go up there, please.

Second message. Also last night. 11:07. Dad.

Call me back. We need to work this out.

Third message. 6:30 AM today.

I smiled and wept.

"Z, it's Rachael—"

"—and Lucas. Bro, you're—"

"—It's us. Please call when you can. We've been up all night—"

"—dude, Dad's flipped his shit, you *gotta*—"

"—shut *up*, Luc. So yes, please call. We're in a bad place over here ... and thanks to your father, so's your blind man. Wicked stuff is about to go down, Z. Call back. I love you."

" 'Dore!" Lucas called.

The voice mail ended. I dialed Rachael's cell. She picked up on the first ring.

"Hey, it's me," I said. I struggled to keep my voice even; I'd been exhaustion's punching bag—the surge of elation was too much. The tears still came. "You're ... you're alive."

"You are, too," she replied. Her voice trembled, and I realized she was doing the same thing, miles away. I smiled through the tears. We were puzzles pieces clicking home, in sync once more.

"Oh Jesus, Zach," she said. "You have no idea ... you'll never, ever know."

I did, a little. A World Without.

"I'm coming home," I said. "I want ... No. Need. I need to see you, be with you."

"Are you okay?"

I glanced at the ghoul's eye staring back at me in the rear-view mirror.

"No. No, babe."

And then I said the only thing I could say. It was stupidly inadequate. Words are sometimes like that—failures of our species, hollow caveman grunts strung together to represent things bigger than the world itself.

"I'm sorry."

"Oh, Z," Rachael said. "Oh, baby. You should be. You'd *better* be. I love you, but you're in the red, don't think for a minute that you're not. Listen to me. If. You. *Ever.*"

I wiped away my tears, nodding. "Yeah."

"No, I need to say this. If you ever do anything like this again, we're through. It's simple math. We're together, Z; we're a couple. That means we're coupled *together*, to each other. You can't just run off. You can't fight a war by yourself."

"I thought I was protecting—"

"I know what you thought, and it was chivalrous and noble and selfless ... and pretty damned selfish. This isn't about *you*, baby. It's about *us*. If you want to keep me in your life, then *keep me in your life*. We're a team. We fight our wars together. If you want to fight on your own, then have the courage and decency to tell me to my face. I like love letters, Z—but I don't truck with lone letters. Get me?"

I did, and told her so. Rachael didn't believe in the Dark Man as I did; she hadn't heard its skitter-slide, hadn't felt its icy breath on her neck, hadn't *seen*. She didn't understand ... but that didn't make her wrong. No, she was absolutely right. I never tried to explain. I abandoned her and Lucas, fueled by obsession and a need, a primal, seemingly-cellular need, to see it done.

I was more like my father—and Richard Drake—than I'd ever imagined.

"I love you, geek goddess," I said.

"I love you back, hottie artist," Rachael replied. "You're in the doghouse, but at least you're loved."

I smiled. "I'll take it."

"And now the bad news," she said. "Your dad called Lucas last night after he tried to reach you. He's pulling Drake out of The Brink."

I stiffened ... and winced. "He's what?"

"He's leveraging yesterday's accident as a reason to transfer Drake."

"Emilio... " I muttered. "He's probably doing it to bolster his case. Literally. Get Drake out of The Brink, make him out to be a violent psychotic, get him away from me. 'Conflict of interest' no more."

"Maybe. Or maybe he wants to protect you. We don't know, but he told Luc that he's bulldozing through whatever red tape to make it happen. He's on a tear, Z, calling in big favors. It's happening today, and there's apparently nothing you or Brinkvale can do about it. At noon, Drake is gone ... and it's over."

"Over," I said. I glanced at my satchel resting in the passenger seat. There was a letter and two photographs inside—things Drake had consciously—or unconsciously—wanted me to find. Why?

"Dunno."

"What was that?" Rachael asked.

I looked back to the road ahead. A green exit sign rose on the horizon: Claytonville.

"I don't think it's over, Rache," I said. "Answers. I need answers."

"What's that supposed to mean?"

A wave of guilt, thick and sickening, passed over me. I couldn't tell her about Uncle Henry. That was black, soul-wracking family history. I didn't believe the revelation would fundamentally change the way she saw me, felt about me ... but it would damn my father in her eyes. And my late grandmother, who had gone along with the plan. And then the secret would fester between us, with Lucas oblivious, intangibly damaging us, all three of us. It wasn't a fair burden to share.

It didn't feel right to tell her. But it wasn't right to *not* tell her.

"Do you trust me?" I asked.

"Don't answer my question with a question, damn it. I said, 'What's that supposed to mean?'"

I cringed.

"I found some things at the Drake house—a letter from the CIA, a photo of the Russian. I don't know what they mean, baby. I don't know what to do. But I know that Drake didn't kill those people, and he doesn't deserve whatever Hell my dad's got planned for him. I ... I know ... I know someone who might be able to help me. I need to talk to him. And then I have to go to The Brink."

"Who's 'him?'" she asked.

And here it was, in the most honest terms I could muster:

"An ... an old friend. Someone who believes in the Dark Man."

Silence.

"You're not going to tell me any more, are you?" she asked.

"I will, if we're on the edge," I said. And despite the misery that would come, I would. "Are we?"

She sighed. "What's *with* you, Zach? Are you *trying* to ruin us? Didn't we just cover this?"

"That's why I'm telling you what I can. That's why I'm asking if you trust me."

"You know I trust you."

"Then can you live with not knowing? At least for right now?"

"Damn it, that's not fair and you know it."

I was rushing toward the exit for Claytonville. I reached for the turn signal out of habit—preposterous, considering the Saturn was the sole car on this stretch of blacktop—but pulled my hand away. This, this moment, was important.

No. This was the most important moment.

"I know," I whispered.

"You're so in the red, kiddo," Rachael said. "Go. Go do your thing and come home safe. We'll fight and then we'll fuck and you'll cook dinner for the next month. And maybe, when we're both ready, you can tell me about this. Deal?"

I loved her more than anything right then. I truly did.

My fingers flipped the turn signal. I merged left.

"Deal."

* * *

I shambled through Claytonville's atrophied limestone halls like the bloodied, filth-covered zombie I undoubtedly resembled. Even this prison's most jaded corrections officers performed bug-eyed double takes at the sight of me: one part of my brain thought I should be proud of that; it was hard to shock the guards in a facility that housed homicidal lost causes—who now happened to be cleaner and better-dressed than me.

The last time I was here, I'd trembled with dread, anxiety, anger and a need ... a need to know. Now, I was too broken, too *spent,* to feel any of those things. I'd been through an emotional atom-smasher. I needed a friend who understood.

"Lemme guess," said the barrel-chested guard as we walked toward the visitor's room. He looked me over and winked. "I should see the other guy. Right?"

I grunted. "I *was* the other guy."

"Ouch."

"Brother, I've got 'ouch' on speed dial."

The rusted door screeched open and in I stepped, alone again in the wide room with its row of semi-private nooks, panes of floor-to-ceiling shatterproof glass, and security cameras. I moaned as I sat, again reminding myself of a George Romero movie refugee. The ghostly reflection staring back at me in the glass was—sweet Christmas—worse than I imagined.

Walking dead, pardner. Brainnnns.

"Hush," I hissed.

And, like two days ago, a fire-alarm bell trilled for a moment ... and then my uncle emerged from the open door beyond the glass. The same guard followed him. Henry sat down across from me. The guard announced that we had ten minutes, and stepped backward, watching us.

Henry gazed at me, his gray eyebrows furrowed with concern. His face did not twist in revulsion as the others' had; I supposed he'd seen worse during his twenty years here.

"What happened?" he asked.

"The path found me," I deadpanned.

Henry's bearded face crinkled into a slight smile. He started to speak again, but I waved my hand: *It's cool, we're cool, let me finish.*

"The man the newspapers call Martin Grace drew a map that sent me to his son's home," I said. "I was sent there to find something. His son did ... well, he did *this*." I shrugged, self-conscious. I remembered the cameras, and didn't want to incriminate myself any more than I already had. "I fought back, took him down. But I did the right thing. Called 911 from the pay phone in the lobby. I think he'll be okay."

"They're resourceful when they're curious," Henry said. "Trace it back here, check with visitor logs."

I nodded. "And if the county lush cares to press charges, I'll happily take my licks. But I don't think he'll do that. He's like his father; it's just not in him to heal. He's lost enough already."

I leaned forward and stared into his blue eyes.

"I saw it."

Henry's face was solemn. "I can tell. You don't fall into the black and come away completely whole." He raised his finger, as if to explain. The charms on his bracelet jingled. "I don't mean physically. There's a very large, sometimes very frightening, world just beside—and beneath and above—this one. That world scraped against you, Zach. It changes you. Like it changed you twenty years ago."

"Yes."

The silence lasted no more than five seconds. It felt like a day.

"Drake said I was marked," I said. "Me and Lucas and Dad. And my girlfriend."

Henry's eyes ticked across my body. He squinted. He nodded very slowly.

"Did you find," he asked, "what you were sent to find?"

"I ... I don't know. I think so, but it doesn't make sense. A photo and a letter from Big Brother. The monster was protecting them, like a watchdog."

I shivered then, recalling the Dark Man's fingers shredding my skin.

"And why doesn't that make sense?" Henry said.

"Because what I found basically nullified the only thing going for me in the Drake case. I thought someone else murdered all those people. A Russian. Why did Drake send me there? I didn't gain anything. Poof, there's the proof, not true."

Henry squinted. "It had a vested interest in protecting them. Maybe there's more power in what you found."

"And maybe Drake sent me there to die," I said. "He knew his son would be there, knew the Dark Man would be waiting and hungry. I was 'marked,' after all. Double cross, kill the threat. I'm the only one, perhaps ever, who's gotten this close to ... to curing him."

I sighed. "I think ... I think I beat it," I said. "It saw the photo of the Russian, the man who'd vowed vengeance against Drake. It should've killed me, but it vanished."

Henry took a deep breath and exhaled. He shook his head as slowly as he'd nodded a minute ago.

"Know this, son. Things like the Dark Man are never 'beaten.' There's nothing in this world that *can* beat them. They're hired guns. They leave when they've done their job."

"You said you were there, back then, when the Dark Man killed Mom. You told me we were under attack. You saved Lucas, you said. It was beaten. It left. How?"

"It did what it was told to do. It took a beloved of Will's, just as Will had … "

He stopped.

"Zach, if it's gone, then you found its secret and put it to rest. Whatever was in that house was the key. The Dark Man has absolutes. It must do what it was born to do. The powers that control these monsters, the terms that govern when an unholy contract has been fulfilled—those are rarely absolute. If it's gone, its contract was fulfilled. You did it. I'm proud of you."

I scrubbed my face with my damaged hands, exasperated.

"But I don't know what to do now," I said. "Everything I've done to help Drake has had … heh … *catastrophic* results. And now he's getting pulled from The Brink. I've got—"

"Three minutes," the guard said.

"—I've got no reason to care," I continued. "I know this. I've done everything I can think of, I've broken every rule there is to break, I've gone emotionally and ethically bankrupt, and look, just look at me. Finally, I'm as banged up on the outside as I am on the inside. This is a job, just a fucking *job*, and no job's worth this. But."

I looked at him, anguished. Could he possibly understand?

"But he's my patient, Henry. Does that make sense, what that means to me? No matter what happens in the trial, no matter what happens to him once he leaves The Brink, I want to help him now. I *need* to. I … I can't … "

" … let it go," Henry finished. He gave a serene, bittersweet smile, and lifted his eyes skyward. "That's why I'm here, Zach. Couldn't let go. Will finally got his wish because I couldn't let it go. It makes more sense than you'll know."

Goddamn it, I had so many questions about that day. About the twenty years that had come and gone. But there was no time.

Always running out of time.

"What's left?" I said.

Henry leaned even closer to the glass. "The Dark Man is an entity of vengeance, son. That's what it was built to be; it never *learned* to be this way. It is what it is. Absolute punishment, retribution that's as compassionless as the sin that brought it here. But is the Dark Man your roadblock?"

"No. It's Drake. His insistence."

Henry nodded. "He wants the blood washed from his hands. Not for the crimes he's accused of ... "

I blinked.

"... but for the ones he'll *never* be accused of," I said. "Red Show."

I finally understood—and my heart ached with the understanding.

"I should go," I said. "But I'll come back. If you'll have me."

For the first time in the twenty total minutes I'd spent with him, my uncle's face brightened and beamed. He smiled.

It looked like his first smile in twenty years.

28

11:30 AM, the scuffed Eterna on my wrist said.

I strode through The Brink's employee parking lot with new-found purpose, sucking in the crisp air, nodding at the gorgeous autumnal spectacle that was Primoris Maximus. And now my feet clomped up the limestone front steps of the hospital, my hands tugged open the two metal doors. I had steel in my veins, and an old friend riding shotgun in my head. I needed his brazen lawlessness, his steel, for the endgame.

I stopped in the doorway. Malcolm stood inside our sorry lobby, his mop in hand. He saw me and gasped. I shrugged—*No time to explain*—and glanced at the glimmering tiles. A yellow sign read, CAUTION: WET FLOOR.

"I owe you a bottle of Grey Goose, right?" I asked.

Malcolm nodded dumbly.

"What ... what the hell happened to you, boy?"

"I owe you two bottles now," I said, moving past him. My mud-spattered Vans left a trail of footprints across the freshly mopped floor.

"Sheeeeeit," Malcolm said.

I passed the scratched window of the Administrator's Office, heading toward the elevator. Lina Velasquez's cat's-eye glasses rose from her computer screen, and her eyes met mine. Her taut face went pale. She peeped a tiny scream.

I kept walking.

Behind me, I heard her slapping the glass, her rings *clack-clack-clacking*.

"Taylor!" she cried.

"It can wait," I said.

"Taylor! Muy urgente!"

I turned the corner, not listening.

More gasps from coworkers as I passed the break room. I heard a coffee mug shatter on the floor.

The elevator doors were directly ahead now. I walked faster down the long corridor, reached them, jabbed the metal "down" button with my thumb. It gave a loud, satisfying *thwack!* against the panel.

Dr. Peterson's voice called from behind me, his perfunctory staccato filling the hall. I'd never heard him raise his voice before. I'm not sure anyone here ever had.

"Zachary!"

The lift beyond the doors began to whine, heading to the attic. I turned around.

The elderly man stood at the corner of the hallway, fifty feet away, his round face glowing pink from the dash to catch up. His belly rose and fell. Peterson's eyes were wide, worried and owlish behind his glasses.

At The Brink, we give a hoot, I thought, and began to chuckle.

The noise died in my throat when another man turned the corner. He loomed behind Peterson like a Brooks Brothers grim reaper, an ill omen. The source of Peterson's worry.

"Dad."

Yes. There to personally oversee the transfer. Behind him stood an NYPD cop, undoubtedly the armed escort for said transfer. The officer's walkie-talkie snarled incomprehensible dispatch fuzz-speak.

Across the tiled void, my father's face was a grim amalgam of disgust, disappointment and determination. He and I were gunslingers again, like we were in the 67th Precinct parking lot, widescreen duelists. Peterson turned and began to say something to the cop.

"Young man," Dad said. "It's over."

The whine behind me grew louder. Almost here.

"High Noon ain't for another half-hour," I said. "Pardner."

My father growled and began his march down the hall. The elevator doors moaned open behind me and I stepped backward, not seeing the person inside the car as I entered, not really caring as I knocked that person aside, folders and papers swirling to the floor like parade confetti.

I punched the button for Level 5.

"YOU STOP, GODDAMNIT!" Dad said, running now. The policeman made to bolt, but Peterson's roly-poly body jerked left, then right, trying to get out of the way, unintentionally blocking him. They looked like fevered, awkward new lovers, attempting a first kiss.

The voice behind me, in the cabin: "What the Christ?"

Dad, ahead: "STOP! IT'S OVER!"

The doors: *Creeeeaaaaaaaaak.*

Me, as they closed, as my father's furious face was less than a foot away:

"Giddy-giddy."

* * *

The metal box sighed and sank into The Brink.

"Taylor, what's your malfunction?"

I spun around. Staring up at me was Dr. Nathan Xavier. His typically immaculately styled hair was now a tousled mess. His hands snatched at the papers that had tumbled from our impact. He saw my horror-show face and barked a horrified "yahh!"

"Hi there," I said.

"Wha ... What ... "

I squatted low. My knees popped. Xavier flinched as if he'd been shot.

"Let me help you," I said, and my dirty hands scraped for the papers, collecting them into a haphazard mess. I passed them over. Xavier's bottom lip twitched and trembled, a pink caterpillar.

I propped my forearms on my knees.

"It's good you're here," I said. The world around us creaked. "You and me should have a heart-to-heart. See, I'm tired. Tired of the games. You wanna gun for me? You want my patients? You want notches in your belt, the spotlight, the media leaving messages on your voice mail. Right?"

Xavier shook his head, aghast.

"Nnn—"

"Sure you do," I said. I hunkered lower, leaning in. "You're hungry, ambitious. You're stuck in this shithole with the rest of us, and you want out, wanna move up, cruise around in your Corvette, live in your Dream House. I dig it. I'm not wired for it, but I dig it. But you listen to me, *Doctor* Xavier. If you're gonna screw me over, be a man about it. Tell me. Or go through proper channels. Hell, have the stones to suggest a collaboration; it might be interesting. But don't slither and scheme and think that I'm not gonna find out about it. And don't think that I won't get pissed off about it."

I stood up now. My finger tapped another button on the elevator panel. I extended my hand to him.

"Do we have an understanding?"

Xavier grimaced at my grubby paw, at the filth under my fingernails. He pulled himself up on his own, ignoring my gesture. The elevator groaned and shuddered as it slowed.

A static-filled roar blared from beneath Xavier's white lab coat. We both looked down, equally shocked by the noise.

"*—ach Taylor must not be allowed access to Martin Grace's room,*" my father's voice barked from the Brinkvale-issued walkie-talkie. "*He's en route via elevator. Say again: Zach Tay—*"

"Aw, shit," I said.

Xavier's face went wicked. "Fuck you, Taylor," he snapped, sidestepping around me, circling toward the doors. "You're gonna be so fired after I'm done with you."

The doors slid open. He turned around to check our location.

I snatched the radio from the man's belt and gave him a quick shove. Xavier yelped, staggering into the hallway of Level 3.

He whirled around, fuming.

"I don't think you'll have the satisfaction," I said as the doors began to close. "Level 3, more than halfway there now. I'll probably be shitcanned by lunchtime. Meet me topside then. We'll scrap in the parking lot then grab beers. My treat, pardner."

Xavier gaped at me, his world turned upside-down.

"You're mad," he whispered.

The doors clanked shut. The elevator chugged on. I glared at the walkie-talkie in my hand, sweating. Seconds. I had seconds to come up with something. My Spock side had apparently taken a vow of silence.

And then the answer crackled from my hand.

"*Belay that. Hoffacker, listen to me,*" Peterson's voice said. "*Zachary has thirty minutes with his patient. You will permit him his ...*"

Unintelligible barks, off-mic. And then:

"*... No, Mr. Taylor. Your meticulous paperwork says noon, and noon it shall be. Hoffacker, I say again: Let Zachary pass. One half-hour.*"

I smiled. Heard a manic titter escape my lips.

You're mad, Xavier had said.

"We'll see," I said, "just how mad I can get."

✳✳✳

The doors opened on Level 5. Max's hallway was blissfully flicker-free. I strode past the nurse's station, passing Annie Jackson, the victim of another double shift, and she called my name, waving her radio, wishing me luck with whatever I was about to do. I waved back and kept moving, now nearing Chaz Hoffacker and Room 507.

The guard's arms were crossed. He gave a surly frown, flabby jowls sagging. He looked like a constipated bulldog.

"Would you feel any better about this," I said, "if I promise to give 'Ziggy' another chance?"

Chaz harrumphed and unlocked the door.

I asked my anti-self for another shot of rabble-rouser indignation, one last trick up my torn sleeve, and stepped inside.

Room 507's lights were on this morning—whether that was due to the impending transfer or Richard Drake's nigh-catatonic state, I couldn't tell. But gone was the ex-spook's haughty pride and ramrod-straight posture. He sagged in his wooden chair, chin resting upon his chest. His graceful hands, usually folded in his lap, hung at his sides, boneless and swaying. His breathing was thick, sleepy sounding.

The living dead. Just like me.

I turned back to Chaz. "Did they medicate him?"

"What do I look like, Trapper John, M.D.?"

"Damn it, did they sedate my patient or not?"

The guard shrugged.

"Dunno. Don't think so. Doesn't look like he needs it." Chaz closed and locked the door.

And then it was me and Drake and the murals on the wall.

I didn't tug the second chair and place it in front of him, like before. I stood.

I *snarled.*

"You cold-hearted son of a bitch," I said. "I told you I'd help you even if it killed me—and it nearly did. I went up to your boy's house, just like you wanted me to. Found a letter with a photo, sent to that address a *year* after you'd abandoned your son. It shot down my pet theory. According to the U.S. government, Alexandrov is dead. Whatever else you wanted me to see is gone. Daniel burned them. Just like you wanted to burn me.

"It tore me to shreds. I couldn't see in the dark, but the dark could sure as hell could see me. Which you probably expected."

Drake wheezed something. Gibberish.

"And that leaves me with two options," I said. "The first is the one you know oh-so-well, the one that pitted me and mine against your monster. Option one? You're insane. You deserve to be doped up for the rest of your days, haunted by that fucking creature, tormented in your stupor. You think *this* is bad? You ain't seen nothing yet, blind man. Yes. Insane. Unsound. Soft in the head."

The patient gave a high moan. He shifted in his chair.

"That's right, Richard. You're not deaf. You heard me. You're a bowl of soggy Froot Loops. You're out of your mind."

Drake began to mutter something. I stopped talking and watched his quivering lips form the words. "*Hhhhh,*" he said.

White vapor streamed from his mouth.

Oh ...

The chill blasted over me like a gale-force wind, and I stumbled a half-step backward, instinctively clutching my arms, suddenly shivering. The air was brittle, so cold it burned.

" ... no," I said. My teeth were chattering.

"*Hhhhh.*" The vapor swirled around Drake's face like cigarette smoke now. He chuckled, a manic, broken sound. "*Hhhhere.* Arrrrk Man. Here. I ... can ... *feel* him."

His head flung back as if he'd been hung from the gallows. His green eyes flashed open and stared at the ceiling, stared at something a thousand miles above. My furor had been supplanted by fear. Chitter-chitter went my teeth.

And the walls themselves replied: *Tktktk. Tktktk. TKTKTK...*

The light above flickered, buzzed, did what it had done three days ago—but there were new things here now, things that weren't here during the last light show, the last hellshow, *I run the red show*, and Jesus Christ almighty, they were moving, turning sour, dying.

I stared in stone-cold terror as the murals' colorful, manic lines and blobs came to life, swirling, breathing and undulating, rippling like water. The colors withered as I watched, transforming into a charcoal gray, two walls' worth of Zach sketches, animated like a Disney film, chaotic and beautiful and terrible.

The gray lines were black now. They coalesced into arm-thick scribbles that twitched and jigged, swirling like giant ghoul's eyes, cinderblock snakes. Some were slow, sliding toward the floor like refrigerated syrup—spoiled, bubbling with black curds.

But much of the dancing blackness was fast. Liquified panther.

The goop, glittering like crude oil in the strobing light, splashed down with a soul-chilling slurp. It became a shifting mass of pain-bringing things as it writhed on the cracked tile floor: barbs, razors, knives, claws, incisors, all black and wet. I lost a little of my mind in that glimmering, shimmering madness.

"Richard ... " I whispered.

The cinderblock snakes flopped to the floor now, quivering and gelatinous, leaving ink snail-trails on the walls ... and the onyx pool rushed to absorb them, hungry to be made whole. It wasn't one voice that spoke now. It was legion.

Tktkpaytktkplaytktkilllnow

The frigid air was thinner now, harder to breathe. The obsidian pool rose and flattened, dimensionless once more. Black flame, charred paper, *Butoh* dance-arms, seesaw-seesaw rocking head.

The light strobed on and on, flashing against black teeth, black pearl, black fingers, long, longer now—growing longer still.

" ... told you you'd die ... " Drake said. " ... *hhhhere* ... with me ... . "

Not going to die, I thought. *No one else is going to die.*

I whirled back to my patient. I hissed my words through blue lips.

"Listen to me, old man. Fucking listen to me."

Tktktkouldkoobemine? Wouktktktbemiitk?

I doubled over, shivering, feverish. I pulled up again, spitting my words through gritted teeth.

"Cuh-cuh-crazy, Druh-Drake. Tha-that's one option. But the uh-uh-other... . "

I heard the thing rising behind me, growling and growing taller, breathing ice on my shoulders. My stomach turned at the sound of slick tongues ticking across fangs.

I heard a whisper, a voice. I ignored it.

"LISTEN to me!" I bellowed. "Fir-first option gone! Nuh-no crazy man would draw myu-mural maps. Ssoo. Sssssane. Yuh gotta be sane."

Drake's limp body jerked, as if electrified. Another whisper, but not from him.

"You all-almost had me fooled, mindbender," I snapped. "Had me thinking it wuh-wasn't you. Ohhh, but it was, wasn't it, Drake? All those peop*auuugh*—"

A dozen icicles pierced my skull, rail spikes in my brain, pumping black liquid into gray matter. The whispers were here now, inside my head, a soaring, roaring symphony of thunder-drums and sinuous snake hisses.

"*Nnnn,*" I said.

Tumbledownthesssteps, tktkartilagessnapping, Zachsnapping

"Nnnno wonder you went blind," I muttered. "Coward."

Drake bucked again, his brow furrowing in confusion. His head titled forward, away from the ceiling, toward my voice.

"What?" he said.

The voices in my mind vanished for a moment. I sucked in a breath, feeble, asthmatic.

"I said—"

But the blackness gushed anew, and I screamed as the voices screamed, and they were the howls of the Golgotha-mad, the psychotics, the lifers, lifting their legion language in unholy chorus:

timeto go, Zaktktk. putyourhand innn satktkchel, pull outktktk your pencilzzzzk.

And God help me, I did. My shivering fingers slid to my bag and found several sketching pencils with uncanny precision. I wasn't driving my hand anymore. No, oh, no. The suicides heard this, I knew it now, twentysomething Rosemary Chapel hanging herself in her parents' garage, black leather belt silver studs ripping her *thrrrr*

India ink was spilling over my eyes, no, *into* my eyes, sliding over my tear ducts, seeping into my retinas. The world was growing dark.

tktktkarmmm. take penciktktktktk. punch hkhkhole innn tktkarmmm.

Like a slave, my fingers plucked a shaft from the bunch in my right hand. The pencil trembled in my iron grip. My fingernails dug into my palms, making them bleed. Damn me, I couldn't let it go.

I raised the pencil high, like a knife, possessed. With everything I—it—had, it arced down, downward, plunging into my right forearm. I screamed. My hand, stupid with its own mind, broke the pencil as it yanked away. A half-inch of wood and graphite remained in my skin.

The air chuckled.

—Tktkchest now.

Yes. God, yes. It was becoming more clear now, here in the dark. Another pencil in my left hand. It rushed toward me, as if I were beating my chest.

It pierced my right bicep, just above the nipple. The pain was exquisite.

And nowktktk. Eyyyyye for tktkeyyyye.

"No," I said, but another pencil was in my hand now ... and it was rising slowly, so slowly, to my face.

I howled, focused my mind on the noise. Used the focus to find words. Directed the words at Drake.

"I know you did it, Richard!" I screamed. "How you did them all!! The whole world is going to know! I'm going to put you away, cold-blooded killer that you are. It's going to be in my report, old man, all of it! YOU KILLED THEM!"

The whispering wasp-swarm died down again, and Drake stirred in his chair once more. The pencil trembled, six inches from my face, as I fought the thing overpowering my body. The muscles in my forearm quivered, as if in an arm-wrestling contest.

The man's sightless eyes quested for my face, and I could see a strange breed of vitality returning to him, bringing color to his cheeks. Tears were streaming down his face now.

But the room's remaining air pressed around us now, wracking me with above-sea-level bends, and I cried out once more. The beast behind me whined, desperate. And then it growled, low and guttural. I felt the sound in my fillings.

The sputtering light above us went black. My heart stopped beating.

And I heard the nightmare millipede skitter-slide rush from behind me to *beside* me ... and then before me. Airless, soundless, dimensionless space separated me from my patient.

I shut my eyes, lost in the ocean, and felt the pencil press forward anew, rejuvenated.

First, I'd lose my right eye. Then my left. And I'd be just as blind as him, the failure he said I was, they said I was, the failure I knew I was.

It inched further still.

No.

I sucked in air. I reminded myself why I was there. I damned my patient, damned myself, and screamed like an unhinged man, an exorcist.

"RICHARD DRAKE! You will PAY FOR YOUR CRIMES! You will PAY for the BLOOD on your HANDS! You will SUFFER, as you made those YOU KILLED suffer! RETRIBUTION, RICHARD DRAKE! YOU ARE GUILTY ... "

The sharp pencil tip dug into my eyelid. The orb behind it constricted, rolling madly in the darkness.

Two roars filled the room now, overpowering my voice. One from the Dark Man, a screeching, brain-splitting howl.

" ... PAY! FOR! YOUR!" I screamed.

And now another scream, from Drake. One word, louder than us all.

Chernobog.

I heard the world tear open: shredding fabric, invisible electricity, a howling wind from anotherspace.

And then, it was over.

The light flashed on above me, steady and true. I threw the pencil to the floor; it clattered and rolled away. Drake sat in his chair, gaping at the light bulb, squinting like a newborn ... and then he looked at me. Saw me.

" ... crimes," I whispered.

He was smiling. Smiling, weeping and nodding. He stood, filled the space between us, and hugged me.

I held him as he trembled and wept. My eyes turned to the walls. The murals had returned, surreal, colorful ... and for the first time, I thought, hopeful.

"Whatever you want," Richard Drake said through his sobs. "Confession, anything. Punishment, yes. Finally, yes. Thank you. Thank you."

I held him tight. Our words and tears blurred together, there in Room 507.

"Thank you."

29

I sank into the black vinyl chair, relishing its aged padding. I'd been nearly dead on my feet for the past two days, so I dared not close my eyes; this moment of being literally "at rest" would likely take me over the edge. The office's dim lighting—and its oppressive scent of coffee and old books—was comforting, too. I ached for sleep. I ached, all over.

The pain meds I'd received in the infirmary weren't helping. The pencil holes in my arm and chest had required stitches, as had one of the gashes on my face from Daniel's attack. I'd come back from Hell, and would have the scars to prove it.

I bit my tongue, opened my eyes wide, tapped my fingers, one after another, against my thumb. Anything to stay awake.

Dr. Peterson closed the door behind me and stepped to his desk. He sat and stared at me with his owlish eyes. His round face glowed pale from the nearby gooseneck lamp. The towers of desk paperwork were a city skyline, it seemed, and Peterson was the moon, judging me from on high, from orbit, ready to mete out my punishment.

He placed the thick folder I'd given him on the desk. Inside was the "Martin Grace" file: the original admittance report, my official conclusions from our therapy sessions, my statement of his competence to stand trial, photocopies of my patient's confessions to the twelve murders—and finally, the transfer documents that released him from Brinkvale care. Noon was three hours gone, and so was Richard Drake.

And now, it was my turn.

"There are things to discuss, Zachary," Peterson said, "the most important being: Are you all right?"

I frowned and sighed. I wanted to say no, no, I wasn't all right; that Peterson's assignment and my crusade—*he's blind, but help him see*—had wreaked a special breed of havoc on my mind and body; that during this adventure, I'd destroyed parts of myself, my job, my family, my relationships; that I'd sacrificed damned-near every shred of myself for a stranger who didn't want my help; that darkness can be a *living* thing, a midnight-ocean shark attack, not a great white, but a Great Black; and oh the things I've seen/not seen in the past week, Dr. Peterson, it's just like Henry said: there's a very large world beside—and beneath and above—this one, and it scraped against me. It changed me.

And for what? I wondered here, as the old man scrutinized me. In so many ways, I hadn't saved Richard Drake at all. He'd be convicted, slam-dunk, just like Uncle Henry's case, twenty years ago.

But I think ... I think I might have saved his soul.

And wasn't that enough? Wasn't that—as I'd said to Drake the day I'd met him—"the goddamned point?"

"I'm all right," I replied, and smiled softly. "I think everything's going to be all right."

Peterson's mouth was a narrow line. He shook his head slowly.

"I disagree, Zachary. I chose you for the Grace case because of your brilliance with patients: your unconventional ability to connect with them. Defying convention is one matter. Being reckless is another."

As his eyes continued to probe mine, his hand slid from the desk surface, out of view. He tugged open a drawer and then placed four videocassettes atop Grace's folder. A three-digit number was written on their labels. Upon each was also scrawled a date from the past week. I noticed that Thursday's date was not represented here.

It was footage from Room 507's security camera.

Whatever glint of hope I'd had of keeping my job died right there. This was no longer about my job at The Brink. This was, quite suddenly, about my career as an art therapist.

My stomach churned, turned sour and acidic. He'd seen it all. I'd damned it all.

"Yesterday's incident with Emilio Wallace forced me to take a closer look at how you interacted with the patient," Peterson said.

His voice was grave. "Martin Grace was a determined man. You were equally determined. There are a great many inexplicable moments on these tapes, Zachary. Your relentless questioning, for instance. Actually, I'm well within my right to call it 'interrogation.' During Wednesday's session alone, your patient said ... "

He glanced at a nearby sheet of paper. His voice dispassionately recited the notes as if they were from a play. I remained silent, sickened.

"... 'No. God damn you, stop. Stop. Leave me alone. Don't. No. Oh no, Almighty God, no.'"

Peterson's gray eyes flicked back to mine.

"And yet you persisted, Zachary."

I wanted to throw up. I wanted to give him a reason, to tell him *why*. I knew I couldn't.

"There are more than a dozen moments like this," Peterson continues, "and as the week progressed, you appeared to descend further and further into what I'll charitably call 'inexcusably cavalier' engagements with the patient. This ... is very troubling."

His mouth now sank into a frown. He tapped the cassettes with a wrinkled hand. Cufflinks glinted at his wrists.

"Equally inexplicable and troubling is what's *not* on these tapes. Hours of footage is missing, or garbled. Any record of Martin Grace during the nighttime hours is gone, as if they were never recorded. His drawing of the wall murals, for instance. Also missing are moments of your sessions together. It appears that the electrical malfunctions on Level 5 affected more than the room's lighting."

I gaped at him, not understanding—and yet understanding perfectly. Perhaps it was the ancient Brinkvale wiring system that caused these blackouts. Perhaps it was something else.

"This footage," Peterson said, "is an incomplete record of your interaction with the patient."

He slid the tapes aside with his hand, making room for another piece of notepaper, which he now placed in the center of the desk. It was covered in his elegant handwriting.

"I have also received information that may interest you," he said. "Despite the District Attorney's office's—and police department's—attempts to quash this rumor, it appears that an individual illegally entered Martin Grace's apartment on Tuesday. This individual was arrested. He was released without criminal charges."

The vinyl around me groaned as I shifted in my seat. All of Richard Drake's personal effects—including the items from the The Brink, the lockbox and his son's home—were inside the manila envelope, locked in my office desk. I'd left them there after I'd filed my report today, not wanting to touch them, not ever again. If Peterson ordered a search of my office ...

This couldn't get any worse, simply couldn't.

"I also received a phone call this morning from the Haverstraw Sheriff's Department," Peterson reported. "Apparently, a Brinkvale employee assaulted a resident of that county. This resident could not recall the name of his assailant, who allegedly visited the day before to question him about his father, a Brinkvale patient. According to the officer, this employee broke into the man's home last night—and quite literally buried a hatchet into the man's leg."

Peterson did not smile at his joke. His eyes slowly, deliberately, cataloged my appearance. He knew, knew everything. Bile rushed to my mouth. I pined for a wastebasket. I was going to puke.

"The deputy asked me if Brinkvale was housing a patient by the name of 'Drake,'" Peterson said. "He also asked me if I knew why the alleged assailant might anonymously report the man's wound from a pay phone at Claytonville Prison."

I stared at my boss. The silence was a roar, if that were possible. Peterson finally spoke.

"I told the deputy we were not treating a man named 'Drake,'" he said.

The old man pushed the paper across the desk, to where the videocassettes rested. He removed his glasses and began to polish them with his tie. His eyes were tiny things now, pebble-sized.

"There is a difference between 'want' and 'need,' Zachary," he said, his thumb working the fabric. "Is there something you want to tell me? Something I *want* to hear?"

I had to clear my throat to speak.

"Uh ... no, Dr. Peterson."

The old man placed the spectacles on his face. He nodded.

"Is there anything you need to tell me? Anything I *need* to hear?"

My mind danced and raced and played hopscotch, calculating this, wondering what—if anything—I should say. Peterson wasn't an administrator anymore. He was my judge, my jury, my executioner. I don't know how long I sat there, my mind screaming in the impenetrable silence of the room—but when the words eventually came, they flowed out as my brain formed them, a manic data dump.

"I ... I try to make a difference, a positive difference, with what I do here," I whispered. "I try to save my people—ah, my *patients*—from themselves, from their torment. I do everything ... *everything* I can to help them. It's what I'm built to do. It's ... "

I looked into Peterson's eyes. My voice was louder now.

" ... It's what you hired me to do. That's what I did with Martin Grace. I helped him. I saved him from himself. I ... I think that's something we both needed to hear."

A smirk flashed onto the doctor's face, and then was gone.

I wasn't actually sure I'd seen it. He picked up the videotapes and his notes with both hands. They trembled slightly above the desk, and then slid away from the gooseneck lamp's glare. He released them.

They clattered into the wastebasket behind the desk.

"The footage was compromised, Zachary," he said, "and any additional information outside of your report is innuendo. Aside from Thursday's tape—which must be archived to accompany the Emilio Wallace incident report—there is no record beyond what you've told me, and what you've filed. This leaves me with your conclusions. I asked you to determine if Martin Grace was fit to stand trial. You did that."

His eyes narrowed now, knowing.

"Your findings were precisely what I anticipated," he said. "Weren't they?"

I recalled what Peterson had said in his office, a million Mondays ago.

"'He wouldn't be here if he was innocent,'" I quoted.

Peterson didn't blink, didn't breathe, for a moment.

"And yet, the patient seems at peace now," he said. "Amazing."

"Amazing Grace," I agreed. I felt stupid, as if I were missing the punch line to a very long, very funny joke.

Peterson leaned back in his chair. He folded his hands, placing them on his belly.

"I want you to go home, Zachary. You're on leave until further notice. I'll review your report—and your conduct—and will soon notify you of your professional standing here at Brinkvale Psychiatric. But in the meantime, rest. I want you to rest. Will you do that?"

I opened my mouth to speak, to plead my case ... but I'd already done that. I nodded.

"That is all, then."

I stood up, quietly grimacing as my body shrieked its pain. I walked to the door, opened it, stepped beyond into the reception area. Lina Velasquez blasted rapid-fire words into her computer keyboard. A hundred-twenty a minute, easy.

"Zachary."

I turned back toward the doorway. Peterson's face was half-lit in the lamplight. He opened another desk drawer and removed a ring of keys. They clinked merrily, in the dim room. He eyed them.

"I acquired these keys through an acquaintance," he said. "There are Braille stickers on every one."

His eyes turned to me now. "Do these belong to Martin Grace?"

I paused.

"No sir," I replied. And that was true.

"Very well then," he said, and tossed them into the wastebasket. "Goodbye, Zachary."

I gave a wordless wave and strode out of the Administrator's Office, down the hall, and out into the world beyond The Brink.

***

I descended Brinkvale's front steps, cringing slightly at the chilly air. Malcolm waited for me at the bottom.

"Zach T," the janitor said, and gave a little salute. He held a rake in his other gloved hand; Primoris had decided to begin its annual shedding during the past hour, it seemed.

"Two bottles, Grey Goose," I said. "I don't know when I'll get 'em to you, but you'll get 'em. I've been suspended, maybe fired. But I'm good for it. Promise."

Malcolm didn't smile. His voice was serious, conspiratorial.

"That's not all you're giving me, is it?"

I nodded, knowing what he meant.

"Didn't forget about that, either," I said. "Tell me. What's going to happen to his effects?"

Malcolm shrugged. The large ring of Brinkvale keys jingled on his hip.

"Nothing, Zach T. Absolutely nothing. The Sub might as well be the deep blue sea. Toss something in, it sinks to the bottom, never seen again. The Brink's basement is where paperwork goes to die."

"Sounds like that warehouse at the end of that Indiana Jones movie," I said. "The one where they put the Ark of the Covenant. I wish I could see it."

Malcolm shuddered; I couldn't tell if it was the wind, or something else.

"It ain't," he said. "You don't."

"The folder's locked in my desk," I told him. "Make sure it sinks."

I extended my other hand. The janitor shook it.

"It was a pleasure working with you," I said.

"Likewise. I always liked you, Zach T. You kept things ... interesting ... around here. "

He eyed me for a moment and then smiled.

"Looks like you learned to pitch after all, huh, kid?"

I grinned back, gave a silent salute, and walked in silence to the parking lot.

Dad was waiting for me there.

***

He stood by Rachael's red Saturn, hands buried in his overcoat pockets, the same undertaker pose he'd had in the 67th Precinct's parking lot. The wind gusted around him, whipped and tugged at his collar, as if unhappy with his presence here. I could sympathize.

"Son," he said.

I glanced around, searching for a police cruiser. There wasn't one. An official-looking black Lincoln was parked nearby; presumably a D.A. office loaner, since my father's BMW was most certainly in a repair shop. The car was empty. My father had made the trek here alone.

"He's gone," I said.

"Gone," Dad affirmed. "Noon sharp. I believe you were in the infirmary. I'm ... I'm sorry you didn't see him off."

I raised my chin, and looked into his eyes.

"I said all I needed to say to him."

"Why, Zachary?"

My father's expression had gone from impassive slate to pained curiosity. I waited for more.

"Why? Why didn't you drop it? Why did you—there's no other word for it—why did you *defy* me? Why, especially now, at the end, when you see that I was right? When you see I wanted to protect you? I ... I don't ... "

I watched him as his voice trailed off, remembering the moment back in the precinct lot when he'd lost control—when he'd screamed his confession to me, his primal snarl, his reason for pursuing the blind man like a junkyard dog. It was then that I'd finally seen my father as a mortal, capable of frailty. The tumblers had fallen then, and he had, too. It had been a painful, necessary thing. It was evolution.

I couldn't tell him that, and I wouldn't expect Dad to understand it. I'd have to learn to live with it.

"I guess you were right," I said. "I'm like Mom. Caring to a fault. Curious, too. Rushing in, asking questions only after it's all done. It's like you said. I needed history."

Dad smiled slightly. It was confident again.

"Context," he said.

I suppressed many things at that moment: The urge to tell him how disappointed I was in him; how I knew the things he'd done two decades ago ... the sins against his brother and sons; how I loathed-yet-still-loved him; how I would silently continue to defy him and visit the imprisoned man who was proud of me, the father-figure I barely remembered, the buried man who lived on.

"Taylor Family Loyalty," I whispered. I glanced from the horizon back to my father. "What's going to happen to Grace?"

His smile faded. His blue eyes went ice-cold, full-bore D.A.

"The confession speeds up everything," he replied. "If he pleads no contest—and there's no reason to think that he won't—the trial will be short. I won't push for the death penalty. The confession, his regret for the murders and this 'conflict of interest' business between us would make that ... strategically difficult."

I ground my teeth. I wanted to grab his fluttering coat collar and shake a sliver of compassion into his obsessed brain. Fucking *strategy*. I could bombard him with so much goddamned "history" and "context" right now his head would spin off his shoulders.

I closed my eyes and sucked in a deep lungful of air. Dad would deliver that which Drake craved. The price his soul demanded. Justice.

I exhaled, and opened my eyes.

"I'm sorry she was killed, Dad. I'm sorry you lost her."

My father blinked. He turned his face away.

"She was beautiful and brilliant," he whispered. "I think ... No. I *know* you would've liked her."

I thought of last night's madness in my Alphabet City apartment, and at Daniel Drake's house—and how that "very large world" above ours had spilled over, if only for a few moments, into this one. I didn't want to know why Drake's cell phone rang when it had. I didn't want to know if it was the corroded battery or something else. I knew only the name on its screen, and that it had been angelic, and that it was now buried with the past, where it belonged.

"I think you're right," I said.

I hugged him and loved him the best I could.

30

"Katabatic!"

I grinned at my brother's exclamation as I placed the last of our spoons into the silverware drawer. He and Rachael were performing some technical tomfoolery in the living room; something involving Lucas' laptop and her monstrous widescreen television. True to my road-trek promise to Rachael, I'd cooked dinner and washed the dishes.

When Luc had learned of this penance, he'd cackled and christened me "The Dish Slut." Har-dee-frickin'-har.

At least Lucas had asked no questions about my bashed-and-patched body earlier this evening. My brisk "Greatest Hits" recounting of last night and this morning—including the standoff with Daniel Drake, Dad at The Brink and my suspension, but excluding details about nearly everything else—had satisfied him. Much like his uncanny ability to know when it was time to depart a social setting, Lucas also knew when it was best to skip the fine print.

He *had* asked about Daniel Drake's condition; I think he felt for the fallen son, just as I did. I'd called Haverstraw's hospital on my way home from The Brink. Daniel was in stable condition.

I leaned into the living room and silently watched my tribe as they giggled at the TV, admiring their creativity and resourcefulness—and loving the *themness* of them.

Lucas had rigged the laptop to the tiny parkour cameras he'd shown me at Well7 on the night of Gram's memorial service. With Rachael's computer sorcery, the Toughbook now streamed wireless video to the television. The jittery footage was separated into four boxes on the screen, one for each of Lucas' feet and hands. It was like the title sequence from "The Brady Bunch" ... if a spastic dog had filmed it.

"Dig it, Dish Slut," Lucas said, pointing at the screen. The contents of one sub-screen jerked, now recording its own on-screen footage. The image was a whirling visual feedback loop, video filming video filming video.

"Awesome," I said, and sat beside Rachael on the couch. She leaned her head against my shoulder. I held her hand. Bliss hopped into my lap and purred. Dali looked on from the well-worn "Zach chair" in the corner.

"How long must I endure this crass moniker?" I asked my brother.

"A whole month," he snickered. He gave Rachael a wink. "That's the deal, right, *Hochrot*? Z's doing 'em for a dirty thirty. You're Palmolive's bitch, bro."

"He's getting off easy, at that," Rachael said.

I nodded, squeezing her hand. Oh, how I knew that was true. Oh, how I loved this woman and her patience—and her acceptance, if not understanding, of how I was wired.

Lucas bounced in place before us; the footage from his toys stuttered and pixelated, trying desperately to keep up. Dali bolted from the room.

"Ahem. Your resident wunderkind has a new creative vision," he announced, beaming. "I'm using my ParkourCams as monster POV footage for ... a horror thriller."

He raised his hands, made them into playful claws and growled.

"Snarl," Rachael deadpanned.

"Is this movie about a black figure that stalks prey who've been 'marked for death' by a blind man?" I asked.

Lucas nodded furiously. His curly hair rocked like a shabby shrub in a hurricane.

"New genre: *parkhourror*. Title: *Obsidian Vengeance*. 'Based on a true—'"

"I'd work on it," I said. "A *lot*."

The three of us laughed. For the first time in days, I felt safe. Warm.

Latin music blared from my brother's pocket. Shakira. The *chica*. Lucas raised his eyebrows appreciatively and fished the cell phone from his baggy pants.

"Heh, nine o'clock sharp," he said, placing the phone to his ear. The TV behind him blurred brown, an IMAX close-up of his shaggy hair. I smirked. I didn't think the technology was quite "there" yet.

He spoke into the phone for a moment, hung up, and began disconnecting the cameras from his limbs. The gear was soon stowed—and the television screen, thankfully, was now black.

"Mustn't keep the brilliant, exotic young lady waiting," he said. "We're catching a new sci-fi movie tonight."

"Ahh, young love," Rachael cooed. She turned to me. "When was the last time you took me to a late-night flick?"

I nodded to the bookshelf near her home theater system. It brimmed with our video collection.

"Up for some James Bond?" I asked.

Now *she* squeezed my hand.

"Kiss kiss, bang bang comes later," she said. "After we fight."

Lucas made a sour expression as he walked to the door.

"Ick. Glad I won't be around for the make-up. You guys have a welcome up night, dig?"

"Dug," Rachael and I said simultaneously.

He grinned and stepped into the hallway.

" 'Dore you," he said.

I grinned. " 'Dore you back, bro."

"Martini shot, everybody."

The door latched shut and he bounded down the stairs, rolling thunder, just as he had when we were kids.

I turned to my woman—my anchor, my sail, the second half of my heartbeat. I gazed into her eyes.

"Are we going to fight now?" I asked. I wasn't playful. I was worried.

"Do you want to fight?" she replied.

"No."

"Doghouse rain check, then." She pulled off her glasses and rubbed her eyes. "Tired."

"Me too."

"Do you really think Peterson is going to fire you?" she asked. "I mean, I can pull in more shifts, more writing gigs if we need the money. See about more sponsorship for Pixel-Vixen707. We'll be okay for a month or so, but ... Z, you can't be out of a job for long."

I nodded, somber. Rachael and I allowed ourselves many luxuries: dinner out, damned good beer, feeding our creative needs for more art supplies and techno-gizmos. But this life didn't come cheap.

"I know, babe. And I don't know. The old man knows a lot. A helluva lot, stuff from well beyond The Brink. I don't know how he got it all. Guess he's not as daffy—or removed—as we Morlocks think he is."

I pulled her close, sighing. Bliss hopped from my lap.

"Listen to me. 'We Morlocks.' Let me put it this way: *I'd* fire me."

"Not good," she whispered. "But you saved Drake."

"In a way," I agreed, and this was true. I kissed her head. I inhaled her scent and closed my eyes, wanting nothing more than more, more of this, for as long as I could. "He needed the blood washed from his hands. The blood of a Russian and his family. Eye for eye, punishment, remorse. Paid in full. I hope."

The silence between us now was both comforting and anxious. His past had been put to rest. My future was in tatters. Had it been worth it?

"Yes," Rachael whispered, as if reading my thoughts. "I hope so, too."

We held each other, silent again, surrounded by our glowing chili pepper halo.

"Did you see it?" she asked. "Did you really see it?"

The Dark Man. Chernobog.

"I'll tell you what the therapist saw," I said. "Paranoia. Superstition saturation. My fear of the dark, cranked up past ten. But if you want to know what Z saw ... and *felt* ... yeah. It was as real as it gets."

"Mmm."

Her breathing became softer, as did mine. Sleep, finally. Sleep.

Bzzzzzz.

We perked up, confused.

My cell phone vibrated against our steamer trunk table again, then stopped. Skeleton song chimed from its speaker.

I pulled away from her, already missing her warmth, picking up the phone. A text message, from ...

"Dr. Peterson?" I said.

We leaned against each other, shoulders touching, as I slid open the phone's tiny keyboard. The message blinked to life on the LCD screen.

LEAVE OF ABSENCE CANCELED. NIGHT SHIFT R.N. REPORTS ERRATIC BEHAVIOR IN YOUR PATIENT, JAMES VAN ZANDT. REPORT TO BRINK, TOMORROW AM. IT WOULD BE PRUDENT...

There was more to the message. I clicked the keypad's "down" arrow.

...TO BRUSH UP ON YOUR MONOPOLY, it read.

"Jimmy Van Zandt," I said. I turned to her, grinning. "They call him 'Park Place.' Autistic, impenetrable, obsessed with that board game."

She smiled back, and leaned in. We kissed.

"So, 'James Bond Will Return,'" she said, quoting the line at the end of nearly every 007 film. "What's this adventure going to be called, hottie artist?"

I chuckled. "I'll tell you in the morning, geek goddess," I said, and we kissed again, more passionately this time.

We stumbled through our apartment, a tangle of rushing hands and half-kisses, far too tired for lovemaking, too far in love to care. The cats scattered, leaving us to the bedroom and our impatient romance. We needed this, this closeness, this *being*.

The bed was cold, but not for long, and when it came time to dim the bedside "Zach light," I twisted its knob further and further, until I could barely see her exquisite face.

"Are you okay?" she asked, gazing down at me.

"I'm learning to live a little dangerously," I said. "I'm okay. I'm ... I'm okay."

And for now, this was also true.

The light clicked off. We glowed bright, in the darkness.